BY MACKENZI LEE

Lady Like
The Gentleman's Guide to Vice and Virtue
The Gentleman's Guide to Getting Lucky
The Lady's Guide to Petticoats and Piracy
The Nobleman's Guide to Scandal and Shipwrecks
Loki: Where Mischief Lies
Gamora and Nebula: Sisters in Arms
The Winter Soldier: Cold Front
Bygone Badass Broads
The History of the World in Fifty Dogs
This Monstrous Thing

LADY LIKE

LADY LIKE

A NOVEL

MACKENZI LEE

THE DIAL PRESS
NEW YORK

The Dial Press
An imprint of Random House
A division of Penguin Random House LLC
1745 Broadway, New York, NY 10019
randomhousebooks.com
penguinrandomhouse.com

A Dial Press Trade Paperback Original

Copyright © 2025 by Mackenzie Van Engelenhoven
Dial Delights Extras copyright © 2025 by Mackenzie Van Engelenhoven

Penguin Random House values and supports copyright. Copyright fuels creativity, encourages diverse voices, promotes free speech, and creates a vibrant culture. Thank you for buying an authorized edition of this book and for complying with copyright laws by not reproducing, scanning, or distributing any part of it in any form without permission. You are supporting writers and allowing Penguin Random House to continue to publish books for every reader. Please note that no part of this book may be used or reproduced in any manner for the purpose of training artificial intelligence technologies or systems.

THE DIAL PRESS is a registered trademark and the colophon is a trademark of Penguin Random House LLC.

DIAL DELIGHTS and colophon are trademarks of Penguin Random House LLC.

Library of Congress Cataloging-in-Publication Data
Names: Lee, Mackenzi author
Title: Lady like: a novel / Mackenzi Lee.
Description: New York, NY: The Dial Press, 2025.
Identifiers: LCCN 2025023966 (print) | LCCN 2025023967 (ebook) |
ISBN 9780593730607 trade paperback | ISBN 9780593730614 ebook
Subjects: LCGFT: Romance fiction | Humorous fiction | Novels
Classification: LCC PS3612.E34476 L33 2025 (print) | LCC PS3612.E34476 (ebook) |
DDC 813/.6—dc23/eng/20250530
LC record available at https://lccn.loc.gov/2025023966
LC ebook record available at https://lccn.loc.gov/2025023967

Printed in the United States of America on acid-free paper

1st Printing

BOOK TEAM: Managing editor: Rebecca Berlant
• Production manager: Jane Sankner • Copyeditor: Faren Bachelis
• Proofreaders: Vicki Fischer, Cameron Schoettle, Nicole Ramirez

Interior art: provectors/Adobe Stock

Book design by Sara Bereta

The authorized representative in the EU for product safety and compliance is Penguin Random House Ireland, Morrison Chambers, 32 Nassau Street, Dublin D02 YH68, Ireland. https://eu-contact.penguin.ie.

with thanks to all my group chats

Remember how tender a thing a woman's reputation is;
how hard to preserve, and when lost
how impossible to recover.
—James Fordyce, *Sermons to Young Women*

There is a nameless tie . . . which blends us
into one & makes me feel that you are mine.
There is no feeling like it.
—Letter from Anne Lister to Mariana Belcombe

LADY LIKE

1

When the letter arrives, Harriet Lockhart assumes it's another death threat, and leaves it on the mantelpiece with the others, unopened, for six days.

Since taking up a life on the Drury Lane stage, Harry has received so many threats of various kinds—death, slander, public humiliation, the like—that she has considered using them to paper a wall in her bedroom. They are all written on cards of a quality denoting the sort of wealth that can afford both a fetish for stationery and to waste it on a virulent missive to a stranger after deeming her existence—or sometimes, simply the rumor of it—so provocative that it threatens their own moral foundations.

The letters all follow roughly the same script: salutations, colored with a hyperbolic descriptor—dear Miss Lockhart, you whore, villain, rascal, bellend, etc.—followed by an accusation of Harry's perceived wrongdoing, whether that be her raffish manners or her chosen roles on the London theater circuit and how often they were written for men or require her to take her top off or both, or her seduction of some such gentry daughter or country cousin or even one or two dowager countesses. Of late, many had touched on how it is Harry's fault that the Duke of Edgewood's good luck at the card tables had come to a close, as it was she who had revealed he had no particular skill at pinochle but, rather, cards up his sleeve.

It was certainly not Harry's fault that he challenged her to duel when she made his trickery known. Nor was it her fault that he was such a poor swordsman he practically fell into her blade. And she hadn't killed him, for God's sake. He'd only lost an eye.

And yet the letters continue to arrive, one of life's few constants being polite society's need to remark upon other people's business.

And an unmarried actress of four and thirty years assaulting a member of the peerage—to say nothing of her penchant for men's suits and short hair—is certainly *business*.

Yes, the threats would make remarkable wallpaper. But it's unclear how long Harry will remain in these Drury Lane apartments now that a great deal of people who seem to want her dead have the address. That, and the theater will evict her if she doesn't sign on for the next production, and she is reaching an age where a career performing bawdy adaptations of Shakespeare's most lamentable tragedies in an oversized codpiece is less funny than it once was. Though considering the increasingly dire straits of her finances since her mother's death, plus her lack of any real skills beyond looking good in a fake beard, she may not be able to afford a noble exit.

All things considered, it would be a waste of good death threats. Not to mention paste.

So The Letter sits unopened upon the mantelpiece for six days until the night she returns from the Palace Theater, her shirt still stippled with sweated-off cosmetics and pigs' blood, and finds it waiting upon the table before the fireplace.

And, in the armchair beside it, her brother, Collin.

Harry stops just inside the doorway and stares—not at the letter so much as at the man who it would seem has plucked it from languishing in obscurity. Unexpected guests are not unusual in Harry's home, often because she invites people when deep in her cups and then forgets once she's sober, but her brother has never been the sort to enter Harry's rooms if he can help it. Something about unwashed socks in places socks have no business being. She also has not spoken to him in almost two years, other than a brief exchange, weak as watered-down gin, at their mother's graveside.

But now here he is, perched on the edge of her armchair like the cushions might stain his suit if he leans against them.

And they might—she never takes off her blood-soaked shirt before sitting to unlace her boots.

"What are you doing here?" Harry demands of her brother. Since she usually tosses her coat onto the back of the chair upon which he's seated, she drops it on the floor instead.

"Good to see you, Sister," Collin replies. Then, as though he can't help himself, he picks up the coat, folds it neatly, and drapes it over the arm of the chair.

Harry sinks onto the sofa across from him, kicking off her boots with her toes pressed into her heels. "What are you drinking?" she asks as Collin raises his glass.

"Tea."

"Sanctimonious. Why's it in a tumbler?"

"Because you don't own any other drinking vessels." Collin takes a sip, then adds with his lips to the rim, "Nor spoons."

"Can't seem to find any of my good hairpins either." Harry retrieves a bottle of whiskey and a glass from the side table and pours her own drink. The bottle is half full, and Harry wonders if that will be enough to sustain her through a visit with her brother. "Do shout if you step on one."

Collin sets his cup beside the folded paper with Harry's name on the front. "You got a letter."

"I get a lot of letters," Harry replies.

"Still an endless string of love poems in your honor?"

"It's been more of an assortment lately. Fruits with the nuts." Harry rubs a strip of sticky wax from her forehead, which had been holding her fake eyebrows in place. She considers peeling off her false beard, but the mustache is fiddly and liable to tear without a mirror. "Why does this one matter so particularly?"

"Because." Collin reaches into the pocket of his waistcoat and withdraws a second letter, which he tosses onto the table beside Harry's. Harry picks up the two pieces of parchment and holds them up for examination. The calligraphic handwriting, the corners creased with military precision, the sapphire drop of sealing wax stamped with a vaguely noble emblem—they're identical. The only difference is that one bears her name and the other Collin's.

And Collin's has been opened. Presumably by Collin.

He watches as she cracks the seal on her letter and smooths it out on the tabletop. In the same monkish hand from the front is written:

Longley Manor, Surrey.
March the twenty-fifth, noon.
Don't be late.

"It seems," Collin remarks drily, "that we are being summoned."

Harry is no great fan of summonses. The last time she was summoned with an official letter on quality paper it was to stand before a Cornwall judge on a trumped-up charge of public indecency. And while it was true she had shown her breasts on stage during a production of *Twelfth Night,* in her defense, it had been an accident. Or, if not entirely an accident, an impulsive decision, which should have counted for something. A crime not so much premeditated as wildly under-meditated.

"Hold on—*we*?" Harry says, her attention snagging suddenly upon his phrasing. "What does yours say?"

Collin flicks his letter open and reads, "'Longley Manor, Surrey. March the twenty-fifth, noon. Do not let your sister be late.'"

"It does not say that." Harry reaches across the table and plucks the parchment from Collin's fingers.

"Whoever sent them must know us," Collin remarks. "As they've preempted your customary tardiness."

"What do you think we're being summoned *for*?"

"Probably to kill us." Collin inclines his tumbler and adds, "Kill *you*, at least. Don't know what score might be unsettled with me."

Harry runs a hand over her hair, shorn short as a gentleman's since her first season at the Palace. "I'm not sure I'm ready for another public scandal. I'm trying to make myself scarce."

"Scarce?" Collin repeats incredulously. "You've been playing Macbeth at the Palace since February."

"Only four nights a week," Harry replies, then adds, "plus matinees."

"Your face is on the posters." Collin produces a handkerchief from his pocket and wipes at some imagined blot on the table before setting his glass upon it. "And that business with Edgewood."

"You heard about that?"

"He's parading around London with a jeweled patch over his eye, swearing oaths against your name. Good God, Hal. Aren't you tired of making your life a public spectacle?"

"Did you come all this way just to criticize me?" Harry retorts. Though she had long ago resolved to care less what Collin thinks, her brother's disapproval has always irked her in a way no one else's does. If anyone should understand her less conventional choices, it should be him. They are rivers that flow from the same source, after all.

"I came . . ." A vein flexes in Collin's forehead as he clenches his jaw. "Because I was concerned for you," he says. "For both of us. And for what these letters might mean."

Harry stares at the handwriting on the page, trying to force herself to recognize it, like picking the face of an old friend from a crowd.

"I thought," Collin adds, "it may be to do with Mother's estate."

Harry laughs. "What estate? She was a whore, she didn't own a manor house in the countryside to which we might be summoned for inheritance."

"She had rich friends."

"Friends? Is that what you call them?"

"That's what she called them."

Harry presses an elbow into her knee, trying to stop its restless bouncing. When that does nothing, she stands, crosses to the basin resting on the window ledge, and pours water from the ewer into it. "Well I can't imagine any of her particular friends decided to honor the memory of their favorite incognita by shepherding her bastard twins into the landed gentry." She scoops up a handful of water and presses it to the back of her neck, scratching at some of the blood drying along her collar. Macduff had stabbed her with great enthusiasm that night, and the bladderful of pigs' blood she kept tucked under her arm during the climactic duel had not so much punctured as detonated. "You're right—murder is the most likely. I'll have to make a list of my enemies and investigate who's in town."

"So you'll go to this mysterious meeting?"

"So long as it doesn't interfere with my schedule. I'm meant to see a gentleman about a horse that afternoon."

Collin frowns. "Don't tell me you're purchasing a horse."

"Don't be absurd," Harry says. "Where would I put it?"

"You certainly couldn't do any more damage to this place."

"It's a pit, isn't it? There's this mold growing along the baseboards that I think might be giving me a rash."

"Jesus Christ, Harry. You need new apartments."

"Not so easy, I'm afraid. The Palace lets me stay here gratis, and I'm not exactly flush in the pockets these days." Harry unfastens her garters and peels off her stockings, one hand on the basin to steady herself. "Where are *you* living of late? I could come stay with you."

They both cringe—Harry at the debasement of having asked, Collin, presumably, at the idea of Harry in such proximity.

"Absolutely not." He waves a hand at her bloody shirt front. "I'd make you undress on the front stoop if you came home in that state."

"Perhaps I'll ask Alexander then. I'm sure he has a room to spare."

"Who?"

"My gentleman with the racehorse."

"How exactly do you know this gentleman?" Collin asks. "And in what sense is he a *friend*?"

"Don't be crass," Harry says, though the last time she saw Alexander, they *had* ended up naked in the Serpentine. "Alexander Bolton is a duke—or, he will be when his father kicks it."

Collin's forehead creases and he purses his lips, but all he says is, "Hm."

Harry scoffs.

"What?" Collin demands. "I didn't say anything!"

"You don't like my friends, Collin, please, don't make a production of pretending otherwise. Nor do you like my rooms or my job or my haircut."

Collin groans. *"Now?* You want to fight about this *now?"*

"Of course not. I'm wearing entirely the wrong outfit." Harry crosses the room and wraps her arms around his neck from behind.

"Is this a fond embrace?" Collin asks, scowl deepening. "Or are you strangling me?"

"I'm still deciding." Harry presses her cheek to the top of her brother's head. He smells of the same cologne he's always worn, earthy and rich like the inside of a wine cask. She sometimes catches a whiff of it in a crowd and finds herself possessed with a fierce longing to see him again.

There had been a time when Collin felt like the only person who could truly know her. They had spent their youth stuck in the middle of two worlds, like crumbs fallen between cushions on a sofa—their mother had been a harlot with patrons who bought her pearls and fine clothes and, when she grew tired of the bordello where Harry and Collin spent the first decade of their lives, a townhouse in Westminster. The other molls always eyed them sideways, but so did the lofty circles in which their money allowed them to run. Harry and Collin had shared the loneliness of displacement, and leaned upon each other when their mother made it clear hers would never be a shoulder upon which they could cry.

But as they grew older, while Harry lived her life on a stage both literal and figurative, Collin had worked his way into the society that had been so unwelcoming to them, and stopped their gossip by making himself above reproach. Anyone who met Collin Lockhart today would be shocked that his mother had been a whore and his upbringing that of a fatherless bastard in a Camden brothel.

Whereas no one was ever surprised to hear Harry's origins. Rather, once explained, most responded with something akin to "Ah, now I understand."

Harry wouldn't have begrudged Collin his choices, had those choices not left her feeling like something Collin was trying to scrape off his shoe, lest the smell follow him. There's a reason they've hardly spoken in two years, in spite of living in the same city.

But here he is, in her room, wearing the same cologne, and she is reminded that missing him is the only thing more complicated than loving him.

She almost asks him to stay. They'll drink tea out of whiskey glasses and play dominos and she can tell him about *Macbeth* and he can explain what he does for a living these days and why it's accounting. He'll ask her to pick up her discarded socks, and she won't, but she will kick them out of sight beneath the sofa, and they will complain about their mother, for even dead, her shadow still blots out the light sometimes. Collin will switch from tea to liquor as they speculate who is summoning them to this mysterious manor house, and it will be easy to pretend they still know each other as well as they once did.

But then, from behind the bed screen, a voice calls, "Harry?"

Harry and Collin both turn as a woman emerges, her long red hair undone and falling to her waist in fuzzy tangles. Full lips part her heart-shaped face, her ample figure made somehow ampler by the fact that she is dressed only in one of Harry's long shirts, the tails rucked up above her navel.

"And that's my cue." Collin stands, knocks back his tea like it really is whiskey, then claps Harry on the shoulder. "We might as well ride to Longley together—shall I meet you at eleven? I assume you can make arrangements for your own mount since you know a man with a horse." He keeps his gaze gentlemanly fixed on the mostly naked woman's face as he gives her a nod. "Miss Swift."

Mariah wiggles her fingers. "Collin. It's been too long."

"Just the right amount of time, I think." Collin retrieves his hat from the stand beside the door before he turns to Harry. "Have a good night, Hal." Then, with the delicate bite of salting meat, adds, "Good to see nothing has changed."

As soon as the latch clicks behind Collin, Harry rounds upon Mariah. "If only your timing was half so good on stage."

The force of Mariah's disdain tips her head to the ceiling. Her hair wraps around her pale shoulders like tentacles. "I was weary of waiting. And you seemed to be approaching sentimentality. I couldn't know how long you might go on."

When Harry doesn't move to her, Mariah steps forward. She presses her body against Harry's, offering a smile and a view down the open neck of her shirt that has caused so many to lay themselves at her feet like a coat over a mud puddle.

Though they have known each other since they were young, there are still days when Harry thinks that only the Virgin Mary, being told she was chosen by God, can understand what it feels like to be blessed with Mariah's particular attention. Mariah has always had a way of smiling, of touching the arm, of saying her lover's name paired with said arm touching and smiling that makes a person feel sanctified. In Camden, gifts would arrive for her in staggering quantities, umatched in both their extravagance and variety—a duke in Gloucester had once sent her a tiger cub, and a French woman she had entertained a fortnight left her a set of sapphire-encrusted gold cuffs, which Mariah had been forced to surrender in a debtor's tribunal the next year.

The Palace house could have been filled to capacity by those who thought themselves in love with Mariah Swift.

But Harry would not count herself among them. She does not love Mariah Swift—some days, she isn't even sure she likes her. But by God, Mariah does make things easy. There is no risk of broken hearts, long attachments, or unreasonable demands like monogamy or morality or washing off all their cosmetics before bed.

"I told you not to come," Harry says. "I said I was tired."

"Poor darling." Mariah teases Harry's shirt out of the waistband of her trousers. "Come to bed and I'll make it better."

Harry drops her head back, staring at the ceiling.

"My God, you are dramatic." Mariah pushes away from Harry, the coo sloughed from her voice like snow sliding from a roof. "I hoped to do something nice for you, since you told me you get so *lonely* after the shows—"

"I never said that."

Mariah drops her voice in an imitation less of Harry and more of Harry as Macbeth, playing to the galleries. *"Oh, Mariah, come stay with me, for I have no one to hold and the nights are long and cold."*

"What I remember saying," Harry says, "is the nights are long and cold because you take more than your share of the blankets when I let you in my bed."

Mariah juts out her bottom lip. "Let me stay. Please."

Harry feels Mariah's knee slot between her legs, and the friction is like sinking into a warm bath. Well, not warm. With Mariah, it's tepid and cloudy, and Harry knows she's probably the third person to wash themselves in it that day.

But still. It's better than the cold.

Harry presses Mariah backward into the vanity, and Mariah braces herself against it with a gasp of delight. "Fine. Go lie down while I get this beard off."

"You could leave it on." Mariah strokes the whiskers, fingers trailing off the ends of the mustache and up to Harry's temples.

"The gray makes you look distinguished. You're going to age so well."

"Oh, I'll never grow old. Deal with the devil, remember? They wrote that Faust play about me."

Mariah kisses her, tongue dipping into Harry's mouth, then turns for the bed with a wiggle of her hips. Harry watches her, already half regretting the concession. Because no matter how fantastic Mariah's ass is, the fact remains that Harry *is* tired. It seems these days she's always tired, especially after five long acts of Shakespearean tragedy performed by a company of women so staggeringly untalented that she has considered a preemptive exorcism to stop the Bard haunting them as retribution for slaughtering his works nightly.

There are days—more and more of late—that the thought of a night that ended before the next day began sounds like a treat rather than a bore. What would it be like not to pick cabbage thrown by the audience from her hair before bed, or realize too late that Mariah's rouge would never come out of her second-best shirt? Or to have someone in her bed each night who was more than simply convenient and transient, and didn't try to impale Harry on stage with a real—albeit blunted—knife when she suspects Harry of eyeing the ass of smiling, bloody Banquo between acts two and three?

When Harry had stood opposite the Duke of Edgewood's sword, even though, judging by his grip alone, she had been fairly certain she had nothing to fear, she had considered for a moment that if she were to die that day, her legacy would be seven years of giving about half of her all on a Drury Lane stage so sticky with various bodily fluids one might catch a venereal disease just by walking across it; an unpaid tab at half the public houses this side of the Thames; and a fair-weather affair with a woman who regularly tried to stab her, and not in the fun, flirty way.

She retrieves the letter from the table and reads the message again.

> *Longley Manor, Surrey.*
> *March the twenty-fifth, noon.*
> *Don't be late.*

She decides she'll leave at half past—no need to wake before eleven.

2

Among the swollen hills of Sussex, in a village called Middleham, so small it is hardly ever marked on a map, Miss Emily Sergeant stands on a bostal path that cuts through her father's land like a scar. In each hand, she holds a fistful of mud, heavy from the morning's rain and clotted with grass, leaves, and excrement—her father's sheep are prodigious shitters. She holds her arms out from her sides, careful not to stain her dress when she squeezes her fists, and the thick mud spurts between her fingers.

"Robert Tweed," she shouts, her head thrown back so far that her straw hat tumbles off, "is a bastard!"

Beside her, her cousin Violet grabs her shoulders and shakes them encouragingly. "Yes! Yes, he is! What else?"

"He's a crook and a cheat!"

"More specific," Violet says. "Specificity is the soul of grievance—is that not a quotation of Plato?" She grabs Emily by the wrist and thrusts her muddy hand to the sky like a revolutionary, though the defiance of the gesture is undercut when they both have to quickly sidestep the stream of wet mud that rains down upon them. A few drops soil Violet's skirt, but she doesn't wince the way Emily would had it been hers. Violet doesn't have a mother to answer to or a town constantly examining the state of her hemlines, along with every other minute detail of her dress and deportment. Just a disinterested husband and a baby whose expectorations almost any stain can be blamed upon. "What else? And really shout it this time."

"What if someone hears me?"

"No one will hear you out here. You must let it out! Oh, but I do love a good scream. It's so healing. Now, what else?"

Emily considers for a moment. Then, "He never—"

"Louder," Violet says.

"NEVER!"—Emily's throat constricts around the word, unaccustomed to being raised to such volumes—"cleans his teeth!"

"Never!" Violet repeats. "His breath would dissolve fish glue!"

"He does not like music or dancing!"

"What a cad!"

"And he shot George Robinson's hound dog when it wandered onto his land!"

Violet gasps, audacious performance falling away in the face of true wickedness. "The sweet old one, who always let us pet her ears?" Emily nods. Violet steps back, giving Emily's wrist one last squeeze. "Throw it."

Emily pulls back her arm and launches the ball of mud toward the alder tree at the end of the path, onto which Violet has affixed a watercolor rendering of the villain Robert Tweed. The sticky mud sails through the air but falls short, landing with a splat against the roots. Only a few dark flecks splatter the painted scoundrel's chin.

Violet scoops up her own handful of mud and steps up beside Emily, packing it like a snowball. "He grabbed my ass at the May Day dance two summers ago."

"He spoke out against universal suffrage because he thinks the poor are too stupid to vote," Emily adds.

"He told me it would be a shame when Martin and I had children because I would lose my figure!"

"He staffs his Brighton building sites with criminals, then does not pay them wages due to them!"

"He hired Thomas Kelly!" Violet turns suddenly to Emily, eyes wide. "Have I gone too far?"

"No," Emily says, though the name sticks between her ribs like a splinter. "Throw it."

Violet turns to their target, squares her shoulders, then launches her mud ball, though it mostly slips through her fingers and drops down the back of her skirt before she hurls it.

Emily squeezes her own mud ball, savoring the satisfaction of mess and dirt she never allows herself.

Clean hands, all the etiquette books say, are the true mark of gentility in ladies. Any woman may don a dress and a fan, but you need only look to her hands to know the truth of her lot in life. A lady's hands are soft, the knuckles uncracked, the nails unchewed but cut short so they do not click when she is playing the pianoforte. Emily takes great pains to keep her nails clean. Emily takes great pains in all things, in hopes that when a suitor calls, he will find a lady so primped, polished, and well-mannered as to render her past irrelevant. As if the Emily of now—nearly five and twenty, sweet and demure and deferential in all things—could blot out any trace of who she had once been, and what that girl had done.

"Robert Tweed," she shouts—*really* shouts this time, so loudly a starling takes flight from the nearby alder—"has bullied farmers for years into selling him their land for his new road to Brighton.

He took advantage of Mrs. Wild's ailing health and tricked her into signing away all her holdings to him before she died."

"Yes!" Violet whispers at her side.

Emily looks out over her father's own land, the view stretching all the way to the white ribbon of the Seven Sisters cliffs unspooled across the seaside. How many times has Robert Tweed come to their house to collect Emily's father so they might walk to his office or the pub to discuss business? Her father would come home ranting of the gall of the man, the pitiful sum he had offered to buy the Sergeants' ancestral lands, eager to pave over their only source of income to make it easier for him to get to the fashionable new seaside resorts in Brighton. Her parents couldn't live off the offer for a year, let alone the rest of their lives, particularly with their only child sinking into spinsterhood and showing no sign of swimming up.

"He's eight and sixty," Emily says.

Violet nods vigorously. "Not a crime, but far too old to be casting his eyes where he has."

Violet scoops up a second handful of mud, takes aim, then seems to reconsider the distance in relation to the strength of her arm. She takes a few steps closer to the tree before releasing. This time, her projectile strikes the corner of the page, pinning it in place with a wet *thwump*.

How very childish it is, Emily thinks, for two women of their age to be standing in a field, throwing mud and screaming. How even more childish to think she is owed a fate more favorable than this, after what she has done.

But she has spent every ounce of energy since she was seventeen trying to make up for her mistake. All her years of starving herself for a waist small enough to flatter a Grecian bodice and wearing cosmetics that make her skin itch, shoving her feet into uncomfortable slippers and burning her hands with Gowland's Lotion, spreading burned cork on her eyebrows every morning—had it all been leading her to this inevitable end? She learned to sew and play pianoforte and draw, swallowing every bitter medicine like it was treacle. She goes to church and bites back her opinions and curls her hair and never speaks first and pretends she does not feel the critical eyes of the town always upon her, waiting for her to stumble or, when she doesn't, sticking out their legs to trip her up themselves.

She has done *everything* right.

But, more important, she did one thing wrong, once. And now she has reached the final station of her cross.

Emily can hardly bear to stare at the painting, so she squeezes her eyes shut. "He beat his first wife," she says.

"Scandalous gossip," her mother had said when Emily had tried to raise the matter.

"She used to come to church with bruises on her neck," Emily had said, and her mother had replied, "She had a large cat that liked to curl there very tightly."

And Emily could only stare at her, wondering if this was how Galileo felt when declared a heretic for his assertion that Earth was not the center of the known universe.

"He beat his wife," she repeats, louder this time, and rising as she presses on. "And he kicks his dogs and his valets and speaks cruelly of others and has spent years trying to cheat my father out of his land and build a road to Brighton that would ruin our community. I have never met a man, woman, or child who had a single kind word for him, nor he for them." Her throat is tight, eyes burning as her rage spills into frustrated tears. "He is rude. He is hateful. He is cruel and cold. And I hate him. I hate him! I hate Robert Tweed!"

"Throw it!" Violet shouts, leaping with both arms thrust in the air.

Emily flings the ball of muck with such strength she almost tips forward. It sails through the air and strikes true, muck and shit smacking the center of Tweed's nose with such force that the painting is ripped from its nail, but remains stuck to the tree.

Violet whoops, running a lap to the tree, where she mashes the mud into the painting with both hands.

Emily looks down at her own hands, coated in filth. *There is a metaphor in this,* she thinks. A woman in a white dress, fashionable and clean, with her hands stained black—surely the poets would swoon for that. And all from soiling a man's image. God, it's positively dripping with symbolism. But how tired she is of being a character in other people's narratives. She wishes she could fall to her knees and bury her hands in the soil, deep enough that the roots would pull her into the earth, slither under her nails and into her veins. She imagines herself growing into wild vines and riotous blossoms, bursting forth from the forest floor every spring, left alone to flower in her own time.

In the distance, skylarks swoop low over the Downs. The Ashdown Forest blots the horizon with its black branches. Her initials are carved onto half the tree trunks there, alongside Thomas's. In the months after the Night That Ruined Everything, she had retreated into those woods, walking for hours and hours alone, feeling like Persephone each time she emerged, slinking back from Hades, her hair still stinking of the sulfurous underworld.

Emily sinks down onto a half-collapsed stile. Violet comes to sit beside her, handing her the crumpled remains of the watercolor. A single brown eye glares up from the page, and Emily crushes her fist around it.

"Did that help?" Violet asks, and though Emily is grateful for the pains Violet took in preparing this whole mad venture, it has left her hollowed out like a scooped melon.

"Do you feel better?" Violet prompts when Emily presses her forehead to her cousin's shoulder. "Now that you've had the chance to berate Robert Tweed in private?"

"No," Emily says. "For I still have to marry him."

3

Emily and Violet trek back to the Sergeant home arm in arm, walking so close that their skirts bunch between them. Violet chatters inanely, attempting to fill the sad silence with complaints about how weary she is of both her husband and her baby. "Am I horrid? You can tell me if I'm horrid," she says. "I'm sure I'll warm to the child in time, but zounds motherhood thus far is a lousy business. Do you know how long it has been since I slept a full night? And Martin still hasn't approved a nursemaid. He is suspicious of the profession as a whole because his childhood nurse used to hold him by the ankles. He claims that's why he never grew."

Though Violet and Emily had written each other endlessly since Violet and Martin moved to London the year before, having Violet once again just down the road, same as she had been in childhood, while they spent the winter in Middleham with Violet's widowed mother, had been a balm for Emily's loneliness. What would she do when Violet was once again a county away rather than at their breakfast table every morning, the baby handed off to Emily's mother and the two of them left to chat and laugh like they had when they were young?

"Don't go back to London," Emily says, pulling her cousin closer to her side. "Stay here forever with me."

"As dearly as I love you, there is nothing that could entice me to remain in this provincial hamlet a moment longer than is necessary."

"You'll come back for my wedding, won't you?"

They have nearly reached the yard, but Violet stops suddenly and turns to Emily. She reaches up as though to take Emily's face between her hands, then seems to remember their recent activities and quickly drops them. Though they had scrubbed at the pump, their palms still bear the faint aroma of farm. "There must be something we can do to stop your marriage. If you were engaged to someone boring but tolerable like Martin it would be one thing, but Tweed is . . ."

"A villain," Emily says. That, she has decided, is the simplest word for him.

"I'll fear for you every day," Violet says quietly. "Do your parents not hear your protestations?"

"My parents want me married." Though her mother often says it's for Emily's sake, Emily suspects that seeing their daughter to the altar will make her parents feel like some of her residual shame can finally be shaken off. "And no one else in Middleham will have me."

"Then you must cast a wider net," Violet says.

"How?" Emily has never left Sussex. Everyone she has ever met lives so close she could walk to their house in a morning.

"There must be some way," Violet says, "to find you a more suitable husband."

Emily looks down at the drawing, which they had brought with them to throw in the fire lest anyone stumble upon it out in the fields. Violet had been loath to waste a sheet of good watercolor paper on someone as worthless as Tweed, so she had done the rendering on newsprint. Society pages from a London rag peer out from between the streaks of mud and paint, the page splashed with reports of parliamentary debate, a review of a lurid Drury Lane production of *Macbeth*, a series of salacious letters from a criminal conversation trial. Midway down, just below the thickest blot of mud—most of which has now dried and caked off—is a list of the young, eligible noblemen who have come to London for the Season looking for wives.

There are a half dozen names in the profile, which is a small hook to hang hope upon, but as Emily scans the list, an idea occurs to her suddenly with crystalline clarity. She seizes her cousin by the arm. "Take me to London with you!"

Violet's face lights and she says at once, "Wait—truly? Are you in earnest?"

"If I go to London—if I find a husband there—where no one knows who I am or what I've done . . ." Emily pauses, thinking. If she can snare a man who does not know the sins of her past but rather sees only the thin, beautiful, well-behaved woman she has worked so hard to make herself into, surely her parents will find it in their hearts to let her seek matrimony elsewhere. Particularly if the alternate gentleman is richer or more titled than Tweed, and does not have it in his heart to pave over their ancestral land. What could they possibly object to?

"We can tell my parents you need a companion," Emily says.

"I do!" Violet cries.

"Someone to help you with the baby and stave off loneliness."

"*I do*," Violet says more vehemently.

"But in reality—"

"You'll be seeking better prospects than that swine." Violet clutches both Emily's hands in hers. "Oh this will be such fun! I can get you into all the parties and introduce you to my friends and hear music and go to galleries and they will all be lousy with eligible men for you to meet and marry! Of course you must come to London!"

"Emily!" A voice calls from the house and both Violet and Emily turn. Emily's mother is stalking across the lawn toward them, a lace collar affixed to her throat that she had not been wearing when they left. "What happened to your dress?" she barks. "You said you were walking!"

"We got stuck in a bog," Violet says quickly. "You know how fickle the paths are this early in the spring."

"Sakes." Emily's mother presses a hand to her forehead, mouth pulled down, the personification of long-suffering. "Come inside and wash—quickly!"

"Why?" Emily asks as she hurries up the porch stairs. "What's happened?"

"Mr. Tweed is on his way to see you."

"Oh." Emily stops. "Violet and I had occasion to—"

"Whatever plans you have can be rearranged!" Her mother is already bustling Emily into the house, waving farewell to Violet over her shoulder as she shuts the door behind them and turns to Emily. "It's done."

"What?"

"Mr. Tweed and your father have reached an accord. He's coming here to make his proposal of marriage."

A formality, Emily knows, not really a question, for there is only one answer though her stomach still drops. Everything is already arranged—negotiations have been in progress for months. All she can do now is let her mother press her up the stairs and to her bedroom to be made presentable.

The same way a body is before a funeral, Emily thinks, though there is only so much color one can add to a corpse's cheeks. Dying can only be made so beautiful.

In Emily's bedroom, her mother gathers a dress over Emily's head. "Remember," she says as she arranges the material, "Mr. Tweed is quite shortsighted, so be sure you sit close to him. He must see for himself how keen you are. And try not to stand so straight. He is not so tall and you know how sensitive men are about a lady's height. You must do nothing to discourage him." Emily starts to turn so her mother can do up her buttons.

Emily stares at her own reflection in her vanity mirror. The pale lilac material makes her feel like a bruise. "Do you think," Emily says tentatively, interrupting her mother's humming, "Mr. Tweed is the sort of man you would wish to be your son-in-law?"

"Son-in-law!" Her mother clucks. "Good gracious, how old it makes me feel to think of him as such."

Likely because Tweed is older than her mother, though neither of them say it. Emily smooths her dress against her thighs as her mother fusses with the frills on Emily's sleeve until they lie flat. "But . . ."

The cold panic is climbing up her spine again. The thoughts of going to London with Violet and of Tweed on his way here to ask her for her hand rattle inside her like knives in a drawer, each sharpening itself against the other. She swallows, then tries yet again. "Do you not find him—"

"I find Mr. Tweed to be a gentleman established in our community who will give you a good life," her mother interrupts.

"Will he?"

"A life better than you would have alone." She pinches Emily's cheeks so firmly Emily yelps. "You're wan. Now show me your hands."

"I shall be wearing gloves!" Emily protests.

"Hands," her mother says again, and Emily places her hands atop her mother's for inspection. "Your hideous nails." Her mother clucks, then tugs at the back of Emily's dress. "And this is still too large in the bust. Here, let me show you a secret." She digs around in Emily's dressing table and comes up with a ribbon and a silver ring, which she squints at. "Is this sentimental?" she asks. "I've never seen it before."

It is easier to pretend she forgot she kept the ring, rather than it is something she stares at daily in her jewelry box. Thomas had given it to her, and since everything between them had to be secret, she had worn it on a chain around her neck, savoring the illicit thrill every time she felt the cold metal between her breasts. He had told her he stole it from the Prince of Wales himself, when the prince regent's carriage had broken down on the rough road from Brighton to London, and he had luncheoned with the workmen to prove what a man of the people he was.

Thomas had always told her stories like that, and Emily had never known how many to believe. The ring had barely fit her littlest finger—she could not imagine it would fit the prince's large hands. More likely he had found it while digging on Tweed's crew, and conjured a story to impress her. And she had been so impressed by everything about him. Even now, she can't recall those days with him clearly enough to know what was real and what was distorted by the hazy veil of new love.

"No," Emily says. "It is not sentimental."

"Perfect." Her mother reaches down the bodice of Emily's dress, pulling the material through the ring and tying it off with the ribbon so it gathers in a way that looks intentional, rather than like she's trying to reduce the size of the garment without paying a tailor.

"There." Her mother comes to stand beside Emily and together they stare at Emily's reflection in the mirror. Emily is struck as she often is by how little she can see of her own face in her mother's. They have been told they look alike, but she can never see the resemblance. Shared blue eyes and fair hair do not make them the same. Emily's mother's face has always been long and lean, while Emily's small features and pointed chin once drew her comparisons to a leaf. Their laughs sound the same, though—at least, she thinks they do. She can no longer recall.

On the drive outside, carriage wheels rattle. Her mother squeezes Emily's shoulders, then rests her cheek against Emily's.

"I received a letter this week," her mother says suddenly, as though she cannot contain the words any longer. "From Amelia."

"Amelia?" Emily watches in the mirror as her own brow furrows. "Aunt Amelia, your sister?"

"Who else?"

"You haven't spoken since . . ." Emily trails off as her mother's grip on her loosens, and she finishes instead, "What did she say?"

"That she had heard rumor of your impending marriage to Mr. Tweed," her mother says. "And the resort is doing well and might your father and I visit her in Brighton before the end of the summer."

"And will you?" Emily asks.

"Why wouldn't I?"

Because she stopped speaking to you, Emily thinks, but bites the tip of her tongue to stop herself from saying it. Amelia had been one of so many who had excused themselves from the Sergeants' lives in the wake of The Night That Ruined Everything. But could Amelia be blamed? Could any of them? Emily suspects that, had it been someone else's daughter fallen from grace, the Sergeants would have shunned them too. It was simply what was done.

"That's wonderful," is all Emily says at last. "I'm glad you're corresponding with her again."

"I never stopped," her mother says, running her fingers through the ends of Emily's hair. "She simply never wrote back."

Below them, Emily hears the front door open. Heavy footsteps in the hall. She turns to her mother again, thinking this time—*this time*—her mother will see the fear in her eyes.

But her mother takes Emily's hands between hers and says, "Thank you for doing this. For me. For all of us."

Shame, her familiar companion now for so many years, cuts an unexpected path through Emily. And here she thought she knew all the routes it traveled. For what she had done that led them here, but now too for the dread in her heart when she thinks of being wife to Tweed. She has already put her family through so much and let them down in every way. Her single choice had cost them the same as it had her. She cannot let them down again.

She considers telling her mother of her plan to go to London with Violet and find herself a better prospect. The kind of man Aunt Amelia would be desperate for association with. Everyone would. The whole town would come crawling back to her, begging for her favor with the same zeal with which they had once turned their backs.

But then, from below, her father's voice calls, "Martha? Is Emily with you? Send her below, please."

Her mother leans in and kisses Emily on the cheek. "It will be better," she says firmly. "It has to be." Then she pinches Emily's cheeks once more for good measure before she runs to the door and calls down, "Give her just a moment to collect herself!"

She need not tell her mother about London, nor her plot to find a different man to wed. *I will find myself a respectable husband*, Emily promises herself. *For us all.*

4

Longley Manor is two hours' ride from London, and when Harry and Collin climb off their mounts, they're both stiff, though Harry found the ride a joy on Alexander's loaned racehorse. The stallion is registered as Matthew Mark Luke and John and he cuts a dramatic figure with his dark coat and mane so blond as to be almost white. When she had gone to collect him, Alexander's groom had warned Harry that the horse was a keen jumper, but Harry had been unprepared for just how fearless he was in his approach to stiles and ditches and fallen logs. She nearly lost Collin twice when Matthew happily vaulted streams that Collin's mount refused to cross.

As they wait for grooms to collect the horses, Collin stretches his calves with one hand on the saddle while Harry stares up at the manor's columned façade.

She has seen a number of grand houses in her day—often under the cover of darkness and only via a bedroom window that dropped, if she was lucky, into a hedge—but, in a contest of stateliness, Longley would soundly trounce them all. The size alone speaks to the sort of wealth that only those born into it ever manage to find ordinary. The façade is sand-colored stone lined with

Corinthian pilasters and wide windows that must cast light into every corner of every room at every hour of the day. Onion-dome turrets stud the top, and Harry loses count of the chimneys at fifteen.

"Well," Harry remarks. "Not a bad place to be murdered, I suppose. Who do you think owns it?"

"Whoever it is, they don't seem to be in residence." Collin points to one of the upper-story windows, where the panes have been punched out. Only then does Harry notice a bird's nest swaddled in the crook of one of the cornices, and runoff from a damaged drainpipe on the roof that has left a dark streak of mineral deposit on the stone.

Something butts Harry's knees from behind, and she turns to find a gray mastiff with so many folds to its skin that it looks like puddled silk. It sniffs her proffered hand, then leans against her leg, and Harry scratches the dog behind its ears. "Someone's been feeding this chap," she remarks, palming the dog on its belly, which thumps hollowly like a melon tested for ripeness.

"Perhaps he's been feasting on the bones of other Londoners lured through the gate," Collin says, eyeing the dog warily. The dog shakes, spattering them both with ribbons of saliva.

Harry claps a hand on Collin's shoulder. "You see to the horses. I'm going to knock."

"What?" Collin calls after her. "Alone?"

"He'll protect me." Harry holds out a hand to the mastiff, which follows her up the stairs to the entrance like a witch's familiar.

It isn't until Harry and the dog reach the top of the long staircase that she notices the door is not only unlatched but already ajar. A prickle of apprehension crawls up her back. Collin's instinct for caution suddenly feels like it might have been a wiser inclination. She had mostly been thinking of how caution clashed with her outfit.

"Once more unto the breach, dear friend?" Harry asks the dog. He stares at her, unstudied in Shakespeare, but follows when she pushes open the door.

The house's entryway is paneled in dark wood, chipped and splintered, though a few spots still shine with expensive lacquer. A stone stairway splits and crawls upward to a second-story landing rimmed by an ornate balustrade, like might be found in a theater to mark the path to the most expensive boxes. A gold chandelier hangs from the ceiling, and above it, a mural of chubby cherubs frolicking amid petal-pink clouds, while nymphs play lyres and eat grapes and enjoy mythological leisure, decorates the dome. The paint has started to peel, so the faces skew more skeletal than divine. Dust collects in the corners of the foyer, crisp leaves and dead beetles tangled in the clods.

Harry steps cautiously inside, the heels of her boots clicking against the flagstones. She rests a hand on the banister and looks up at the high windows, from which sunlight spills across the dark floor in liquid panels.

"It's a beautiful house, don't you agree?"

Harry whirls and claps a hand to her heart. "Son of a bitch." The dog, which had nearly completed the sixty-five circles needed to lie down comfortably, leaps to its feet and barks once.

A man is leaning against the doorframe off the entryway. He's nearly as tall as Harry, who towers over most, though the height of his raffia top hat works in his favor. His dark hair has gone mostly gray and his cheeks are round and red, the complexion of a man to whom port is always available. His simple linen suit feels both too plain and too clean for the dusty surroundings.

"Thirty-five major rooms on the ground floor," the man says, as though he hasn't just manifested like a spirit with a complete account of the property statistics. "Seven hundred and twenty-five acres. It was built in 1592 by courtiers as a prodigy house to serve Queen Elizabeth when she traveled her realm. What do you think?"

"It's certainly excessive." Harry hooks her hands in the pockets of her frock coat, squinting at the man. "Is it yours?"

The man chuckles, and Harry thinks that no sound is more frustrating than a gentleman chuckling enigmatically instead of explaining himself. "I suppose so."

"Well felicitations, you've a lovely home."

"It could be yours, Miss Lockhart."

The sound of her name cracks the air between them like a whip. Harry frowns. "Who are you exactly?"

The man's smile goes maddeningly broader. "You don't recognize me?"

"Should I?" In her experience, most men possess an overinflated sense of their own remarkableness. Though the slope of his eyebrows and narrow nose niggle at something inside her, she cannot place where she might have seen him before. He's a handsome man, though age has softened his features like a vegetable left too long on the vine, and he's more of a paunch than his doctor likely finds advisable in a man his age. "We didn't shag, did we?"

"My name is George," says George.

"Half the men in England are called George, and the other half are Edward," Harry replies. "God save the king, and all that. What's your family name?"

"Ah." The man considers this, and Harry wonders what kind of imbecile has to give such a simple question this much thought. "I suppose," he says after a moment, "it would be Hanover." He doffs his hat and repeats, "God save the king, and all that."

Good lord.

It's no wonder he looks familiar. She's seen a portrait of a face remarkably like his in every government building and Anglican church and public house and library and post office and upon every sixpence coin she has ever pulled from her pocket.

This man is George IV, Prince of Wales, Earl of Chester, Prince Regent in his father's incapacity and recent ascendent to the throne, soon to be crowned the goddamn king of England.

And—*Christ on toast!*—she asked him if they'd shagged.

Harry fumbles into something like a curtsy, though having no skirt, instead takes the tails of her coat and holds them out at an angle their tailor never intended. She hears something rip.

The prince takes a quick step forward, extending a hand to her. "Please, Miss Lockhart, you need not bow to me here."

"I rather think I do, Your Highness," Harry says, eyes determinedly fixed on her boots. "The rules about showing proper respect to a king are not dependent on geography."

"I am not the king."

"I hear there's going to be a party soon that will change that."

"I beg you not to think of me as such," he says, his voice pinching. "Think of me instead as your father."

"Am I meant to take that figuratively," Harry asks. "In the way that as king you will be father of the whole nation?"

"Miss Lockhart."

Harry raises her head. The prince still has a hand extended, like he's asking her to dance. And suddenly, she knows the real reason his face is familiar. It's Collin's face. It's *her* face. The thick eyebrows and patrician nose that could never be attributed to their broad-featured mother. The dark hair, salting in the same patches as Collin's. Her own thin lips that had always felt like a rebuke to her matrilineal line's full mouths, smiling at her from the face of the Prince of Wales. His eyes squint when he smiles too, just as hers do.

"If you'd come sit with me," the prince says, "we have much to discuss and I'm afraid I haven't much time. I was expecting you earlier."

"Should I fetch my brother?" Harry asks. "It will save you time if we can react simultaneously."

"Let's you and I talk alone first," the prince says as he turns for the parlor. "Surely he knows that, were there real danger, your hound would give chase."

The answer doesn't bode well for her fate as the favored twin in whatever drama she's sure is unfolding, yet Harry follows, dropping the tails of her coat, but remaining in a low crouch, like she's under fire. The dog watches her go, and when its eyes meet hers, Harry beckons it fiercely. The mastiff may look like a drawer of ribbons, but he is a kind of second, should she need one, and Harry has been in enough fights to know the value of reinforcements, even ones of questionable merit. But the dog merely eyes her extended hand, then drops its head back onto its paws.

The furniture in the parlor is covered in sheets, their edges furry with dust. The prince yanks one off a couch and immediately coughs as dust blooms in a cloud around him. He is, Harry thinks as she sits on the bench of the pianoforte and waits for him to finish asphyxiating, likely unpracticed at coming into contact with anything that has not been prepared for him by four or five people. What very different lives they have lived, she and her father.

The question of parentage has never occupied much space in her mind. Once or twice in her youth she had made a halfhearted attempt to pry open the locked doors of their mother's heart and learn the secrets of who her father might have been. But before long, Harry realized it was best to accept that who her father was made no difference to who she was now—her mother certainly didn't give a fig after him, and Harry shouldn't either.

However, even in her bandit youth, it had never occurred to her that her mother might have been consort to the prince regent himself. Let alone that those liaisons may have begot Harry and Collin, or that such lineage might one day lead her here, to a meeting she has a suspicion is about to change her life, though in what way she can't be sure. Is it so outlandish to imagine that she might leave here a princess? Why else would he have called them both? Certainly not just to introduce himself. She wants to ask where this revelation puts her in line for the throne, but it doesn't seem the right moment.

"You're my father," she says as the prince at last settles himself upon the sofa.

"I am," he replies. "And allow me to offer my condolences on your mother's passing."

"Yes, I'm sure you mourn all your whores." Harry sticks her thumbnail between her front teeth, a habit from childhood she always thinks broken until she finds herself under duress. Should she offer similar sentiments on his own father's death, though the mad king had been ailing for so long, Harry wonders if it was a relief to finally have him gone. Still, some sympathy might go a long way. But in moments of emotional stress, she has always found herself reaching for cruelty rather than compassion, which is why she instead says, "Would you like my thanks for not having dropped my brother and me in the Thames as infants?"

"You could thank me for your mother's allowance," the prince replies, and when Harry raises an eyebrow, continues, "Did you never wonder how an incognita could afford the rent on a renovated townhouse in Westminster? New dresses every Easter, tutors for you and your brother, presents at Christmas?"

Harry feels her nail crack between her teeth. "I thought she was a good lay."

"And now that she's gone, I'd like to offer you the same support." The prince pauses, waiting for a reaction. Harry doesn't offer one. "This house is yours, as well as the land and title. I have a second manor set aside for your brother, about a furlough west of here."

"Why?"

The prince must have been expecting grateful tears and blubbering and kissing of his rings, rather than suspicion, for he has to consider this for a moment before answering. "Because I was fond of your mother," he says at last. "She gave me companionship when it was dearly needed. And no matter the circumstances, you are my daughter. I have several children besides you and your brother to whom I am extending similar offers."

"So you can't have loved her *that* particularly," Harry says. She knows there is risk of speaking thus—especially since her current living situation is only slightly better than the workhouse—but suddenly her mother's distrust of the upper classes seems justified. Surely no offer such as this has ever come without conditions.

The prince regent inclines his head. "I hope to fill the nobility with allies."

"What are the conditions?" Harry asks. "Should I accept your offer."

"Did I say there were conditions?"

"There are always conditions. No one has ever given their bastard children a house and a title and asked simply for their word that when the time comes they'll take up your cause. What if I'm a criminal and I use this place as a cache for stolen loot? Or I donate the house to some disgruntled Sapphist cult intent on overthrowing you? I would never, obviously. I'm very gruntled." Harry presses a hand to her chest. "But the Sapphists."

The prince folds his hands in his lap. Presses his thumbs together. Scrutinizes his nails. "I would like to help provide for you, Miss Lockhart," he says. "Your brother as well. I do not wish to see you destitute."

He glances up at Harry, and she can sense a clause creeping up on her like a thief down a dark hallway.

And then the prince finishes, "As long as you are married to a respectable husband by my coronation."

"There we are." Harry slaps her knees and stands, dusting off the seat of her breeches before fishing in her coat pocket for her riding gloves. She'd rather he said she'd need to shackle herself to the colonnade. Literal imprisonment would be far preferable to the prison of matrimony, particularly with that *respectable* carrying so much weight. "As flattering as it is to be one of your loose ends, I must decline."

She starts for the door, but pauses when the prince asks, "How do you plan to keep up your current lifestyle?"

"I earn a living."

"You earn enough to occasionally cover a round of drinks after your matinee," he replies, and Harry almost asks him how he knows her profession before she remembers—goddamn future king of England. "But you live off the remaining allowance your mother provided for you. Or rather, that *I* provided for you, as she had no savings."

Damn. Her mother had so little regard for her children in life Harry realizes she should have been more suspicious about her generosity in death, meager as it was.

"You're a hobby actress," the prince says. "A hobby duelist. A hobby horsewoman. None of those earn much money, do they?"

Hurtful, Harry thinks. Though not untrue.

"All I ask is that you marry and keep up a respectable façade," the prince continues. "Your name will not be publicly attached to mine, but with the bequeathal of the house, assumptions will be made, so I would ask that you exercise discretion. No more duels. Or affairs with nobles. Or thespian pursuits."

"You're asking me to quit the theater?"

"I'm asking you to conduct yourself with more . . . modesty. Though with the house and land, there would be no reason for you to work. The income from the estate would more than support you."

Of all the devil's bargains! She'd rather he'd invited her here to murder her. He might as well have, for these preposterous conditions will leave her so little of herself. Such terms could only have no impact on a life as dull and conventional as Collin's.

Collin.

"Are you making this same offer to my brother?" she demands.

"Yes."

"Under the same conditions?"

"I will require the same discretion and behavior befitting his new station," the prince says. "But there is no marriage clause. The question of ownership and inheritance is less complex, on account of his sex."

"And you would rather perpetuate this inequality between the sexes than address the institutional failing in your capacity as regent?"

The prince smiles. The familiar squint of his eyes is so much less endearing than it was in the entryway. "I'm sure you've heard stories. I myself had a rather misspent youth."

A misspent middle age as well, for by all accounts, kingship has done nothing to curtail Prinny's fondness for drink and gambling and expensive parties. The rags were reporting that for the upcoming coronation, the new king had commissioned a robe with a twenty-seven-foot train, and as many kitchens would be needed to prepare the feast.

"But if, as king, I am to create crucial allies for myself in the nobility, you must understand that their morality cannot be questioned. It would reflect badly upon my own reputation."

"So that is what you want me to be?" Harry asks. "Some kind of respectable buttress so you can keep carrying on however pleases you?"

He considers this for a moment, before he nods. "Yes, that about sums it up."

Harry drops her chin to her chest, hands mashed into her jacket pockets.

The prince stands and faces her. The height Harry had had over their mother suddenly makes a great deal more sense, for she and the prince are nose to nose They stare at each other, and Harry wonders if the prince too is considering how strange it is to meet someone you had before only known in your own reflection.

"Is there anything you'd like to say?" he asks at last.

Bollocks—that's what she'd like to say.

The idea of marriage—not just a hasty one, but marriage at all—makes her want to lie facedown upon the floor. And the bloody morality clause! If she accepts his terms, her life will forever hinge upon what this arbitrary god deems appropriate. Though the prince's ideas of propriety would be secondary, for a reputable husband is better than any morality clause for keeping a woman within the bounds of convention. She suspects that, like so many royal bastards before her, some length could be let out of her father's contractual chain if she exercised a certain amount of discretion. But what husband deemed respectable enough for marriage would want a wife who outfitted herself in trousers and cropped hair?

"What I'd like to say is *damn you*," she replies at last. "But that might get me executed."

"I'll allow it," the prince replies.

"As my king?"

"As your father. You needn't say yes or no definitively today. But I suggest you consider it." He places a hand upon her shoulder, and Harry lets it stay. "Please, consider it, Miss Lockhart. Even if you doubt my intentions, I promise, I am only thinking of you."

"Do I actually have a choice?" she asks. "Or is this simply theater?"

The prince inclines his head. "That depends on what you *really* want from your life."

In the foyer behind them, Harry hears the squeak of the front door, then Collin's voice calls, "Hal? Are you dead?" A scrabble of paws on stone, then Collin cries, "No, get away from me! Don't lick me, no!"

The prince smiles. "Well then. Shall we call your brother in?"

5

"July will be too hot," Robert Tweed says. He is seated on the opposite end of the sofa from Emily with three pillows between them, as many as Emily could place before her father gave her a look. Tweed coughs, then reaches into his pocket for a handkerchief. The loose skin around his neck wobbles. "My gout is always worst in summer. It must be May."

"May is far too soon," her father says. "There will hardly be time to have the banns read. And her mother will want to embroider the dress."

Emily has been sitting quietly since Tweed arrived, as he and her father discuss the particular details of her engagement—if they will have a party, what sort of cake will be served, when they should see the lawyer about the contract that will render her father's land and only daughter Tweed's legal property—but hardly listening. Soon, none of it will matter. She is thinking of London. The noise, the heat, the smoke. And the men—the men! Scads of eligible men who are not currently hacking up phlegm on the other side of the couch from her. Eligible men who have no idea who she is.

"Emily," her father says, and Emily looks up. "What say you to a June wedding?"

"Why should it matter to her?" Tweed wedges a fingernail between his front teeth, digging something free. "She is simply happy to be wed. She'd marry me tomorrow, wouldn't you, lamb?"

Emily blinks. Attempts a smile. Thinks of mud dripping down his watercolor face and all the men in London who will be tripping over one another to ask her to dance. "I'm afraid," Emily says, "that I have a commitment this summer." She turns to Tweed. "My dearest cousin Violet has just had a baby, and I have agreed to travel to London with her and lend my assistance."

"Emily," her father says. "You're not a maid."

"Of course not," Emily says. "I'll be Violet's companion. It's been arranged for months—didn't Mother tell you? Oh, but you know how forgetful she can be. She may even have forgotten herself." She affects an anxious tone. "I gave Cousin Violet my word. It would be terribly inconvenient for her and Martin if I had to withdraw my offer now. They leave at the end of this week."

Her father frowns. Emily prepares to fabricate further, but Tweed speaks first. "Do not trouble yourself." He reaches across the settee and takes one of Emily's hands. His palm is damp, like a spot of earth beneath a stone that never sees the sun. Her skin breaks out in gooseflesh. "There is no need to rush, now the engagement is set. We will be married in September, when you return from your sojourn in London."

"That is very generous of you—" her father says, but Tweed interrupts.

"Mr. Sergeant, would you give me a moment alone with your daughter?" His eyes linger on Emily's neckline as he says, "There are some things I would like to discuss with her."

"Oh." Her father's eyes dart between them. Emily isn't sure which of them her father trusts less—her or Mr. Tweed. "Is that . . . wise?"

"It will only take a moment," Tweed says.

"I would prefer—" Emily says, but Tweed squeezes her hand so hard and so suddenly she almost yelps.

"Leave us," Tweed commands, and Emily's father skitters for the door.

As soon as they are alone, Tweed pushes the pillows between them onto the floor. "Come sit beside me."

"I'm here," Emily replies.

"Closer," he says. "My eyes are not what they used to be. And I should like to see your face."

Emily cannot think of a reason not to, other than the rising of the hair on the back of her neck. She scoots closer, and he smiles. His teeth are flecked with spinach like the black keys on a pianoforte. They must be false. No man of Tweed's age still has all the teeth in his head, and each so white and straight.

"I have always found you beautiful," Tweed says. "You are so slim and pale, like a child."

Emily thinks of the soldiers on the fields of Waterloo, whose teeth were pulled from their heads after they died to make dentures for the ton. Each time she kisses him, she will be kissing a dead man's mouth. Not just one, but many. A smile made of ghosts.

"I know how much you have to gain from this marriage," he says. "Financial security—for you and your parents, and proper management of their assets. A fine house and fine clothes and a staff of servants. And most importantly, since you do not have one of your own, you will have my reputation. But I am not a man who lends his name wantonly."

He pauses, and Emily realizes she is meant to respond. "Of course."

"So hear me when I say that should you do anything that brings shame upon me," he says, his voice lowering, "I will do whatever necessary to see your actions have repercussions."

"I would never," Emily says, "endeavor to bring shame on myself or anyone."

Tweed smiles icily. "Well, we both know that isn't true." He runs his hand along her thigh, and she finds herself frozen, unable to push him off. She has never before considered how large Robert Tweed is. Advanced in age, yes, but still with broad shoulders that suggest an athletic youth hefting hunting rifles.

"A city like London can provide a myriad of temptations for a young woman alone," Tweed continues. "So be mindful of your behavior there, young madam."

"I will not be alone," Emily says.

"Ah yes, this cousin. Though if she has kept company with you all these years, I assume she is no paragon of virtue herself."

"I do not think—" Emily starts, but Tweed interrupts her.

"I don't suppose you've ever been on a rabbit hunt, Miss Sergeant."

"No, sir."

He slides down the sofa, their legs pressed together. His hand, still resting on her thigh, slides upward, closer to her hip. Her muscles are so tense they throb—surely he feels it. "Did you know," Tweed says, "that a rabbit will scream when it is cornered? It's a sound that can be heard for miles. We used to have competitions among the boys—who could extend the noise the longest. Though I never won." He smiles. "I was never one to clip the leg and let it wail. Better to have it done in one clean shot." He pantomimes holding up a pistol and raising it to take aim, but then, rather than fire at an imagined target at the distance, he turns and points the phantom barrel at Emily.

"Do not forget, my dear," he says, and squeezes her thigh. "Rabbits always scream when they are cornered."

6

Harry sits in the Palace Theater's most expensive subscription box with her feet wedged against the rail and her pipe lit. The audience won't arrive for hours, but on the stage below, painted Scottish landscapes are already being rolled from the wings. Inverness, Dunsinane, and Birnam Wood all exaggerated so as to be seen from the galleries, though now that she's in those galleries, all Harry can think is how they really should pay a set painter rather than have her and Mariah doing it themselves, several bottles deep at two in the morning.

Beside her, Collin is folded over like a pocketknife, the tips of his fingers steepled and his elbows resting against his knees. His measured breaths are drowned out by the mastiff lying between them, snoring. The dog trotted after their horses their whole ride home, sometimes falling behind when he was distracted by dandelion puffs, but always reappearing over the next knoll, and now he sprawls in the box between them, snorting in his sleep like a truffle pig on the hunt.

Collin sits up suddenly, running his fingers through his hair, and Harry watches him from the corner of her eye, hoping to find in his expression a yardstick by which to measure the day's revelations. But his face is blank as he watches the stagehands roll Forres Castle off the rail. Either he's taking the whole "bastard children of the prince regent" business better than she is, or she has simply forgotten how very good he is at sucking all his feelings in, like squeezing into a too-tight jacket.

"What day is the coronation?" Harry asks.

"The nineteenth of July," Collin replies without looking at her. "Four months."

"We don't have to go along with this," Harry says, trying to sound more certain than she feels. "Can't we extort him into giving us the houses outright? Or muster an army against him? I suppose that would be treason. Though with our claim, we may be able to play the Henry the Seventh defense and pass it off as a righteous seizure for the good of the nation."

"Please, Hal." Collin leans back in his seat, matching his posture to hers. "You've only just become royalty, surely you can't be a tyrant already."

"The nerve of the man, to barge uninvited into our lives like it's a public ball and force us to follow some arbitrary code of behavior because he thinks having a court of respectable nobles around him will make him look less profligate next time he empties the royal coffers building an Indian palace in Brighton!" Harry says. "To say nothing of forcing me to wed."

"Well, you are a woman of some years—"

"I would recommend you do not see that sentence through to completion."

Collin raises his hands. "Marriage is hardly an outrageous idea, that's all. And he did say we could decline."

Harry had assumed that detail, hastily and halfheartedly pasted on to the meeting, was more of a formality. You *can* turn down your inheritance, in the same way you *can* rob the blind or steal from the elderly. You *can*, but it's rather bad form.

And you *can* live in a pit above the Palace until the boards collapse and you fall through the floor. You *can* keep living on less and less, shackled to a bawdy theater company to survive even though you really had hoped that by this age you'd be doing something that made you proud, rather than peevish and indeterminately itchy.

And the money. It was always about money. She had done a quick accounting of her finances as they rode and realized that without her mother's allowance, she could continue with her current lifestyle for approximately two and a half weeks. Playing the men's roles in Shakespeare has not left her an enviable dowry, and actresses have the average life of daffodils. If she had any sense, she'd have swallowed her pride and agreed before they left the manor.

Below, the musicians make their way onto the stage below, unpacking their instruments for rehearsal. The tonal click of softly jostled strings underscores the stagehands' footfalls. A linkboy is trimming the wicks along the front of the proscenium, lying on his belly and sliding across the floor.

"We will likely both wed eventually," Collin says inadvisably. "You only need speed it along a bit. What is so objectionable to you about that? Besides the legal inequality of the sexes," he adds, preempting a tirade on women's rights from Harry. "You don't think there is a man in England you could marry tolerably?"

"Come now. You've met me." Harry sweeps a hand over her gentleman's duds. "The aesthetic alone. You think any proper husband would let me to sit down to Christmas dinner with his family? And what are the chances that, should I somehow find this lightning strike of a man, I feel in any way tenderly toward him? And, believe you me, if I am to hand over everything I own, including my body, to someone, I must, at minimum, like him."

Collin holds out his hand for the pipe and Harry passes it to him. "There is a compromise between marrying someone you love, and marrying a stranger to appease the prince regent. You might marry a friend."

"Like Mariah?" Harry runs her foot along the dog's silky belly, and he snorts in his sleep.

"If liking your partner is of the upmost importance to you, that may disqualify her."

"I like Mariah!" Harry says. Collin busies himself with the pipe.

What neither of them need say aloud is that legally, she can only marry a man. She will forever be a woman who has loved and desired and lain with the fairer sex. She will never not be a woman who prefers gent's clothes, a whore's daughter, all the things she has worked her whole life to wear like medals rather than a scarlet letter. Those pieces of her will not simply disappear, even if she marries respectably and changes her entire personality, and neither does she want them to. They are her foundations. The things that in her youth she had thought made her strange are now the parts of herself she holds dearest. If the prince, or whatever husband he approves for her, forces her to tuck those things away to make herself more palatable to society, there would be nothing left of the life she had built herself. Just knowing that the prince considers them such—that he thinks of her very existence as immoral—stirs her old insecurities.

Harry presses her hands over her face. "I like my independence," she finally says. "That's all."

"Yes, but that independence will be dealt a significant blow once its financial backing is pulled." Collin puts the pipe between his teeth, then adds, "And perhaps you might think of this as more than a material opportunity."

"An opportunity to what, exactly?"

"Let go some of your more unsavory proclivities."

"Ah." Harry presses a hand to her forehead. "Now I recall."

"Recall what?"

"Why we don't speak anymore."

"I only mean," Collin says, grabbing her arm preemptively should she try to storm out, "there's a halfway point between marrying a man you hate and one you love, and there exists a similar stop between *this*"—he sweeps a hand up and down, indicating her frame, same as she had, but it's so much more annoying when he does it—"and stuffing yourself into lace and petticoats and learning to watercolor. You don't have to give up your whole self in order to be considered more savory. But you may perhaps express it in a way that befits your age. And new station."

Harry stares at him, debating what vicious name to call him before she storms out, but then Collin clears his throat and says, without looking at her, "My apologies. That came out rather coarser than I intended."

"Thank God," Harry says. "Because you sounded like an ass."

"What I meant to say is, let me help you."

"Help me become more *savory*?" Harry asks, smacking her lips around the word. "Like a quiche?"

"The Season is still in its infancy," Collin says. "I'll do the circuit with you. I know enough of the right sort of people that I could get us into the parties and balls, and I can make introductions. Not every member of the ton is dull and prim—you may meet someone you like."

Harry considers this. The idea of having to rely upon Collin for anything rankles her, to say nothing of what his idea of a suitable husband is and how irritating it will be to watch him force that definition on her like a prophet bringing down his gospel. But if the prince is determined to see her a bride, and she is unwilling to marry a stiff-shirted lesser noble who calls her things like *my lady wife*, a suitor deemed appropriate by royalty will likely only be found in the particular drains her brother orbits.

Though if she is to endure her brother's company, she refuses to get nothing out of it other than a dull husband. "Let me stay with you," she says. "I'll be tossed out of my rooms at the end of *Macbeth* unless I sign on for the next one."

"Won't you reup?"

"The prince asked me to resign. Well, not asked, but he strongly implied he doesn't approve of Sapphic Shakespeare. And if I'm to be respectable now, I can't be taking callers in some rank Drury Lane garret. Oh, I could even bring Havoc!"

"Who?" Collin asks.

"Havoc!" She nudges the mastiff with her foot. "That's what I've decided to call him. It's the line from *Julius Caesar*: 'Cry "Havoc!" and let slip the dogs of war.'"

She expects Collin will roll his eyes, but instead, this terrible pun earns one of his rare laughs. "You'd have to promise—"

"No blood, I swear to it. At least not once *Macbeth* is over. Speaking of." Harry stands and stretches with her hands behind her head. Havoc stands too, dipping into a bow with his tail in the air and his toes curled. "I've got a beard to adhere. You should stay and see the show!"

Collin laughs again, colder this time. "As fetching as you look in those whiskers, Hal, I refuse to sit through five acts of lamentable

Shakespearean tragedy performed by women with oversized codpieces."

"Ah, but you see," Harry says as she picks her way to the back of the box, Havoc at her heels. "That's the joke!"

"It's *Macbeth*," Collin calls after her. "There shouldn't be *any* jokes."

7

The following afternoon, Harry goes to see Alexander Bolton, Duke of Rochester, for their postponed ride.

The last time they saw each other, Harry's hair still fell to her waist, and Alexander had been a pimpled, poorly proportioned youth who had overcompensated for his meager looks and short frame with a biting wit and too much energy.

He had also been piss drunk and reciting Homeric poetry to a hedge he had mistaken for a lady.

Now, as he trots from the barn and across the paddock to where she is waiting for him with Matthew Mark Luke and John, face split in a grin, she hardly recognizes him. In their years apart, he has transformed into the picture of clean-aired, warm-blooded country living. Blond hair with a soft curl frames his wide, pleasant face—all he needs are panpipes and a line of soft-eared ewes trotting after him down a country path and you could drop him comfortably into a Boucher painting.

"Harry!" He throws his arms around her, the strength of the embrace lifting her off her feet. "Where have you been?"

"Off riding a horse some daft gent's groom let me walk away

with," Harry replies, her face squashed against Alexander's shoulder. "I was tempted not to bring him back."

"You came so early! I was still in bed."

"What do you call him?" Harry asks. "The full name is far too long."

"Just Matthew, usually," Alexander replies. "The breeder christens all his horses after books in the Bible, but the Gospels had to be combined for registration purposes."

"You're lucky you got in early in the New Testament. If he was called Philippians, no one would bet on him for fear of misspelling it on a racing form."

Alexander laughs, then slaps her on the shoulder. "Come, let's ride. I want to see you on Matthew."

Harry notices he leaves his hand on the small of her back just a little longer than is natural, his eyes sweeping her frame before he turns, the same way she is admiring the cut of his breeches, so tight they nearly render him an anatomical drawing. The curve of his ass as he climbs astride his horse is the first thing to truly distract Harry since the revelation of her lineage.

Harry and the duke ride most of the afternoon, Alexander on his Arabian, trotting on the heels of Harry and Matthew. Now that she need not regulate Matthew's speed lest Collin grumble about being left behind, Harry lets the horse show off the extent of his youthful athleticism. He's keen to be told what to do, and responds well to Harry's directions when she stands in the stirrups, knees bent, and leads him to the next jump.

Alexander finally calls for their return to the stables as the sun is beginning to set. Harry could have ridden longer, and suspects Matthew could have as well, though he slurps gratefully when water is offered. Harry too drinks deeply from the bucket hanging off the fence, then splashes her face, watching as Alexander leads his Arabian into the yard to meet them.

"I've had an idea," Harry calls to him as he dismounts. "What if you give me Matthew? It will save him the trouble of running away from home to be with me and breaking your heart."

Alexander strips off his jacket before dunking his whole head into the trough. Harry watches as he shakes the water from his hair like a dog. His shirt clings to his shoulders, and when he turns, Harry can see the muscled cords of his back through the translucent material. When had her daft friend become so fit?

They'd first met when Harry was twenty and Alexander only six and ten—a young aristocrat washed up at the brothel where Harry's mother used to work, in hopes a night with a Camden fen would make him a man. Harry had stumbled across Alexander in the common room, sweating and stressed and still a virgin, for their first attempt had ended with Mariah shouting that fucking him was like trying to shoot billiards with a rope. Harry had calmed his nerves with a few hands of cards, and the next day he had sent her flowers at the Palace in thanks. They had become fast friends after that, haunting the same seedy London circuit until Alexander left for the Continent on a tour his father hoped would tame him.

Harry isn't certain it had the desired effect, for now he's fit *and* charming, and though she had never before numbered him among the very short list of men she finds attractive enough to bed, she suddenly finds herself wondering if she had simply never seen him clearly before. Maybe it's the confidence with which he now carries himself that's sending pleasant tremors through her belly.

Or maybe it's his thighs.

Perhaps both.

He catches her staring and grins. "I like your hair."

"I like your ass," she says, and he lets out a surprised bark of laughter. "Don't laugh, it's true! I might have written you more if I knew you'd gotten so fit."

"I played a lot of cricket," he says, ducking his head as though bashful, but Harry knows him well enough to spot the performance.

"In Paris?"

"In Sussex. I've been back at my father's estate for a year."

"Ah, well that's probably better for your health than staying up all night betting on cards and drinking cheap gin."

His lips quirk. "I still do a lot of that too."

They lead their horses to the barn and into their respective stalls. Alexander has grooms that can do the work for them, but Harry insists on removing the tack and picking out Matthew's hooves herself.

As she pries mud from the horse's shoes, Alexander calls to her over the wall separating the two stalls. "Tell me how you've been, Harry! How's the Palace?"

"Likely to be condemned any day now," she replies. She considers telling him about her mother's death. The gulf between her and Collin. Even the recent revelation about her paternity and that she may not be much longer at the Palace because of it. But she and Alexander have never been on terms *that* intimate, and she cannot imagine what such a sudden change in atmosphere might do to the mood. She had once tried to talk to him about tension in the Palace company over the casting of *As You Like It* and he had, quite literally, run from the room to avoid unpacking that emotional carpetbag. The sporadic letters they had written to each other after he left to tour had never included more than the set dressing of their lives. Alexander, she had long ago learned, was not a man to whom one bares their soul.

Though neither had he been a man with such an impressive ass. Perhaps all things could change.

She opens her mouth to continue, but he begins speaking before she can. "My father won't stop nagging me about my spending. I'd renew my subscription box but he's put me on an allowance while I'm here."

"Were you not getting an allowance before?" Harry asks.

"No," Alexander says, sounding genuinely surprised. "I simply had access to his accounts."

Harry tosses a chunk of what she expects is a bit more than just mud over at him. "I cannot imagine why he regretted that decision."

"Ho there, my whist game has improved considerably. And this horse breeder I met in Essex—the one who sold me Matthew—has taught me a much wiser strategy than my previous method for playing the ponies."

"Which was?"

"Bet on the prettiest one."

"The same method you use for ladies."

"Well, it serves me, doesn't it? You're here." Alexander's head appears over the stall divider, arms folded and chin resting on his hands. His hair, half dry, is the color of just-harvested honey. Harry does her best to appear nonplussed. She knows Alexander is a prodigious flirt, though that had never before amounted to anything more than a few teasing pecks. Harry never wanted it to. That she is even considering it now is new and thrilling in a way that is almost indistinguishable from fear.

"Harry," Alexander says, reaching over the stall to flick one of the cropped strands of her hair against his thumb. "Do you know what I thought the first time I met you?"

"How much fun it must be to have a face this fine?"

"I knew I wanted to sleep with you at least once."

"Good God." Harry drops the pick and stands to face him over the stall wall. "Are you trying to woo me?"

Alexander grins, and Harry is gratified to see his cheeks color faintly. "Is it working?"

"Assuredly not," Harry says, lying. "Thank God you only got fit—if you were suave too, the ladies of London would be murdering one another in the streets to get a swing at you."

Alexander catches her by the arm as she turns back to Matthew and pulls her to him, both of them pressed to their respective sides of the stall wall. "What about you? Do you want a swing?"

There is, Harry thinks, a good chance that sleeping with Alexander is a decision that will age like milk. But if she is about to be forced into monogamy against her will, she is determined to see as many people naked as possible beforehand.

Which is why she takes Alexander by the collar, says, "Now who could resist an offer like that?" and kisses him.

AFTER, THEY LIE naked together, wrapped in Alexander's luxurious sheets, and though Harry is far from satisfied—Alexander, it would seem, has become so good-looking that sexual proficiency isn't really required—she's still pleased by the evening's turn. She dozes with her head on Alexander's shoulder, only waking in earnest when he kisses her on the forehead, then pries himself from her and begins to dress.

She watches from the bed, and when Alexander catches her eyes in the dressing table mirror, he grins. "I had a fine time today."

"As did I." Harry arches her back, pointing her toes to relieve the cramps in her muscles.

"We should ride again."

"In which sense?"

"Either. Both."

"I'm on as Macbeth the rest of the week, but I could stay the night."

Alexander splashes cologne onto his jaw, then retrieves a neckcloth from where it's draped over the bedpost. "I'll be out until the wee hours, I'm afraid. A dance at the Argyll Rooms."

"A dance?" She flops backward onto the pillows. "Oh hell, are you in London because you're looking for a wife?"

He grimaces. "Not by choice, believe you me. More an obligation my father thinks I have put off long enough." He straightens his jacket, then gives himself a long, admiring look in the mirror. "Perhaps I could just marry you," he says as he reaches up to fix his hair. "Spare me from the miserable grind of the Season."

Harry smiles, watching as he fingers the thick locks at the nape of his neck. Then suddenly she finds herself thinking . . .

Well, why not?

If she and Alexander were betrothed, her search for a spouse would be over before it had begun. They'd dance together once or twice at public balls, be seen riding in Hyde Park, and no one would think it anything but love when he proposed marriage a few convenient days before the coronation. And surely the prince couldn't find anything unsuitable about a duke.

Within their holy bonds of matrimony, she could do what she liked, and so could Alex. As husband and wife, they would have good conversation, maybe sex sometimes, but it would never be odd to introduce him to her lovers at the breakfast table. She wouldn't ask him to give up gambling and drinking and late nights at clubs, and he would never raise a fuss if she did the same. She'd still need to exercise some discretion, but at least the enemy would not be lurking in her own home under the guise of a suitable match.

Crikey, Harry thinks. Has she just solved marriage?

Alexander retrieves a fresh pair of boots from the wardrobe, then comes to sit on the side of the bed beside her as he pulls them on. She slips a hand around his stomach, then into the waistband of his breeches, crooking her thumb and first finger around the shaft of his cock. Alexander's hands slip on the buckles. "You devil," he murmurs, and leans over to kiss her, his mouth spiced with cardamom tooth powder. She bites his lip.

"Harry," he murmurs. "I think I have a proposal for you."

"How interesting." Harry slides into his lap, straddling him with her arms around his neck. "I have one for you as well."

"I suspect mine is a bit more . . ." His eyes stray from her face to her breasts. She can feel him getting hard against her. "Unconventional."

God but her heart is pounding. Is she the first woman in England to go pudding brained over a marriage of convenience? She is already imagining what she'll paint over that fat angel on the ceiling of her new manor. She'll throw the windows open every morning and read Shakespeare in the sunlight. She'll take Havoc for long walks on grounds that are hers and let him piss wherever he likes. She'll only see Alexander when one of them needs a friend—or a shag.

And then Alexander says, "Harry, would you ride Matthew in the Milton Derby steeplechase?"

Harry had been so ready to cry *Yes, yes, a million times yes!* she has to swallow several times to force the words back down her throat. "I beg your pardon?"

"It's a novelty race," Alexander says. "So all the jockeys are ladies. But they're quite the competitive bunch, and it's no easy win. The lass who was going to ride him took a fall in training and won't be in the saddle again until at least August, but the race is in June."

And suddenly, Harry finds the face she had been so fond of mere moments ago so aggravating she wants to slap it. She slides off Alexander's lap and falls backward onto the pillows.

"I know it's sudden," he continues, oblivious. "But I've been going mad over finding someone who can manage Matthew. He's no challenge for the professional jockeys, but most women can't handle him on the hedges. And it's rather important to me that he performs well, this being his first outing. I'll surely have money on him. As will some of my friends." He pauses, then pats her knee over the blankets. "But here I am going on. You had something to ask me?"

Harry raises her head. Alexander's eyebrows knit in concern and yes, that jawline is sharp enough to halve fruit, and perhaps she is still under its spell, for she still asks, "Will you marry me?"

Alexander coughs, loosens his tie, then loosens it further. "Pardon?"

"I need to marry as a matter of some urgency," Harry says. "And if you're also on the prowl, we might as well help each other."

He rubs a hand over his neck, then says with painful gentility, "Harry."

Harry's stomach drops. Nothing good has ever followed such a tender intonation of a name. Before he can gently direct her elsewhere, Harry hurtles herself onto the conversational footpath and cuts him off. "It would be a marriage in name only. We needn't be faithful or monogamous or even involved in each other's lives."

Alexander collapses next to her on the bed, his boots leaving dark streaks of polish along the sheets. Harry rolls over onto her side, propping her head on her elbows to face him. "But we'd *enjoy* each other! I've always liked being around you—we get on. We are both accustomed to our particular lifestyles. If we wed, we wouldn't have to compromise that. We can even write it into the vows. *Till death do us part, and until then let us never hold the other to a respectable time to rise from bed.* What say you?"

Alexander rolls toward her, dinner jacket bunched up under his arm. His immaculate cravat is starting to come undone, and Harry is struck by a sudden urge to reach out and fix it. "You know I adore you, Harry," Alexander says. "But I need someone a bit more conventional. Or who can at least pretend to be. I'm already on the rocks with my father, and I've promised him I'll find a suitable wife this Season."

"If it's about an inheritance—" she starts, ready to tell him about the recent revelation of her parentage, but he interrupts.

"It's not that. You simply don't fall under any father's definition of suitable."

Her skin prickles. Suddenly she feels too exposed, and pulls the sheet up over her breasts.

Alexander frowns. "Have I upset you?"

"No," Harry says, her tone at odds with the sentiment.

"Come, Harry, we both know you're not the sort of woman one can take to church or home for tea. And you'd hate being made to do such things—you'd start to chew through the walls."

"Weren't you leaving?" Harry snaps.

"You're right." Alexander sits up, reties his cravat, then leans down for a final kiss. Harry knows it's petulant, but still turns her head so his lips barely glance off her cheek. "You're welcome to sulk here as long as you like."

"I am not sulking," Harry replies. "I'm pouting."

"What's the difference?"

"If you marry me, you'll learn very quick."

"Good night, Harry."

"Good luck finding a *suitable* wife!" She rolls onto her stomach. She feels Alexander's fingers ghost over her shoulders, but she ignores him, and a moment later, the door latches as he departs.

She lies in bed until the sky outside the window is black, wearied by the rapid slide from elation to despair. Still, she doesn't allow it to keep her company long—she has seen the only happy ending that might be written for this story, and she will not surrender hope so easily. The prospect of marrying Alexander, however brief, has forced her to begrudgingly admit to herself that she not only wants the house and land and money, she *needs* them, lest she find herself watching her father's coronation from a kip under Blackfriar's Bridge. Without her soul being the price, the best she can hope for is to marry someone outwardly respectable who will not ask her to change a thing about herself, nor run to the prince to report on his wife's behavior. And since the only man she can think of who fits the bill is Alexander, he must be convinced to marry her.

She stands and crosses to his dressing table. A card has been wedged into the space between the mirror and the frame, and she fishes it out. An invitation to a private ball hosted by the Majorbanks family this Friday. Harry sinks down onto the bench, snapping the card against her palm.

If Alexander needs a wife he can take on his arm to a ball, she's prepared to show him she can be that woman.

She has no invitation of her own, but Collin knows the ton and Harry knows forgers. She is almost certain Alexander will be tired of waspy girls in Grecian gowns before the second quadrille of the night. And with whom will he seek solace? Whose very presence will be thrown into extraordinary relief by the contrast of so many dull, vapid women he imagines to be the sort he wants to marry? She'll wear a dress and a wig and paint her face—proof she can be prettied up and let out in public. She may even bring a peafowl on a leash, if she can find one on such short notice.

Harry will be at the Majorbanks's ball—gorgeous and suitable and goddamn irresistible. When she tells him the truth of her parentage, she'll look every bit the part of royalty.

She and Alexander will be married by the coronation.

8

"I promise you," Violet says. "I was told there would be men here."

Emily stares dully across the drawing room, a sea of skirts and bonnets and curls. "At a *ladies'* tea?"

"Nowhere on the invitation did the word *ladies* appear," Violet says. "I was told it would be a mixed reception!"

"By whom?"

"I don't remember! I haven't been getting much sleep." Violet presses her gloved hand to her forehead. "I'm sorry. I know this isn't what you hoped."

"It's fine." Emily looks around, wondering if it's too soon for them to leave. She feels nauseous, and not only because of the three glasses of lemonade she has gulped down since arriving. The room is hot, and she plucks at the front of her dress. She has employed her mother's trick with the ribbon and Thomas Kelly's ring again to gather the material of her bodice, but even with Violet's help, it was not so elegantly done, and she's concerned it might fall at any moment.

"I've been out of the social scene for a while," Violet says.

"I understand," Emily says, and she does, though it hardly tempers her disappointment.

This might be enjoyable were a marriage not waiting at the end of it. This party—this whole London sojourn—would be delightful had she not felt the need to inventory every man in her presence, and weigh their worthiness of her time accordingly. The city itself—her first time outside of Middleham—would have been thrill enough had every day she passed there not simply been one closer to marrying Tweed.

She had thought, based on the stories the dowagers of Middleham trotted out every summer about their own London Seasons thirty or forty years previous, the city would be lousy with noblemen prowling the streets, each in search of a pale, blond bride with small opinions and a smaller waist. To hear them speak of it, Emily had thought she might get press-ganged into courtship by an eligible viscount on her first short walk from the carriage to the Palmer's front door.

But after a fortnight in the city, she has yet to cross paths with even a minor baron. Violet's social circles are more robust than Emily's, but those particular muscles haven't been flexed since before her baby was born. The Season has been in bloom since January, and though it's barely April, all eligible prospects seem to have already been snapped up. So, in spite of Violet's valiant efforts to secure them invitations, they have thus far been only late additions to a single picnic and two sewing circles. They had squashed themselves into the back row of a public violin recital, at which Violet had been unable to stay awake and Emily had been too fearful of impropriety to talk to men without her cousin to make an introduction.

And now they are passing another afternoon at another useless reception. Not a man for miles.

Violet leans against the wall, stirring her tea absently with her pinkie finger. "It's nice to talk to adults, though, isn't it?" she says. "Everyone uses sentences. And words. No one vomits on you."

"Admirable traits," Emily agrees.

"And everyone is so self-sufficient! No one needs anything of me! Did I tell you I accidentally locked the baby's room with keys and baby still in it?"

"And so you had two copies made of every key in the house," Emily says, for she has heard this story several times, though she doubts Violet remembers telling it.

"I'm still afraid it wasn't entirely an accident." Violet stares sightlessly ahead for a moment, then begins tipping slowly sideways.

"Are you falling asleep?" Emily asks.

"I might be," Violet replies. "I'm not sure I'm ever fully awake anymore."

"Ladies." They both straighten as Lady Dennis, the imperious hostess, approaches them. Her daughter floats behind her silently like a ghost. Both of them smile in the same manner, with their lips pulled tight, showing no teeth. "Mrs. Palmer," Lady Dennis offers Violet her hand, then turns to Emily. "And who is this?"

"My cousin Emily Sergeant," Violet says. "Visiting me for the summer from Middleham."

Instinctively, Emily tenses up, the way she always does when her name is trotted out for the first time. But Lady Dennis smiles, and Emily takes a deep breath, reminding herself that no one here has any reason to think her anything but a proper young lady.

"Have you come for the Season, Miss Sergeant?" Lady Dennis asks. "You seem of too advanced an age to be on the marriage market."

"My coming out was delayed by . . ." Emily swallows. "A local tragedy."

"You poor dear. Would that I could share with you some of Anna's invitations." She nods to her silent daughter behind her. "We have received more than we can attend. I had to send regrets to the Majorbankses this morning, can you imagine? *The Majorbankses!* But we had already agreed to sup with the Irwins in Hampstead that night, and their son is so keen on Anna. He brings in four thousand pounds a year!"

"A shame," Emily and Violet say in unison.

"Indeed!" the dowager replies. "I heard the Majorbankses have secured the attendance of the Duke of Rochester."

"Duke?" Emily repeats.

"Have you yet seen him?" Lady Dennis asks eagerly. "He's quite the catch of the Season. Just returned from a spell abroad. Very wealthy. And keen to be wed, so I've heard."

Well, Emily thinks. *Tick, tick, tick.*

"There are so many fewer Dukes in London than amatory novels led me to believe," Emily says, hoping the sentiment might inspire Lady Dennis to offer tips for how to make this meeting occur, or perhaps even their spot at the Majorbanks's ball to Emily in her stead. "I should love to meet one in the flesh."

Lady Dennis simply says, "My dear, wouldn't we all?"

As the dowager and her daughter float away, Violet slumps against the doorframe, fanning herself. "Do you think anyone would notice if I lied down?"

"Depends where you lie," Emily replies, taking Violet's cup from her hands. "I'm going to get more lemonade."

Emily leaves Violet and starts toward the dining room where refreshments have been laid out, but pauses for moment at the hallway intersection, where she can see the front door, nearby which presumably lie the stack of cards and letters to be sent out. Including the invitation to the Majorbanks's ball with the Dennis's regrets, in spite of the assured presence of a duke.

She couldn't.

She must.

She abandons her empty cups on a sideboard and sneaks to the front door, slippers quiet on the polished floor. The stack of cards is substantial—Lady Dennis hadn't been exaggerating her daughter's numerous calls—and Emily flicks through them quickly.

"May I help you, madam?"

Emily jumps, nearly dropping the stack of letters, and whips around. A valet stands behind her, a parcel of letters to be added to the stack in one gloved hand.

"Lady Dennis asked me to fetch an invitation for her so we might confirm our arrival times are the same." The lie tumbles out of her with surprising speed. "May I check your stack? I can't seem to find it here."

The valet hands Emily the cards to examine, and—yes! There it is. Emily pulls the Majorbanks' stationery from the stack. "I'll take this one for her, thank you."

Emily waits a moment after the valet departs, then cracks the wax seal on the invitation. She pulls her glove off with her teeth and spits on her thumb, then rubs out the pencil marks spelling out regrets.

She can send it from Violet's house, with their reservation. They can pretend to be the Dennises for the evening—and what difference will it make to the Majorbankses? Besides, it's not as though she's attending with plans to steal the silverware or lift a bottle from behind the bar like she and Thomas once had.

Thomas.

The memory is sharp and unexpected as a pinprick: her and Thomas sneaking into a magistrate's private party only to be chased off by one of the valets. They had hidden for nearly an hour in the gardener's shed, giggling and shushing each other until they were found and escorted out.

In the stillness of the empty hall, she can almost hear his voice, inviting her to slip away. Find an empty room and make their own fun.

No good has ever come from her own choices in men. Perhaps she should trust her parents. Marry Robert Tweed.

But then she thinks of Tweed's damp hand on her thigh, the way he had pointed the imaginary pistol at her chest, and she clutches the invitation more tightly.

She slips the reservation card into her reticule, then goes in search of a pen.

9

Harry leans against the glass wall of the Majorbanks's orangery, a vision in burgundy, sipping fortified punch. She's half listening to the man at her elbow, who is wearing so many shades of pink as to resemble a salmon canapé, as he recounts with agonizing specificity the time he met Edmund Kean at a cricket match. Though the further he gets into the story, the more Harry suspects he actually met a cove who happened to have the same small, pointed mustache as the famous actor.

This night, she thinks, is nothing like she hoped it would be.

For one thing, Alexander has not yet appeared, and she is beginning to doubt he'll come at all.

For another, upon securing the invitation, Collin insisted on accompanying her in order to make introductions to eligible gentlemen. She told him plainly that she was only interested in Alexander, but Collin insisted. Though she has avoided her brother most of the night, he has still sent a parade of dull gents her way, of which the canapé is the latest.

Harry surveys the crowded ballroom, potted trees lining the perimeter dotted with bright colored birds in gold cages. A gallopade has just finished, and the musicians are taking a recess. And there—at long last!—is Alexander, bobbing like a swan in a sea of mothers extolling the virtues of their unwed daughters.

"Will you excuse me?" Harry says to not–Edmund Kean's friend and leaves before he can respond. "Alexander!" she calls, relishing the brandy-sweet taste of addressing him by his invited name.

The mamas' heads all whip toward her, like flags in a wind that has abruptly changed directions. Alexander looks too, brow furrowed for a moment before he recognizes his rescuer.

His eyes widen. "Harry," he says, then catches himself and amends, "Miss Lockhart."

"May I steal you away?" She fastens her hand around his arm, dragging him gently toward the refreshment table. "I have a question about this camellia by the punch bowl."

"Ah yes, I do love a good camellia." Alexander falls into step beside her, letting her lead him behind one of the exotic fruit trees that line the dance floor. Once they're out of sight, he collapses with his head against her shoulder in relief. "You didn't actually have a question about camellias, did you?"

"Don't be silly. Here." She scoops up two glasses of punch from the table and presses one into his hands. "Cheers."

Alexander clinks his cup against hers. "What are you doing here?"

"I'm attending a ball in hopes of securing a spouse," she replies, resisting the urge to punch him on the arm, as she suspects the gesture will not make her look particularly wifely. "The same as you."

"Oh. Well. That's . . ." Alexander is staring at . . . not quite her breasts, but breasts adjacent. It's like looking at someone's forehead instead of their eyes when speaking. He reaches out suddenly, almost like he's in a trance, and takes the pearled hem of her sleeve between his fingers.

"Alex," Harry says, and he drops his hand quickly.

"Right, yes." He shakes his head, like he's trying to rouse himself. "Well, Godspeed, I hope you find this man."

"Alexander." She catches his hand. "Don't be dim."

He rolls his neck, staring up at the ceiling with a sigh. "Harry. I can't."

"Look at me!" She spreads her arms, indicating the dress, the hair, the breasts, all of which was chosen specifically to convey, *I can be suitable. I can be respectable. I can be equally favored with your stuffy parents and the Sapphist set of the London theater.*

Alexander does indeed look. His tongue darts out to wet his lips. "You are a sight tonight, I daresay."

"Aren't I?" She touches her wig, the same warm brown of her hair. One of the dressers at the Palace helped her pin it so expertly it's almost impossible to tell it's a piece.

"Is it too forward to say you look beautiful?"

"Far too forward. You can make up for the impropriety with an equally inappropriate waltz." She plucks the pencil from her reticule and opens her dance card. "Now, is it Alex with an *A*?"

"Saucy." He slaps the card playfully so it falls to the end of its ribbon around her wrist. "Go on then. Let's have a dance. Put me down for—"

But he is interrupted when someone knocks his shoulder from behind. Alexander turns to apologize to a slight blonde in a white dress, just as she drops her fan. He retrieves it for her and returns it with a smile. She curtsies, cheeks red, and departs.

The entire interaction is minuscule. Ordinary. It should be nothing.

But Alexander's eyes linger on the woman, mapping her thin frame, her white gown, her modest blond hair swept into an elegant arrangement. Beautiful and conventional and as different to Harry as sun and shadow.

"Alexander," she prompts.

"Apologies." Alexander rubs the back of his neck. "What were we . . ."

"The waltz," Harry says. "That you'll dance with me."

"Yes, of course. I'll . . ." Alexander turns around again, and hellfire and damnation, he's looking for that slight blonde in the slight dress, she's sure of it. "Do you know who that was?"

"Who?"

"That woman. The one who dropped her fan."

"Oh, Bathsheba?"

He's practically standing on his toes, pawing at the foliage for a better view of the floor. "Do you know her?"

"I can't recall, her face was so forgettable." Harry flicks his shoulder with her dance card. She meant for it to be playful, but she thumps him hard enough that he flinches. "What about my waltz?" Harry says, though it feels like she's bailing out a sinking ship with a teaspoon. "I think it's customary to put your name down."

"Yes, right, I'll just . . . give me a moment, will you?"

"Alex—"

But he holds up a hand and says, still searching the floor, "I'll find you later."

Harry watches him go, unable to think of something to say that would make him reconsider his pursuit of that tiny blond ladybird. She blows a sharp breath through her nose, pressing down on her back teeth. Can she intervene? Should she? Surely once Alexander actually talks to a diamond of the first water, he'll realize how much better Harry is in comparison.

But before she can decide, a hand fastens on her elbow, and Collin's voice tickles her ear. "I managed to secure you an invitation tonight. The least you can do is acknowledge me."

Harry tries to twist from his grip, but he holds firm. "Consider yourself acknowledged."

"Come, there's someone I want to introduce you to."

"No need—I found Rochester."

"Your beau? He's here?" Collin looks around. "Then you can introduce me to him."

"I'd prefer not to."

Collin frowns. His dark suit looks expensive, though Harry notices a spot of what is almost certainly Havoc's drool on his cuff. "Why not?"

"Because you'll find a thousand tiny flaws that disqualify him from marrying me, when the only real thing that's got you in a twist is that you didn't pick him."

"I will not."

"You already don't like him because he and I are friends."

"Well." Collin's eyebrows twitch. "Even you must admit you aren't the best judge of character."

"Jesus Christ," Harry says, forgetting for a moment she's meant to be respectable. "I shan't introduce you. And don't go looking for him."

"I won't—"

"Promise me." Harry presses a fist to his chest, over his heart. "You'll meet him in time. I just need to clear up a few details first."

Collin stares at her for a moment, then fastens his hand around her fist. "I promise, I will not speak to your Duke of Rochester without an introduction from you first." Harry is about to thank him, but Collin interrupts her. "But if you're looking for someone our father will deem acceptable, you need to look beyond your own circles. Which is why—Mr. Barker!" Collin calls, and Harry realizes that her brother is waving over a middle-aged man with so much hair growing from his nose it could be fashioned into a mustache.

Harry tries to run, but Collin still has her wrist in a genteel shackle. "Mr. Barker, allow me to introduce my sister, Harriet Lockhart. Harry, this is Mr. John Barker. I thought you two might get along, as he's a great admirer of the Bard."

"Collin," Harry says, but Collin is passing her hand to the gentleman like he's handing over the lead of a dog. "I must find—"

"The lady does too much protesting, methinks!" Collin says to Mr. Barker with a hearty laugh.

"That," Harry says, "is not the quotation."

"Ah well, I'll let you two recite it correctly on the dance floor." And, with a last vicious smile, Collin scampers back into the trees like a matchmaking squirrel, leaving Harry alone with a thoroughly unappealing suitor.

"Miss Lockhart." Mr. Barker gives her a small bow. "Shall I compare thee to a summer's day?"

"No, no, I'm quite all right," Harry says. At that moment, she feels herself more a frosty night in an interminable January.

"Perhaps you might accompany me for the next quadrille. I can favor you with a recitation from *Coriolanus* while we dance."

Of course that's the play he would select. There is no way she can be expected to dance a whole set with this man and not make an anus joke. The injustice of being a lady! The cruelty of her father the prince! She wishes she could hand this Mr. Barker off to one of the other women here, like a present at Christmas received and then given again at the next holiday.

Or. Perhaps she can.

"Mr. Barker," she says, the idea still forming as she speaks, "Have you yet seen *Macbeth* at the Palace Theater?"

"Ah, you mean the Scottish play?" He presses a finger to his lips, invoking the theatrical superstition, and Harry indulges him by mimicking the gesture. "It is my favorite of the Bard's tragedies, though I've never had the opportunity to see it staged."

"Alas, there are not many performances left, and I hear it's hard to secure a seat. However." She pauses, feigning consideration. "I am well acquainted with one of the actresses."

Mr. Barker's nose hair twitches. "Are actresses not"—he lowers his voice—"all whores?"

"Of course," Harry says seriously. "I met her through a charitable foundation that gives them Bibles, for which I volunteer my time."

"I see." Mr. Barker nods, his moral objection to actresses in no way extending to a moral objection to the theater itself.

"As thanks for teaching her Scripture and needlework, the actress in question offered me a box at the final performance, but a lady such as myself would never set foot in such a den of iniquity." She presses an aggrieved hand to her chest. "Might you want to take my place?"

He runs a hand over his chin. "If the seats would otherwise go to waste, I would be happy to—"

"Ah!" Harry holds up a finger. "But wait, Mr. Barker. There is something you must do for me first."

10

Is anything worse than walking into a party? Emily thinks as she stands shoulder to shoulder with a potted lemon tree and tries to look more at ease than she feels.

The room is stifling. A hothouse, it would seem, is still a hothouse even when repurposed for a ball. Violet had vanished what must be a quarter of an hour ago, having promised to return with punch and a man to introduce Emily to. In the meantime, Emily is holding up the wall. She's been clutching her fan so tightly since that gentleman knocked it from her grip that she's starting to sweat through her gloves. What does one do with their hands at a party? She looks around, trying to find some other attendee standing alone whose behavior she can mimic, but everyone is broken off into twos and threes, chattering and laughing and trading dance cards. An old panic gutters in her, the memory of standing on the fringes of the social hall dance floor in Middleham and pretending she did not know everyone was whispering about her. *No one here is talking about you,* she reminds herself, but still the buzz of conversation around her seems to solidify and shape itself into those familiar rumors. *Did you hear about Miss Emily Sergeant and that man she—*

"Excuse me."

Emily turns. It takes her a moment to recognize the gentleman behind her as the one whose shoulder she knocked—she had hardly registered his face, too distracted by the Amazon of a woman beside him wearing a wine-colored dress in a cut that can only be worn by the exceptionally brave or the exceptionally well endowed, of which Emily is neither and that woman seemed both. A woman in a dress like that likely never wonders what to do with her hands.

But the gentleman—here he is again. He dips his head as he takes her hand with a genial smile. "I do hope you'll find my impertinence charming, for I could not bear letting you pass me by without knowing your name. I am Alexander Bolton, Duke of Rochester."

Crikey, has she accidentally been doing the correct thing with her hands after all? For not only has she been approached, but by a duke no less! *The* duke, the one Lady Dennis had called the catch of the Season. If she came home on the arm of an age-appropriate, handsome duke, her marriage contract to Robert Tweed would surely dissolve like salt in water.

Rochester smiles, and his teeth are white and straight and all his own. And yes, Emily knows that her list of desired attributes in a man is short—*not coupled* and *not Robert Tweed* being really the only two—but he might be the most handsome person she has ever seen.

"I did try to find someone to make an introduction," he says. "But you seem to be a mystery. I'm happy to fetch the master of ceremonies to introduce us, if that makes you more comfortable."

"Miss Emily Sergeant," she says quickly. "I am recently arrived in London, visiting my cousin."

He touches his lips to her knuckles, and she silently repents for every time she ever rolled her eyes at girls in amatory novels who swoon at the single touch of a man, for she feels her legs turning to jelly. "Let me be the first to welcome you. How does this night compare to the many other balls you've surely been attending?"

Emily laughs. She had hoped it would come out girlish but instead it sounds rather manic. "This is my first in the city, and the town I come from is so small that I have never walked into a party and not known nearly everyone there."

"Well then, allow me to show you some London hospitality and find you a glass."

Rochester takes her hand again, and though they're both gloved, Emily is certain his knuckles are slick with expensive lotions, and his nails manicured, for surely this is a man with great regard for his personal hygiene. "Wait for me," he says, then kisses her hand lightly before he disappears into the crowd.

As soon as his hand leaves hers, Emily realizes how damp her palms are. Her gloves are stuck to her knuckles. She starts to fan herself with her hand, then remembers she has an actual fan and whips it open. *Who,* she thinks, dabbing at the sweat along her hairline, *chose a goddamn hothouse for a ball?*

"Emily," she hears Violet call, and she turns, eager to tell her cousin about the handsome duke who had approached *her,* of all the ladies here!

But Violet is not alone. She's accompanied by a man near Emily's father's age, with bristles of wiry hair creeping out of each nostril.

Violet is smiling but widens her eyes at Emily, a silent apology. "Emily, this is Mr. John Barker. Mr. Barker, my cousin, Miss Emily Sergeant. Mr. Barker saw you across the room and asked to make your acquaintance."

Emily extends her hand, and as Mr. Barker kisses it, his nostril hair brushes her wrist. "Good to meet you, Mr. Barker."

"Miss Sergeant," he replies. "You look most exquisite in white. May I have the next dance?"

"Oh. I . . ."

She would like to wait for Rochester to return, but she also knows a lady never says no to a dance, and what would the duke think if he found her rejecting men because of some one-sided allegiance to him? So Emily pins on a smile like an ugly brooch gifted by an elderly aunt. "Yes, of course, Mr. Barker. I'll pencil you in for the next quadrille, shall I?"

"Or perhaps this one?" he asks, and damn, yes, the musicians have just picked up their bows for another set.

"Of course." She glances over her shoulder at Violet as Mr. Barker leads her to the dance floor, and Violet mouths *Sorry!* before taking a sip from one of the two punch glasses in her hands.

Once the dance begins, Emily expects Mr. Barker will make inquiries about her health or parentage, or even the weather—all the niceties he had neglected before sweeping her onto the floor. But he makes no attempt to converse. Instead, he dances like it is a competition, and he is determined to finish first. At the end of the set, Emily is pink-cheeked and out of breath, searching the room for Violet. Or a chair.

But there is another man with Violet asking to make Emily's acquaintance, this one plump and ruddy-cheeked and introduced as Mr. Chesterton. She isn't certain he gets her name before he leads her back onto the floor.

After Chesterton, she pencils in Messrs. Wilde, Harris, Burton, Bell, Tottenham, and Shufflebottom. All the men of London seemed suddenly lined up to dance with her. Some enlist her cousin for an introduction before whisking her out to the dance floor. Others charge in alone. This sudden interest should bode well for her marriage prospects—except that once engaged in the reel, not one of the gents seems to have any interest in conversing with her. They don't offer to take her on a turn about the gardens after, fetch her a drink, or even sit with her while she recovers her breath. One spends the whole time telling her about the girl he intends to marry, which is only marginally better than the one who explains the process of breeding swine, with gestures.

When the final set before supper is called, Emily's toes throb. Her dress is plastered to her back with sweat, and she has lost several feathers from her hair, like a molting bird. She finally manages to spin away from the dancing and collapses on a bench beside the refreshments, struggling to catch her breath.

"You look as though you need this now more than ever."

When Emily raises her head, Rochester is standing before her, holding out the long-ago-promised lemonade.

"Have you been waiting all this time?" Emily asks, taking the glass gratefully.

"Well, I confess, I drank the first cup I retrieved for you," he says. "And the second. Possibly a third, I can't recall—there is quite a lot of brandy in it. You seem to be a popular partner tonight. I don't suppose there's room for me?"

"Oh I'm sure . . ." Emily flicks open her card, only to find that somehow every space is already filled. She nearly screams in frustration. This time next week, she'll still be here, turning mindless circles around this orangery on the arms of men who don't give a fig about her.

"I'm sorry," she says, but Rochester waves away the apology.

"Perhaps you might meet me in the garden before supper instead?" he asks. "Under the pergola? Fresh air should do you good."

"It would be my pleasure," she says just as her next partner takes her by the arm and drags her back onto the floor.

To her great surprise, as the musicians raise their bows, she realizes she is once against facing Mr. John Barker. His nose hair is somehow even bramblier.

"Mr. Barker!" Her tone falls short of the pleasure she hoped to convey and instead lands somewhere between surprise and disappointment.

"Ready to go again?" he asks as the musicians begin.

Mr. Barker bows, then reaches for her hand, but Emily pulls backward. "Mr. Barker," she says again, struggling to remain civil when what she would really like to do is grab him by his nose hair and shout. "Forgive my impertinence, but we have already danced a reel tonight and you seemed disinterested in getting to know me better. Why exactly is it that you seek another turn?"

She expects he will deny his lack of interest, or at the least offer some blustery explanation. The best she can hope for is that the question alone will cause him to storm off the floor and she'll be free to chase down Rochester.

But instead he says, "A woman gave me tickets to the theater."

Emily blinks. "Beg pardon?"

"She gave me tickets to a Drury Lane show. All I had to do was ask you to dance." He sniffs, and his nose hair quivers. "I'm mad for the Bard. Particularly when the ladies' troupe does it. You know sometimes they take their tops off. Of course, I avert my eyes, but it can come on most unexpectedly—"

"What woman?" Emily interrupts.

"She's there, in the burgundy dress." Barker points, and Emily turns, just in time to spot the woman she saw earlier with the duke slipping from the hothouse. And with Emily's dance card full and Rochester nowhere in sight, it isn't hard to reason who she's off to meet.

"Son of a bitch," Emily mutters.

11

Behind the hothouse, a long pergola is draped in yellow wisteria, blooming riotously. Pollen of the same color drifts through the air, and fuzzy bees weave drunken paths between the blossoms. The air seems to hum with them.

There is no one there when Harry arrives, though, after purchasing her way into filling the dance card of her rival—Miss Emily Sergeant, Mr. Baker had reported to her in exchange for an upgraded box at the Palace—she had gone looking for Alexander and found him absent. A gent in the card room finally mentioned that last he heard, Rochester was meeting someone in the garden. Which is when Harry realized that Miss Segreant too had vanished from the dance floor, and Harry may be rubbish at sums, but even she can do math that simple.

The pergola seems the likeliest place for a rendezvous, secluded and romantic as it is, and indeed, within only a few minutes of arriving, Harry hears footsteps on the gravel path behind her.

She turns.

"Oh." Miss Emily Sergeant steps into a patch of moonlight, buttery and warm as it filters through the foliage. "I thought you were someone else."

And Harry—for a moment—is struck dumb.

The immaculate Miss Sergeant from the dance floor is gone, replaced by a ferocious fury. She has unfastened her hair so that it falls in sweat-damp cords over her shoulders, and her dress is creased. Her cosmetics have been wiped from her face, leaving only her mouth stained faintly red, like she has just taken a bite of a ripe pomegranate.

Harry recovers enough to raise her hand and call jovially, "Good evening. Have you just been pulled from a lake?"

The muscles of Miss Sergeant's throat tighten as she swallows, though, to her credit, when she speaks her voice remains demure. "Forgive me, but I must ask you to leave."

"Why is that?" Harry asks.

"I'm meant to meet someone here."

"As am I."

"Perhaps you might meet them somewhere else."

"Perhaps *you* might," Harry says, "as I was here first, and I suspect you followed me."

Miss Sergeant's cheeks pink. "I think I'll wait," she says. "If you don't mind."

"I do," Harry replies. "But I don't suppose that will stop you."

Miss Sergeant gives her a smile so withering it could salt the earth. Harry almost takes a step backward, out of swinging distance, but she's certain the cut of Miss Sergeant's dress would not allow her to raise her arms above her shoulders. "I don't believe we've been introduced," she says, offering Harry her hand. "Miss Emily Sergeant, at your service."

"Who is he?" Harry asks, ignoring the gesture of friendship. When Miss Sergeant looks confused, she says, "The man you're meeting. A lover? It's not—but I shouldn't speculate." She presses her fingers to her lips. "Gossip is such a low vice. But I saw you with so many men tonight it's difficult to choose just one."

Emily's cheeks go from pink to red, and Harry knows the implication has poked a particular bruise.

"What is it he likes about you?" she continues. "Desire can be a heady substitute for self-worth, you know."

Harry expects a jape in return—she certainly set herself up for one, just to see if Miss Sergeant would trip the snare—but Emily turns away, back toward the gilded light of the hothouse. Good lord, has this chit given up already? Harry thought she might put up a fight, and she would be forced to try a different approach, such as whipping off her own wig and exclaiming, *Do you know how many suitable men in London would let me keep my hair this short? There is only one, and he's here, and I'm sorry, but I must do everything possible to marry him, even if it means sacrificing your prospects!*

"Or," Harry asks, "is it his estate you're so keen on?"

Emily Sergeant turns her face upward to the wisteria like she's calling on God for patience.

"Has anyone called you a *fortune hunter* yet, or may I be the first? Do they have those in whatever provincial hamlet you come from? Or," Harry continues, unable to resist digging in her heels, "maybe it's just that he looked at you. All some ladies want in a man is a pulse, a title, and a giant—"

"Oh sod off!"

Miss Sergeant whirls around, her modesty shed suddenly as a dressing gown dropped to the floor. Harry is struck dumb. She had expected tears, not a virulent curse paired with smoldering eyes.

"Yes, you, you contemptible twat!" Miss Sergeant stalks forward and pokes Harry in the chest, each word sharp and savage as that punctuative finger. "I want you to sod off and leave me alone, you meddling, cow-faced harpy." Emily reaches down and wrenches off her slippers. "I hate these shoes and I hate this dress and I hate the imbecile who decided to host their goddamn ball in a goddamn hothouse. I hate you and I hate every inbred, mouth-breathing, clap-ridden fruitcake who went along with your pathetic"—and here she flings one shoe at Harry—"juvenile"—the other follows—"scheme to ruin my evening."

Harry raises her hands. "Steady on."

But Emily isn't finished. "Does it make you feel better about yourself? To treat me like dirt and embarrass me and ruin my chance at happiness? I'm sorry I'm thinner than you and prettier than you and have better posture and teeth and don't need to dress like a common whore to catch a man's eye. How justified you must feel in being a childish bitch!" Miss Sergeant throws her arms wide. "Well congratulations, you ruined my night, now kindly sod off and leave me alone."

Harry gapes. She has never heard a ton lady use language so blue. Even the brothel bullies at the Covent Garden houses would have blushed at such vocabulary. And what diametric opposition, all those vulgar words tumbling from the small, rouged mouth of a slender lady in classical white. Harry could not have been more surprised if one of the caged canaries around the hothouse dance floor had asked her for a cigar.

It is also maddeningly—*maddeningly!*—arousing. Harry is never so drawn to a woman as when they are yelling at her. The cursing, it would seem, is an even more powerful aphrodisiac.

"That," Harry says, "was beautiful."

"Oh God." Miss Sergeant raises a small hand and presses it to her mouth, eyes wide with horror. "Please don't tell anyone."

"Tell what? That you lost your temper and called me a fat, ugly, cow-faced whore?"

"I can't believe I . . . I promise, I never . . . I apologize, I don't know what came over me."

"What would your suitor say about that? Ah, here he is now!" Harry raises her hand to the pretend figure down the path, and Emily spins around with a squeak of terror. Finding no one there, she whirls back on Harry, and Harry thinks for a moment she might cry. Or start cursing again.

"Please," Emily says seriously. "That is not a reflection of my character. I am tired and overheated and I am . . . not myself."

And her eyes are so big and wet and pleading that Harry feels an unexpected stab of guilt wiggle between her ribs like a blade. She has the distinct impression that Emily's outburst was the equivalent of champagne, shaken and shaken and shaken for years until the cork finally popped. Nothing to take to heart—she just happened to be the one holding the bottle when the pressure became too much.

It should be Harry who apologizes—she *has* ruined this woman's night, after all, whether or not her ulterior motives were benevolent. Self-servingly benevolent, yes, but the two were not mutually exclusive. But admitting wrongdoing, no matter how righteous, will force her to surrender any high ground she has won. And she cannot surrender Alexander just yet. Miss Emily Sergeant, with her small waist and delicate hands and flat chest that sits perfectly in a Grecian gown, will have many men who could make her happy. For Harry, there is only one.

"I'll keep silent," Harry says, "if you leave."

Emily glares up at her. A petal falls from the wisteria and lands on her shoulder. Harry almost reaches out to brush it away.

Emily bends slowly, retrieving her shoes from where they landed on the path. She takes a step forward, face turned up so she and Harry are nose to nose, and for a delirious, delusional, absolutely insane moment, Harry thinks Emily might kiss her. She feels suddenly light-headed and reaches to steady herself on the pergola.

But then Emily says, "Go to hell," before she turns and stomps away, leaving Harry under the wisteria, dazed, alone, and still maddeningly—*maddeningly!*—aroused.

12

Emily flees the pergola, face hot and dress plastered to her with sweat. Her heart is pounding in her ears, so loud she can hardly think through the din. She wants away from here. She wants to be back in Sussex, in her small room in her small house years in the past, on the Night That Ruined Everything. This time, she'll stay beneath the covers. She'll ignore the stones against her window. This time, she'll do everything right. She will not be the sort of woman who calls a stranger a twat and throws her shoes. What had come over her? She has not lost her temper in years. She long ago barricaded that door, jammed it, locked it, and threw away the key, papering over that darkest, most unladylike piece of her.

She feels suddenly light-headed and stops to steady herself with a hand on a Grecian statue. Years of anger at the unfairness of life had exploded from her, Pandora's box flung open in the smug face of *that woman*. It feels like a rotted tooth finally pulled from her head, but the relief doesn't negate the pain.

The nerve of her. Anyone, Emily assures herself, would have lost their head in the face of such a . . . well.

Even had she not been commanded to depart, she can't bear the thought of returning to the party. Surely Violet will work out what's happened if she returns home. Emily is nearly to the drive, prepared to make her escape on her own two bare feet if she can't find a cab, when she hears someone call her name.

She turns, and there, of course, is the Duke of Rochester, and she is shoeless and her hair is down and she can't decide if she's actually crying or simply so angry it feels like it. He diverts his course from the pergola and jogs across the lawn toward her with a broad smile. "I was afraid you had left," he calls, "and I had missed my waltz."

Emily blots at her forehead, trying to sound as poised as she had earlier that evening, when lemonade and the crowded dance floor loomed largest in her mind. "Not yet, my lord. Should we have it now?"

"I think there's about to be a recess for supper." Alexander stops before her with a smile, which Emily fails entirely to return. "Are you well?" he asks, his eyes drifting to her slippers clenched in each hand.

"Quite." She can think of nothing else to do, so she holds up her slippers and says, with light hysteria, "Just resting my feet."

"Of course. You were quite the sought-after dance partner this evening."

"I was lucky to share the company of so many excellent men."

"And a few undesirables as well, I'm sure," he says with a conspiratorial wink.

Every piece of etiquette Emily was ever taught flits around her brain like flies trapped in a jar. Do not frown, it puckers the skin. Do not laugh, it creases the eyes. A smile is a lady's best weapon. A scowl is as good as a chink in the wall, and to speak ill of others is to only speak ill of oneself. Do not mention the man who smelled of fish or the one who stuck his finger up his nose before taking her hand or the one who said her dress made her look rather wan.

"All the men were lovely and kind," she says.

Rochester looks again at her shoes, and Emily wonders if she should put them back on. What had she been thinking taking them off? That vile woman had goaded her—had she? Emily can hardly remember anymore.

"Were you meeting—" she says at the same moment Rochester asks, "Would you care to sit with me? Oh—you first."

How to ask now without sounding jealous? But also how to continue this acquaintance if he has his sights set upon that woman under the pergola? "Were you meeting . . . someone else?"

"A gentleman—for business talk, nothing for you to mind. Come, sit with me a spell. I was going to suggest a turn about the garden but if your feet are aching—"

"I'm happy to take a turn," Emily says, resisting the urge to hurl the damned shoes into a nearby hedge. "Whatever you wish, my lord."

She knows she's working too hard to compensate for actions Rochester didn't witness, but she's worried that if she lets herself slip even for a moment, she'll fly at him the same as she did that horrible woman. She cannot falter. Not now, not with him.

But the duke insists they rest, and Emily lets him lead her to a stone bench at the lip of a lily pond where they sit a chaste foot apart.

Rochester smiles, and he is very handsome, she thinks. Or at least pleasant looking. Or wealthy, which can often be mistaken for handsomeness. "Tell me about yourself, Miss Sergeant," he says. "I'd like to make better acquaintance."

"I am quite a simple creature," she replies, a deviation memorized from *The Lady's Book of Etiquette*. "But if you tell me what you enjoy, I will endeavor to make your interests mine."

Rochester laughs like she's made a joke.

Emily waits. Conversation, the book had advised, relies on a lady to originate, and then sympathize. Whatever he says next, she is going to sympathize the hell out of.

Rochester stares at her for a moment, then his eyes widen. "Oh, are you in earnest?" He rubs the back of his neck, glancing from side to side. "Come, surely you can think of at least one thing about yourself I should know."

Oh God, she can't. She can't tell him where she's from, or the names of her parents or what her father does lest her secret be exposed. And she has been so dedicated to the hobbies of preparing herself for marriage and trying to reassemble her ruined reputation that she has had little time to cultivate other interests. She could tell him she enjoys embroidery, but what if he asks her to explain what exactly she likes about it and catches her in a lie, for there is nothing to be enjoyed about embroidery? Ruining her eyes so she has a plausible excuse for not reading the Bible? Or pricking her finger hard enough to justify skipping her practice of the pianoforte—is that anything? Is this the nature of an interest?

She could tell him something innocuous to throw him off the scent. Maybe her height, but perhaps he will think her too tall.

"Miss Sergeant," Rochester says, and she realizes she has been quiet for too long. "Do you enjoy dancing?"

"I . . ." Why does every question feel like a trap? She wants to pluck at the front of her dress and separate the sweaty shell from her skin. She wants to rip the whole thing off, lie down in the soft grass, and let the earth absorb her. "Do you?"

"It is not my preferred way to spend an evening, but with good company and a few rounds of cards, a dance can be a jolly good time."

Emily nods. "I agree."

Silence again. Rochester picks at a loose string on the cuff of his coat. Emily contemplates suicide.

"Do you like horses, Miss Sergeant?" Rochester finally asks, his tone the conversational equivalent of a wild leap for a gangplank being drawn onto a departing ship.

"No," Emily says, and that, at least, is the truth.

Rochester purses his lips.

"But if you do," she says quickly, "I could develop an appreciation. Of a sort."

It is . . . something, at least. Enough that Rochester accepts the bone she has not just thrown him but positively pressed into his hands and begged him to take—*please, just take the goddamn bone!* "Well, I recently purchased a racehorse," he says. "Very lean, very fast. I thought I was going to have him running circles at the Downs like his prestigious ancestors. Only to get him home and find he has an unexpected knack for jumping. Can't keep his feet on the ground."

"Perhaps he was a Pegasus in a previous life and remembers he once had wings," Emily says, so goddamn grateful to be having *something* resembling a conversation that she realizes too late the reference meant to be a joke may instead make her seem overeducated, and what man would want that in a wife?

Rochester's brow creases. "What?"

"A . . . Pegasus," Emily repeats, then, in hopes of reframing the comment as an opportunity for him to teach her something, adds, "Is that not the winged horse from the Greek myths? I must be remembering wrong."

"Ah, so you like mythology."

She swallows. Liking mythology is a bit of a leap from making a single reference to Pegasus, but Emily doesn't want to contradict him. What she wants is water—the nearby pond taunts her, for she can neither sociably drink from it nor drown herself in it. She inclines her head in a way she hopes passes for a nod and will thus close the subject, then asks, "What does one do with a jumping racehorse?"

"Well, he has his first outing next month in the Milton Derby steeplechase," Rochester replies. "Have you been to a horse race?"

He must truly think her a sheltered country mouse to ask such a thing. But perhaps if she says no, he will thrill to take her on a new adventure. She can feign wonder at how fast the horses run, and say daft things like *I'll bet on that one because he's gold like my hair*! "I haven't! I don't think we have them in Sussex."

Oh hell. She had not meat to reveal her home county. And before she can hurry the conversation past it, Rochester repeats, "Sussex? Is that where your family is from? Mine as well—perhaps I know your father."

"I can't imagine you do," Emily says. "He's a simple farmer. And I," she says, regretting the ridiculous words as they leave her mouth but unable to corral them, "his simple daughter."

Rochester sighs tightly, then pushes himself up from the bench with his hands on his knees. "Well, Miss Sergeant. It has been lovely to meet you, but I think I should return to the dance."

"What?" Emily's heart jumps and she nearly seizes Rochester's hand to pull him back down to the bench beside her. The conversation hadn't exactly been sparkling, even she can admit that, but she hadn't expected it to end so abruptly. Where was her invitation to join him for a waltz? Sit by him at dinner? His question of when might be best to call upon her? She had done everything right!

"You've leaving?" she says.

"Only going back inside," Rochester says, though he might as well have declared himself en route to the moon for how hopeless and small the words make Emily feel. "We can have our dance another night, yes?"

"But . . ." Panic rises in Emily's chest, the suffocating, trapped feeling of being stuck inside a too-small sweater. This cannot be happening. She has a duke alone in a London garden, for God's sake! He sought her out! What in their meager interaction has soured him to her so quickly? "What have I done wrong?"

"You haven't done anything wrong," Rochester says. "You're, ah . . ." He clasps his gloved hands before him, considering his next words carefully. Though unless they are a proposal of marriage, Emily knows she'll be incapable of receiving them as anything other than a criticism. Just another way she is ill-suited to be a bride, her past be damned. "Miss Sergeant, you are very beautiful. And with manners like yours, I'm sure you'll have no trouble finding a man who would love to make you his wife. But you're just so . . . dull."

The word *dull* strikes her like an apple thrown at the back of the head. The surprise registers more than the impact. "Dull?" she repeats.

"I wish you all the best," Rochester continues, his obliviousness another apple, this one straight to the nose. "Perhaps our paths will cross again this Season."

"And upon that crossing of paths," Emily calls as he begins to make his way back to the hothouse. She knows desperation does not flatter a woman, but she cannot let the Season's most eligible duke slip away so easily. "Might we continue our acquaintanceship?"

Alexander raises his hands in exasperated acquiescence that

Emily chooses to read optimistically as at least adjacent to continued interest, until she hears his response. "Of course, Miss Sergeant. Seek me out again should you find yourself a personality. Or meet a horse."

Emily still has her wits enough about her to wait until Alexander is out of sight before she tips sideways onto the bench, pressing her face into the stone. She shoves her fist against her mouth, suppressing a scream while also wondering what it would matter if anyone heard her.

"Miss," she hears someone call behind her, footsteps crunching upon the gravel path. "Miss, are you quite well?"

For a wild moment, Emily thinks Alexander has changed his mind and returned. But when she sits up, she sees a different gentleman, this one dark haired where Rochester is blond, trotting toward her with a hand extended in concern. "Yes, thank you," she says, quickly brushing off the front of her dress.

The gentleman stops, hand still extended though he does not touch her. "Has someone hurt you?"

Yes, Emily thinks, *many years ago.*

"No," Emily says. "I'm quite well."

The gentleman looks unconvinced, for which Emily cannot blame him—she's a poor actress and can hardly play off a face-forward plunge into a stone bench as an expression of contentment.

"Will you allow me to sit with you for a spell?" the gentleman asks. "Until you've recovered."

"I'm afraid I'm a poor conversationalist at the moment."

"We needn't converse." He takes the spot on the opposite end of the bench from her. The cast-off light from the orangery highlights the gray around his temples, though he cannot be past forty. "I'd be a poor gentleman if I left a lady in distress."

And then he smiles, so kindly that Emily finds herself speaking without sufficient consideration. "Are you married?"

His mouth twitches. "I'm not. Though I'm afraid I'm not looking for a wife at the moment."

"But if you were looking," she says, "what qualities would you say you find becoming in a woman?"

"Ah. That's . . . quite a broad question." He ponders for a moment, hands resting on his knees, then says slowly, "I suppose I myself am drawn to women who are kind and intelligent. Who speaks freely but not wantonly, and can admit when she's wrong. Who does not act with haste or carelessness, but when she does, makes sincere attempts to make amends. Who is forgiving of herself and others."

"What traits do you want in a wife then?" Emily asks, for that answer was almost entirely abstract and thus terribly unhelpful, and made no mention of skills on the pianoforte. She almost lets out a bubble of hysterical laughter at the thought. How much time she had wasted on that blasted pianoforte.

"Someone I enjoy being with," he says. "A partner. A friend. Someone I laugh with, but to whom I can also confide in. When something happens in my life, she should be the first person I think to tell, be it good or bad. And I should want to share everything with her. Someone interesting and clever and funny and remarkable. When standing in front of the Colosseum in Rome, my thought should not be of its majesty, but how much better it would be if she was there to see it with me."

Damn, where was all *that* in the etiquette books? Emily slumps. "You mean you don't want a quiet mouse with no character of her own?"

"I beg your pardon?"

"It's nothing." Emily presses her feet into the grass, savoring the chilly prick of the blades. "Only, I'm afraid I've spent a good deal of time learning to be all the wrong things. That's all."

"Did someone say something to you? About your demeanor?"

Emily nods. "A gentleman I had an interest in called me dull. Apparently girls need hobbies and opinions and a knowledge of horses, or at least a knowledge of why she doesn't like them." She sniffs, then adds, "Which I suspect doesn't negate the fact that she also must have a tiny waist and a perfect bosom with no effort or artifice."

"Is this gentleman so important?" the man asks. "I do not wish to make assumptions, but I noticed you spent quite a lot of time on the dance floor this evening with a great number of men. One man is not the world."

Perhaps not, Emily thinks. *But only one man's land and title this Season can trump Robert Tweed.*

"Are you in love with him?" the gentleman asks.

"Good heavens, no, I just met him," Emily says. "Though I suppose I am in love with the life he could offer me." She presses her wrists delicately to the corners of her eyes, though she knows her cosmetics are already ruined. "But I will continue to pursue him. I cannot be discouraged so easily, even if it means I must alter myself entirely to tempt him."

The man stares up at the sky, considering for a moment, then asks, "Are you living here in London?"

"For the summer."

He runs a hand along his chin, then glances at the house, like he is checking to be certain no one is coming their direction, before turning his body toward her and saying confidentially, "Forgive me if this is forward, but I have a bit of a mad idea. I think I know someone who could help you. If you really are the conventional lady your gentleman seems to think, she—my sister—may provide a counterbalance. She could show you a bit of London you wouldn't see otherwise. And you might be good for each other—God knows she could use some refined company."

"That would be helpful," Emily says, when really what she wants to say is *Yes, please, show me the woman who has mapped the expanse between what men say they want and what they actually want in a wife!*

"Perhaps you could come for tea at mine tomorrow and meet her? You're welcome to bring a chaperone. Influence aside, it might do your heart good to have friends in the city."

"That would be lovely. I'd be glad to attend." Emily holds out her hand to him. "I'm Emily Sergeant."

"Collin Lockhart—a pleasure, Miss Sergeant." She expects he might kiss her knuckles, but instead he shakes her hand as he might another gentleman's. He looks her up and down, then nods, chuckling quietly. "My Harry is going to love you."

13

The morning after the Majorbanks's ball, Harry wakes in an unfamiliar bed in an unfamiliar house with an unfamiliar shape atop the covers beside her.

It takes a few moments of blinking around at the puritanical lack of decoration before she remembers where she is—Collin's spare room. He had taken pity on her when she begged him not to make her go back to her apartment, where Mariah Swift was likely waiting to coerce her into some kind of debauchery that was unbecoming of new royalty. That, and she was well foxed.

The mass nestled beside her, she realizes, is Havoc, snoring gently.

Harry stretches with her hands above her. Havoc does too, massive toes curling as he rolls onto his back. His jowls flop over his eyes, exposing his pink gums and slack tongue. Harry runs a hand over his belly, staring up at the ceiling. Her head throbs. Too much wine drunk too wantonly the night before, particularly after dinner, when she had interrogated Alexander about every woman he had spoken to that night and he had played coy, not even mentioning Miss Sergeant.

Miss Emily Sergeant, whose hair can't possibly have been as honey gold as Harry remembers. Perhaps that was a trick of the light and the pollen and so many bees. Emily Sergeant, with her turned-up nose and long neck and ridiculous slippers. To think Harry had been concerned she was any kind of rival.

Harry drags herself out of bed, steps over her red dress puddled on the floor, and retrieves a set of breeches from the back of the writing desk.

Poor Miss Sergeant, Harry thinks as she dresses, then follows the smell of breakfast belowstairs. She's likely somewhere having her bleeding feet amputated after all that dancing.

Which is when Harry enters the dining room and finds Collin at the table, breaking literal and figurative bread with the very same Miss Emily Sergeant.

"Oh good, Harry, you're up." Collin tosses his napkin onto the table as he stands. "We were just talking about you."

Miss Sergeant turns as well. When she catches sight of Harry, she freezes.

Now what, Harry thinks, unable to stop the grin spreading across her face, *are the chances?*

Emily does not stand as Collin introduces them. Harry, for her part, remains in the doorway, leaning against the frame and smirking, two things at which she is obscenely talented. Miss Sergeant's upturned nose tilts even more skyward as they regard each other.

If Emily indulged in any of the Majorbanks's boozy lemonade, Harry would never know it. She looks as perfectly coiffed as she had when she'd dropped her fan in front of Alexander like a goddamn exhibitionist. And yes, her hair is somehow truly so golden Midas would have coveted it. Harry's imagination had not exaggerated it.

Collin looks between them several times, then asks tentatively, "Are the pair of you acquainted?"

"We've met," Emily and Harry say at the same time.

"Well then, this will be . . . easier?" He looks to Harry, eyebrows raised, as if to ask, *Will it?* "Would you sit down, Sister? Miss Sergeant, should you wake your cousin?"

"Let her sleep," Emily says, and Harry notices for the first time a woman near Emily's age, tipped over on the settee with her mouth open. "It was a late night, and she has a new baby."

Harry feels a butt against her knees, and Havoc, lured from bed by the sound of company trots into the parlor and begins investigating the table with his nose.

Collin rescues the pitcher of cream before it tips. "Hal, control him, would you please?"

"Hello darling!" Emily holds out a hand to the dog. "May I?"

"He's very vicious," Harry replies, but Havoc has already collapsed onto the floor and offered Emily his pink belly to rub.

"I met Miss Sergeant last night," Collin says. "She has her eye on a gentleman you might help her win over."

"Oh *has* she now?" Harry asks.

Collin eyes her. "You're being terribly odd."

"Is she?" Emily asks primly. "I assumed that *this*"—she waves a hand through the air, indicating Harry in her entirety—"was an act."

Harry shrugs. "Bit of both."

"What about the haircut?" Emily asks.

"What about it?"

"Who accosted you with shears between last night and this morning?"

"You flatter me with the particular attention you've paid my hair."

"I'd have to be an imbecile not to notice it entirely gone."

"The question of your intelligence had never occurred to me."

"Whereas I wondered after yours several times last night."

"Was that before or after you were considering my cow-like twatishness?"

"Should I go?" Collin interupts.

"No, I should." Emily tries to stand, but Havoc rolls onto her feet. "I appreciate your offer, Mr. Lockhart, but I cannot see this arrangement progressing."

"Sit down, Miss Sergeant," Harry says.

Emily, held captive by Havoc lying on her feet, replies curtly, "I am."

Harry takes the chair beside Collin and pours herself a cup of tea. "First, I have a very fine collection of wigs. A *coiffure à la Titus* is very fashionable in France, and it does exceptional things for my bone structure."

"Is that French for *an executioner's dream*?" Emily asks.

It's such a clever retort Harry has no choice but to ignore it. "Secondly, what possible assistance could I offer you in the courting of a gentleman?"

Emily glares at Harry, her jaw flexing though her mouth is closed, then glances at Collin, as though hoping he will supply the answer for her. "The gentleman in question," she says after a moment, "told me I am beautiful and well mannered—"

"Of course he did," Harry mutters.

Emily ignores her. "—but that he found me quite conventional and . . . dull."

Had Harry been midsip of tea, she might have spit it out in surprise. After her performance beneath the wisteria, *dull* is not the descriptor Harry would have imagined disqualifying Emily Sergeant from the marriage market. The mask of demure gentility must not have slipped with Rochester as it had with Harry. "You? Dull?"

Miss Sergeant's delicate nostrils flair. "Your brother offered your companionship while I'm in London, in hopes that I might prove to this gentleman that I am a lady of class and breeding but also one of spontaneity and independent thought, who possesses a sense of humor and . . ." Her eye twitches. "Fun."

"My companionship?" Harry turns to Collin. "You want me to be the metaphorical hatchet she takes to her reputation?"

Collin glares at her. "That's not quite what I—"

"Have you any paper?" Harry asks Collin. Then, turning to Miss Sergeant, she says, "We should write a list, I think, of the many ways to make you interesting. First, you'll have to see a penis. You can always tell by the set of a woman's chin if she's seen a phallus in the flesh."

Emily pales, and Collin mutters, "Harry, for God's sake."

"Isn't this what you want?" she says. "This is why you invited her here. So I can ruin her."

"I thought you could take her to the theater," Collin says. "And introduce her to people. You two might be good companions for each other this Season, as you're both . . ." His eyes glance off Harry. "New to these circles of London."

"But Miss Lockhart seems so traditional and reserved," Miss Sergeant says, her tone so salty it could have flavored soup. "I cannot imagine what she might teach me on the subject of becoming unconventional."

"Harry might take you to a coffeehouse," Collin goes on, seemingly determined to ignore them both. "Or Speakers' Corner. You said your gentleman mentioned horses in particular—Hal, you could take Miss Sergeant riding!"

"We'll have to start much simpler than that," Harry says, then leans over to Emily and asks, "How are you with the alphabet? I hear learning is bad for a woman's brain and I'd hate to make assumptions."

"Maybe this is an ill-advised idea," Miss Sergeant says.

"Maybe it is," Harry says with a shrug.

"No, it's a fine idea," Collin says. "If you would both cooperate!"

He bangs his open hand upon the table, upsetting the tray of scones. Havoc makes a dive for them, taking the tablecloth with him. Emily manages to rescue the pot before it tips, but all four teacups fall to the rug, spilling their contents.

On the couch, Emily's cousin sits up. "What's happened?" she asks. "Emily, are you being ravaged?"

Collin stares at the table, his cheeks sucked in so tight his ears twitch. "Hal, can I have a word please?"

He doesn't give her a chance to reply, just seizes her by an arm and press-gangs her from the room. Behind them, she hears Emily's cousin ask, "Should someone get a cloth?"

In the entryway, Collin still doesn't release her, so Harry slaps him with her free hand—not hard, and yes, it's childish, but so was Collin tackling her into the hallway.

Collin yelps but doesn't let go. "What has gotten into you?"

"Stop mauling me," Harry whines. "I dipped far too deep last night and my stomach is not constant."

Collin lets out a huff of disapproval, but releases her. He straightens his shirt where it has come untucked from his breeches in their scuffle, then casts a glance at the parlor before leaning into Harry and hissing, "Help her."

"Help her do what?"

"Help her open up. She isn't dull—she's shy and lonely and far from home. She could use a friend. And so could you."

"I have plenty of friends."

"I think," Collin says, "that you could be good for each other."

Harry crosses her arms. "So you invited her here in hopes she might be a good influence upon me, and I might be a ruining one upon her in return?"

"Stop misunderstanding me on purpose," Collin snaps. "You could help her come out of her shell. And yes, I did consider that she might help you integrate yourself into some more genteel circles."

"Isn't that your job?"

"Harry, I'm just trying . . ." He presses his face into the crook of his elbow and Harry can hear the vibrations of the silent scream he releases into it. Then he drops his arm and says, "If you take her riding, you can stay with me until the coronation."

Harry perks up like a tulip in water. "Here? In your house?"

Collin grits his teeth. "Yes, here."

"Havoc too? And you promise you won't make me wash any dishes?"

Collin rolls his eyes. "You're such a child."

"If you let me stay here, I will invite Miss Sergeant to go riding with me," Harry says. "It's not my fault if she doesn't accept."

"Fine. Now go talk to her." Collin claps her hard on the shoulder, steering her back toward the hall, then storms off to the kitchen, where Harry presumes he'll put his head in the oven.

When Harry returns to the parlor, Emily's cousin has vanished—presumably to find somewhere less chaotic to nap—and Havoc is trying to wedge himself under the couch to suck up an errant scone. Miss Sergeant sits alone at the table, the teacups reset but empty. She turns when Harry enters the room, and her face hardens.

"Would you go riding with me?" Harry asks with no inflection. "So Collin will be appeased?"

"Would I . . ." Emily turns back to the table and glares at the teapot. "Of course not."

"Then why did you come here?"

"I would not, had I realized Mr. Lockhart was your brother."

"Of course."

She glares at Harry. "And *of course* I will not require your assistance in any matter, particularly those of courtship."

Harry drops into the seat across from her. "Why not?"

"Shall we start with the fact that last night you tried to ruin my chances with the very man you are now purporting to help me court? Yes, I know you and Rochester are friends," she snaps when Harry feigns surprise. "I saw you giggling and playing the coquette. Are the two of you intimate acquaintances, I wonder?"

"I don't see how that's . . ." She trails off, unsure of how to finish. Relevant? Any of your business? Something Emily could have possibly guessed?

To which Emily replies, her tone feather light, "You can always tell by the set of a woman's chin."

And Harry, so surprised to have her own words thrown back in her face, laughs.

Emily scowls. "Is that not why you were jealous?"

"Jealous? Of you? Don't be absurd."

"Of his attention. And now your brother thinks *you* can help *me* fashion myself into a more desirable match? Don't make me laugh." Emily snatches her bonnet from where it is resting on the arm of the sofa and jams it onto her head as she stands. "I will win Rochester myself. You cannot stand in my way. Nothing can."

"Except your personality, it seems," Harry says, and Emily's fingers slip on the ribbons of her bonnet. "Why him in particular?"

"He's a duke," Emily replies. "Need there be further reason? Now, have you seen my other glove?"

"You removed your gloves? How intimate. Were you planning to stay?"

"I removed my gloves," Emily snaps, "because I thought I was about to eat scones with a kind new friend, not some sneering Amazon!"

"You think I'm an Amazon?"

"That is irrelevant!" Emily whips a pillow from the settee. "Come, neither of us want me here. Help me look so I can be on my way."

Harry spots a white fingertip stuck to Havoc's haunches and peels it off. She clears her throat, and Emily looks up from the cushions.

"Thank you." Emily extends a hand, but Harry flicks the glove backward out of her reach.

"If you are so desperate to be married, why not seek out another man?"

"Please give me my glove."

"A duke is a catch, to be certain, but a lady like you can't be short suitors."

Emily sucks in her cheeks, then says, "My parents have selected a fiancé for me who is not a good match. His only interest in me is for access to my family's land."

"As is the foundation of many marriages. What do you find so objectionable about this poor bloke? Is he short? A redhead? Or—God forbid—is he—" And here Harry drops her voice into a horrified whisper. "Poor?"

Emily stares at the glove in Harry's hand, then says bluntly, "I fear he would do me harm."

Harry feels the words like a cold bucket of water to the face. Here she had thought Miss Sergeant shallow in her pursuit of a duke, but instead, there is real fear behind her words. Emily Sergeant is afraid. And she is trying to do the only thing she can—the only thing any woman of good breeding can do to protect themselves: marry up. Harry wishes suddenly she had not spoken so flippantly. What reason had she to assume the worst of Emily Sergeant, other than the fact that she was pretty in a way that said she cared about her appearance, conventional and feminine in the manner of etiquette books, and exactly the sort of girl who had mocked Harry her whole life for being none of those things?

Emily turns away, and Harry can see the tension in the rise and fall of her shoulders as she takes several deep breaths. "If I return home with a better prospect, my parents will have to reconsider the arrangement. I have studied the society pages, and I know Rochester is one of only a few men in London for the Season who is eligible, courting, and endowed with sufficient title and inheritance that my parents could not possibly object to my marrying him in place of Mr. Tweed. There. Now you know the truth. I hope you're bloody pleased with yourself."

She starts toward the door but when Harry calls, "Miss Sergeant," she turns.

Harry holds out the glove. Emily stares at it for a moment, as if determining whether this is an olive branch or yet another baited trap. She slowly reaches out to take it, but Harry doesn't let go.

"Alexander rides most mornings at Regent's Park," she says, assuring herself there is no harm in sharing this. Should Emily work up the nerve to visit the duke, her good breeding will likely overtake her senses, and when required to choose a side of the gulf between what men say they want and what they actually want in a wife, she will present the same dull girl Alexander met at the ball. But at least Harry might sleep easier—*and* in Collin's spare room, for she can tell him honestly that she tried. "His is a dark horse with a white mane—easy to spot. You might catch him as he finishes, and walk with him as he cools down."

Emily tugs the end of her glove, and this time, Harry lets it go.

"And I am sorry," Harry says. "For how I treated you last night. You are correct in your assessment that I was jealous over the attentions of my friend, and my emotions got the better of me. Please forgive me."

Emily pulls her glove on slowly, only looking away from Harry's face when her fingernail snags on the lace. "Thank you for the information about the duke," is all she says before she goes looking for her cousin.

It is as close as Harry suspects she'll get.

14

A chance run-in with Alexander Bolton will look too calculated should it occur only two days after the Majorbanks's ball, so Emily waits a sennight before she and Violet take the baby walking through Regent's Park, along the path that goes by the stables. She uses the time in between to read more about horses, though everything she learns only confirms what she already knows, which is that they are large, unpredictable, and untrustworthy.

Violet keeps up a stream of conversation as they cross nearly the whole heath to reach the paddock where the horses are exercised, mostly about how little the baby slept and when the baby last ate, and Emily does her best to pay attention to her cousin instead of her own anxiety at the thought of seeing Alexander again.

They pick a bench near the stables, from which they can see the jockeys taking their horses through the jumps at a distance. Overhead, the sky is a woolly gray, rain threatening to break from the coffered clouds.

Violet hoists the baby from his carriage and begins to thump his back. "Which one is he, then?"

The riders are too far away to make out their faces, but Emily recognizes the dual coloring of Alexander's stallion Harry had mentioned. She points. "That one."

Violet nods—or perhaps she is simply bouncing herself along with the baby. "He looks to be an exceptional horseman."

"Indeed." Emily watches, breath bated, as Rochester steers the horse to the fence, adjusts his stance, then digs his heels into the horse's flank. The stallion takes off at a gallop toward the assembled stiles, which, with the duke's steady hand, he clears easily.

Perspiration breaks out upon Emily's neck. At the ball, she had taken note of Alexander's handsomeness in the way of hearing an opera sung—though not to her taste, she could appreciate the skill required to produce it.

But now, she is captivated by the sight of him on that horse. The lines of his body, highlighted in the gray light from the sky, are elegant as strokes of calligraphy. The dip in his back as he leans into the neck of his mount, the curve of his ass in his tight riding breeches. The muscled girth of his thighs, too far away to be seen clearly, but her mind fills in the gaps as she watches him rise off the saddle and balance in the stirrups.

She should look away. No, she can't bear to. She must. Her throat is suddenly dry, and she feels a pulse in her legs that ripples all the way to the bottom of her feet. She thinks of marble nudes by great Italian artists, and suddenly sees the appeal in dedicating one's life to the depiction of the human form. If it took the creation of a statue to justify this level of study, she would have learned to carve. She would eat the form of man from rock with her teeth if she had to.

Eventually, the riders finish their circuit and set course for the stables. When they reach the paddock, Alexander, lit from behind by the overcast light, swings himself from the saddle. Emily's breathing quickens. God, his calves! The cocky angle of his shoulders! The dip of his neck, the strong profile! The short dark hair curling around his ears—

But Alexander is a blond. She remembers noting how similar in color his hair was to her own.

The rider turns, removing their cap, and—

"No." Emily speaks aloud without meaning to.

"What?" Violet sits up. "What is it?"

Emily leaps to her feet. "We have to go."

"What?" Violet stands, confused. "What about your duke? You came all this way to speak to him."

"We have to go—now."

"Give me a moment." Violet begins to bundle the baby back into his buggy and good lord, infants come with so many parts, why can they not be moved swiftly from one location to the next?

Emily keeps her back to the stables, as though that might make her invisible. "Make haste, please!"

"Just give me a moment—"

"Catch up with me, then." Emily starts to walk, even as Violet is still bundling the baby.

"What has gotten into you? Emily, wait for me!" Violet calls, but Emily has already started across the lawn, as quickly as one can in a skirt that tightens around the knees and with feet that still throb at the memory of the Majorbanks's ball.

But then another voice calls from the direction of the stables, "Miss Sergeant!"

And, out of either deeply ingrained politeness or outright stupidity, Emily turns.

Across the paddock, striding toward her, is Harriet Lockhart, all calves and cocky shoulders and that stupid, smug grin as though she knows Emily had been staring.

Bastard, Emily thinks, wondering if she can plausibly pretend she has not seen Harry, even though their eyes are locked.

Harry hops the paddock fence and jogs to Emily, and God, those riding leathers are obscenely tight, though *of course* Emily had only admired them when thinking it was Alexander's firm rump to which they clung. Harry pulls off her gloves, pushing her sleeves up to her elbows, and Emily feels beads of sweat trickle down her spine.

"Miss Lockhart," Emily says, inclining her head. She can feel herself going red as she thinks of the way she ogled Harry on that horse—*thinking her Alexander, of course!*

"What a strange chance we should meet here," Harry says.

Emily presses the tips of her gloved fingers to her forehead, wondering how much moisture they can possibly soak up. "Almost like you told me to come."

"Ah yes, I did mention Rochester would be riding, didn't I?"

"Another ruse, I see."

"It is not!" Harry laughs. "He's with the mare—just there." She points to where Alexander—Emily sees him now—is leading a small bay into the stable. "He had me on Matthew this morning since I'll be riding him in the Milton Derby."

"A lie by omission, then."

"No lie at all!" Harry replies. "I did not expect you to wait a fortnight before you made an appearance."

"It has been seven days at most."

"You counted the days?" Harry presses a hand to her heart. "You're a romantic."

They are interrupted when Violet pushes the buggy in between them, looking from Emily to Harry. "Good morning. Have we met?"

"Yes." Harry offers her a hand. "Though I believe you were asleep."

"Oh yes." Violet squints. "Was there a bear with you, or was that a dream?"

"You're thinking of my brother, I expect."

Violet adjusts her grip on the carriage. "Emily, we should go."

"I want to see the horses," Emily says quickly.

Violet squints at her. "First you talk all week of coming here, then you want to run away like you're being chased, and now you want to stay again?"

Emily swallows hard, staring determinedly away from Harry, who she's sure is grinning and making assumptions, all of which are probably true. "Well, now I want to stay."

"I'm happy to take Miss Sergeant home when she's finished here," Harry says.

"Oh, that isn't—" Emily says, but Violet interrupts.

"Wonderful, thank you." She leans in to kiss Emily quickly upon the cheek. "Good luck, darling. Have a good time with your duke."

"He's not my—"

But Violet is already pushing the carriage away, wheels clacking on the uneven path, leaving Harry and Emily alone.

"Lovely woman," Harry remarks.

Emily is certain if she goes any redder she'll catch fire. "Where's Rochester? I best get this over with."

Harry claps her hands together and gives them a victorious shake over her shoulder. "That's the spirit. Now—steady on." Emily has started toward the paddock gate, but Harry catches her arm. "Would you like me to make an introduction? I might pretend I don't know that the two of you are already acquainted. We can play off this meeting as a fated coincidence."

"Release me," Emily says. "I do not require any help from you."

Harry lets go, then looks down at her palm, like she's worried something on Emily's dress might have stained her, though the opposite is far more likely.

Emily takes a few steps toward the stables, then stops. The truth is, she hasn't considered what exactly she will say to Rochester when she sees him, her arrival unannounced and uninvited.

Emily turns back to Harry, who is now leaning upon the fence at an aggravatingly jaunty angle. "Fine," Emily says, her voice tight. "Will you walk me?"

Harry presses a hand to her chest in feigned surprise. "Me?"

"Since you are so in Rochester's favor."

"Am I?"

"And since my association with you might cause him to reconsider his preconceptions about me."

"Very well. Would you like an arm?"

"Piss off."

"There she is."

Emily scowls, then takes off at a trot toward the stable, her shoes squelching in the swampy turf.

15

The stable is muddier than the lawn, straw and muck congealing into a tarry laminate, and Emily knows within steps that she has ruined a second pair of shoes thanks to Harriet Lockhart.

"Alex," Harry calls, slipping past Emily into the narrow walkway between the horse stalls, and Rochester looks up from where he's running a brush over his mare's flank. His eyes go from Harry to Emily, then widen in surprise.

"Miss . . ." He looks to Harry again, and Emily can almost hear Harry mouthing her name to Alexander in reminder. "Tarpit!"

"Sergeant," she says. "It's good to see you again, my lord."

Alexander straightens, brushing straw off his trousers as he surveys her and Harry, side by side. "What an unexpected pair the two of you make."

"There's no pairing," Emily says quickly.

"You don't know each other?" Alexander asks.

"Well, yes," she says. "We are . . . acquainted."

Alexander gives her a queer look. "What brings you here, Miss Sergeant? You don't strike me as the sort of woman who passes mornings at a stable."

"Oh, but I would like to be," Emily replies. *Loose*, she thinks. *Be calm. Be relaxed. Be interesting.* "I wanted to see your jumping racehorse!" She thinks about sharing one of the facts she learned about horses, but decides it's best to dole them out in moderation. No need to vacillate so quickly from bland as unsalted soup to deranged encyclopedia.

"Of course." Alexander doesn't look nearly as excited as she hoped he would be. She had thought that regardless of his interest in her viability as a long-term companion, he would at least be cheered by the opportunity to put his hands upon her waist under the guise of helping her into a saddle.

He gestures to his mare, though one of the grooms is already seeing to her. "I'm afraid I'm quite occupied. But perhaps Harry here can give you a primer. She's a far better rider than I."

Emily begins to protest. "I would much rather—" but Rochester interrupts.

"What say you, Harry?" Alexander claps her on the shoulder. "Fancy teaching the girl to ride?"

And Harry has the audacity to remain straight-faced as she replies, "It would be my honor."

Emily follows Harry across the yard to where her horse is drinking sloppily from a trough. At his side, Harry's mastiff slurps with equal vigor and saliva. When he sees Harry, he trots over, dribbling water from his jowls like a wrung-out dishrag.

"All right." Harry adjusts the collar of her shirt, and Emily catches a flash of the pale curve of her breast. She looks away. "Shall we stand out here for perhaps ten minutes and pretend to talk about horses? I'll give you three things you can take back to Rochester, astonish him with your new education, and they'll be reading the banns by tomorrow morning. Is that what you want?"

"What I want," Emily says, "is for you to show me your horse."

Harry lets out an exasperated laugh. "You're safe with me, Miss Sergeant. You can admit you were just putting on a show for Alex."

"Surely *you* were," Emily retorts. "All that peacocking around in your tall boots and hopping fences and playing with your hair. All your *Alex this* and *Alex that,* just because he's asked you to call him by his familiar name."

Harry runs a hand over her forehead. "God, that's me exactly. I *do* hop a lot of fences and wear a lot of tall boots."

Emily glowers at her. "Tell me about your damn horse."

The corners of Harry's mouth turn up, and lord, the audacity of this woman, to take such pleasure in chaffing her.

"What's funny?" Emily demands.

"Nothing," Harry says. "Only, Rochester would like you better if you spoke to him the way you speak to me."

Emily almost laughs. Men think they want a spirited lady until they actually meet one. Then all they want to do is break her. That's what Thomas had taught her. And Emily does not have time to be spirited anymore—no matter how fantastic Harriet Lockhart's ass looks in those riding breeches.

Looked, she corrects herself. And only when she thought it Alexander's ass.

Harry pats the horse on the neck, then says, "Well, this is Matthew Mark Luke and John."

Emily nods to the horse, who eyes her with unsettling, slanted pupils. "Pleasure to meet you." Then, back to Harry, "Four names for a single horse?"

"He comes from a long line of biblical stallions," Harry says. "The nomenclature of racehorses is such that they must be registered under a unique name, and each of the four Gospels alone were too common."

"Well then he's very lucky he was not born later or he might have been called Philippians." Harry gives her another of those sideways looks, and Emily crosses her arms. "What?"

"I made the same quip to Alexander," Harry says. "That's all."

"Well, it's obvious," Emily says, unwilling to admit that she and Harry might have anything like a sense of humor in common. "Philippians is the hardest of all New Testament books to spell. It doesn't have as many double letters as it should."

"Thessalonians would disagree," Harry says, adjusting a twisted strap on the horse's bridle. "Shall we start with what you *do* know about horses?"

"I know they grow all their teeth by age five," Emily says. "They usually live to be between twenty and five and thirty years of age. They cannot breathe through their mouths, and are often described by their colors—palomino, bay, chestnut, gray, roan, piebald. And you measure them in hands."

"I thought you said you didn't know anything about horses."

"I took it upon myself to learn."

"You are dedicated to your craft. Or, craftiness, I suppose, is more apt."

"I am simply trying to make a better impression upon a man I wish to know."

The sky flashes with lightning, chased almost instantly by low thunder. Harry looks skyward. Emily feels it too—the gentle patter of the first few raindrops striking the back of her neck. Dark spots pebble the ground around them, turning the warm umber paddock the color of cold coffee. Matthew tosses his head, ears flicking in a helix, and Emily leaps backward, nearly crushing Harry's foot.

"You should go inside," Harry says, a steadying hand on Emily's elbow. "One of the grooms can find you a curricle back to your cousin's."

"What about you?"

"I have to see to Matthew."

"In this weather?"

"Someone's got to. And I don't mind the rain."

Emily glances back to the stables. What might Rochester say upon seeing her dash inside in girlish fear of getting her hair wet? It would not provide the impression of bold nonchalance she hopes to convey, particularly if Harry, in contrast, works out in the rain, unbothered and focused. But to what end? Creating another version of herself just to draw Rochester's eye? Pretending to be someone else she's not in order to trade one version of captivity for another?

Emily feels suddenly foolish, a lady in the rain trying to spin hope out of straw.

But a lifelong charade is still preferable to a marriage to Robert Tweed. Emily squares her shoulders and imagines herself returning to the stable, wet and fetchingly mud splattered, and when Alexander comments upon the storm, she will toss her hair over her shoulder in a damp arc and say *I hardly noticed, as I was so enthralled with your beautiful stallion. Someday soon, sir, you and I should . . .* And here she will execute a suggestive but not lewd cock of her eyebrow, *ride*.

She has not come this far to be deterred by something as mundane as the weather.

"I don't mind the rain either," she says. "May I help?"

Harry takes in Emily's thin morning dress and cotton jacket, and Emily thinks she may refuse. But then she tosses Emily a rag and says, "Take off your gloves and give him a rubdown then." Her cotton shirt, already damp with sweat and now nearly transparent with rain, sticks to her. Emily notes the thick muscles of Harry's forearms, and how they flex when she hefts the saddle from the horse's back.

"Don't stand behind him," Harry says. "And watch out for his mouth."

"So where am I meant to stand?" Emily asks. "If not in front nor behind him?"

"To the side."

"Then he's looking at me."

"Jesus, Mary, and Joseph." Harry hefts the tack onto the fence, then troops over to where Emily is hovering beside Matthew, well out of reach of teeth and hooves and wiping down. "Here." Harry puts a hand on the small of Emily's back, pushing her gently forward.

Fear grips her suddenly, and Emily digs her heels into the mud. "Wait just a moment!"

Harry stops. "If you're truly that afraid, you'll do nothing but spook Matthew and get underfoot."

"I want to . . ." She trails off, unsure how to finish. *I want to impress Rochester* or *I want to appear less dull* are both fitting, though so is *I want to do this with you.*

"It's all right," Harry says, her tone surprisingly gentle. "You don't have to. You've nothing to prove."

Emily looks from the horse to the stable, then to Harry. The concern in her eyes is frustratingly sincere. *Don't look at me like that,* Emily wants to say. *You are not supposed to care about my well-being, it makes this all much more confusing.*

Or maybe it's the horse Harry's fretting after. That seems more likely, and Emily feels suddenly flushed and foolish for thinking it was her.

"I want to help—" Emily says again, but then Matthew tosses his head, and she leaps in surprise, dropping the cloth. Harry grabs her before she falls, one hand at Emily's waist like she's pulling her in for a waltz.

"Steady on," Harry says, and now those muscled forearms are against Emily's shoulders. The small of her back. She can map the shape of Harry's arm where it presses against her.

"Did I startle him?" Emily asks, turning to Harry. Their faces are very close.

Harry leans suddenly into her, so close their cheeks almost brush, and Emily's heart skips. All the blood leaves her head, and she's worried for a moment she might swoon in earnest.

But then Harry simply retrieves the dropped rag.

"It was only the rain," she says.

As though it had been waiting in the wings for that cue, the sky opens and thick torrents of rain gush down. Havoc sprints back toward the stables. Matthew tosses his head again. One enormous hoof paws at the mud.

Harry holds up a hand to shield her face. "Miss Sergeant, I must insist you return to the stables."

"Give me—a moment—" Emily's voice is almost drowned out by another peal of thunder. She is trying to pry herself from the swamp she had stepped hard into, but the more she struggles, the more the mud seems to suck at her.

Harry lets out an exasperated sigh. "For God's sake, you're going to catch pneumonia, which is far less interesting than the poets make it sound. And you can't marry Alex if you're dead."

"It's not that—I'm stuck!"

Harry holds a hand up to her face, shielding it. "What?"

"I am stuck in the mud!" Emily tries again to free herself, only to nearly lose her balance. Harry grabs her by the arms, pulling until Emily is able to pry her feet out of the mud and stagger back onto solid ground. She has so little sensation left in her toes, it takes a moment for her to realize one of her slippers is gone, leaving her in only a soiled stocking, slipped free of its garter.

Harry notices too and asks, "Where's your shoe?"

"If I knew, it would be on my foot!"

"Oh hell. Here, I'll find it. Hold on to Matthew for balance."

The sky flushes white with lightning. Thunder rumbles.

Emily puts a tentative hand on the horse's flank, hopping to stand at his side as she had been instructed. Harry is on her knees, rooting around in the mud like she's tunneling. "Son of a bitch," she hears Harry mumble. "Enough of this." Harry staggers to her feet, wiping her muddy hands on her muddier pants. "I'm afraid your shoe has gone to its great rest. Put your arms around my neck."

Emily obeys, even as she asks, "What are you—"

But before she can finish, Harry loops an arm around Emily's knees, the other around her back, then picks Emily up, cradling her like she's a child. Harry bends her head against the rain, face low over Emily's to shelter her as she carries her to the stables.

Emily wants to flinch away from the touch. But more than that, she wants to settle into it like a hot bath.

For Harry is so warm. Like sitting beside an open flame. And yes, Emily understands objectively that as living beings, all people emit warmth, and yes, perhaps it is the closeness and her own chill and the delirious shimmer of the rain that is skewing her sense. But Harry is also a mystifying combination of hard and soft. For, as previously noticed, her muscled shoulders and sturdy arms—but also the soft swell of her breasts, which Emily must not look at, no matter their proximity and the translucency of Harry's riding shirt. She must not look and she must not think of them pressing against her, and God, Emily feels light-headed. Though perhaps that's to do with the cold.

Rochester. She must think of Rochester.

But when they reach the stables, the only men there are the

grooms, their oiled hoods thrown up as they brace themselves to step out into the rain.

"Where's the duke?" Emily asks one as he passes them.

"Gone," he calls. "He had a luncheon appointment and wanted to be off before the storm."

The scales tip suddenly, and Emily finds herself sliding into the absurdity of this preposterous set of events. Her, with one shoe, soaked and splattered in mud, trying to impress a man who has already left. Instead of cursing as she had at the ball, she laughs. She turns her face into Harry's neck and *laughs,* feeling lightly hysterical.

"Are you crying?" she hears Harry ask tentatively. "Or have you gone insane?"

"Put me down, please."

Harry obeys, and Emily immediately regrets the request. Without Harry's body against hers, she feels cold and small and suddenly very alone. She wraps her arms around herself, but that only doubles the amount of wet material against her and she begins to shiver in earnest. Even her chemise is wet, and her petticoats are strangling her legs. Her ribs feel too tight around her lungs, and her breath hitches.

"Here." Harry retrieves a heavy coat from a hook beside the door and wraps it around Emily's shoulders, then rubs her hands up and down Emily's arms. "Where is it your cousin lives? I'll take you home."

"Chelsea," Emily replies, teeth clacking.

"Good lord. You were determined to see Alexander in his riding leathers, weren't you?"

"I can walk myself there," Emily says. "It's not so far. And look, the rain has nearly stopped."

"No chance. You'll be frozen solid before you've crossed the park, even in a curricle. You need dry clothes. And some soup. Perhaps for someone to set you on fire. Let's find somewhere you can recover."

"You needn't perform any longer," Emily says. "Rochester is gone—a show of compatriotism is not necessary."

"Show?" Harry repeats. "Miss Sergeant, your lips are turning blue."

Emily can hardly deny this—she's struggling to form plosives—but still she protests, "I need no charity from you, Miss Lockhart."

"Please, don't be stubborn. It's adorable, but it's goddamn wearing me out. Stay here while I find a carriage."

"I can walk, thank you." Emily knows she's being ridiculous—and how desperately she wants that soup and fire and dry socks and to not have to walk home in this state. Christ, this coat is so warm and worn in at the elbows. She wants to be buried in it. But she still has her pride, and will not be coddled by the likes of Harriet Lockhart. Out in the paddock, she was horse-struck and wild with the thought of Rochester so near. Drunk on the rain and mud and Harry's substantial forearms, she had lost herself for a moment, but she has returned, and she will not be lured further into the woods of Harry's kindness. Surely wolves wait amid those trees. This is, after all, the same woman who so irritated her under the wisteria that she lost her temper for the first time in years. She can't risk that kind of proximity.

She tries to twist out from beneath the coat, but one of the buttons catches on the stitching at the sleeve of her dress, and when she attempts to disentangle them, finds her fingers are too cold to undertake such delicate work. She shakes her arm, hoping that button and stitching will magically uncouple themselves. Or rip—perhaps she should just tear them apart and run.

"Calm down, you infernal pixie!" Harry pins the coat around

Emily, fastening the top button at her throat and rendering her a prisoner. "Heed me—there is a tea shop near here, where I'm known. We can walk there together, then you can sit by their fire and dry off and you will not be charged so you won't owe me a thing and your pride will remain undamaged. Please, if only to ease my guilt should you die of a chill. Let me believe I did everything I could to save you."

Emily would clench her jaw, but her teeth are chattering too badly. She nearly bites her own tongue. Dry clothing is such a daft thing to fight against—and pride such a daft thing to die for should she catch cold.

"Fine," Emily says. "But I still expect you to shoulder substantial guilt at my passing."

"If that's what it takes," Harry replies, "I promise to make you my greatest regret."

16

Though Harry assures her the establishment at which they will take shelter is a teahouse, they have barely crossed the threshold before Emily begins to have her doubts.

While the interior is painted in pinks and greens like any respectable tea-serving establishment, and china cups are laid out on each table, turned upside down on their saucers, it feels like the set of a play, accurate but unlived in. Emily has the impression no one has ever pulled back any of these chairs from their respective tables to sit down to share a pot with a friend, nor unfolded the paper menus and perused the offerings.

The shop is empty but for a woman at the counter, her bodice displaying a fair amount more breasts than is typical of even a barmaid. Her hair is an unnatural shade of red, like new-laid brick. She shrieks in delight when she sees Harry and comes out from behind the counter to greet her. "Darling Harry, my love!" She cups Harry's face between her hands and kisses her upon the forehead—Harry, who seems to anticipate this, stoops down to receive it, like a blessing from the pope. "It has been ages! Where have you hidden yourself? And you're soaking wet, the pair of you!" The woman turns to Emily. "Who is this?"

"A friend of mine," Harry says. "Miss Sergeant, may I present Miss Pearl White."

In Harry's oversized coat, Emily is certain she looks like a rag shop granted the wish of becoming a person, but she still offers a hand in genteel greeting. "How do you do."

"We were caught riding in the rain," Harry says. "Do you mind if we kip up here for a bit?"

"You've rotten timing," Pearl replies. "I've gents coming down any minute, so you'll have to make yourselves scarce. But you can warm yourselves in the Cunt Cavity for now."

"The . . . what?" Emily splutters, but Pearl must not hear her, for she holds out her arms.

"Let me hang your wet things for you."

Harry helps Emily peel off her heavy coat, then passes over their duds to Pearl. When both their backs are turned, Emily discreetly hooks a finger around one of the menus on the nearest table and flips it open. Each thick page is etched not with baked goods and beverages, but rather with a different woman's likeness and a list of their rates and particular skills, accompanied by revealing illustrations and phrases like *discreet flagellation* and *luscious posterior* in fancy calligraphy.

Emily is almost relieved to have had all her suspicions about Harriet Lockhart confirmed. Of course this wicked woman brought her to a brothel, and of course she is well known by the proprietress here.

"Miss Sergeant?"

Emily snaps the menu shut and turns. Harry, one step behind Pearl, is holding open a door at the back of the shop, waiting for her to follow.

"Coming?" she asks, and Emily barely bites back a bubble of hysterical laughter.

The hallway behind the shop is as anatomical as its name would suggest, with curved ceilings melting into arched columns, and everything painted in varying shades of pink. The curtains lining the hallway too are pink, some drawn back to reveal the alcoves behind them, lined with paintings. It is blessedly warm—though perhaps, Emily thinks, that too is meant to invoke a certain je ne sais genitalia.

But she is beginning to feel her toes again, so Emily follows Harry and Pearl down the corridor.

"You can take Exquisite Dandies, or The Dairy Maid's Delight—I've the stove lit there," Pearl says, pointing to each of the alcoves in turn. "I think the Arse Bishop of Canterbury's free as well, though it's farther from the fire."

"The Dairy Maid's will be the warmest," Harry answers. She holds out a hand to Emily, seems to reconsider the context of leading a lady into one of these secluded chambers, and withdraws with a simple "After you."

Pearl flips a sign beside the curtain, then says as she departs, "Let me see to my gents and I'll be back."

The Dairy Maid's Delight is an alcove decorated with three paintings, one on each wall of the recess, and a small stove in the center. Its belly smolders with thrillingly warm coals. As Emily strips off her wet jacket and wraps herself in one of the quilts offered them by Pearl, she examines the paintings as discreetly as possible. In the first, a dairy maid coyly churns butter while a gentleman in a soldier's uniform enters her from behind. The movement requires her round ass to be thrust out at such an improbable angle that it takes Emily a moment to work out whether it *is* one woman or two, for surely no one can stand so upright while contorting their hips so as to provide such easy access. And all while vigorously churning.

"I wouldn't advise you sit there."

Emily turns. Harry is barefooted, though she's standing on her boots. Her cheeks are red, and she coughs into her fist before nodding to the bench beside the stove onto which Emily had been considering swooning, though whether in shock at the art or from the lingering cold, she isn't sure. "Pearl does her best, but some things never wash away."

Emily takes a quick step away from the bench. Then, just for good measure, a second step. "Right."

Harry slings her stockings over the stove tray, which sizzles as the water drips down. "Upholstery may not have been the best choice."

Emily's reply dies in her throat as she notices the painting behind Harry, in which two women frolic together in a pastoral landscape. *Are they* both *women?* she wonders, but yes—the anatomy is unmistakable. Emily scans the painting, searching for the man that is surely pleasuring himself in the nearby tall grass or concealed in a tree and about to leap upon them, but it's just the ladies. One wears a tricorn and tails, though her hair is long and loose. Her improbable bosom on full display as she hefts up the skirt of the presumably titular dairy maid.

"Miss Sergeant," Harry says, and Emily blinks.

"Beg pardon?"

"I asked if you'd like me to hang your socks."

"Oh, that would . . . yes." Emily steps out of the oversized boots she borrowed from a groom for the walk to the tea shop. Harry turns away as Emily pulls her skirt up over her ankles to slide off her socks, the gesture a harmless courtesy, yet, in the presence of the ladies in the painting, Emily feels suddenly indecent.

"It's nice, isn't it?" Harry nods toward the painting as she takes Emily's socks and drapes them beside hers. "There was a fire here several years ago and Pearl had the damaged art replaced with something a bit more elegant." She indicates the painting of the two ladies, in contrast to the opposite portraiture of the butter churner with the enormous ass.

"Do you frequent this place?" Emily asks before she can stop herself.

Harry's eyebrows rise. "Meaning what, precisely?"

Before Emily can reply, Pearl appears through the curtain behind them. "Here's some warm wine!" She sets her tray on the bench, then wraps an arm around Harry's neck and nuzzles into it like an affectionate cat. "Darling, we have missed you. Mariah says you've been splendid in *Macbeth*."

Emily's surprised to see that rather than take the compliment in stride, Harry instead looks as though it hangs heavy around her neck. Her shoulders sink, and she mumbles, "Mariah also thinks Byron is an understated poet, so she is no great arbiter of taste."

"She also said you're speaking to Collin again. Sweet lamb. How is he?"

"What need have I to come around," Harry mutters, disentangling herself from the embrace and swiping a bit of Pearl's powder off her cheek, "when Mariah keeps you so informed of my every move?"

"Why have you stayed away?" Emily asks sweetly. At last—*at last!*—it is her turn to embarrass Harriet Lockhart, not to mention prove she is a degenerate. "Miss Lockhart, you shouldn't deprive Pearl of your business."

"Business?" Pearl asks, oblivious to the glare Harry shoots Emily. "No, just missing our little girl! We've hardly seen her about since her dear mother passed."

Emily feels herself go red. Harry looks down at the floor. Pearl, immune to the discomfort perhaps as an occupational necessity, kisses Harry again, checks the coals in the stove, then departs.

Silence, so deep and long Emily feels she could have swum in it.

Then Harry says, without looking at her, "Collin and I grew up here. My mother was a Cyprian, but she quit the business when a benefactor bought her a house in Westminster. We moved there when I was ten." She takes a sip of the wine Pearl left, winces at the heat, then adds, "You can pass any judgments you'd like, but I'll warn you, I've heard it all before. I'm hard to wound."

Harry looks away, suddenly sheepish, which, Emily thinks, she should be, for bringing Emily to a nanny house without any forewarning, then having the audacity to choose the exact room in the Cunt Cavity with *this* painting of *these* ladies, but turn away when Emily took off her socks like some kind of goddamn gentleman. While they're on the subject, it really should be Harry apologizing to Emily for looking so fit on the back of a horse that Emily mistook her for the duke, and for the loan of her coat and carrying Emily in the rain in such a way that Emily couldn't help but feel how soft and warm and bosomy she was, like a buxom loaf of bread.

What, Emily thinks, *a confusing day this has been.*

Emily pulls the quilt tighter around her. The stove has at last begun to warm her, and when she reaches for her glass of wine, her fingers do as she asks without hesitation. She doesn't know what to say. She wants to apologize, but instead asks tentatively, "Was it strange, growing up here?"

"You don't have to—" Harry starts but Emily interrupts her.

"I want to know. Truly."

Harry lets out a small breath—almost like a sigh of relief, though she quickly holds her hands to her mouth, and Emily wonders if perhaps she was simply blowing upon them for warmth. "I couldn't say. People used to ask me the same thing about having a twin—is it strange, what's it like? The answer being that, as it's the only thing I've ever known, I have no comparison. It was my home. I can look back now and see it was unstable and volatile and it will muck you up if you and your brother have to hide under the bed as your mother takes clients. But we were sheltered and protected and the women here were my family. I probably would find whatever ordinary place you grew up in as strange as you'd find this place."

"Sussex," Emily says. "I grew up on a farm in the South Downs."

"And what was that like?"

"Suffocating," Emily says before she can stop herself. It is the word she had always felt best described the confines of her town, but never dared voice, and she corrects herself out of habit, lest she be scolded as ungrateful. "Beautiful and peaceful and idyllic and..." She struggles for another word, but Harry finishes for her.

"And suffocating. You can be honest." Her mouth quirks. "I won't tell Alexander."

"It was a small community," Emily says, "with many opinions on the business of others."

"Ah, you were raised among gossips! Say no more, I understand. There are no bodies busier than the denizens of a brothel."

Emily curls herself over her glass of warm wine, letting the steam dampen her face. Let Harry think she understands—it saves Emily having to explain how one choice ruined her life. "Do people really mock you for your parentage?"

"They used to, when I was in school," Harry says. "Now if they do, they're wise enough to only speak behind my back. And I've learned not to let it bother me."

God. If only it were that simple.

Emily takes another sip of wine. "May I ask you one more question? It's quite sensitive."

Harry leans forward. "Go on."

She looks so earnest Emily almost feels bad for replying, with as much gravity as she can muster, "What's it like, having a twin?"

Harry laughs, and Emily feels the warmth hit deep in her belly as she swallows, like she's taken a gulp of whiskey.

Harry leans over the stove, holding her hands just above the steaming tray. Emily remembers how, at the ball, she had thought Harry's features severe against her red dress and elaborate hairstyle. The idea seems foolish now. In the glancing gold light, the hard corner of Harry's jaw and divot in her chin look perfectly matched to the rest of her. A frame so strong and well fashioned could not be done service by features any softer. Her lips, now thawed from the cold, are poppy red.

Harry, Emily realizes, has managed the peculiar alchemy of transforming the things that might make her strange into things that instead make her exceptional. The daughter of a whore, raised in a brothel, that ridiculous haircut—all of it carried off with such nonchalant confidence that makes her seem like a character in an adventure story, and these details merely the sort of rare origins that are required in any self-respecting heroine. She is opposite Emily—opposite what any of the etiquette books teach—but on Harry, it feels right. Like some peculiar garment that suits her frame and figure, but would swallow Emily.

This, she realizes, is what she needs Harry to teach her—not how to be a more interesting sort of woman. But how to carry the woman she is without apology.

Perhaps Collin Lockhart was right in thinking they should know each other.

Emily takes a deep breath. Swallows her pride—and the rest of her wine—then asks, "May I propose a hypothetical scenario?"

Harry peels one of her socks from the tray and tests its dampness against the back of her hand. "You may propose anything you like."

"I have been considering your brother's suggestion that you might help me become a more appealing marital prosect for the Duke of Rochester. This is not an admission that I *need* your help," she adds quickly.

"Spare me the reminder that you still don't trust me."

"Less than I trust a horse," Emily replies. "But, hypothetically, if I were to enlist your tutelage . . . what would that entail?"

Harry studies her for a moment, head cocked, then asks, "What did Rochester say to you, exactly?"

"That I'm beautiful and well mannered—"

"Yes, you mentioned."

Emily blushes. They were the only compliments he had given her, and she has been clinging to them like a lifeline. "And that he and I could make a fine couple."

Harry raises an eyebrow.

"But that I seemed duller and more conventional than the type of woman he finds himself drawn to," Emily finishes.

Harry studies her, one thumb pressed to her chin. Emily feels inventoried, and tries to hide her face behind another drink of wine, only to remember she's finished her glass.

She is about to withdraw the question, or claim she had only been joking, of course she doesn't need Harry's help. But then Harry says, "To start, your appearance must be altered."

"What's the matter with my appearance?"

Harry holds up her hands, like she's framing Emily to hang her in a gallery. "The virginal white classical draping nonsense has to go."

"It's fashionable!"

"It's common. I can take you to my modiste—she'll make you a gown that will turn heads. Second, when you seek out Alexander again, you need a topic of conversation with which to engage him. Perhaps one relating to an enigmatic hobby of yours."

"I have no enigmatic hobbies," Emily says.

"Yes, well, I can help you with that. What else?" Harry presses the tips of her fingers together and studies Emily over top of them. "You need an anecdote about a sordid outing that you tell with great nonchalance, as though you frequently rob erotic bookstores while dressed as Don Quixote. Not that exactly, but we'll think of something."

"And when will I have occasion to meet the duke in this unusual dress and tell him about my sordid hobbies and enigmatic anecdotes?" Emily asks.

"Reverse those." Harry snaps her fingers. "At the Milton Derby. Now that he knows we're acquainted, we can tell him you're there to see me ride in the steeplechase. A tenuous connection, but plausible. And it makes you seem a bit indifferent to him, which will make him keener to give chase."

"Will you truly help me?" Emily asks. She hates the note of supplication that pitches her voice, but she is not above begging. She's a spinster of almost five and twenty about to be forced into marriage with a fiend, for God's sake, *she will beg*. "So that next time Alexander and I cross paths, he finds me more pleasing?"

Harry flicks a sock off the stove and hangs it over her shoulder. "Wouldn't you rather marry a man who likes you for who you are? You're simply trading one artifice for another."

"And what artifice is that?"

"That you're a demure, shy little daisy who is desperate to please a man."

"You hardly know me. How can you be so sure that isn't who I am?" Emily's eyes again drift to the two ladies in the painting, snuggled up just over Harry's shoulder. "You're not in love with him, are you?"

"Who, Alexander?" Harry snorts. "Don't make me laugh."

"I'm not bothered if you've been intimate," Emily says, trying to sound as though she casually discusses such matters on the regular. "I assume he's been with a lot of women."

"I wouldn't put money on that," Harry says. "He hasn't always been so handsome."

"If we are to be in partnership," Emily says, then pauses, for this, she is sure, is the last stile they must clear, "I want you to swear to me you are not harboring any romantic feelings for him that might conflict with our arrangement."

"Why does it matter so much?"

"Because if this is to work," Emily says, "I must trust you."

Harry stares at her for a moment, then takes up her wine from where she set it upon the stove. Her hands flex around the glass, and Emily cannot help but notice the way the small movement ripples her biceps. Her shirt has dried enough as to be restored to opacity, but Emily can still see the shape of them, like a fish below the surface of a pond. A strapping, toned fish that Emily cannot tear her eyes from. "At the ball, I was jealous of the attention he paid you, but not because of some unresolved infatuation. I'm simply unaccustomed to sharing him."

"And that's all it was?" Emily asks.

Harry puts a hand to her heart and, gaze fixed on Emily's, says, "I am not in love with the Duke of Rochester. That I will swear to."

And Emily believes her. Perhaps unwisely, but Harry does not strike Emily as the type to lose her head over a man, nor does she seem a woman for whom marriage is a great priority. She has already aged seemingly unrepentantly into spinsterhood, and chosen a haircut that likely deters men both in style and the confidence required to carry it off.

And, she assures herself, even if Harry *is* harboring some unresolved feelings for the duke, what should Emily care? She only wants to marry Alexander. It's not as though she plans to love him too.

"Very well," Emily says. "Then let us make me interesting."

17

Mariah waits until she's astride Harry to announce she's been evicted from her boardinghouse.

"The old bitch who owns the place says my language is too crude!" Mariah readjusts herself on the dildo strapped to Harry's waist. "Can you believe that?"

"And you're certain," Harry asks between panted breaths, "this isn't because you've been tupping her daughter since the New Year?"

"She didn't mention that. Now come on!" Mariah seizes Harry's hand and slaps it against her ass. "Like you mean it."

Harry grits her teeth. The only reason she let Mariah in tonight was because *Macbeth* had gone poorly, and Harry was brooding. She had to return to her room to pack her things for Collin's and found herself caught in an eddy of mourning the last days of life as she knows it, to say nothing of the fact that those last days are being wasted on dramatics that are more mishaps than actual haps. When Mariah had knocked upon her door, Harry had been gasping for a reprieve from being alone with herself.

But now, Mariah is scheming. Harry can sense it.

"Go to Pearl's," she says. "She'll put you up."

"Can't I stay with you?"

"You can stay in the room while I'm away," Harry says, adjusting her position on the bed. Mariah's weight is heavy on her hips.

"Away?" Mariah sounds nowhere near as grateful as she should upon being offered shelter from the proverbial storm. "Away where?"

"I'm staying with my brother."

Mariah perfectly arches an eyebrow. Harry can remember her practicing the expression in the mirror when they were young, holding one side of her forehead in place until her brows had learned to operate independently. "But you hate Collin."

"I do not hate Collin, *he* hates *me*."

Mariah pushes herself up on her knees, and the dildo slides out of her, flopping in its harness against Harry's belly. "You're going to quit the company, aren't you?"

"Now why would you think that?"

"You'd only let me stay here if you weren't planning to come back. And why else would you go live with horrible Collin?" Mariah slaps her hard on the breast. Harry flinches with a yelp. "Admit it!"

"Can we discuss this later?" Harry asks through clenched teeth. She reaches between her legs but Mariah grabs her wrist and pins it to the mattress. Her curtain of loose red hair falls in a tent around them.

"You think you're too good for the Palace company."

"I think we are all too good for that rot," Harry replies. "You cannot tell me you enjoy wearing wigs made of dry noodles."

"If you're leaving, I'll come with you."

"That's not what I meant."

"Why not? I'll quit too. Wherever you sign on next, so shall I."

Harry sighs. Another company? She might as well lie down and die. She had once entertained grand designs to become a serious actress celebrated for playing men's roles. She'd be Lear and Prospero and Hamlet, strutting around the stage in a fur-trimmed cloak and a scabbard at her waist. She would buy a house in Leicester Square where roses would be left upon the stairs by her many fanatical admirers. She'd have to hire guards to keep them at bay. She'd be known for walking her pet tigers on jeweled leashes and the runs of her plays would sell out within the day of their announcement.

But she could never muster the courage to pursue those dreams with any real enthusiasm. She always feared what might happen to her hard-won confidence if she stood face to face with the possibility of real rejection.

"I may not join another company," she says. She's loath to tell Mariah the truth about why she's quitting. She can only imagine how Mariah might abuse the knowledge that she is consort to a royal bastard, to say nothing of Harry's certainty that any secret Mariah possesses would not stay secret for long.

"Then I'll do that too." Mariah sits back on Harry's thighs, rolling the dildo between her hands like it's flesh.

"Or," Harry says carefully. "We might spend some time apart."

Mariah stops her kneading. "Why would you say that?"

"Because we fight all the time and drive each other mad."

Mariah's lower lip juts out theatrically. Her cosmetics leave a faint red shadow on her upper lip. "Yes, but then we have incredible sex."

"Believe me, it's not *not* a consideration."

Mariah crosses her arms in what might be an attempt to look petulant, though it only serves to push her breasts up. "Is there someone else? I don't give a fig if you tup other people. But you can't leave me for someone else!" Her voice pitches in a way Harry is sure is all artifice. Harry sighs, pressing a hand to her eyes.

Harry knows she will never have to explain herself to Mariah—she never has, not since she and Mariah met as children at Pearl's, both of them daughters of Cyprians. Harry had been reminded just how exhausting emotional intimacy was when she had taken Miss Sergeant to Pearl's a week past—it is so much easier to be glib and unavailable, which is all Mariah ever asked.

But Mariah is too comfortable, like a pair of old shoes walked full of holes she can't throw out for fear that the next ones won't fit the same. Better, Harry's always thought, to sleep with the shoes you know. At the end of the day, Mariah will keep her warm and sated and will never ask her to be kind or sincere or emotionally intimate.

In return, all Mariah asks is to be the only person to whom Harry ever pays attention.

Which was fine for their youth—even thrilling. Harry had never wanted anything more, and the highs and lows of their turbulent relationship had made her feel desirable.

But it isn't just the shadow of the prince's offer that has dulled the shine.

"Who will take care of me if you leave me?" Mariah asks.

"You'll find someone."

"They won't be good to me like you are."

"I don't—" Harry stops, the protest dying in her throat. She remembers when Mariah worked for Pearl, the bruises Harry would find on her collarbone when she undressed her, the scratches on her back, and the way she would sometimes wake in the night and find Mariah crying quietly beside her.

She reaches out, but Mariah slaps her hand away, snuffing Harry's sympathy like a candle. "Ouch!"

"There *is* someone else, isn't there?" Mariah demands, pounding her fist against the mattress. "You fancy someone!"

"I do not," Harry says, though Emily Sergeant's face rises unbidden to her mind and she cringes. She does not fancy Emily Sergeant—or rather, she only fancies her in the way anyone with eyes would. Emily is beautiful. And confusing and strange and surprising, which feels like a different thing entirely.

It is more that an unexpected admiration for Emily Sergeant had snuck up upon her. Harry had not expected Emily to show up to Regent's Park at all, let alone on a morning Harry was riding, but arrive Emily had, in a mood as foul as the storm. She had been flushed and fussy and desperate for Alexander's attention in a way that made Harry certain that her own pursuit of Alexander was not threatened. Nothing drives a man away faster than the scent of desperation.

But then, Emily had stayed out in the rain with Harry, frozen and wet and failing to pretend she wasn't livid. And Harry had made the sort of enormous lapse in judgment that she only ever makes when faced with a beautiful woman in distress and had taken her to Pearl's.

But Emily hadn't laughed at Harry for her upbringing, nor made cutting remarks once she knew the nature of her relationship to the teahouse, and that unexpected decency had knocked Harry off course. That, and Emily's single-minded determination. The way she had stood in the rain, defiantly drowning. And Harry has always loved spirit. It's why she's agreed to meet Emily again that week, for an appointment with Harry's favorite modiste and an evening of debauchery at Ranelagh Gardens. Harry is going to buy Emily a glass of dark liquor and bribe one of the dancers to come sit in her lap. And then Collin will be sated by Harry's efforts and the prince will be impressed by her proximity to gentility and Harry will continue her courtship of Alexander. Emily is no threat. Just a mild distraction.

Mariah leans over Harry, fuzzy curls tumbling over her shoulder and tickling Harry's breasts. "Promise me you won't quit the company."

"I can't."

"Then promise me you'll tell me before you do." With her small mouth stained with Harry's wine and eyes as large as the saucers they had drunk it from, Mariah looks like a puckish imp, wandered out of the forest searching for humans to enchant into giving her their hearts.

And that, Harry thinks, is why she must be rid of Mariah Swift. For though it is so much easier to walk through life, enchanted and oblivious, half asleep under some spell, it's time to wake up.

She grabs Mariah around the waist and pulls her back down on top of her. Mariah shrieks in delight and surprise, toppling over in what Harry is sure is feigned weakness that allows her to fall directly back onto the dildo.

"Don't break my dishes," Harry says, voice cracking as Mariah grips Harry's hips between her thighs. She grabs Mariah by the ass and presses up into her, and Mariah throws her head back. "And if you find any of my good hairpins, put them on the tray by the washing basin."

HARRY MEETS EMILY at the Piccadilly entrance to Hyde Park, and they walk together to the tailor's shop in Leicester Square. The proprietress—a mean Scottish woman called Lucy McGowan—is the only dressmaker to ever successfully cut a silhouette that makes Harry's broad frame look shapely and fashionable. Most gowns make her look like a ham hock swaddled in satin. It was Mrs. McGowan who supplied Harry with the red dress she wore to the Majorbanks's ball, as well as the one she wears to Emily's appointment in hopes Mrs. McGowan will recall fondly their previous collaborations, to say nothing of the shillings Harry had already melted at her shop, and offer a cut price.

But instead, when they enter the shop, the modiste gives Harry a critical up and down, then remarks on what poor care Harry has been taking of the seams. Harry begins to argue with the fervor of the guilty, but Mrs. McGowan ignores her, and instead takes Emily by the arm and leads her behind a screen to be fitted.

"Is white entirely unacceptable?" Emily calls to Harry as McGowan's shadow flits about her, out of Harry's sight but presumably pinning the muslin over Emily's underthings.

Harry, who is busy testing the number of feathers she can add to her wig before it slides off her head, calls, "Yes."

"Perhaps a cream might—"

"White is no longer being discussed, Miss Sergeant," Harry replies. "It has been packed up and shipped across the Channel to France with every other banal fashion trend to which London is so slavishly devoted."

Emily glares at her over the top of the screen. Harry sticks another feather in her hair.

There's a rustle of pattern paper behind the screen. The toe of a discarded shoe pokes out beneath it. "Then what color would you have me in?" Emily calls.

Harry picks another feather from the vase. "What say you to a yellow?"

"I'm amenable to yellow," she says. "Like a champagne rose?"

"I thought," Harry says, "more a champagne dandelion."

Emily's forehead creases. "Dandelion?"

"Naturally." Harry selects a bolt of vibrant saffron from the wall and holds it up for Emily's examination.

"I can't wear color that bright. I'll be so . . . noticeable."

"Isn't that the idea?"

"It's far too bold! Besides, who wants to be compared to a dandelion? You'll have Rochester thinking me invasive and common."

"Hateful."

"Are you here to defend the honor of the common dandelion?"

"Someone should! Dandelions are tenacious! Impossible to kill—and they overtake everything they touch."

Emily loops her arms over the top of the screen, which must require her to stand on her toes. "They're certainly stubborn."

"An understatement," Harry says. "Dandelions are bright little rascals who love nothing more than disrupting a tidy lawn. They are abhorred by cantankerous gardeners and loved by friendly bees, as we should all aspire to be. Dandelions," Harry says, pointing one of the ostrich feathers in Emily's direction, "are outstanding foliage."

"Now then." Mrs. McGowan steps out from behind the screen. "Up on the block before the mirror now, please, Miss Sergeant, and mind the pins."

Emily follows her, adjusting the muslin self-consciously as she takes the instructed spot. Harry stands beside Mrs. McGowan, both of them looking Emily up and down and considering the dress, held in place only by a handful of straight pins. The material is so thin that Harry can see the lacings of Emily's stays beneath it. She feels the back of her neck grow hot, and would like to look away, but finds that if she doesn't look at Emily's stays, she then has to look at something else, like Emily's elegant neck or the dip of her clavicle, to say nothing of the expanse of milky skin beneath said clavicle.

Is there any aspect of this woman that is not modeled from a *Repository* fashion plate? And, more important, why does the sight do so much for Harry? She had never thought her tastes skewed so conventional, but Emily is just so . . . beautiful. She can think of no other word for it, though it feels too simple.

"I think it needs less around the shoulders," Harry says, and her voice comes out hoarser than anticipated.

"The shoulders?" Emily meets Harry's eyes in the mirror. "No words for the neckline?"

"What sort of words were you expecting?"

"I assumed I could have come out bare breasted and you'd deem it too high."

"Low necklines are common," Mrs. McGowan says, and Harry nods. "The shoulders are the great underappreciated feature of a woman."

"And this bit, right here, where the neck becomes the shoulder." Harry traces the spot on Emily with the feather. Emily wrinkles her nose and Harry is relieved that needling Emily provides adequate distraction from admiring her. "That is the exact expanse of a woman's bare flesh that inspires men to conquer cities in her name."

"I don't need cities," Emily replies.

"Just a small dukedom?" Harry winks. Emily scowls.

McGowan folds the muslin sleeve up until it barely covers Emily's pale shoulder. "Maybe a little lower here as well, though, as a contingency," Harry says, dusting Emily's breasts with the feather, and when Emily scowls, chucks her under the chin with it.

"You'll pay for those if you break them," Mrs. McGowan warns, and Harry quickly replaces the feather in its vase. The modiste pinches Emily's slender arm, and Emily flinches. "Stop clutching the material. It won't fall off you."

Emily takes a deep breath, then relaxes her hands from fists around the skirt. "Will there be so little when it's finished? You can see the shape of my legs."

"They're good legs," Harry says, then adds to Mrs. McGowan, who is still fussing with the sleeves, "Could you put something frillier on the bust to plump it up?"

"What's the matter with my . . ." Emily trails off before the word *bosom,* her cheeks pinking. She has such a lovely blush, Harry thinks, almost like it has been painted onto her cheeks.

"Men like a bit more dairy than you've got."

"Well we can't all be so . . ." Her eyes stray to the neckline of Harry's gown.

Harry feels the corners of her mouth turn up. "Go on."

Emily's eyes snap back to Harry's face. "Nothing."

"You were going to tell me I have fine breasts, weren't you?"

"That is irrelevant!" Emily snaps, now blushing to her ears.

Mrs. McGowan places a final pin in Emily's sleeve, then considers her unfrilled bust. "What will the color be?"

Harry looks to Emily, eyebrows raised. Emily rolls her eyes, then mutters, "Yellow."

Harry grins. "The color of a tenacious dandelion."

Mrs. McGowan looks thoroughly unamused by them both. "Very well. Take the muslin off carefully," she instructs Emily. "Do not disrupt the pins. Now you." And here she points to Harry and barks, "Take that off as well."

"What?" Harry looks down at her own dress. "Why?"

"I must fix that hem before you rip it out. Go on!" Mrs. McGowan chases Harry behind a second screen on the opposite side of the room and unbuttons her before hefting the heavy dress over her shoulder and tromping off to repair the hem.

Almost as soon as the modiste has gone, Harry hears Emily call timidly, "Madame? Might I have your assistance?"

"McGowan's gone to the back," Harry answers. "What do you need?"

"Nothing," Emily says quickly. A pause. The sound of something ripping, then Emily curses not quite under her breath.

"Everything all right?" Harry asks.

"She put me in stays that suited the pattern better and now I can't get them unlaced." Harry hears Emily take a heavy breath, then she asks, "Would you help me get them loose, please?"

"Ah, yes. Give me . . ." Harry casts around her corner for something to cover herself with—she's dressed in her thin chemise, but having so recently stared at Emily's fine neck and fine clavicle and fine *everything,* it feels unbearably indecent to unlace Emily's undergarments wearing so little. Seeing nothing but the bolts of cloth from which the tenacious yellow was selected, Harry swaddles herself in a length, wrapping it around her waist and then breasts before clamping down her arms to hold it in place. Then she trips across the room, stockinged feet collecting scraps of material. The long tail of the unfurling fabric drags behind her like a wedding train. She hears the *thump* as the bolt falls off the shelf.

"What are you wearing?" Emily asks as Harry ducks behind her screen, which seems rather judgmental for someone standing in only a thin slip under the tight stays imprisoning her from her breasts to her waist.

"Only my finest," Harry replies. "Now let's have a look at these laces that have you captive."

Emily holds out her arms, even as Harry clamps her own to her side to hold her bundled fabric in place. She bends over for a better look, keenly aware that she is doing little more than staring at Emily's breasts. Well not breasts, but the stays covering them, which are extremely breast adjacent. Harry grows so hot she almost drops the fabric from around her, lest the sweat coating her back should soak through.

While Harry has admired many different breasts on many different women, something about Emily's—about Emily—about her scowl and her gall and her dogged determination to grab her own future by the throat—makes Harry want to lean forward and press her lips to the shadowed dip between them.

"Any luck?" Emily asks, and Harry snaps from her reverie. *God!* Has it been so long since she was with someone other than Mariah that she is *this* stupefied by a beautiful woman asking her to unlace her stays—and not even in prelude to fornication?

Harry hooks a finger into the laces and tugs experimentally. Emily's body rocks, though Harry didn't pull hard, and she grabs a nearby shelf to steady herself. "My." Harry fiddles with the bow, which is somehow thrice knotted. "You've really mucked this up."

"It wasn't me! It was . . ." Emily glances over the screen like Mrs. McGowan might be lurking. "Just undo them for me, please."

Harry begins to work through the knots, hoping that the task at hand might distract her from Emily's breasts and body and heat and *nearness*. She thinks Emily must be looking elsewhere until she remarks, "Well your nails are worthless for this," and Harry glances up to find Emily is watching her work. "Look how short they are! Hardly good for anything."

"They're good for some things." Harry clenches her teeth, eyes crossing as she tries to focus. Emily's breasts are small, but the soft swell of them pushed up by the boned stays is impossible *not* to look at, and, for God's sake, they're *right there*. She's practically making eye contact with her nipples. And Emily is staring at her, like she suspects Harry of thinking unholy thoughts and must remain vigilant. Harry should look away—but isn't it stranger *not* to look? Surely if they were irrelevant breasts, it wouldn't matter if Harry looked at them. But how is she meant to look at them like they truly are irrelevant? God, this is a nightmare.

"No luck?" Emily asks. Harry tugs again, hoping to create some kind of gap from which she can approach the knots at a different angle. Emily hunches over, sucking in her stomach. Her elbow knocks a capped jar of buttons off the shelf behind her, which Harry catches before they hit the ground. Her fabric swath nearly slips out from under her arms.

"I'm sorry, but you may have to be buried in these stays."

Emily presses a hand to her forehead. "Crikey, just cut the laces. I'll pay her for new ones."

"No, hold on, I have an idea." Harry slips one of the pins from the muslin dress draped over the screen and manages to work it in between the laces, and at last the knots loosen. She hooks a finger through and tugs them free from their grommets, just as Emily says, "Let me," and their hands bump, knocking Harry's off course and resulting in her accidentally pinching Emily's breast.

Emily jumps with a yelp.

Harry steps backward and holds up her hands. "Sorry, sorry!"

To her surprise, Emily pinches Harry's breast in return.

Now it's Harry who yelps. "Ow! What the devil?"

"You did it first."

"It was a slip of the hand."

"So was mine."

Harry slaps Emily's breast.

Emily grabs the front of Harry's makeshift swaddle and yanks. Harry suspects she intends to only pull down the fabric, but the tug is sharp enough that Harry's chemise goes with it, exposing both her breasts.

Emily claps her hands over her mouth. "I'm so sorry! I didn't realize—"

"You devious creature!" There's little reason to protect her modesty any longer, so Harry lets the fabric fall around her ankles, leaving her standing before Emily in only her cotton chemise, thinner than even the muslin pattern and with nothing underneath. "If you wanted to see my breasts you could have just asked."

Now Emily has her hands over her eyes. "I'm so sorry!"

"No you aren't! Look at you, you're laughing like a maniac!"

She is—Emily's cheeks are bright pink and she seems unable to stop her giggling. "How was I supposed to know—" Now she is laughing so hard she can't speak clearly. Each word bumps like a cart on a potholed road. "You're the one who came here . . . dressed like Julius Caesar."

"Ah yes, famously bare-breasted Julius Caesar."

Emily doubles over, collapsing with laughter until she is crouched on the floor. Harry laughs too—mostly at Emily's wild, infectious cackling, which warms Harry's whole body like she's stepped into a sunbeam.

"I really . . ." Emily manages a shuddering breath at last, then lets out one final burst of laughter before she tries again. "I am truly sorry."

"It's fine." Harry extends a hand to Emily, helping her back to her feet. She pulls her up with more force than Emily must have expected, for Emily oversteps and tumbles into Harry. She grabs Harry's forearms to steady herself, but not before her chest collides with Harry's. And with both of them in only slips, Harry can feel Emily's breasts against hers.

And suddenly, Harry feels like she has dropped below the surface of a lake. The sound of the shop and from the street outside muffles. Her vision pulsates. She tries to take a breath but it feels like her lungs are full of water. Before she can stop herself, Harry looks down at Emily's breasts. With the stays fallen away, Harry can see the blush of nipples under Emily's slip.

She hears the soft hitch of Emily's breath, and realizes that she has been standing for too long, Emily in her arms, staring at her. God, she has got to get her head on straight.

"Apologies," Harry says quickly. "I'll let you finish dressing." She tries to step backward, only to find that Emily is still holding her arms, staring at the place where her skin touches Harry's.

"How are your arms so . . ." she says, then blinks and looks up at Harry, like she hadn't meant to say that aloud. Harry wets her lips before she can stop herself.

"Pardon?"

"Yes," Emily says, and she lets go of Harry. "You'd best let me finish dressing on my own."

18

Outside the shop, the high street is bustling. The smell of sugared fruit just on the edge of burning wafts off a nearby cart, and Harry considers that a pie on the walk home may be just the thing.

"The yellow gives me pause," Emily says, stopping to retie her bonnet.

"You'll carry it with aplomb," Harry assures her. "If Rochester doesn't compliment you on the color of your dress at the Derby, I'll eat it."

"Are we still going to Ranelagh Gardens tonight? For my interesting anecdote about an interesting outing?"

"The box isn't reserved until half seven," Harry says. "Shall I walk you back to your cousin's?"

Emily frowns. "What for?"

"Respite from my company."

Emily rolls her eyes. "Oh stop."

"What? You're surely weary of me."

"I know what you're doing." Emily juts her chin up toward Harry, bonnet slipping backward. "You can't make me say it."

"Say what?" Harry asks, feigning ignorance. "That you enjoy my company?"

Emily presses a gloved hand upon her lips. "I shan't."

"If you stay silent, it's the same as a lie."

"Is it?"

"Come now." Harry grabs Emily by the wrist, prying her hand from her mouth. "Just say it once. Tell me you enjoy me."

Emily shrieks, half surprise, half laughter as Harry pulls her in. "Release me."

"You do, don't you?" Harry presses Emily's wrist to her heart, and Emily bends against her like a tree braced into the wind. This flirtation is growing more blatant by the minute, but Harry can't help herself. Emily's cheeks are pink, mouth curled in a smile, and Harry is still thinking of the moment they shared in the shop, the way playfulness had become suddenly charged. How easily she could grow addicted to that feeling. Even now, she knows she's courting it to a dangerous degree. "Say it just once and I'll let you go."

Emily twists in Harry's grip, though the fight is weak enough that Harry is certain it's just for show. "I find you irritating!"

"And?" Harry drags out the word. "Say it."

Emily purses her lips, gaze darting downward before glancing up at Harry through her lashes and God, but Harry is possessed by the mad desire to kiss her upon the wrist. Were this any other woman but Emily Sergeant, she would have, even if it earned her a slap for the boldness. But Emily Sergeant is made of a different matter. Harry finds her preferences skew toward flinty women—usually those who despise her—so the attraction doesn't surprise her. It is that as Emily's cold exterior begins to thaw, Harry finds herself leaning in closer.

Which is . . . different.

"Miss Lockhart," Emily says slowly. "While it pains me greatly to admit it—"

"Go on."

"And though I fear I shall come to regret these words—"

"Such preamble."

"And thus reserve the right to rescind them at any time." Emily wiggles her wrist in Harry's hand, but Harry holds firm. Emily throws her head back. "I concede that perhaps it is true that today, and today only, I find I have somewhat enjoyed—"

But she is interrupted when something hits Harry in the chest.

One minute she's standing next to Emily, the next she has been thrown several steps backward from impact and her front is dripping with red. Blood? Has she just been shot? She remembers one of the stagehands from the Palace—a veteran of the Napoleonic Wars with a dead arm from a bullet at Waterloo—who told her he never felt the pain, just the impact.

"What happened?" Emily cries. Her face is freckled with red. "Are you all right?"

Harry reaches down and touches the front of her dress, only to realize it's not blood smeared there, but fruit. She's not been shot—she's had a cherry pie flung into her chest. Looking around, she spots a figure fleeing the scene, a hand thrown over his face to conceal his identity.

Harry holds up one finger to Miss Sergeant. "Will you excuse me?" she says, then takes off at a run after her attacker.

Two blocks later, Harry manages to snag him by the back of his jacket as he turns down an alley. She shoves him into a window, rattling the casements.

She isn't surprised that she catches the pie assassin—she's fit and long-legged, and he's small and chuffing. What does surprise her is that Emily Sergeant appears by her side, winded, and that carefully knotted bonnet free and flopping against her shoulder.

Before she's even properly caught her breath, Emily cries, "What the devil is the matter with you?"

Harry thinks for a moment Emily is shouting at *her*, then realizes that no, she's scolding the assailant.

And she isn't finished. "You strike my friend with a pie and then flee? The very least you can do is apologize, if this was an honest mistake, and if it was intentional, then I must ask, are you cruel or stupid or both? Was this meant to be some kind of demented prank? Apologize now, or I will alert the constabulary to your maleficence and see that you are disciplined sufficiently."

"Easy, that's enough." Harry holds up a hand to stop Emily. As enjoyable as it would be to continue watching her verbally fillet the scoundrel, she needs him to explain the motivations behind his senseless but absurd crime.

Emily huffs, arms folded, then barks at the man, "Explain yourself, sirrah!"

The man—God, he's only a boy, just out of short pants by the looks of him. The top of his head barely passes Harry's shoulder—how he managed to fling the pie high enough to strike her directly in the breast is as great a mystery as why. "The Duke of Edgewood sends his regards!" he cries, his defiance undercut by how close he is to tears.

"Oh Jesus Christ." Dread punches its way through the buzz of alarm and confusion ringing in Harry's chest. She had thought enough time had elapsed that the duke's thirst for revenge had passed. They had dueled in February, for God's sake, and now it was nearly May! Duels were meant to end feuds, not progress into protracted pastry-based revenge—though Harry supposes burying the hatchet is easier when one of the parties ends up dead.

Harry lets go the boy's collar and shoves him away from the

wall. "Get lost, pup. Tell your duke I got his message and I'm terribly afeared."

As the boy takes off at a sprint, Harry turns to Emily, ready to give a hand-waving dismissal of the peculiar attack they just survived.

But before she can, Emily asks, "Are you hurt?"

"I don't think so. Irritated, mostly." Harry touches the point of impact, only to find that her hands are shaking. *If this were a bullet,* she thinks, hand folded over her heart, *this is when the pain would start to set in.* Best to keep chatting like nothing is wrong to convince them both. "I paid a shilling for that new hem and now the whole dress is ruined. To say nothing of the waste of a good pie."

Emily lifts a hand, like she might attempt to brush the pie off Harry, then reconsiders, as the mess is beyond brushing. "I can get the stain out."

"With all due respect to your domestic abilities, I don't think anything short of a cleansing fire will affect this dress."

"Let me try. With a bit of vinegar, I'm sure it can be salvaged." Emily folds her hand into the crook of Harry's elbow, and leads her back to the street. "Come on. Let's get away from here."

And Harry, God help her, stunned and dazed and dripping in pie, lets Emily Sergeant walk her home.

19

Havoc greets them at the door to Collin's house, his usual enthusiasm amplified twofold when he discovers that Harry has not only returned to him, but returned soaked in pie. He and Emily follow her abovestairs, Havoc licking the back of her dress, and wait in the hall until Harry tosses out the soiled garment for Emily to soak belowstairs.

Once she's scrubbed and changed and unwigged, Harry finds Emily in the kitchen, sleeves rolled, up to her elbows in soapy water and Harry's dress, while Havoc sits on her feet, prepared to catch any stray pastry that might fall. The smell of vinegar in the air stings Harry's eyes, though Emily appears to have moved on to attacking the skirt with a cube of soap from the stand beside the basin.

"We can mark the time of death and feed it to the fire," Harry says. Her wet hair drips into the collar of her banyan.

"Then the enemy wins!" Emily loses her grip on the soap, and it sails into the air. Havoc makes a dive for it before realizing it isn't pie. "Did you know that man?" Emily asks as she retrieves the bar. They had spoken very little on the walk to Collin's, and Harry is not prepared for the flush the question raises in her cheeks, nor the realization that she doesn't want to tell Emily this story.

She picks a piece of crust from her hair, considers eating it, then throws it to Havoc instead. "No, but I know his employer."

"The Duke of Edgewood," Emily says.

"Indeed. He and I fought a duel."

The space between Emily's brows creases. "You were in a fight?"

"A duel—surprisingly different." Harry runs her fingers through the hair at the nape of her neck, trying to break up the tacky strands and wondering how so much syrup managed to get through her wig. Dress ruined, wig ruined—what a horrible, expensive day. "And it hardly qualified as even that—we fought with tipped foils, for God's sake! The same ones we use on stage. I've been accidentally stabbed a dozen times and never lost an eye."

"Dueling is illegal," Emily says. "What could you possibly have quarreled over that came to blows?"

"We were playing cards at White's and he didn't like that I accused him of cheating."

"Was he?"

"Cheating? Absolutely. Half a deck fell out of his sleeve when he stood to overturn the table. But he denied it, threw a glove at me, and stormed out."

"Gracious." Emily hefts the dress from the basin and rings it out. Pink water spurts from the material. "What I wouldn't give for just a smidge of your confidence."

"Confidence?" Harry laughs. "Collin calls it insolence. My mother had crueler names."

"Whatever it is," Emily says, "I'd give anything for it."

Harry pulls back the bench at the kitchen table and sinks down upon it. Havoc comes to her side and begins licking her hand. "Don't make that devil's bargain just yet. Confidence is hard won."

"How do you mean?"

Harry thinks of the girls at school who called her names and drew pictures of her mowing their headmistress, all of which found their way into her schoolbag. Of the boys at the stables, who pissed in her boots and grabbed her ass whenever she picked her horses' shoes. Of the first morning in their new townhouse, when the windows were pelted with eggs, and Harry had cried until her mother slapped her.

"I was mocked for so much when I was young," she says. "My mother, my height, my affinity for trousers and horses and theatrics. I fought back for a long time—got my eyes blacked so many times Collin was concerned it would affect my vision—before I discovered that if I didn't care, or acted as though I didn't care what anyone thought, everyone would leave me alone."

Emily frowns. "Why?"

"What fun is poking a dog that doesn't snap? People want to know they hurt you."

"But did you still care what people thought of you?"

"At first. Now I'm so sincerely apathetic that I truly do not give a fig for anyone's opinion. Is this the haircut of a woman who cares what others think of her? If you pretend for long enough, you fool even yourself."

Emily shakes her head, still staring down at the dress. "I can't imagine."

"Imagine what?"

"Being so secure in myself. I'm far too concerned with people liking me."

"But there are so many better things to be than liked!"

"Such as?"

"Despised. Loathed. Abhorred!" Emily laughs, and Harry finishes, more gently, "Ardently and passionately desired."

Emily stops scrubbing and turns to Harry with a soft intensity to her gaze, and Harry finds that in the light of someone listening to her—really listening—for the first time in so long, she wants to keep talking. She wants Emily to know everything about her.

Which would be a very poor idea, because she plans to wed the man Emily has set her sights upon. Best not to accidentally give up any information that Emily might someday use against Harry, no matter how good it feels to speak freely or how intoxicating it was when Emily had held on to her at the dress shop, their bodies pressed together.

Harry flings the towel from her neck at Emily, who flinches with a laugh. "Don't look at me like I'm a tragedy."

"It sounds lonely." Emily dries her hands on her skirt. "To have no one but yourself upon whom to rely."

"*Lonely.*" Harry waves a hand like she might swat away the word. "I don't need anyone to love me in order to love myself."

"But someone should."

"Should what?"

"Love you. Someone should love you." Emily ducks her chin, turning from Harry as she holds up the dress, tilting it to the light. She has only managed to turn the crimson stain pink. "I may have overestimated the strength of vinegar and soap."

"Your efforts are appreciated regardless." Harry rolls her shoulder in its socket, feeling the ache of a bruise forming there. "I know that I promised you a trip to Ranelagh tonight, but I don't think I have the strength after all this. Can we schedule for another day?"

"Of course. Are you sure you're all right here tonight? Do you want me to send for a doctor?"

"No, I just need a bath and a drink and then bed."

"Will Collin be home soon? I hate to think of you here alone."

God, has she ever wanted to be alone less than she does now? Harry thinks suddenly of the manor house in the countryside the prince has set aside for her, its countless empty rooms. What a vast space she'll have to fill with no one but herself and her hard-won confidence.

And Alexander, she reminds herself.

And if she is to have Alexander, she shouldn't be spending time with Emily.

If Alexander knew the real Miss Sergeant, not the prim façade she seems to think she needs adopt, Harry fears he might fall in love with her in earnest. Emily could be the perfect bride for him. Far from dull, as Alexander pronounced her, she is smart and funny and interesting and thoughtful. Who wouldn't want to marry her? Harry should be doing nothing to aid Emily in pursuing Alexander.

Rather, she should cut Emily loose now, tell her she cannot be the one to help her woo Alexander. Take this day as a sign any further companionship is doomed. At the very least, Harry should be passing this time with Alexander, proving to him she can be demure and responsible when the need arises. She could go see him now. He'll be back from his morning ride. She could put the pie-stained dress back on and arrive on his doorstep in distress, seeking a manly shoulder upon which to cry. She could even let him walk in on her while she's in the bath, and then a shoulder to cry upon might become a shoulder to sleep with. She'd let him think he had consoled her, sheltered her, protected her, all those things men want to do for women. And she wouldn't be alone.

Yet Harry finds herself saying, "Perhaps we might go out tomorrow. Not to the Gardens. A different scandalous outing."

Emily nods. "Your brother mentioned Speakers' Corner. Might we meet there?"

"Noon?" Harry says, and Emily smiles.

"I'll see you then."

20

At Speakers' Corner, Harry learns that after a lifetime spent on a Sussex farm, Emily has a great deal to say about the need to increase land rights to tenant farmers. Even more after she has been plied with rum punch, which she tells Harry four times with increasing volume she likes quite a lot.

The following day, in a coffeehouse they visit to locate a leaflet written by one of the orators, she learns Emily drinks her coffee black and hot, and without cream, and manages to charm the bacon-faced clerk into sending them a plate of scones without charge. When they pay for the leaflet and the coffee, Harry learns that Emily has a tendency to round up any number to the closest multiple of ten rather than have to do arithmetic in her head.

At a talk on farmers' rights the next week, Harry discovers Emily has a habit of fidgeting when she has something she'd like to say. She loses an earring midway through the talk and they spend almost half of an hour after everyone has gone looking for it under chairs.

Afterward, on their way to a bookshop the lecturer recommended, Harry learns Emily has no sense of direction. She's also stubborn, refusing to accept help, and they end up wandering increasingly unsavory streets for nearly two hours before finally finding themselves, in some improbable trick of London geography, outside Pearl's tea shop, and it's Emily who suggests they stop. They drink small beers and eat peanuts and oysters until Harry realizes she is overdue at the theater and has to rush out.

It is Emily too who suggests they visit a casino where Alexander likes to play, and though he isn't there, Harry leaves one of her cards with a note that she and her friend from the south—no names, must remain a bit mysterious, he'll get the hint, she assures Emily—were sorry to have missed him and, by the way, won quite a bit on chance games, which they had. Emily, it seems, is improbably good at hazard, a game that Harry had assumed it was not possible to be good at, as it is entirely chance based. When Harry comments on how much she likes a figurine in one of the card rooms, Emily pockets it for her, not revealing her theft until they are halfway home. Harry finds herself torn between delight and concern that they'll be arrested. Which might be a scandalous outing too far.

As spring tumbles forward, blossoms falling from the trees to make way for green leaves, Emily comes by the stables thrice to see Harry ride, though Alexander is never present, and none of the visits do anything to warm Emily to horses. Harry makes a valiant effort, but Emily refuses to get in the saddle herself, insisting she would rather sit on the fence and watch Harry prepare Matthew for the steeplechase. One morning she brings Harry's favorite pastries, which Harry only remembers mentioning once in passing and yet Emily had remembered. And though Matthew is saddled, the ride never happens, for their morning is taken up with sitting on the grass and eating them all, though Emily had brought enough for a family.

Harry knows herself well enough to admit she is developing quite an infatuation with Emily Sergeant. But that's fine. She has passively fancied a lot of beautiful women who once shouted at her. There is no danger in the pleasant buzz of desire. It's the emotional equivalent of one glass of wine too many. And Harry plans to enjoy the high, but drink no more.

It is a month to the day of their first attempt to visit Ranelagh Gardens when Harry finally makes the promised reservation, and though Emily has racked up more than enough adventures to impress the duke, they both continue to pretend the outing is essential.

The sun has hardly set, but Ranelagh Gardens is already lit brilliantly when Harry arrives with Collin, who had insisted on joining to witness this unlikely friendship firsthand. They pay their shillings and cross the rotunda. Two girls lurking about the entrance to the hall of statues wave to Harry and Collin, and Harry, recognizing them from Pearl's, waves in return. Collin looks the other direction. When a cry to watch your pockets goes up from somewhere in the crowd, Harry and Collin raise their hands, an old joke from youth signifying there's nothing on them worth stealing. Harry laughs, and Collin gives her a grudging smile.

Emily isn't scheduled to arrive for another hour, so they find a box in the gallery and Harry orders wine for them both. When the bottle arrives, Collin nods at the label. "You remembered."

"Of course," Harry replies.

They have drunk most of the bottle when the organist in the next balcony clunks from an interminable ballad into the first notes of "There's No One Can Love Like an Irishman." Harry and Collin groan in unison.

"Do you remember—" Collin says at the same time Harry says, "That Irish beau of Mother's—"

"He used to sing this to her before they—"

"—couldn't carry a tune, he never hit a note—"

"—you'd think he'd get one right every once in a while, just by mistake—"

"—you could hear them through the whole house—"

"—he always left the window open, the whole street could probably hear—"

The organ reaches the last lines of the verse, and Harry, remembering suddenly the words of the cursed tune, sings, *"And I know she'll say, from behind her fan."*

Collin sits up, the words seeming to come to him as well, and he turns to Harry as they sing together, melody devolving into a chant, *"That there's none can love like an Irishman, like an Irishman, like an Irishman!"*

Harry seizes Collin's arm to keep herself from falling out of her chair with tipsy laughter. Collin snorts, tilting his glass back to drain the dregs. "God, he was a prick," Collin says at the same time Harry says, "He was one of Mother's better beaus."

Collin swats at her. "In comparison only. Why are we laughing?"

Harry shrugs. "Easier that way, I suppose."

Collin tips his glass back again, as though checking it really is empty. "She always liked you more than me."

Harry scoffs. It was true their mother had paid her more attention than Collin, and attention and love are easy to misconstrue. Collin had been better at keeping his head down and his mouth shut, two things Harry had never mastered despite how often her mother slapped her. "I don't think she liked either of us much."

"Certainly didn't want us."

"And neither did our father!" Harry raises the bottle. "Cheers to the unwanted royal bastards."

Collin laughs, clinking his glass against it. *"Royal bastards.* So strange."

"How is your nonconditional inheritance shaping up?" Harry asks. "Have you picked out drapes for your house yet? Exorcised the ghosts?"

"Literal or metaphorical?"

"That house is most certainly haunted by something. Longley, I suspect, will always be home to the ghosts of everyone I might have shagged had I not been forced into a union against my will."

Collin runs a finger over his bottom lip. Harry can still make out the faint scar that splits it, from when, as a child, he had tripped on the uneven stairs at Pearl's and bitten through it. "Not that what I think matters," he says, "to you or His Majesty. But I think it's absurd."

"What is?"

"His condition that you marry. He'll be the bloody king! He could write a provision of inheritance for a single woman into the deed if he chose to. He can pretend it's well intentioned and for your own good, but you've been taking care of yourself for years. You don't need a husband."

Harry is so surprised by this admission—and, strangely touched that he's taken her side for perhaps the first time in their lives—that the only thing she can think to say is a foolishly simple "Thank you."

Collin nods sharply, and Harry has a sense they're both uncomfortable with this allegiance. Though perhaps that's simply because it's new. "When is Miss Sergeant meant to arrive?" Collin asks.

"Half ten. I should go find her, actually—and something more to drink." Harry stands, pushing her chair back as she heads for the hall, but pauses on the threshold and turns back. "Collin?"

He drops his head over the back of his chair. "Hm?"

It's been good to see him more, and she almost says so. He

leaves home early and returns late, always muttering something about his work, but their paths still cross in their shared lodging more than Harry thought she'd prefer. But it's been surprisingly nice to have her brother near. He's a bitter tea, but she's drunk it since childhood, and sometimes still finds herself with a particular craving.

But Collin's love has always felt conditional, same as their mother's had been, though Harry knows he'd be loath to hear the comparison. The fact that he had just acknowledged a disparity in their father's treatment of them because of their sexes doesn't make him a suddenly changed man. So instead, she says, "Another bottle of the same?"

And he replies, "Please."

Harry takes the short flight of stairs down to the bar two at a time, feeling buzzy with the wine and the atmosphere and the impending reunion with Emily. She turns down a corridor behind the bar, passing a shadowed hallway leading to an empty card room marked no entry with a rope, when someone reaches from the darkness, grabs her by the arm, and yanks her to them.

Harry is torn between a well-timed scream and a well-placed knee driven into her assailant. Her first thought is that the Duke of Edgewood finally had the good sense to hire a true assassin rather than one who can't be trusted with a weapon more dangerous than a pie.

But then her assailant fastens his mouth over hers and she catches a whiff of familiar cologne.

Harry pulls away, her back colliding with the wall. "Good God, Alex."

Alexander pushes his mop of blond hair from his face, smile momentarily illuminated when a waiter passes the entrance of the hallway with a lamp. "Did I startle you?"

"I should say so, you bellend. Jesus." Harry presses a hand to her heart.

He catches her chin between his thumb and forefinger and tilts her face to the light. "I saw you sitting across the way, and when you got up I thought, Wouldn't it be a lark to surprise Harry?"

"You are fortunate I'm a bottle deep, or I might have broken your nose," Harry replies flatly. "What are you doing here? Besides pulling unsuspecting girls into dark corners. How many women have you tried that on, by the by?"

"Tonight? Only you." Alex leans into her again, and Harry, whose still-slamming heart has left her feeling less than charitable, steps away. Alexander catches himself against the wall behind her. His coat falls open and a few stray shillings fall from his pocket.

"Are you gambling?"

Alexander grins, scooping up the coins. "A bit."

"A bit?" Harry hefts the pocket of his coat between her hands. It jingles like a Morris dancer. "You're going to fall through the floor. Come buy me a drink if you're having such a good night."

"Or what if we had a quick knock and then get back to our respective parties? I'm loath to leave this game."

"Unless it's for a stroke?"

"Precisely." He grabs her breast through her shirt, squeezing it like he's testing a fruit for ripeness. "Come on, Harry, just a quick go."

"Not now—I'm here with my brother. And Miss Sergeant should be joining us soon. You remember her, don't you?"

"Well then, I'll have to buy you both a drink." He kisses Harry on the cheek. "How's Matthew handling for you? Think you'll be ready for the Derby?"

"You'd know if you ever bothered to show up to training."

"I know, I'm sorry. I've been occupied."

"With what?"

"Let's ride tomorrow," he says instead of answering, and loops an arm around her waist. "Just you and I. Come to mine after luncheon?"

"God, Alex, your breath."

"All right, you harpy." He bites her shoulder, then pushes her playfully back into the hall. "Show me your box. I promise I won't tell Collin we've a date for tomorrow."

Harry had been reaching behind her to take his hand, but stops at the sound of her brother's name, and turns back to Alexander. "You've spoken to Collin? When?"

"He introduced himself at the Majorbanks's ball and we've gone out a few times since. He said he wanted to know the fellow his sister had designs on. He's an interesting man. Asked me all sorts of questions. I wish you'd told me what he does." He reaches for her, but Harry bats him away. Alexander frowns. "What's the matter? We can go to mine now, if you'd rather. I won't talk to your brother. Or Miss . . ." He trails off, struggling to conjure the name. "The blonde, yes? The small one who looks like a doll? Harry, what's the matter? Where are you going?"

But Harry is already storming away. "I need some air."

"Are you coming back?"

"Who knows? I'll see you tomorrow."

"Harry, don't go. Harry!"

Harry pushes through the crowd toward the exit. She doesn't realize how hot she's grown until the cool evening air strikes her face and she stops at the gate, breathing heavily.

Of course Collin had to stick his nose in her business just so he could turn it up in judgment, after she had asked him to trust her on this and stay away from the duke. *Of course* he'd have sought out Alexander—how foolish she was for even giving her brother the duke's name! And *of course,* now he will find Alexander wanting in some way, as he's always found everything about Harry wanting. Why couldn't he have trusted her judgment, just this once, or at least pretended to? Rather than seeking out Alexander and making her business his? He was always so certain he knew what was best for her, when, in truth, he doesn't know her at all.

She slumps back against the wall as, somewhere above her, chimes strike the hour. She presses her hands to her flushed cheeks.

"Hello there."

Harry straightens, turning sharply, to find Emily Sergeant, in an embroidered dress with a shawl draped elegantly over her shoulders. Harry runs a quick hand through her hair, like a stray lock might be the thing that betrays her distress rather than everything else about her. "Miss Sergeant."

"I thought I was meant to meet you at the clock." Her smile fades as she looks Harry up and down. "Is something the matter?"

Harry considers deferring—there is no need for Emily to know their business, and if she delves too far into this explanation, she'll have to concede her own marital designs on the duke she has assured Emily she has no interest in. "My brother is being an ass," she says simply. "But it's no matter. Go in without me—I'll give you the box number."

"Are you coming?"

"Not just now. I need to stand out here until I can be civil." Harry sticks her hands into her pockets and balls them into fists around the material. "I was considering leaving, though I understand the bind that would put you in as a lady unchaperoned. Sorry, I'm being . . ." She runs a hand through her hair again, takes a steadying breath, trying to shake off her anger like rain from a coat. "Let's go inside and forget any of this happened."

"Or we can leave," Emily says.

"Leave?"

"Go back to my cousin's."

The invitation is so surprising Harry almost laughs. "And do what?"

"Have a quiet night in."

"I am not made for quiet," Harry says. Her anger will only get louder if she's made to sit with it in silence. At least the noise and shine of the Garden would be a distraction.

"I'm sure you can bear a single night away from the demimonde." Emily takes Harry by the arm, leading her gently back toward the street. "Come, it isn't far. And it will be quiet. Well, except for the baby."

"I'm sure it can't be worse than Collin's squalling."

Emily shakes her head, smile twisting her lips. "Hateful."

21

"Now?" Emily throws a pillow from the settee, which Harry bats out of the air, nearly sending it sailing into the fire. "This very moment? You are in a play this very moment and you neglected to tell me?"

"Well not this very moment, as I'm sitting in your cousin's parlor eating cake."

"Do not misunderstand me!"

Emily watches as Harry scrapes her fork around the edge of her empty plate. Violet and Martin were already abed when they arrived and the staff gone home, so Emily had suggested they nest in the formal parlor rather than the drawing rooms adjacent to Violet's bedroom. The fire there was still high enough to be restoked, and Martin's liquor cabinet unlocked. Harry had admired its contents when they arrived, but they haven't poured any. Instead, Emily had brought them two slices of cake from tea on mismatched saucers from the kitchen, which they've been eating slowly in front of the fire.

And now, improbably, here is Harry, with her jacket off and her feet pulled up under her, eating cake off Emily's cousin's china. It feels like seeing a tiger at a tea party, a strange disjunction of person and place. Emily had feared as soon as she offered the invitation that she had made a mistake. Even if Harry accepted, surely she'd be bored within ten minutes of arriving. What did she have to offer by way of entertainment, particularly when the alternative was the shine of a pleasure garden?

But not only is Harry here, she is relaxed and smiling and shows no signs of searching for a flimsy excuse to go.

Emily leans backward on the settee, bare feet burrowed in between the cushions. The unladylike posture makes her feel hedonistic. She wants to stretch across all three cushions, undo her hair from its arrangement, and drop her head back over the arm so it falls into long cascades. She wants to know Harry is watching her without looking. She wants to feel her gaze hot as the fire.

Harry retrieves the errant pillow and shoves it under the chair in which she's reclining. "Where did you think I was going every night?"

"I thought you were rehearsing. All you ever said was that you were needed at the theater!" Emily throws a second pillow at her, though it falls short and lands between them. "I assumed if you were in a production that was playing on stage at this very moment, you'd have told me so I could come see it."

Harry sets her plate on the side table, then leans forward with her elbows on her knees. "Miss Sergeant, you may not under any circumstances come see my play."

"Why not?"

"Because it's horrible. *I'm* horrible. My troupe exclusively performs horrible theater."

"Surely you exaggerate."

"You'd think otherwise if you had seen our balletic reimagining of the St. Crispin's Day speech in *Henry V.*"

"There are songs?"

"Oh they must have songs—it's the way we get around the drama bans."

"Who did you play in the Henriad?"

"Hal, obviously. The dashing prince-rake turned great king of England."

"Is that why Collin calls you Hal? Since it's a diminutive of Henry, as is Harry?"

"Got it in one."

Emily settles back into the settee again. Exhaustion is creeping up on her, but for now, it only serves to make her feel loose and silly, and she asks before she can stop herself, "Could *I* call you Hal?"

"You can call me anything," Harry replies with a sideways smile, and Emily feels her heart stutter.

She looks down quickly, dragging a finger around the edge of her plate to pick up the crumbs. Even though she has passed most days of the past month with Harry, so much time that it almost felt silly to still call her Miss Lockhart, it's too much to use her family's pet name.

"I should like to call you Harry," Emily says, surprised by the giddy shudder that goes through her when she says the name aloud. It strikes her tongue like a bud of poppy, and she feels suddenly so intoxicated it frightens her, so she adds quickly, "But you may continue to refer to me as Miss Sergeant."

Harry sketches a bow. "As you wish."

Emily puts her finger between her lips, sucking crumbs off it. Harry watches her, teeth pressed into her bottom lip.

"Why carry on performing if it's so terrible?" Emily asks.

"I have to earn a living somehow and I'm no good at anything else."

"You're good at lots of things," Emily protests.

"Such as?"

"You're charming and clever and you ride horses and know so many references. You're thoughtful. You're fashionable."

"Am I?" Harry interrupts. "Or do I simply own a lot of brocade coats?"

Emily rolls her eyes. "You could find a better company."

"Well, the Palace is all Sapphists, which is nice."

"What does that mean?"

"What does what mean?"

"Sapphists. Is that a kind of thespian?"

"No it's . . ." Harry coughs and rubs the back of her neck, and when she glances around, Emily has the sense she's searching for a candle to tip in hopes a small fire might divert the subject. "It's a reference to Sappho, the Greek poetess."

"I've never heard of her."

"I can't imagine you would have." Harry presses the tips of her fingers together, hands between her knees. "She's been largely bowdlerized by modern censors, as she had a bit of a fondness for writing erotically about other women."

Emily looks down quickly at her hands. The crescents of her nails are dotted with cake crumbs. "Oh."

A moment of silence between them. The cushions rustle as Harry shifts in her chair, and for a moment, Emily wonders wildly if Harry is about to close the space between them and take her hand. But then she says, "Miss Sergeant. You know I couple with women, don't you?"

Emily isn't sure if the ripple of surprise that goes through her is because of the confession, or because she isn't more shocked by it. She feels it in her thighs. Her hips. An illicit twinge in both body and soul. She's heard sodomy and such debauchery obliquely referenced in church, but never met a Sapphist before. *Sapphist*. The word feels slippery and soft as silk, and she finds herself thinking of a gaggle of young women she and Violet had passed that morning at Hyde Park sharing sweets. Two of them had reached inside the bag at the same time and withdrawn the same piece between them. One had laughed, but the other had blushed, and quickly dropped her hand away, like she had been burned. Why had she noticed them so particularly? And why think of them now?

"I assumed you realized," Harry continues, "or I would have said before. I wasn't trying to hide it."

"You know," Emily says slowly. "I think I did know. You never told me outright but . . . it's like when you hear a song and you know you've heard it before but you can't remember where. All you know is that you recognize it. It was like . . . I knew you." She looks up at Harry. A dark curl has fallen across her forehead, a perfect imitation of a question mark. "That sounds absurd."

"No," Harry says, and Emily feels the now familiar sunbeam warmth of being caught in her gaze. Or perhaps it's footlights. Perhaps they are together on a stage, and perhaps it is written in a script that this is the part where they kiss. "It makes sense."

"Does it?" Emily asks.

Harry smiles. "Perfectly."

"And everyone in your theatrical company shares your preferences?"

"It's a qualifier to join." Harry settles back in her chair again. "A lady I was bedding when I was nine and ten was one of their patrons and she introduced me to the company manager. I was looking for a way out of my mother's house and I was a dramatic youth who loved Shakespeare, so it was a good fit at the time."

"It must be nice, to be with such women."

"It's not a perfect arrangement. Everyone has slept with everyone and someone is always quarreling or refusing to act across from someone else who has slighted them. Either that or trying to bed each other for preferential role assignments. But it's nice not to worry about revealing yourself. You can just. . . . be."

"I'd never thought what it might be like to have to hide your desire."

"It doesn't usually feel like hiding. I don't often put much effort into it. But then I'll be at a company meeting and hear someone talking openly about some girl they met and are smitten with and realize it's just . . . different. For it to feel ordinary. The Palace was where I first started wearing trousers. Then I started wearing them everywhere because they felt so much more suited to me."

"How did you know you preferred women?" Emily asks. "Have you ever been with a man?"

"A handful. I felt like I had to at first. I grew up around a lot of sex, but it was all between women and men so it was the only sort of intimacy I understood. Then Pearl brought a lady into her house who wore trousers and took both men and women to bed, and she drew me some illuminating diagrams."

"And bedding men doesn't disqualify you?" Emily asks. "From being a . . ." She cannot say the word, now that she knows the meaning. It feels too decadent.

Harry's mouth quirks. "There's no test you must pass, you know. I have never found it unpleasant to sleep with men. Sometimes it's good. Sometimes it's dull. It is always inferior to even the worst night I've spent with a lady." She swipes her fork around the edge of her cake plate, then says, "Have you ever considered it?"

Emily's heart jumps into her throat. The thrill she has felt every time she is around Harry suddenly has a name, and names have power. She knows that from every fairy story of her youth. "Considered what?" she asks, and her voice comes out too high.

When Harry raises her head, their gazes lock. Harry smiles. "Nothing," she says. "Pay me no mind."

Harry swipes the corner of her mouth with her thumb, and Emily wonders suddenly, against her own will, what it is like to be one of the women standing across the stage from Harry, speaking rehearsed lines in her gaze, instructed to sweep across the stage toward her, fall into her arms, kiss her.

"Miss Sergeant," a voice says in the hallway, and Emily jumps, whipping around.

"Martin!" Violet's husband steps from the shadows of the hall, coat over one arm and hat still in his hand, as though he has just arrived home and found his routine aborted by the sound of their voices. Emily cannot believe she hadn't heard the door, but she hadn't expected she needed to be listening for it. It's not as though she's been caught in a compromising position, though why had he arrived just as she was thinking of Harry's mouth? Had he heard them speaking of Sapphists? The unchastity of it feels written all over her. Even her bare feet feel obscene and she tucks them under herself. "I thought you were above with Violet."

"I'm sure you did," Martin says, taking a step into the room, and Emily feels a prickle of apprehension. "Or else I can't imagine you would have invited a gentleman unchaperoned into my home."

"Oh, no." Emily laughs with relief, which only makes Martin's frown deepen. "Martin, this is Harriet Lockhart. She's a friend of mine. She knows Violet too."

Harry climbs to her feet quickly and extends a hand to Martin, though he doesn't take it. "How do you do."

"You are acquainted with Violet?" he asks. "Perhaps I should have a word with my wife as well about her choice in companions."

"Don't be cruel," Emily says.

"Then do not bring degenerates into my home."

"Hold on now—" Harry says, but Martin interrupts, taking Emily by the arm and dragging her up from the sofa.

"May I speak to you alone?"

Emily follows Martin into the hall, casting only a quick glance over her shoulder at Harry, who looks like she might follow, but Emily holds up a finger for her to stay.

In the hall, Martin turns to Emily, leaning in to speak confidentially though Emily can't imagine who might overhear them. "Do you have any idea the time?" Martin says. "Or the impropriety of your company?"

Emily folds her arms. She does not know Martin well, and what she has heard of him from Violet has inspired in her little desire to learn more. A man with a weak stomach, Violet often called him, both in reference to his lack of convictions and his finicky digestion. She suspects that should she glare hard enough, he'll slink up to bed and leave them be. Perhaps he'll try to raise the issue at breakfast the next morning, though Violet will not care, and really, what is there to complain about? "We're two ladies spending the evening at home together," Emily says deliberately. "What's so improper about that?"

Martin's mouth tightens. "Perhaps I should write to Mr. Tweed about how you spend your time."

Emily laughs before she can stop herself. Of all the improper things she has done since arriving in London, the idea that *this* is the one that would get her reported to Tweed—skipping an evening at a pleasure garden to instead eat cake at home with a female companion? Even Tweed would certainly throw that letter into the fire.

"I can hardly see what he'd object to," Emily says. "My actions would have to be highly sensationalized to raise alarm."

"Perhaps I'll write to him anyway," Martin says.

"Please do," Emily replies. "Send him my regards."

Martin glares at her. Emily glares at him in return.

"I do not like the influence you have had in my household," Martin says.

"And what influence is that?" Emily says. Maybe it's the darkness that has made her bold, the heady feeling of all conversations that happen at night. Perhaps it's Harry. Perhaps it's the cake.

"Violet has been preoccupied with your company."

"Because I have gotten her out of the house? Is that why you're upset?"

"I am not upset. I simply wonder as to the nature of these outings. And what company you are keeping." His eyes stray to the drawing room. "You have proved yourself not to have the most discerning eye in companionship."

"If you're so worried for my virtue, perhaps you should come with us next time Violet and I go out."

"Perhaps I shall."

"I'm sure Tweed will be thrilled to hear your salacious account of our shopping and tea."

Martin lets out a huffy exhalation. "Keep your voices low," he says. "I would not want you and your . . . companion to wake the baby." Then he turns and hangs his hat on the rack beside the door before heading abovestairs.

"Everything all right?" Harry asks as Emily returns to the parlor. She's still standing, knees slightly bent like she's ready to drop into a boxing stance.

"Fine." Emily falls backward onto the sofa, eyes closed. Her skin buzzes, like insects have been crawling across her, and she takes a deep breath, one hand pressed to her chest.

"Are you well?" Harry asks.

Emily opens her eyes. Harry is peering down at her with her forehead puckered in concern. "Yes, of course."

"Have I gotten you into trouble?"

"No," Emily says. "I did that myself a long time ago."

"What do you mean by that?"

"Nothing." Emily forces herself to sit up and smile at Harry. "Martin was simply concerned for me."

"Because I'm a bad influence on you? Based on, I assume, only my appearance."

"No you're—"

"He's right. Though in my defense, I was recruited specifically for the purpose of leading you astray."

For a moment, Emily thinks she means astray from the path that has been laid before her—marrying a man, settling on her family farm, having children and living out her simple life, and her heart gives a flutter of delight.

But then Harry adds, "For Rochester."

"Ah yes." Emily gives a small laugh. "For Rochester."

What queer disappointment, she thinks. And what a brisk reminder, like a cup of cold water to the face, that she must be thinking of Rochester in all things, and what might make him want her more! Not what might please Harry. Not what outings she might enjoy or what she might think of the outfits Emily wears or how Emily might stand when she arrives first to an appointed meeting so as to appear most casual and beautiful and not giddy with anticipation when Harry comes upon her. All things for Alexander. How had she lost sight of that?

Harry stands and stretches with her hands behind her head. "I should go."

"No," Emily says too quickly.

"I didn't plan to stay out this late at Ranelagh—let alone loaf about here with you."

"Then surely it's too late for you to walk," Emily says. "And the cabs will all be in." She has no notion if this is true, but it feels right, and Harry's brow furrows in consideration. So Emily says tentatively, "Why don't you stay the night? I could find you a nightgown."

It's not an absurd offer—Emily knows plenty of ladies who share beds and quarters with other ladies before marriage. But extending the offer feels indecent, particularly in the shadow of Martin's frown. Even more particularly when Harry takes so long to consider it. Perhaps it's only because Emily is unaccustomed to having any friends to invite to spend a night, and she has done it clumsily. She's been alone for so long.

"Don't be silly," Harry says. Emily feels her face redden with embarrassment, but then Harry says, "Any nightgown of yours won't reach my knees. I'll sleep in my shirt."

22

Emily dreams of Sappho.

Or, not Sappho, but a woman her mind tells her is Sappho, cobbled together from component pieces of the day and Emily's own imaginings, shades of Eve and Rapunzel and Persephone, with the world blossoming at her touch. She's an actress, a woman with many faces, strutting the stage in a Shakespearean doublet. She's the painted women calling to her from the balconies of Ranelagh Garden, the older cousin of a neighbor who had spent a summer in Sussex and fascinated Emily with her coarse, curly hair and freckled arms. She is Harry. She is Emily. She is a rabbit, cornered and shrieking as Tweed stands over her, rifle to her breast.

Emily sits up. The wan light of morning cascades through the rippled glass windows. She had fallen asleep while Harry was still undressing, and assumed Harry would crawl into bed beside her, so she's surprised to instead find Harry squashed into the armchair beside the hearth, her legs drawn up to her chest, like a present wrapped in a too-small box. Emily is struck by the sight of Harry so unrefined, with her feet bare and her white calves peeking out from the blanket in which she is wrapped.

Emily puts a hand on the covers beside her, not sure what her disappointment can be mapped to. It flows inside her, a river without a source. The last time she had slept with someone beside her, it had been Thomas. She had woken beside him in the new daylight, expecting to feel changed and instead feeling hollowed out and alone.

She has never told anyone what happened with Thomas. She had never thought of it as anything but a secret to guard. Middleham would think what they wanted no matter what she said. Every person she has met in London only knows the genteel version of herself she has put forward—and she's hoped that's all they will ever know, the duke especially. If all goes according to her plan, no one will ever know everything about her.

Before she left home, the thought would have been a relief.

Now, it makes her feel as though she is standing by herself in a crowded room.

She has a choice, she realizes. A choice to tell someone the truth. To tell someone the worst thing she's ever done, and know that they know it.

Emily scoots to the edge of the mattress, quilt wrapped around her shoulders, and says quietly, "Harry."

Harry jolts awake, wiping her mouth. Her hair sticks straight up on one side. "Good morning."

"Are you awake?"

"I can be." Harry stretches with her hands linked above her head and smiles at Emily, though when Emily fails to return it, she sobers. "What's the matter?"

"I have to tell you something."

"Go on."

"I'm afraid."

"Of what?"

"To tell you. That you'll think of me differently."

Harry sits up, leaning forward to Emily. "You can tell me anything."

Emily licks her lips. Perhaps she is delirious with exhaustion. With memories of Thomas. With Sappho still dancing through her mind, unbridled and wild. And she knows suddenly, with absolute clarity, that she wants Harry to know. She wants Harry to know all of her.

"When I was eighteen," Emily says, "I killed a man."

"You . . ." Harry blinks hard, then shakes her head, as though to make certain she really is awake and has not dreamed this startling sentence. She scoots forward to the edge of her chair until her knees nearly touch the footboard of the bed. "You . . . what?"

"His name was Thomas. I met him at a village fair when I was seventeen. He was working as a builder in Brighton, and he was like no one I'd ever met before. He bought me dirty books and dosed me with whiskey and taught me things about science that God doesn't want us to know. He was charming and witty and I thought he was kind."

Harry doesn't say anything. Emily takes a breath. Perhaps this was a mistake, but she cannot stop now. She began with the ending for exactly that reason. "He wasn't kind to his dogs, though. Or servants. Or most women. Or me, really. I know that now. But he paid me attention, and I mistook that for love. And when he asked me to marry him, I said . . ."

Emily stops. Her chest is trembling, like her bones are pressing in on her lungs to stop her breath and keep her silent. She cannot tell if the nausea crawling up her throat is a sign to keep it to herself, or the feeling of a poison finally leaving her.

Harry reaches out suddenly and puts her hand atop Emily's, where it rests on the bed. Emily lets out a sound like a sob, though her eyes are dry. Harry presses her hand around Emily's, thumb against the center of her palm. She waits. Emily takes a breath.

"I said yes," Emily says. "My parents wouldn't stand for me having anything to do with him, which only made me want him more. So we decided to elope. We arranged a night he'd come and fetch me, and we would abscond to Scotland together. On the appointed night, he climbed up through my window, but he was . . . different. Coarse and gruff and so rough with me. Or I suppose he was always that way, but I hadn't noticed before. Or it hadn't mattered. Or I thought he'd never turn his hand on me. I don't know."

"You don't have to explain," Harry says. "I understand."

Emily almost sobs in relief. She wants to fall forward with her face in Harry's shoulder. "In that moment, I finally saw him for who he really was. So I told him I had changed my mind and didn't want to marry him."

Emily takes another breath, expecting it will tremble the way the previous ones had. But her chest feels suddenly looser. Her lungs have unclenched and she takes her first deep breath that morning—perhaps her first deep breath since Thomas crawled through her window.

"He called me a whore," Emily says. "And a tease and said I had already shown him the best china, so to speak, so what did he even need to marry me for? He pushed me down on the bed, and I knew he meant to hurt me."

Emily puts a hand to her face. Harry still cradles the other, her skin soft and warm against Emily's palm. "I kicked him," Emily says. "Or struck him, somehow, and he fell and he hit his head on the bedpost and . . . he stopped moving."

She closes her eyes and presses her face to her knees. After a moment, she feels Harry's hand on the nape of her neck, the touch so gentle and tender Emily feels undeserving. She wants to shout at Harry, *Did you not listen to everything I said? You should not want to touch me with such tenderness!* As if in defiance of the thought, Harry reaches out and takes Emily's face in her hands. "You defended yourself. You protected yourself. There is no shame in that."

Emily lets out a wet laugh. "You needn't spare my feelings."

"I'm not—Emily, he was trying to coerce and attack you. Even if he was not, you should have been able to refuse him without consequence."

"He was there because I asked him." She sits up, rubbing a hand over her eyes. "I invited him in. You can't make a deal with the devil if you don't open the door to him."

"Who told you that?" Harry asks.

"Everyone," Emily says.

"Was there an investigation?"

Emily nods. "I told the magistrate he had come to take me away, then fell and struck his head, and it was ruled an accident."

"Did you tell them he tried to take advantage of you?"

"Well, he didn't. I had already given myself freely."

"That isn't—"

She cannot bear to argue this point, and when she holds up her hands, Harry goes silent at once. "It wouldn't have mattered. Thomas was suddenly a good man with a family and bright future that I'd stamped out. No one would speak to me or associate with me after that, let alone marry me. No one but Robert Tweed, because he wants my father's land for his road. I'll be as beaten down at his hand as I would have been at Thomas's. I escaped a bad marriage only for it to send me into another one." She holds up her hand. "*Out damned spot.* Isn't that how the line goes?"

"Emily," Harry says. "I'm so sorry."

"What for?"

"I'm sorry anyone made you think you were any less for the way a man treated you."

Emily meets Harry's eyes. Though she cannot yet make herself believe those words, something about the sincerity in Harry's voice makes her feel, for the first time, that someday she might. "You can go back to sleep now. I shouldn't have woken you."

"I'm glad you did."

"But now you'll . . ." Emily pauses. Now someone knows all of her, and even though there's relief in that, she also wants to know how she may have changed Harry's opinion of her. She's spoken the truth, and she wants it in return. She clears her throat. "Now, will you think of me forever as the woman who killed her intended?"

"Hardly. I'll think of you as the woman who licks your cake plate." Emily laughs, but Harry isn't finished. "Who shouts at that boy who threw a pie at me. I'll think of you as the woman stuck in the mud with one shoe. I'll think of you as you are. As I know you to be."

Emily presses her palms to her cheeks to stop herself shaking her head. It's too much—for Harry to know it at all, but even more so for Harry to respond in fierce defense of Emily, as though what she had done was righteous. The idea of having to reconfigure herself around that idea is too overwhelming, and too dangerous. She cannot let this kindness warp her self-image into something false. She cannot let herself off so easily. "Every single thing I've ever done is because I was the woman who killed Thomas Kelly. I'll never know who I might have been otherwise, and if I'm not that, I don't know who I am."

"You can be whoever you want. You're hardly the first woman to run away to London to escape a past she's been unfairly saddled with. Nor the first to remake herself in defiance of others' expectations." Harry runs a hand over her face, then says, "Why don't you try it on for one night? Try being exactly who you want to be with no hesitation?"

"What opportunity would I have for that?"

"*Macbeth* ends next week. There's always a company party after a show closes. Why don't you come as my guest? You can see the show and then come drink too much with people who don't know you and you can present to them whatever version of yourself you want. You can be anyone, real or pretend."

"Are you inviting me to meet the Sapphists?" Emily asks, and she manages to muster a smile.

Harry smiles in return. "I'll make sure they go easy on you. I'll be there, looking out for you. But let me give you this: one night of doing whatever your heart tells you."

Emily considers this. The idea thrills her. She could be anyone. She could say yes to anything. Eat what she likes. Drink whatever she wants and in any volume. Wear a ridiculous dress or sing while standing on a bar top or dance with a stranger. All the things she had once thought she might like, but after Thomas, could never imagine doing for fear of rumors collecting on her like burrs. "I'd like that," she says.

"But I swear to God, Miss Sergeant, if this was all a pretense to see me humiliate myself as Macbeth—"

Emily laughs. She feels suddenly exhausted, as though she hasn't slept at all. "Come here," she says, scooting backward and patting the mattress beside her. "We can both get a few more hours of sleep."

Harry smiles. "I'm all right here."

"You could have gotten in bed last night," Emily says quietly. "Even though I was already asleep—you wouldn't have woken me."

And Harry, silhouetted against the white pane of sky, turns her head away, so Emily sees only her strong profile, backlit by the morning light. The sunlight is luminescent on her round cheeks, turning her skin the liquid gold of honey just lifted from the hive. "With the greatest of respect, Miss Sergeant," Harry says, "I could not."

23

Harry returns to Collin's the next morning after luncheon with Emily and Violet—Martin, thankfully, having already gone to his firm. She assumes Collin will similarly be at his office, staring at documents with a furrowed brow or whatever he does every day to afford this house and his expensive suits.

But just as she reaches the door to her bedroom, Havoc nudging his enormous head against the back of her knees, the door at the opposite end of the hallway opens and Collin emerges, looking like a man exhumed.

He freezes when he sees Harry, one hand still on the knob.

"Good morning," Harry says, and Collin winces as if she'd shouted.

"Is it morning?" he croaks. The hair on one side of his head stands up straight, and he appears to be wearing the same shirt he had on the night before.

"Why aren't you at the office?" Harry asks. Then, because she is still smarting from his betrayal and can't resist the urge to twist the inebriated knife, "Where *is* your office, by the by? I should know, in case I need to inform them of your untimely death after a night of wild debauchery. And what do you do exactly? And would you explain it to me right now in excruciating detail? Shall I speak louder?"

Collin winces, massaging his temples, and Harry smirks. She has never seen Collin so flattened by a night of drinking.

"I must have . . ." Collin runs his fingers through his flat hair, frowns, then draws his hand away and gives it a confused look, as though he found something unexpectedly sticky there. "Overslept."

Harry pulls a face of exaggerated sympathy. Collin looks as though he'd like to push her down the stairs, were his balance not so impaired he'd likely tumble straight after her. "How was your night?"

"I . . . can't recall."

"Did Rochester find you?"

"I think I might have told him . . ." He trails off, realizing suddenly that he's shown his hand.

Harry folds her arms. "I asked you not to seek him out."

"I know you did, but—"

"I asked you to trust my judgment."

Collin slumps sideways with his face against the wall. "Can we please not fight about this right now?"

"I don't need your approval to marry Rochester."

"I wasn't seeking him out to give you my approval."

"Then I don't need your opinion of his character."

"That's not . . . I simply wanted to know who you're courting. I'm interested in your life; why is that so hard to believe? I care for your happiness." A pause. Collin rubs his nose, then casts Harry a quick glance out of the corner of his eye. "But Harry, I must say . . ."

"Good lord." Harry drops her head back and laughs. "You are a parody of yourself."

Collin pushes himself off the wall and manages to stand straight for a moment before he slumps the other way, clutching the banister for support. "I don't think he's good for you."

"Why, because he's too much fun? Because he got you foxed and you had a good night for the first time in your goddamn life?"

"Please trust me. I don't think he's the right man for you."

"Your opinion on this matter is irrelevant." Harry holds up her hands. "You don't have to worry about marriage. You don't have to consider shackling your life to someone who won't try to take it from you."

"I will not apologize for having your best interests in mind."

"Oh believe you me, I never expected you to." And she storms into her bedroom, nearly tripping over Havoc sprawled on the rug, and slams the door behind her as hard as she can. She hopes it will rattle Collin's brain out of his skull.

Havoc jumps onto the bed, and when Harry flops down beside him, bats at her until she begins to knead his neck like bread.

Any residual warmth from the night she and Emily had spent together has slid away like a wet hillside. She had only asked one thing of Collin—well, two things, though he had offered her the room in his house most of his own free will. But she had asked he not meddle with Alexander. Trust that she knew what was best and she had found the man who would both meet the prince's requirements and let her protect herself. Does he think so little of her judgment? Or does he simply not understand what kind of cage marriage might be for a woman like her?

She's meant to go to Alexander's this afternoon. She had only come home to change into her riding things. They'll pretend they're going to run the horses but then he'll kiss her against a stable wall and she'll take his cock between her hands and he'll come far too quickly and it will all be so predictable and easy and *fine*.

And what a relief fine would be! It would be so easy to marry Alexander, to use him as a shield for her own peculiarities. To let people respect her for her house and husband and connections to the king. Why is she working so hard to make things even more difficult for herself by letting herself grow sweet on Emily Sergeant and contemplate what might happen if she doesn't take the offer from the prince? Her protestations before she met Emily felt halfhearted, now that she really has something to lose, rather than just the hope of it.

Predictable and easy and fine, she thinks. And not enough.

The prince shot a cannonball through life as she knew it, yet here she is, trying to rebuild the same house she lived in before. Why is she working so tirelessly to make everything the same as it has always been when that was never anything better than fine? When was the last time something had made her truly happy?

The night previous, she realizes, when she had done something entirely out of character and gone home with a woman she had no intention of sleeping with. The night she spent with Emily, the quiet, the comfort, waking in the night and seeing Emily's shape breathing in the dark. Even Martin crashing in and acting a prick hadn't dampened things—though it was a sobering reminder to Harry that she would never be wanted in homes like his.

And then Emily's confession—the intimacy of it all! They had hardly touched, no more than a comforting hand to the back of the neck, but Harry cannot remember the last time she felt so close to someone. So trusted. Harry had always thought that opening up to someone was like holding a finger closer and closer to a flame—eventually one would get burned.

But fire too could warm. Fire was good for making tea and baking bread.

The timing could not be worse. There has never been a less convenient time for Harry to realize she is falling in love with an impossible woman. Less well timed for her to realize that she wants something new for her life. Something different.

She cannot think this way. It's insane, the idea that she might sacrifice a lifetime of security for one woman. She must do something to force herself to stay the course. She'll go see Alexander today. She'll write to the Palace and tender her resignation. She'll give up her work and with it her room, and she'll have no safety lines to catch her. She'll leave herself with no choice but to take the prince's offer.

And she will tell Emily the truth about her pursuit of Alexander. See if the question of love is even still on the table once Emily knows the truth.

HARRY LEAVES TICKETS for Emily and Violet at the theater box office, along with an envelope for the company manager containing her official resignation.

And though she does the latter in secret, hoping the letter won't be read for another few days in the flurry of closing night and the excessive celebratory drinking, by the end of act two, somehow everyone seems to know that Harry has quit the Palace.

The news has likely reached Mariah, but Harry doesn't make herself available for an earful. She fears Mariah might be angry enough to make a spectacle on stage—Harry checks all the prop daggers at the interval to be sure none of them are sharp enough to pierce flesh—but Mariah seems to be on her best behavior. She says all her lines correctly. Doesn't wear the nightgown with the back cut out of it. Even cries real tears in the arms of the doctor.

It's far more unsettling than a spectacle. She must have something planned, and Harry decides the wisest strategy will be to head it off. When they leave the stage after the final curtain, Harry catches Mariah's hand, stopping her progress to the dressing room. "Could I have a quick word?"

Calmly—has the word ever before been used in the same sentence as her name?—Mariah pries Harry's fingers from hers. "About what?"

Oh yes, Harry thinks, she's absolutely fuming. "I thought maybe you'd heard I'm leaving."

"I heard."

"And you're not . . ."

"Not what?"

"I don't know—adding arsenic to my wine?" When Mariah doesn't react, Harry asks quickly, "Or have you? Though I suppose I'd already be dead."

But Mariah simply says, "You'll be missed."

Harry narrows her eyes. Either Mariah has been swapped with a changeling version of herself, or she's plotting. And before Harry can figure out which it is, Mariah is sauntering off to the dressing room, waving backward to Harry as she goes.

But Harry hasn't time to dwell upon it, for one of the stagehands is at her shoulder, informing her she has a guest at the door, and Harry feels her heart pick up.

She'd like to clean herself up before she sees Emily—the excitement of the final performance, plus a finger of whiskey before the curtain, had caused the stagehand to dump blood over her head in such a thick stream it had dislodged her mustache. She had felt it slip midway through Macduff declaring herself from her mother's womb untimely ripped, which really is no way for a king of Scotland to go. Nor is half mustached any way for her to greet Miss Emily Sergeant. But she's far more worried that if left unattended backstage, Emily will step on a nail or fall through a trapdoor or be accosted by the three witches—played by a pair of septuagenarian sisters and an unsettling doll they have given both a name and a tragic personal history—and be scared off.

So Harry follows the stagehand to the door, where waits Miss Emily Sergeant with a small bouquet of poppies and a bottle-shaped parcel wrapped in brown paper.

"Well," Harry says as she approaches Emily with bloody arms open. Emily shies away with a laugh. "You saw the play."

"I did!"

"And?"

Emily presses a hand to her mouth. "It was bad."

"How bad?"

"Quite bad."

"God." Harry pulls her shirt up over her face, forearms squelching against the bloody material. "I did try to warn you."

"I thought you were exaggerating! I didn't understand a lot of it."

"Neither do we."

"You're excellent, though. Even when you're just standing on stage, you're hard to look away from."

"Truly? Or are you just tossing Spanish coins because you regret coming?"

Emily's mouth twitches. "Bit of both. Oh! And I brought champagne!" Emily peels the paper back from the bottle to show Harry the label. "Violet said to tell you the champagne is hers—

she was here with me, but had to relieve the nurse before Martin got home."

"Well, please give Violet my thanks."

"The flowers are from me," Emily says, color high in her cheeks. "And the champagne is really from the both of us."

Oh God, Harry thinks. She should tell Emily about Alexander now, for that little wrinkle of Emily's nose as she smiles cuts Harry straight to the quick.

"Would you like a tour?" Harry asks. "Everyone has to change before they go to the taproom. And we can drink a bit of this before anyone else gets to it. Do watch where you step. And your head. And where you put your hands. Lots of exposed nails."

"Then why don't you lead me?" Emily asks, and takes Harry's hand.

Harry leads Emily through the labyrinthine backstage and into the wings, where the banquet table is still spread with the prop dishes and half-eaten bits of the roast made out of gelatin so none of the actors will actually eat on stage, though all of them do anyway. "Fetch me those glasses, will you?" Harry asks, and Emily retrieves the goblets as Harry clears a spot for them to sit.

Emily sniffs the stained interiors. "Was there real wine in these?"

"Yes, King Duncan likes to get a little tap-hackled before she kicks it. Helps her get an early start on napping through acts four and five." Harry presses the heel of her hand to the champagne cork, and it pops with much less resistance than she had anticipated. She leaps backward as the warm foam drips over her hand. Emily squeals, shoving the two sticky goblets under the bottle like she's filling from a tap.

Glass in hand, Harry perches on the edge of the table, while Emily sits in the red velvet throne at the head. "To Shakespeare," Harry says, raising her glass. "With deep regret."

"To Harriet Lockhart," Emily replies, lofting her own with such enthusiasm some of the champagne sloshes over the sides. "The worst king of Scotland to ever grace the London stage." Harry clinks her glass against Emily's.

Emily takes a long gulp, like one might a beer, then draws back, coughing.

"Easy." Harry laughs. "Do you like it?"

Emily presses a hand to her chest, running her tongue over her teeth. "I didn't expect it to be bubbling."

"That's a bit less alarming when it's cold—you're meant to serve it chilled."

Emily taps a finger against her chin, pretending to consider this. "Isn't there a saying about gift horses and not looking them in the mouth?"

"Might as well count the teeth while I'm in there." She offers Emily her arm. "Now the tour?"

"That isn't your blood on your shirt, is it?"

Harry hops down from the table, brushing her hands off on her trousers. "Not tonight, though we're not known for our aim with those swords."

Harry lets Emily run her hand along the fly lines in the wings and poke around in the costume rack. She tries on a range of hats from past productions, and leaves the closet sporting a feathered tricorn and an Elizabethan ruff tied loosely around her neck. As they walk, Emily finishes the champagne, drinking straight from the bottle until there's none left.

By the time they reach the proscenium, Emily is well on her way to drunkenness.

"Is this the stage?" she gasps as she runs ahead of Harry. "It's so small!" A few of the stagehands still lurking in the wings glance at them. One of them gives Harry a suggestive eyebrow wiggle with his tongue pressed against his cheek. Harry flips him a two-fingered salute as she crosses to where Emily is leafing through a rack of backdrops like they're the pages of a book. She pulls back one far enough that Harry can see too and exclaims in delight, "It looks just like a castle!"

"That is the idea. Steady on." Harry grabs Emily and pulls her backward before she learns the hard way not to put too much faith in the structural integrity of canvas.

Emily is distracted by a piece of scenery just shifted from the wings and grabs Harry's hand, dragging her over to it. "And a balcony! There's a real balcony! What's the famous bit with the balcony?"

"*Romeo and Juliet?*"

"Here, help me up." Harry guides Emily onto the platform the structure is built upon, then up the hidden stairs to the balcony itself. It's only a few feet off the ground, but Emily looks out over the empty audience like she's at a great height. "I'll be Juliet," she says, then points to Harry. "Hide in those bushes there." Harry obediently conceals herself in what is not a bush but rather a sheep moldering from *As You Like It* refashioned into a bush. Emily turns toward the audience, empty bottle pressed to her chest. She takes a deep breath, then hollers, *"Romeooooo! Helloooooo, Romeo!"* She turns to Harry and says in a stage whisper, though whether the volume is an actor's choice or a drunken miscalculation, Harry can't be sure, "I don't know the lines."

"You've got it in one," Harry says. "Juliet says, *Helloooooo, Romeo,* and then Romeo says—" And here she cups her hands to her mouth and hollers upward in imitation of Emily: *"But sooooooft! Whatlightthroughyonderwindowbreaks! It is the east, and Emily the sun!"*

"That," Emily says with great seriousness, leaning so far over the rail that Harry almost reaches out to catch her preemptively, "is not the line."

"*Arise, fair sun, and kill the envious moon—*" Harry hoists herself up so she is standing on the balcony beside Emily, the rail between them and Harry's feet wedged through the posts. Emily shrieks in surprise as Harry lets go the balustrade, grabbing her around the waist and pinning them together, Emily's weight in counterbalance to her own holding her in place. The bottle falls from Emily's hand and rolls to the edge of the balcony.

Harry expects Emily will squirm free, but instead, she relaxes, her body soft against Harry's. Then she reaches up and wraps her arms around Harry's neck. All the lines—if she ever knew them—are driven from Harry's mind as her senses flood with the smell of Emily's hair. The curve of her hips. The fine bow of her lips. "Something . . . something about the moon. I can't recall the rest."

Emily lets out a soft laugh. "That's a shame."

"But there's a bit later where she leans her hand upon her cheek." Harry takes Emily's hands in her own and guides her like she's a doll, pressing their cupped palms to Emily's cheek. "And Romeo thinks to himself, damn, I wish I were a glove, then I too might touch her cheek." She unfurls her hand over Emily's, and when Emily looks at her, Harry can't ignore how this position, with Emily's face cradled in her hands, feels like the prelude to a kiss.

"And then?" Emily asks. She wrinkles her nose just a little, and her lips are petal pink and her skin is so soft and Harry has a hand upon her cheek . . .

She has waded further into these waters than she ever intended. Harry is suddenly not just out of her depth, but has stepped off a shelf into open ocean, turning to find no sight of land. She is going to drown at only the feeling of her hand atop Emily's on her cheek. She can't hold her breath any longer.

The trouble is not that she wants to kiss Emily Sergeant.

She, though, has wanted to kiss Emily since they first met, because Harry has always fallen a little in love with any woman who yelled at her, abstract and hypothetical and mostly confined to her fantasies of being tied to a bedpost and bossed about.

The trouble is that she wants to make her dinner. She wants to fasten Emily's necklaces for her as she lifts the hair off the back of her neck, and argue about trivial things like Harry's inability to put anything back where it belongs. She wants to plant flowers in a garden outside a house where they both live. She wants to button her dresses and share a hairbrush, finding Emily's long gold strands there among her own. She wants to lie quietly together every evening in bed, let Emily steal the blankets and ruin Harry's sleep. She wants her whole life studded with remnants of Emily Sergeant. She wants to trip over Emily with every step.

And that banal domesticity, that longing for more than Harry ever thought she wanted, tugs deep inside her.

Think of Longley, she tells herself. *Think of a house, and money, and constancy. Think of what your life could be.*

But it's Emily ringing like a bell inside her heart, smiling up at her and leaning in so her nose touches Harry's chin. "Go on, I want to hear the next bit."

"Emily Sergeant," Harry says, and she almost doesn't recognize the timber of her own voice. "I don't know what to do now that I've met you."

Emily's brow creases, and Harry is gripped by cold fear that she has been too bold. "That's not Shakespeare."

"No, that's me."

"You in the play?" Emily asks. Their hands are still stacked upon her cheek. "Or you in real life?"

And this, Harry thinks, is surely the moment. Take the feral thing she has never truly let into her heart and domesticate it. Let it come into her house and lie before her fire, eat at her table, and sleep in her bed. Let it shred her window treatments and tear up the carpets. Let love ruin her. "Which do you want it to be?"

Which is when, from the wings, Mariah Swift's voice calls, "As there seems no good time to interrupt, I suppose I'll step in now."

24

Mariah is standing on the edge of the stage, just far away enough that Harry isn't sure whether or not she's heard her soft words. She's wearing a frilled red gown, the one she wears when she wants Harry to take her to bed. Her red hair is down, and her arms are crossed, pushing up her breasts.

How desperately Harry wishes for a well-placed trapdoor to open up beneath Mariah at that moment. The Palace's mechanisms have never been reliable, and it wouldn't be the first time the floor had spontaneously dropped away. She holds up a finger to Emily, then hops down from the balcony and jogs across the stage, wondering if it's too late to shove this proverbial jinni back into its lamp. "What do you need?" she asks Mariah.

"Nothing. I heard voices is all."

"I don't believe that."

"I have more right to be here than you." Mariah gives Harry a smile so syrupy it would have rotted teeth. "You've quit."

"Good evening!" Emily calls to Mariah from the balcony.

Mariah waves with just the tips of her fingers. "And who," she says out of the corner of her mouth, "is that provincial virgin?"

"That dress makes you look like a haunted sofa," Harry hisses in retort as Emily trips down the balcony stairs and across the stage, presenting her hand to Mariah.

"Emily Sergeant. I'm a friend of Harry's."

Mariah puts her hand in Emily's, knuckles up, like Emily might kiss it. "I'm sure you are."

"Goodness," Emily says, gazing at Mariah. "You are so beautiful."

Mariah presses a hand to her breast in a display of false modesty that is really a pretense to pull the neckline of her dress lower. "How kind."

"Your skin," Emily says, awe soaking her voice. "Your hair! I've never seen natural hair this color."

"You still haven't," Harry mutters.

Emily takes a strand of Mariah's hair between her fingers and flicks it like she's cleaning a paintbrush. "You look like a goddess in a fresco."

God, Harry thinks. She is so accustomed to Mariah's beauty that she often forgets what a powerful aphrodisiac it can be. Particularly when Mariah is putting on the show she is now, chin dipped, as though her beauty is a dress she had forgotten she owned and simply thrown on before coming down. "How sweet of you. Isn't she sweet, Hal?"

"And a bit foxed," Harry says.

"Not that foxed," Emily says.

"Did you come to see the play?" Mariah asks.

"Yes, and you were so wonderful in it!" Emily says. "Better than Harry."

"Oh, Harry's rubbish," Mariah says.

"And she had so many lines!" Emily presses her hands to her

cheeks, a gesture of outsized horror befitting the critiqued performance.

"Well at least she's quit now," Mariah says. "So we won't have to endure her again."

Emily turns to Harry, eyes wide. "You quit?"

"I . . ." Harry attempts to set Mariah on fire with her eyes. This is not how—or where, or when, or in the company—that Harry planned to tell Emily about the prince and her plan to marry Alexander. "I did."

"But you love the company!" Emily says. "You told me!"

"Love is not the word."

"Because they're all Sapphists!"

"Well, you're not so innocent as I thought," Mariah says. "Are you a Sapphist, Miss Sergeant?"

"I might be." Emily bites her lip. "For tonight."

"Perhaps tomorrow morning as well?" Mariah asks, and Emily giggles.

Harry gapes at Emily. This would have been helpful information to have several nights previous when Harry had gone to absolute battle with herself over the impropriety of climbing into the bed beside her, and whether Emily's bare feet touching hers on the sofa were meant to be flirtatious or not. Even just now, atop the canvas castle, what was she meant to make of that? A declaration of real love or a scene in a play?

"Miss Sergeant." Harry squeaks out the words through gritted teeth. "Could we go somewhere private and speak?"

"I thought we were going to the taproom," Emily says.

"Oh!" Mariah touches Emily upon the arm. Both Emily and Harry stare at the spot. "Are you coming to our party?"

"Perhaps that's not wise anymore," Harry says.

Emily's brow furrows. "Why? Because I'm only free to make choices when you agree with them?"

"That's not what I'm saying. I'm trying to look out for you."

"By controlling where she goes?" Mariah asks.

Harry's jaw throbs. "Mariah, please, this is not your concern."

"You are so very controlling, Harry." Mariah turns to Emily, their arms suddenly looped. "She's always been this way. You cannot let her push you about."

"Mariah—" Harry starts, but Mariah thrusts a finger at her.

"There, see? She's doing it again."

Harry throws up her hands. "Fine. Miss Sergeant, would you like to accompany me to the taproom? We're overdue."

"Why don't we all go?" Mariah asks brightly. "I'm headed that way myself." She holds out her other arm to Harry. When Harry doesn't take it, Mariah says, "Suit yourself, then." And tucks her hand into Emily's instead.

Which is how Harry comes to walk behind Mariah and Emily to the taproom, listening to the two of them titter and chat the whole way.

AT THE TAPROOM, Harry watches Mariah and Emily sit together in the middle of the raucous party, an oasis of quiet conversation with their heads getting closer and closer until both their faces are shadowed by the tricorn hat Emily is still wearing. She watches them dance when musicians take up a fiddle and bodhrán, the way Mariah snakes a hand around Emily's waist, fingertips pressed to the small of her back and their hips together. She notices when Emily disappears for a moment, then returns with both their jackets, holding Mariah's for her to shrug into. They link hands as they slink together from the taproom, toward the doorway, where Mariah pauses and glances back. Her eyes find Harry's as though they are connected by a string, and her painted lips pull into a slick smile. She kisses the tip of one finger, then wiggles it at Harry before she follows Emily from the taproom.

Harry stares up at the ceiling and wishes one of the rotted beams would fall onto her head and knock this whole bloody night from her memory.

For yes, she is well and truly in the soup now.

25

Emily imagines Mariah Swift's room will be an elegant boudoir—draped in velvet the same red as her hair, strands of false pearls and fringe dripping from the golden furniture. Nothing will be as expensive as it looks, all the adornments bearing the false elegance of a theater set.

Instead, the room is cluttered and cozy. There are still embers glowing in the fire, easily revived, and though there's certainly too much furniture for a space so small, it makes the room feel pleasantly busy, like arriving at a party and finding it already full of friends.

Mariah takes off her wrap and sits in front of the dressing table to unpin her hair, while Emily runs her fingers along the curiosities laid out on the windowsill and hearth. There is a collection of gentleman's facial hair, as well as several wigs, displayed on stuffed head forms, and a box of false jewels. Lifting the lid on it feels like opening a chest of pirate treasure. There is a collection of Shakespeare's plays, each bound in its own volume. The spines of *As You Like It* and *Twelfth Night* are broken, but the history plays and a few of the tragedies look almost new. A folded broadside is tucked into the corner of a mirror, along with a poem carefully copied onto a sheet of vellum and tacked on the side of the wardrobe.

"Do you like Sappho too?" Emily calls to Mariah, tapping the spot where the poem's attribution is written.

Mariah spits out a mouthful of pins. "What?"

"Sappho. The poem."

"Oh, that's Harry's."

"Harry's?" Emily repeats.

"It's all Harry's. I've been staying in her room while she's at her brother's."

"This is all Harry's?" Inexplicably, Emily's skin breaks out in gooseflesh. She turns a slow circle, looking around the room with new eyes. Suddenly it feels more like a museum, every object a meaningful representation of some new facet of its owner. And she wants to know it all. She wants to open every book, count the dog-eared pages and the scored lines. She wants to put her hands into the pockets of the coats and find loose change and old handkerchiefs, half-smoked cigars and probably a wad of dog hair. She wants to put her mouth on the chipped rims of the cups and use the cosmetics. Run the brushes through her hair.

"Not for long, now that she's quit—it's on loan from the theater." Mariah stands from the dressing table and goes behind a screen to change. "Pour yourself a drink," she calls. "Harry doesn't believe in tea or I'd offer you some."

Emily opens the cabinet in the corner where the dishes and cutlery are stacked and stares at the mismatched tumblers. There's a faint smear of rouge on the rim of one, and she picks it up, holding it up to the firelight for a better look at the color.

"Aren't you darling?"

Emily turns. Mariah stands in front of the screen, draped in a dressing gown that looks like liquid metal poured over her frame, so closely does it fit her form. She drags her hair over one shoulder, then gestures to the sofa. "Won't you sit down, Miss Sergeant?"

Emily tumbles backward into the settee, and Mariah comes to perch beside her. There is a patch of makeup she failed to wipe away just below her ear, and Emily thinks of Harry on stage, blood running down her face. The way she tipped her chin so the gaslights wouldn't hollow her cheekbones, the faint smirk playing about her lips, even in her own climactic death, like she was about to turn to the audience and say *Isn't this silly, to pretend?* The deliciousness of being in her confidence. She thinks of Harry when she had first seen her riding, those same athletic shoulders and audacious thighs that had strutted around the stage tonight, offensively untalented but having a good time nonetheless. How delightful it would be, Emily thinks, to see her every night. To share a stage with her. To share anything with Harriet Lockhart.

Oh God, why hadn't she stayed with Harry? The champagne has started to wear off, and her momentary irritation at Harry with it. Harry would have apologized if given the chance, and Emily would have admitted she was just looking for a reason to snap back. They could have sat upon that balcony all night, beneath painted stars and the shadow of an imagined castle, Harry's head resting on her knees. Why hadn't she rubbed the snarls out of Harry's short hair, where the blood had clotted?

But instead, she is here, and is determined to prove to herself... though what and to whom, she isn't sure. That she can make decisions for herself without catastrophic consequences? That she can drink liquor and let down her guard and kiss someone without the world falling down around her?

She can. She will.

Before she can think any more about it, she lurches forward

and presses her mouth to Mariah's. She has lately felt so hungry to be touched, to lean her cheek into the warm curve of another's hand—*oh that I were a glove*—that she expects it to feel like waking from a deep sleep.

But it's cold and impersonal. Closer kin to a stamp on a document than a tender caress. Mariah's skin is slick, and smells of grapeseed and tea tree, and the sensation moves Emily not at all.

Mariah's lips flutter beneath hers, and she realizes Mariah is laughing. She puts her hands on Emily's shoulders and pushes her away. "Oh good lord, please, don't."

Emily's courage evaporates, and she slides to the opposite end of the sofa. "Forgive me," she says quietly. "But I thought . . . is that not why you've invited me here?"

Mariah laughs. Not unkindly, but not *not* either. "Of course not."

"Then why?"

"Because I'm cross with Harry for quitting the company," Mariah replies. "Though I admit, I didn't think it would be quite so easy to steal her girl."

Emily blushes, so suddenly and deeply she feels as though her skin is vibrating like the surface of a pond after a stone is tossed in. "I'm . . . she's . . . what do you mean?"

"She's quit the Palace company," Mariah says.

"That's not what . . . Harry and I are not . . . we have no . . ."

"Ah yes, those coherent protestations are certainly believable." Mariah unearths a pipe from a heap on the side table and lights it with one of the candles. The spicy smell of tobacco perfumes the air. "However platonic you may consider your relationship, it's obvious that Harry is smitten with you. And from the way you've been looking around this place like it's a temple to her, I suspect it's mutual."

Is it? She certainly likes Harry. She likes the things they do together—though primarily, she likes them because they are done with Harry. She likes the sound of Harry's voice. The shape of her mouth. Those absurd biceps and muscled thighs. She likes the way Harry needles her. The way she gets under Emily's skin. The way she listens to the things Emily has to say, and remembers them. The way that, when they had heard a band play in the music hall, Harry had thrust her fist in the air in delight when the cymbal was struck. The quickness with which she reaches for a joke and shares her life and books and food and ideas, the confidence with which she carries herself, the way the whole world reforms around her when they are together and . . .

Oh hell. Surely not.

"So she'll spend the night sweating about you being here with me," Mariah continues. "And since she's Harry, she won't ask you about it, and you'll be too shy to clarify, because that's presumptuous." Mariah pulls her feet onto the sofa and rests them on Emily's lap. The slit of her robe falls open, exposing her pale calf. "Would you like me to tell you every embarrassing story from her youth? She went through a period where she asked everyone to call her Byron and tried to run away to Switzerland."

"I can't be in love with Harry," Emily says quietly.

"Why not?"

"Because I am supposed to marry a wealthy man. It's the only thing I've ever wanted."

Mariah raises a drawn-on eyebrow. "It is?"

Emily stares at her.

What does she want? Truly? It had been so long since her own desires factored into her plans for the future.

She wants a second chance. She wants to go back in time and stop worrying what everyone else wants of her and start listening to her own heart. She wants to stop punishing herself because the rest of the world is. She wants not to fear her own heart so desperately, certain it will only lead to her ruin. She wants to be entirely herself, not a shadow version hidden behind the girl she thought would be most appealing to men, and be loved for it. Loved and desired for who she is. She wants to know herself and trust herself well enough to think of loving Harry and not have it frighten her.

She wants to come home to someone who makes her feel like a bottle of champagne.

Suddenly her eyes flood with tears.

Mariah sighs. "Come now. Don't cry. It's not so terrible, is it? You could do far worse in love than Harriet Lockhart."

"But I cannot love—" How to finish? A woman? An actress? A reprobate? Someone I cannot bring home to my parents? Anyone less suitable than Robert Tweed? Her entire future is lost if her heart's compass spins its needle to Harry.

But then again.

What had ever appealed to her about a life as some man's docile wife other than it would satisfy her compulsive need to please everyone else before herself? Life is an ocean, but love does not have to be an anchor weighing her down. It can be salt enough to float. She can drift through easily on the current, floating on her back, face turned to the sky. She can let the light flood her skin once again.

"If I am in love with Harry," she says quietly, pushing a tear off her cheek, "what am I to do?"

"Oh, you sweet thing," Mariah says, and blows a ring of smoke into the air between them. "You really are thick as shit."

26

The morning of the Milton Derby dawns overcast and damp. Dew sits on the grass like a skin on cold soup, and the gray light turns the Downs flat. In the stands, Emily and Violet huddle together against the unexpected chill, both fooled by the late spring date into thinking a shawl was unnecessary. Martin had been dressed and ready to accompany them that morning, apparently making good on his threat to observe their outings, though he crossed paths with friends on the way to their seats and let Violet and Emily go ahead on their own. At least horse races are an acceptable outing. Had he been home the night of *Macbeth* and insisted on accompanying them, Emily's claims of propriety would have been on shaky ground.

"Perhaps the punch is being served mulled," Violet says, and Emily takes it upon herself to find out.

It is refreshment only that she goes searching for, she assures herself, and not Harry.

The race is overdue to start, the flag held for half an hour in hopes the sun might appear. The riders are sequestered with their mounts in the stables, and Emily wonders if she might possibly find her way there before the start. To wish Harry luck, but more than that—she wants to explain what happened with Mariah. Or rather, that nothing had happened. Emily had slept on the sofa and let herself out the next morning before Mariah even woke. She had gotten a cab back to Violet's and spent every moment since wondering if Mariah is right, and Harry is in love with her. And, more important, if she is in love with Harry.

It has been a week since the night of the play, and they haven't spoken. It is their longest stretch apart since the Majorbanks's ball. Emily has begun writing a half dozen cards to send to Harry, but can never find the right way to ask, *Can we discuss Mariah's queer notion that you are in love with me?* What tone was one meant to adopt for such a missive—casual, but urgent, neither too asinine nor too sincere?

In the end, Emily gave up. She would see Harry at the race, she had told herself, and balled up her final attempt before tossing it into the fire. They would talk then.

But now here she is at the race, in the yellow dress Harry dreamed up for her, and she can't find how to get to the stables, and knowing Harry is here but not with her this moment is making Emily break out in hives.

She is stopped upon the path running the length of the track when she hears someone call her name. For a delirious moment, she thinks it's Harry, but turns to find Alexander Bolton, Duke of Rochester, peeling himself from a conversation and coming toward her. *Not now*, she thinks as she bobs a quick curtsy.

But then Alexander takes her hand and Emily seems to wake up to herself, because oh blast—it's *him*. The person she's supposedly here for. And yet she doesn't have time for him because she has to find Harry.

"I didn't know you were coming today," Rochester says. "But mistake me not—your presence is most welcome." He kisses her knuckles, and she notices him give her dress a second look—once when he bends, and again when he stands. "You look *well*," Rochester says, the word heavy with intention, and goddamn Harriet Lockhart, Emily thinks with a secret smile. Riotous dandelion indeed.

"Thank you," she says.

"Truly, you look . . ." He takes a step back, still holding her hand, and for a moment, Emily thinks he will ask her to twirl so he can see her from every angle. "Somewhat changed since I last saw you."

"I feel somewhat changed," Emily replies. "London has been good for me."

"Evidently. You may be the first person to ever find their health improved by time in the city."

"I will be cheering on your Matthew Mark Luke and John from the stands," Emily says. Then, she adds like the idea has just occurred to her and is of no urgency, "Have you seen Miss Lockhart this morning?"

"No, my arrival was delayed and now I'm too late to wish her luck!" He indicates the track, and Emily turns to see the riders beginning to assemble on the track. *Blast*. No chance to talk to Harry now.

"Matthew looks fine, does he not?" Rochester adjusts the brim of his hat as he casts an appraising glance over the horses. "See how his coat shines in the sun."

"Indeed, my lord. I've already put money on him."

"Have you really?"

"I read his statistics and find him the most likely winner." She pushes a strand of hair from her eyes, and watches as his eyes follow her gloved hand. Emily touches her neck, along the sweep Harry had promised the dress so highlighted. Rochester's eyes follow her fingers, and God, does he actually wet his lips? Emily almost laughs. Surely it cannot be so easy.

"Paddington has the longer stride," the duke says.

"But Matthew a higher jump."

"And the superior jockey, wouldn't you agree?"

Emily feels her face color—*does he know?*

Someone whistles on the track, and Rochester seems to wake from his reverie. "Have you been to Almack's yet?" he asks, and she shakes her head. "They hold public balls there on the full moon—anyone can attend, so they crowd quickly. But the music is very good. I'll be in attendance next Saturday. Perhaps I'll see you there."

"You will, my lord."

"Then we can finally have that dance," he says, eyes flashing. "So long as Harry allows me a space on your card this time. The two of you have become so close."

"Not that close," Emily says quickly and possibly too loudly.

"I wonder." He puts on a show of consideration. "Has she told you of her parentage?"

Is this some sort of test? Or is he asking because it's unknown to him? Emily had assumed Harry and Alexander were close enough friends—and the duke liberal minded enough—that Harry would have shared her mother's profession with him. Certainly if Harry shared it with Emily, Rochester would have been taken into confidence. "What specifically about it, my lord?"

"The terms, mostly."

"Terms?" Emily frowns. "I'm not sure what you mean."

Rochester swipes off his top hat, presses down his hair with the flat of his hand, then replaces it. "Mr. Lockhart had asked me for some advice on land management. And I wasn't aware . . ."

Again he trails off, looking at Emily as though waiting for him to finish the sentence or intuit his cryptic meaning, but Emily just stares back blankly. At the Majorbanks's ball, when they first met, she had thought Harry a rival for Alexander's affection, and it occurs to her now that if she really wants insurance against their pairing, she could tell Alexander what she knows about Harry's mother, as he seems not to know. Alexander might find Emily herself more interesting for her proximity to—but not direct implication in—purchasable company, and he'd see her allegiances lie with him, not Harry. After all, it's him she's going to marry.

But what would be the point of that, besides humiliating Harry? An idea that once would have been appealing to Emily now leaves her cold.

"I'm sorry, my lord," Emily says. "If you want more details, perhaps you could ask her yourself."

"Yes, I think I might do just that." A bell clangs on the track, and Alexander glances to the riders. "Will you excuse me please, Miss Sergeant? The race is about to begin."

"Of course."

"But I'll see you next Saturday at Almack's."

"I look forward to it, my lord."

"You should . . ." And here he casts a hand up and down her frame. His eyes again linger along her neckline. "Dress like this more often."

He strides away, but not before turning to give her one more appraising glance, and Emily thinks how giddy she should feel, while feeling it not at all.

By the time Emily returns to the stands, Martin has rejoined

Violet and their bench feels overcrowded. Bright pins of sunlight are poking through the clouds, glancing across the backs of the riders waiting on the starting line. The horses paw at the ground as the race official climbs to his box. Emily tries to convince herself she is giving all the riders an equal glance, going down the line in order, rather than specifically seeking out Harry.

When she finds her, Emily's heart... well, she had been expecting some kind of thrill, the same way she has felt every time in recent memory she has seen Harry, the antithesis of the awe Rochester failed to inspire in her. But Harry is shifting in her saddle, and Emily finds the hair on the back of her neck rising. Has she ever seen Harry so obviously uneasy while riding? Harry adjusts Matthew's bridle, then reaches behind to tug the strap of her saddle, turning forward only to twist back again. Something has disturbed her—Emily is sure of it.

Or, Emily reminds herself, perhaps she simply hasn't seen Harry in moments of stress like this. Maybe her shoulders take on that hard set every time she stands in the wings of the theater before the curtain. Maybe Emily doesn't know her well enough to recognize the clench of her jaw, and why should she? They're only friends. Emily is not, as Mariah suggested, in love with Harry. No matter how much she had been thinking about the moment they shared on the theater balcony, when she had been certain Harry was going to kiss her and her pulse had risen like bubbles in the glass of champagne.

At the flag, the racers erupt down the track and the crowd is on its feet almost at once, everyone screaming and waving hats and hands in the air. Emily stands too, her program clutched to her chest. Someone behind her whistles, shrill and loud. Violet seizes Emily by the arm, letting out a tremendous whoop as the horses approach the first hedge.

The riders are shoulder to shoulder, their horses' flanks gleaming in the gray sunlight. Emily's breath catches as she watches Matthew launch himself over the hedge. He is truly built for jumping—the stretch in his legs, the height he achieves, the clean distance over the hurdle while other horses catch the leaves with their back hooves. The jump is perfect. Emily takes a deep breath and wills herself to relax.

After the third privet, Harry and Matthew hold a shared lead with a speckled horse and his rider. As the next jump approaches, Harry pulls ahead, driving her heels into Matthew so he jumps earlier than is necessary. She knows his length. His stride. She knows he'll clear it, and they'll land ahead.

But at the apex of the jump, Harry lurches sideways in the saddle, like the gravity of the Earth has changed for her alone. A strap of the saddle whips up from beneath Matthew's belly and suddenly the whole saddle tips, flying loose from the horse's back.

And Harry falls with it, one foot still tangled in the stirrups, and hits the soft ground of the racetrack so hard Emily swears she hears the impact, even over the sound of the crowd. She watches, helpless, cold horror dripping through her, as Harry rolls, tumbling directly in the path of the other horses just clearing the jump.

Emily screams.

All she sees is Harry, on the ground. Harry, trying to curl her body away from the thundering hooves as the other riders clear the hedge, unable to see her and correct their mounts to avoid stepping on her. Harry, lying in the dust of the privet as the pack of horses gallop on without her. Harry, on the ground unmoving.

Emily screams Harry's name, though she can hardly hear herself over the blood pounding in her ears. Someone grabs her arm and she thinks maybe she's swooned. The sudden rush to her head is certainly enough to send her staggering. She has to get to Harry. She has to make certain she's all right. She has to make certain Harry knows—Emily is in love with her too.

Emily breaks free of whoever is holding her and runs down the stands, pushing people out of the way, nearly tripping on the benches, knocking off hats and bonnets and overturning glasses of lemonade. She only stops when she hits the fence designating the stands from the track, the hard blow knocking the wind out of her. She staggers backward, and someone catches her before she sits down hard on the lowest bench of the stands. Whispers ripple through the crowd.

Emily hears a crash behind her, and someone shouts "Let me through!" She turns in time to see Collin Lockhart shove through the stands before hopping the fence and sprinting across the track. He kicks up tufts of grass as he runs to his sister. Harry still hasn't moved. Was she trampled? Stepped on? Thrown so hard it cracked her skull or broke her neck?

"Emily! Emily!" Suddenly Violet is beside her, taking Emily by the arm and pulling her from the rail. Emily wants to cling to it—she has to watch, she has to know, if she does not see it with her own eyes, she will never be able to make it feel real. But Violet winds an arm around her shoulders, pulling her back with a whispered admonition of, "Come away."

Martin appears behind Violet. "What's come over her?"

"She's upset—"

"Clearly, she's making a scene. Get her out of here." Martin reaches for Emily's other arm, but Violet slaps his hand out of the way.

"Martin, leave her alone."

"I'm concerned—"

"Then get out of our way."

Martin glares at Violet, but retreats, and Violet, one hand still clamped on Emily's arm, leads her away. And Emily, weak from fear, lets herself be led.

Violet stops them in the shadow of a nearby tent, away from the view of the crowd and without a line of sight to the track. She folds Emily's hands in hers.

Emily's eyes are dry, but her chest heaves like she's sobbing. "I have to see her."

Violet's hands pulse around hers. "Her brother's with her."

"She's hurt!"

"Try to breathe."

"She's my friend."

"I know."

"I care for her."

"I know."

"I think I'm in love with her."

Violet gives her a gentle smile. "I know that too."

And now the tears flood Emily's eyes, late arrivals to this miserable party. "You do? How?"

"Emily." Violet pats her hand, the gesture somehow both knowing and scolding. "Please. You speak of her constantly. You've spent all your time with her. She's always playing the coquette with you and you glow every time. Her attention lights you up. I've never seen you like this."

"Why didn't you tell me?"

Violet presses a hand to her mouth with a small laugh. "I thought you knew."

Emily starts to laugh too, but the sound breaks into a sob. Violet wraps her arms around her, and Emily clutches handfuls of the back of her cousin's dress. "I need to tell her," Emily says, her face pressed to Violet's shoulder.

"You can."

"What if—"

"None of that." Violet pulls back and wipes Emily's wet face with her thumbs. "No reason to waste time on ifs. Let's find out."

And she leads Emily out of the shade, just as the sun breaks properly through the clouds for the first time all day.

27

Harry is shocked to discover she isn't dead.

Probably not dead. She *might* be dead. She's in an alarming amount of pain that seems to be coming from everywhere. Her brain feels as though it's been rattled in her skull, and her face burns like it's been pressed to a hot stove—and she is certain that, should there be an afterlife, it will be all fire and brimstone for her.

But if this is hell, it looks very much like the Milton Downs.

"Where is Rochester?" someone says from above her. "Go fetch him—tell him to control his goddamn horse."

It's Collin, Harry realizes. Collin is kneeling over her—possibly two of him—she cannot be sure of the number of Collins. Her vision is swimming. No, not two Collins—one Collin and a second man with him. One of the race officials. The one who dropped the flag.

Or perhaps it is two Collins—one her actual brother, and the other a counterfeit version of him that gives a damn about her.

"Jesus Christ, Harry," says the false Collin. "Open your eyes."

"They are open," she murmurs. Her mouth tastes like she's been sucking coins.

A pause as he peers into her face. "So they are." Collin catches her chin as it slumps onto her chest and shakes her. "Stay awake," he says, his voice gentle, before he turns and bellows over his shoulder, "There *must* be a goddamn doctor here!"

"One's been sent for," says the race official at Collin's shoulder.

"Where's the blood coming from?"

Which yes, seems like a good question, and the race official replies, "Her nose—" and, "bit her cheek—" Each sentence steps on the heels of the one before it, and Harry wants so badly to go to sleep.

Collin hooks Harry's arm over his shoulder. "Come on, Hal, try to stand."

"Here, let me—" The race official is on her other side, but when he tries to move her arm, Harry's body flinches from him like oil in a hot pan. Pain ricochets through her, so intense her vision blurs. She collapses back to the ground with a scream.

Collin screams too. She tries to sit up and swoons, slumping over into his chest.

"She's separated her shoulder," the official says, prodding the socket. Harry wants to swear at him but instead spits a mouthful of blood into the grass. "I can reset it—hold her tightly." Collin obediently fastens an arm around Harry like he's trying to hold her back in a barroom brawl. Harry grits her teeth, braced, but still unprepared for just how much it hurts when the race official wrenches her shoulder back into its socket.

Harry screams again. Collin's arms go tight around her, pinning her to him. She bites hard on his gloved thumb, and he curses, but doesn't let her go.

"Give her a moment," the race official says. "And then we'll stand her up."

Her body feels as though it's convulsing, hot tremors of pain running through her like the resonance of a struck bell. Though perhaps it's Collin who's trembling. Harry thinks suddenly—unexpectedly, deliriously—of the way violin strings will sometimes resonate when a neighboring string is plucked.

"Sympathetic resonance," Harry murmurs, and Collin's grip loosens.

"What was that?"

"Where's Emily?" Harry's face throbs, and she tastes blood. "Is she here?"

"Who?"

"Emily."

"Em—" Collin breaks off, cursing under his breath, then takes Harry by her uninjured arm. "Come on, let's get you away from here. And I need to find Rochester."

"I don't want to see Alex, I want—"

"Emily, I know," Collin says, and hauls her to her feet. "I'll find her, Hal, I promise."

THE RACE OFFICIAL installs Harry and Collin in one of the betting tents, the long table cleared of cards and pencils so Harry can lie upon it. Her shoulder pulses persistently, and she wants desperately to sleep, but every time her eyelids droop, Collin prods her. When the doctor arrives, he examines the reset shoulder, instructs her to keep it in a sling and rest for the next several days, as she's likely concussed. He cleans the scrapes from the impact, and gives her laudanum for her shoulder, her face, her cracked ribs, her concussed head, her pride—all the general pain. All the while, Collin paces and frets at the doctor's shoulder, tearing at his hair and agreeing so emphatically with every instruction it feels like he's arguing.

When the doctor leaves, Harry raises her good arm to her face, testing the taut skin of her forehead. The swelling is already beginning to tunnel her vision. "I can't work out what went wrong."

"And you needn't," Collin says. His hair is puffed up like dandelion fluff from all his distressed running of fingers through it, and Harry notices a spot of blood that she suspects is hers on his collar. "Not now. We'll worry over it later."

"I think it was the saddle—"

"Harry—"

"I didn't know the grooms, and they wouldn't let us do it ourselves—"

"There will be time for investigations later," Collin says firmly, prying her fingers away from her forehead. "Stop touching your face, you'll make it worse."

The tent flap is drawn back suddenly, and Collin leaps to his feet, ready to banish any bystanders who may be hoping for a glimpse of the possibly dead jockey, but it's Rochester, his jacket unbuttoned and his top hat missing. He's pale and wide-eyed, like he's seen a ghost—or possibly, Harry realizes, like he's seen his friend and sometimes lover fall from his prized racehorse and possibly die before an assembled crowd of the ton. That's more likely than the ghost thing.

"My God, Harry." Alexander barrels past Collin to her side. "Are you all right?"

"Where the hell have you been?" Collin demands.

"I had . . ." Alexander waves absently to the tent flap. "To see to the horse."

"Is Matthew all right?" Harry asks, pushing herself up on her good elbow.

"He's fine," Rochester replies. "He was having such a good time running without your weight, he finished the race on his own."

"Bastard. I'll have him boiled."

"It is too soon," Collin says sternly, "to jape about death."

"Mr. Lockhart," Rochester says without looking at Collin. "Do you think I might speak to Harry alone?"

"Speak to her?" Collin repeats. He opens his mouth, seems to chew on what he would like to say for a moment before swallowing it down and instead saying, "About what, exactly? What is so pressing that you must speak to her *now*?"

"The race."

"The race?" Collin repeats, his words feathered by an astonished laugh. "You want to talk to her *about the race*?"

"I want to know what happened."

"She was thrown from your goddamn horse, that's what happened."

"She seems all right," Rochester says.

"She's hardly all right," Collin says. "Look at her."

Harry holds up her hand, trying to come between them as much as she can from a supine position. "Can someone find me a looking glass? I'm absolutely champing to see the damage."

Both men ignore her, which is infuriating, if not surprising.

"But she's alive," Rochester says, casting a hand toward Harry in demonstration.

Even Harry frowns at the flippancy in his tone, though she's willing to chalk it up to no one being their best selves in the wake of a great shock.

Collin, however, gives Alexander no such lead. He gapes at Alex, and for a moment, Harry isn't sure if her brother is going to slap the duke, or laugh at him, or perhaps slap him while laughing. "*She's alive?*" Collin repeats, and his voice trembles. Then the laugh Harry had predicted bursts from him, though she vastly underestimated the lunacy of the pitch. "*She's alive?* You're ready to call this a win because we cleared the absolute goddamn minimum of

Harry *not being dead*? She's alive, thank God—but please, don't start pretending to give a damn now. Let's talk about the race and your bets and the money we've lost and thank God she's alive so nobody's going to pressure you into shooting your racehorse because he threw her!"

Harry closes her eyes for a moment, wondering if this is her head injury making itself known and she is hallucinating her calm, measured brother going absolutely mental at the Duke of Rochester. Alexander takes a step back from Collin, raising a hand in defense. "Steady on, mate," Alexander says, but Collin jams a finger into his chest.

"Don't you *mate* me, you profligate scapegrace."

"Collin," Harry says.

Alexander's eyes flick skyward, and he mumbles, "The horse didn't throw her, let's get that straight."

Which is when Collin puts his foot through the side of the tent. The canvas rips with a sound like a gunshot.

Harry and Alex stare at Collin, while Collin stares at the damage he has just done, fist pressed to his mouth. Then he turns back to the two of them, and declares with scattershot desperation, "I'll pay for that."

"Collin—" Harry says again, but he cuts in.

"I don't know what came over me. I apologize—Harry, Your Grace, I'm so . . . I'm so very sorry."

Alexander turns away, a hand over his mouth not quite covering his smug smile.

"Collin," Harry says firmly before her brother burns the whole tent to the ground. "Could you fetch me a drink—I need the taste of turf out of my mouth."

Collin drops his apologetic deference like kicking off a pair of slippers. "I don't want to leave the two of you alone."

"Jesus Christ," Rochester mutters.

"Go on, Collin," Harry says. "I'm not awake enough to be a good lay right now."

Collin's cheeks redden, and Harry thinks he's going to yell again. But then he swipes his hat off the end of the table, smashes it onto his head, and stalks from the tent.

Alexander grimaces as he retrieves one of the stools left by the bookies and pulls it to Harry's side. "God, what's come over him?"

Harry sits up, immediately regrets it, for her head and ribs and face and shoulder and whole goddamn body throb, but is too exhausted by the idea of trying to lie down again. "You look terrible," she says to Alex.

He wrinkles his nose at her. "And you look like you just fell off a horse."

"I did not fall!"

"Well, you weren't thrown. It seems the saddle was damaged. The girth was worn thin and at the jump, it snapped."

Harry frowns, though it hurts her forehead. "That can't be. Surely the grooms would have noticed. Who would have saddled a horse with a damaged tack?"

"An unfortunate accident," Alex says. "These things happen."

"I should have called for a hold," Harry says. "I knew something was wrong, I should have—"

Alexander shushes her, and she doesn't smack him for it only because he takes the hand of her uninjured arm. "That's not what's important right now."

"Are you going to tell me what really matters is me resting up and saving my strength for getting well?"

Alexander's brow furrows. "Yes, that's important too, I suppose. But I came because I need to talk to you. About . . ." His throat bobs as he swallows hard. Harry tries to ignore the tug of sleep and pay attention. "Do you remember when you first rode Matthew?"

He must have well and truly thought her dead if it has inspired sentimental reflection. "Say your piece, Alexander. I cannot follow a rambling course."

Alexander knits his hands behind his neck. "You made a proposal to me that evening."

"A literal proposal, if memory serves."

"You asked if I wanted to marry you," Alexander says, like she hasn't spoken, and Harry has a sense he has rehearsed this speech and can't be thrown from the script for fear he'll never find his place in it again. "At the time I said no, but I spoke too quickly. And in light of recent events my feelings for you have become clear. I would like to reevaluate the answer I previously offered and perhaps reconsider."

"Alex." Harry throws her arm over her face. "Please, I've just hit my head—"

"My answer is yes, Harry." He pries her hand from in front of her face and presses it between both of his. "Yes, I'll marry you."

28

Outside the tent flap, Emily hears each of Alexander's words like the fall of an ax.

Yes, I'll marry you.

All this while, Harry wanted to marry the man Emily had set her sights upon, and let Emily chase him like an idiotic puppy, for what? Her own amusement? It may have taken the duke time to accept Harry's proposal, but clearly they had been enjoying each other and clearly Harry had known it was leading toward this and yet she had still—*still!*—pretended to offer assistance in Emily's matrimonial designs on Alexander Bolton.

Every goddamn thing Harry had told Emily has been a trick meant to sabotage her, from the whiskey to this stupid yellow dress. She feels suddenly foolish and ungainly in it. How could she fall for all that fearless dandelion bunk, and Harry's cruel tricks, and *have a scandalous outing, men find it thrilling* twaddle?

At her side, Violet says, "What are they saying?" effectively drowning out Harry's response to the duke, though Emily is certain she can guess it. Emily shakes her head, hoping Violet will understand and fall silent, but instead her cousin says, "What is it? Can you hear what they're saying?"

"They're getting married," Emily whispers.

"Who is?"

"Harry."

"Harry? Your Harry? To whom?"

"She's not my Harry," Emily says. She feels small and lost as a bead dropped on a dirty floor. She should have known. She'd suspected from the start that Harry's attack upon her at the Majorbanks's ball was fueled by jealousy. How silly she had been not to listen to her own instincts. Instead, she had let this woman get her drunk on fine wine and theater and bloody Sappho and now she was full of regret with no one to blame but herself.

"Miss Sergeant," someone says behind her.

Collin Lockhart is standing at her shoulder, one hand extended like he had been about to touch her. She jumps in surprise at his nearness, and he startles too, spilling the cup of punch he had been carrying down a shirt already spotted with blood. "Apologies, I thought you heard me. I did call your name."

Emily can think of nothing to say. Her head is spinning. Her heart is throbbing in her chest. She finally manages to squeak, "Harry..."

"She should recover fully," Collin says, misinterpreting her anxiety. "A separated shoulder and a crack on the head that we'll watch closely. She'll be glad you're here—she was asking after you."

Emily feels as though she might faint. All she can think to say is, "Your sister and Rochester are paramours."

Collin stares down into the empty punch glass. "Of a sort."

"He wants to marry her."

"I'm not sure that's entirely—"

Violet interrupts. "He's just proposed."

"Has he?" Collin pales, then clears his throat and says stiffly, "Well then. Congratulations are in order, I suppose."

"How long have they been coupled?" Emily asks.

"Since March, I think," Collin replies. "Harry made a play for him at the Majorbanks's ball, though they've known each other for years. Please, come in. Harry is keen to see you."

And before Emily can tell him that she'd rather sink into the earth and die a maid than have to face Harriet Lockhart and the Duke of Rochester gazing adoringly at each other, Collin has pushed back the flap of the tent and ushered them inside.

29

"So if I understand, you won't marry me . . ." Alex's face contorts, like he's doing a complicated sum in his head. "Because you don't want to sleep with other people? Or because you don't love me? I'm afraid I've lost the plot."

"I won't marry you," Harry says for the third time, though Alexander still seems unable to understand that she has rejected his acceptance of her proposal. And while, yes, even she can admit that is a bit confusing, she feels that if he were really trying, he would have grasped it by now. "*And* I don't love you. They are unrelated, but both true."

Alexander stands, looping his hands behind his head, which, Harry thinks, is a bit of a cruel reminder of her own limited mobility. "Well." Alexander laughs, humorless. "I'm afraid that might not be the only consideration—"

But before he can explain, they're interrupted by Collin's voice at the flap of the tent.

"Harry, you've a visitor." He steps aside, and there is Emily, in that goddamn yellow gown like a ray of sunlight. A rebellious dandelion with a fuzz of blond hair curled around her face. She looks marvelous. She looks like herself. She looks . . .

She looks more heartbroken than Alexander, but just as vexed.

Beside her, Violet is glaring at Harry like she wants to make her into boots.

"As promised, Miss Sergeant," Collin says, then extends a hand to the duke, and says, "Alexander, shall we give the ladies a moment? Then perhaps you and I can have a private word."

Emily stands still as Alexander and Collin leave the tent. She looks small and withdrawn in a way Harry has never seen her, like a piece of paper curled by a flame. "What's the matter?" Harry asks.

Violet lets out a bark of empty laughter. "How dare you."

"Perhaps," Emily says, turning to her cousin, "you might give us a moment alone as well."

"Are you certain?"

"Please, Cousin."

With one last glare over her shoulder at Harry, Violet departs, leaving the two of them alone. The space between them—four steps from the entrance of the tent to the table where Harry is sitting—feels vast as the distance to the moon.

Emily rubs a hand over her eyes, and for a moment, Harry dares hope all she will say is that she was worried for Harry after the fall. But instead, she squares her shoulders and demands, "Have you enjoyed making me look the fool?"

Harry swallows. The muscles in her back tighten. She can feel the pull in her injured shoulder. "What you heard—" she begins, but Emily cuts her off.

"You planned to marry him all this time." Emily fists her hands by her side. "I should have known you would always be the woman who filled up my dance card at that first ball. I was so stupid to believe otherwise. You hadn't suddenly found the milk of human kindness in you. You haven't even the watery broth of basic decency! You know my situation—you know I am desperate—you know everything, you let me tell you *everything*! I thought you were my friend."

"I was," Harry says, her voice hoarse. "I am."

Even if Emily lets her explain, she knows it's too late. She should have told Emily the truth from the first day in Collin's parlor. How did she ever think keeping this a secret would save her the pain and shame and having to admit she was goddamn stupid for not recognizing from the moment they met that Emily Sergeant would be a wind of hurricane strength in Harry's life? She could tell her now, about the prince and his stipulations, and Harry's bone-deep fear of being asked to compromise herself to survive. But she doubts Emily will hear her. And it's all meaningless. No matter the justification, Harry knows she has erred. Still, she at least owes Emily the truth.

"Before we met," Harry says, "I asked Alexander to marry me. I needed someone who wouldn't try to stifle me or make me into someone I wasn't, and I thought Alexander could be that."

Emily stares at her, mouth quivering. Then she says, "I don't want to see you again."

Harry wants to argue, to beg, to go back to the day they met and do everything differently. To rearrange her whole life to make certain that when Emily Sergeant arrives, there is room enough for them to dance. Life is too short and choices too finite for how long and fragile love is. But more than that, she wants Emily to stand up for herself—to ask for what she wants—and have someone respect it. "All right," Harry says, and each word feels like a splinter of glass pried from her heart.

"Don't try to see me."

"I won't."

"Fine," Emily says.

"Fine," says Harry.

And then Emily turns and storms from the tent, leaving Harry alone.

30

Emily doesn't leave her room for days after the steeplechase. Violet brings up meals on a tray, and tries to entice her into eating, talking, opening her curtains, sitting up in bed, before finally surrendering and offering comfort in the form of lying quietly beside Emily, letting her sob herself to sleep.

It's not until now that Emily realizes how much of her life in London is tied to Harry. Everything she has done in London is somehow a spoke on the wheel of which Harry is the hub. Everywhere she's ever been is somewhere Harry took her. The books she's halfway through reading are ones Harry gave her. Every dress she owns was worn once on an outing with Harry. Every dog she sees pass on the street below her window reminds her of Havoc, who reminds her of Harry. She can't look out the window at all without thinking of a time she once saw Harry *near a window* and good lord, the whole goddamn world has been ruined for her. Love is nothing but a kind of insanity.

Since Harry has been pried from her life like a rotten floorboard, Emily is forced too to confront the reality that she has not made any progress at finding a husband who is not Mr. Tweed or Alexander Bolton—and that even her pursuit of the duke dropped off somewhere along the way. She told herself that everything she has been doing with Harry has been for Rochester, but when she lines them all up and looks from the height lent her by perspective, she cannot deny. It was all just Harry.

And now, Emily will marry a man who will probably throw her down the stairs and barely have the decency to make it look like an accident. What had she been doing, wasting her time in the city on a woman who could do nothing to secure Emily's future—only complicate it further by offering glimpses of a life she could never have in the long term? It's as though she has been striding confidently through a foggy landscape since she arrived in London, and suddenly the clouds have cleared only for her to realize she has been walking in place all this while.

After a sennight, Violet sits on the edge of the bed and asks if Emily would like her to make arrangements for her return to Sussex.

Emily sits up for what feels like the first time in days. "I can't."

"Don't mistake me," Violet says. "I am not dismissing you. However." She reaches into the pocket of her skirt and withdraws a letter. "Your parents wrote."

"To you?"

"To Martin, and he shared it with me. Apparently he is concerned you're sabotaging your chances of a marriage by your behavior here, and passed those concerns on to them. He has no real evidence," she says quickly when Emily looks alarmed, "other than something about passing your nights with unsavory company, but your parents want you to come home before Tweed catches wind of any of this." She hands Emily the letter, then adds, "And perhaps some distance from the place where you and she knew each other may help heal a broken heart. Soon you won't even remember her name."

The idea that Harry could be recovered from, love nothing

more than a bad cold, makes Emily start to cry again. "I cannot go," she mumbles. "I still need a husband."

"You're not going to find one like this. Let's get you up and dressed," Violet says. "Take a bath. Wash your hair. And then we'll look at the schedule for the public balls. There's plenty of time to find a husband!"

And Violet, Emily knows, is right. She dries her eyes, takes the hot towels Violet brings her to wrap about her face and take down the swelling, and readies herself to plunge once more into the breach.

Though of course the breach thing is a quotation from *Henry V*, which reminds her of Harry, so she has one more solid cry.

Then she's off.

Emily has been so preoccupied by grief that she has garnered no invitations to private balls, nor asked Violet to help with her social connections. So, at the next full moon, though Violet cannot accompany her due to the baby's colic, Emily throws propriety to the wind and takes herself to Almack's Assembly Rooms.

There is little risk she'll encounter either Harry or Rochester at the public ball. Though it was Rochester who told her about the ball, now that they are happily coupled and likely swanning around naked on top of his beautiful racehorse together, he has no reason to attend society balls any longer unless it is to flaunt their love. Which isn't *not* something Harry would do. But hopefully she'll be too busy snogging Rochester somewhere else.

She dresses in white again—the same simple Grecian gown she wore to the Majorbanks's. The yellow dress is at the bottom of her trunk, folded as small as she could manage. She would have burned it, had it not been so bloody expensive. She wears her sturdiest slippers too, the ones least likely to torture her feet when she is asked to dance.

If she is asked to dance.

She looks around the crowded hall, trying to smile at anyone whose eyes meet hers, praying she might know *someone* here who can make introductions. The clock chimes, confirming she has been standing alone and uninvited to the dance floor for a full half hour. If no one will approach her, she will take matters into her own hands. She notices a group of people near her age standing near the punch bowl and starts toward them, intent on introducing herself no matter how forward it seems. She has almost reached them when one of the women catches her eye. But instead of waving or inviting her over or giving Emily any indication she would be welcome in their company, she nudges the girl beside her and they both turn and stare at Emily.

Emily stops. One of the women puts her fan to her lips to better hide whatever she whispers to the man beside her, who then turns and stares at Emily as well, like she's a scandalous painting on display in a gallery. It reminds her of the way people stared at her in Middleham, openmouthed and with no shame, after . . .

She scans the room.

Her gaze lands upon a pair of gents propped against the wall, pointing openly at her. And not in a way that says *Look at that handsome lady with the great neck, I think I'll ask her to dance.* More in the way one might point at a two-headed cow—the mix of fascination and revulsion, terrifying to approach but also impossible to look away from. When Emily stares back at them, trying to look more defiant than she feels, they grab each other and quake with laughter.

Emily can feel her cheeks coloring. The only thing she wants more than to leave is to a way out of marrying Tweed. She'll just get some fresh air and she'll return, a new woman.

Turning, she collides with a redheaded gentleman carrying a cup of punch he nearly spills down himself in surprise.

"Oh dear, forgive me!" she cries.

"No, the fault is mine. Though I suppose there are more subtle ways to introduce yourself to a beautiful woman."

"What?"

"I was bringing you this punch," he says, his smile revealing gapped front teeth. "As a pretense to make your acquaintance."

"Oh that's . . . thank you."

"Edward Hughes, at your service." He extends the second glass of punch to Emily. Not a lord, no title, at least not one he offered, but his suit looks expensive and his shoes shine, so perhaps there is enough money behind his name to appease her parents—and hell, how she despises this marriage math, a lifelong partnership reduced to calculations. The chance of love in a marriage had always felt far out of her reach, but she has never been so resentful of its absence. The best she could hope for was tolerance, and even that had felt a lofty aspiration. But then there was Harry, and now she knows what it is to want to rearrange the furniture of your life just to pull up another seat to the table for someone to sit beside you.

She hears Harry's voice in her head: *Wouldn't you rather be ardently and passionately desired?*

This is all Harriet Lockhart's fault. As much as one can be blamed for having excellent forearms and a searing wit and kind eyes and—

"—your name?" Mr. Hughes asks, snapping Emily back to the ballroom.

"Emily Sergeant," she says quickly, taking his hand. "At your service."

"Emily . . ." He pulls back his hand, leaving Emily with hers floating empty. "You're the lady from Sussex."

"I . . ." Emily feels the color leave her face. "Do we know each other?"

Mr. Hughes holds up a finger, as though scolding a naughty child. "No, but I've heard stories of you."

Emily's heart is in her throat. Is everyone in polite society talking about her association with Harry? Her rounds at the political rallies or being tipsy on champagne at the theater? Suddenly the work she thought had been to win Alexander seems to be a tick against her. "I'm not sure to what you are referring."

"You're the woman who killed her intended," he says. "Aren't you?"

Oh God.

Not this. Not here, not now, not again. Not another world shutting its doors to her.

"W-what?" is all Emily manages to stammer in return.

"And you've come to London in secret," Hughes continues, as though she needs her own plan explained to her. "Hoping to trick some poor bloke into marriage."

Emily feels suddenly light-headed. She's afraid she might drop her punch glass. That would be a bit too on the nose—her white dress splattered with blood red. "That's not true."

"So you're not the Middleham Murderess?" Hughes asks.

Emily wilts. That horrible name from the local papers—she hasn't heard it in years, at least not spoken to her face. "I didn't . . . I mean, I'm not . . ."

Mr. Hughes smiles coldly, then takes the untouched glass of punch from Emily's hand. "Have a good night, Miss Sergeant. Good luck finding a man more foolish than I."

How do they know? She's told no one.

No one but Harry.

Panic rises in her throat, quick and overwhelming as floodwaters. She presses a hand to her mouth, afraid she might be sick. The edges of her vision wobble as she watches the hateful Mr.

Hughes cross the floor and extend his hand to a blond woman who, Emily notes, her panic sharpening into savagery, looks *just like her*.

How foolish to think she could escape Thomas's ghost. It has stuck to her like a burr on a woolly jumper, impossible to pull off without leaving the stitching forever mangled.

Perhaps this is what she deserves—fate's reminder that there's no escaping her shame.

But Harry had held her gaze while she told her story and had not flinched. Harry had told her she was still worthy of happiness and life and love.

As she watches Mr. Hughes guide his partner onto the floor, Emily thinks how stupid she was to believe her.

31

Harry is not usually inclined toward philosophical musings, but the chief question occupying her mind as she sorts through the contents of her room—*What is the point of anything anymore?*—skews distinctly esoteric.

Emily is gone. Harry hasn't seen Alexander since she turned down his proposal, which effectively severed both their relationship and any chance of her qualifying for her father's inheritance. She's been studiously avoiding Mariah—easier now that they don't have to share a stage each night, though it's kept her from Pearl's as well. Collin has been absent too, disappearing from the house for long stretches of time and returning at odd hours, lingering just long enough to change his clothes or demolish a block of cheese and bread standing up in the kitchen. And now that Harry has quit the Palace, there is no theatrical disaster with which to distract herself each night. The sudden loneliness overwhelms her, in the same way she is overwhelmed by the length of life. All too big and not enough at the same time. Not until these weeks with Emily had Harry begun to understand the difference between company and companionship.

Even Havoc has little use for her, as he's tall enough to knock plates off the counter and finish whatever food Collin leaves behind. She had brought the dog with her in hopes he might be excited by a new location and all the many crumbs that could be snuffled out from between the cushions of the sofa, but instead he's fallen asleep in front of the wardrobe, his snores sounding like a teakettle full of soup.

It is difficult to separate the oddments she wants to keep from the oddments to be thrown out—the importance of every item questioned in the way it only is when being fitted for moving house. So many of the things she has accumulated, which once felt precious, suddenly seem silly and unimportant. Empty bottles of scent she thought she may one day find a use for. Flowers given her by a countess she had bedded during a run of *As You Like It*, dried upside down in her wardrobe. A silk handkerchief of her mother's which, as a youth, Harry had carried in her pocket every day. Pointless sentimentality, all of it.

Harry makes quick work of the room, only pausing occasionally to massage her sore shoulder. The doctor prescribed rest, but instead she has been wallowing, which may have made things worse due to how often she sprawled in bed with no regard for her injury. She has fallen into a deep pit of self-pity, and upon reaching the bottom, has no inclination to do anything other than find a spade and keep tunneling.

As Harry starts plucking strands of jewelry from a tangled heap, trying to remember if any of the jewels are real, Havoc sits up suddenly and lets out one loud *woof.* Harry thinks he must have woken himself from a dream, but then she hears the door open.

"Harry?" Mariah's voice calls.

Havoc leaps to his feet and dashes to greet her, tail thwacking Harry on the back of the head as he passes.

Harry turns back to the knotted necklaces, pulling two apart with more force than is necessary. "Did you come to gloat?"

"Gloat?" Mariah repeats. "About what? I heard you were hurt."

Harry still doesn't look up. She's certain Mariah is reclining against the wall and wearing something cut low. "Yes, well I'm much better now. It was only a separated shoulder. Now that you've seen for yourself I still have both arms, do your gloating and then leave me be."

"What am I meant to gloat over?" Mariah asks. Havoc grumbles his support, though Harry is sure it's because Mariah is scratching his ears.

"You got Miss Sergeant to go home with you." Harry abandons the knot of jewelry and tosses the whole thing into a pile she has mentally labeled *rubbish,* then turns to the door. Havoc is standing between Mariah's legs as she massages his head. The movement jiggles her breasts, which are in danger of spilling out of her low neckline. "Go on," Harry says, climbing to her feet and squaring her shoulders like a boxer. "Let's get it over with."

"Oh hell, are you *still* jealous?" Mariah lets out a tinkling laugh. "I assumed the two of you would have worked things out by now. I had no idea it would eat at you for this long." Mariah slides her hands under Havoc's ears and flips them back and forth. Havoc lets out a contented rumble. "I didn't know you had been thinking of us together all this time. Did you imagine it? She and I, lying in your bed?"

"Don't—"

"Have you been sleepless over thoughts of where we touched each other?"

"Yes, see, this is exactly the gloating I meant."

Mariah laughs again, disentangling herself from Havoc and picking her way across the room to stand before Harry. "I can't believe she didn't tell you."

"We aren't speaking," Harry mumbles. "She found out I had

designs on the same fellow as her and thought I'd been having her on."

"Were you?"

"At first," Harry says. "But things changed."

"And you just let her go?"

Harry bristles at Mariah's derision. "I'm not going to crawl back to her with protestations of why she owes me forgiveness she does not want to give. I hurt her. She owes me nothing."

Mariah rolls her eyes. "And here I thought you loved her."

"I did," Harry says. "I do. Not that it's any of your concern. But it's because I love her that I'm letting her go."

Harry tries to move to the wardrobe, but Mariah leans backward against the door, pinning it shut and keeping herself between it and Harry. "God, what sentimental amatory novel did you get that tripe from?"

"If you had ever loved anyone you might understand," Harry retorts.

"I love *you*."

"You do not."

Mariah gasps, slapping an open palm to Harry's chest. "How dare you!"

"You do not love me, you want to possess me," Harry says.

Mariah crosses her arms, bosom spilling over her neckline like bread rising over the lip of the pan. "What's the difference?"

Harry throws up her hands. "And that alone is proof."

"Of what?"

"That you do not love me. Mariah, we are so badly suited to each other. We both know it and we are neither of us happy when we are with each other. We're just comfortable being miserable together."

"What's so wrong with that? God." Mariah flops down onto the bed, sending a pile of Harry's shirts cascading to the floor. "You're so cruel to me."

"I am not being cruel, I'm being honest."

"Well then be a little less honest!" Mariah picks up a pillow and flings it at Harry, who bats it out of the air. "If I'm so horrid—"

"I did not say that—"

"Why invite me in your home and your bed and your life?"

"Because we're friends—"

"Don't patronize me." Mariah flings another pillow, then a third, which Harry manages to catch. "If I didn't let you use me for your pleasure, you'd have cut me loose long ago."

"And you're only with me because of some bizarre desire to own me so no one else can."

"Yes, well that's because everyone likes you, but you're the only person who likes me." Having no more cushions, Mariah throws herself across the mattress, rolling over with her face to the wall.

Harry considers throwing the pillow at her in retaliation, but as this is the closest she and Mariah have ever come to a true conversation about their relationship, she doesn't want to risk undermining it. "Well, if you were a bit nicer."

"And let everyone use me as they please?" Mariah sits up and glares at Harry. Her long, loose hair flops over her face, and she swats it away. "I was at Pearl's too long to fall for that. I must protect myself from the people who would misuse me if given a chance, and love and sentiment and that tripe are not compatible with that." Her hair falls in her face again, and this time she does not touch it. Her shoulders sink, and she drops her head to her chest. "I thought you of all people understood that."

"I do," Harry says.

But Mariah shakes her head. "No you don't. It's never been the same for you. You always had your mother to shield you."

"My mother never shielded me."

"She kept you from the work," Mariah says. "You never had to do what I did to survive."

Silence falls between them. Havoc slinks across the room and rests his melon-sized head on Mariah's knee.

"Have I?" Harry asks quietly.

Mariah sniffs, though her eyes are dry. "Have you what?"

"Have I taken advantage of you?"

"Yes." Mariah rests her hand on Havoc's back. "But only because I let you."

"I'm sorry."

"Go on." Mariah laughs. "Neither of us have used the other well."

"I am though," Harry says. "Truly sorry."

"Oh shut it." Mariah swipes a hand under Havoc's chin, then wipes the collected drool on Harry's bedclothes. "Aren't you going to ask me?"

"Ask you what?"

"About what happened between myself and your Miss Sergeant." Mariah tips her face up to Harry, batting her eyelids. "Aren't you gasping to know?"

"No, please, don't." Harry presses her face to the door of the wardrobe. "If you have any compassion for me—"

"Oh for God's sake, you milksop! Miss Sergeant and I never slept together."

Harry turns sharply. "What?"

Mariah leans back on the bed, kicking her legs like a delighted child. "Did you really think she was my sort of girl? I invited her home because I was cross with you for quitting the company. I never intended to bed her."

Harry doesn't trust her own relief—nor, more important, does she truly trust Mariah. Besides, what does it matter to her anymore whom Emily goes home with? She was never Harry's to lose. But still she must know. "You never did anything—"

"She tried to kiss me." Mariah laughs. "It was as romantic as snogging a wall."

"Are you lying to me?"

"Why would I lie about *that*?"

"I don't know, you like to lie."

"It's your choice if you believe me, but it's the truth." Mariah lies back on the bed again, with less theatrics this time, though she does spread her hair over the mattress in a corona, then stares up at the hangings. "She's a fool for letting you go. She of all people should know that wanting to marry someone and being in love with them are two different things."

Harry frowns. "What do you mean by that?"

"Have you been in bed so long you haven't heard?" Mariah presses her hands together over her breasts, like a heroine died tragically lying in a coffin. "Your little Miss Sergeant is a murderess."

It takes Harry a moment to realize what Mariah has said. The word feels so divorced from the Emily she knows it is hard to match them. Then she realizes, and the room seems to tilt around her, like a ship in a swell. She almost sits down. "How do you know about that?"

"So you *have* heard."

"Mariah." Harry drops to her knees beside the bed and seizes Mariah by the hand. "Tell me."

"I was at an assembly dance last week and someone told me there was a woman who had come to London to find a husband after she killed her fiancé. Only to then discover it's our own Miss Emily Sergeant." When Harry doesn't reply right away, Mariah pokes her in the stomach. "Are you listening? I said she's disgraced."

"I have to see her."

"I thought you were finished."

"We are, but I have to tell her it wasn't me. I don't want her to think I had some vengeful intention to ruin her because of what happened between us."

"No, don't—"

But Harry is already on her feet, batting her way through the detritus of her worldly possessions in search of what she needs. "Will you take the dog back to Collin's for me?"

"Why can't you?"

"I have to go to her. Have you seen my dinner jacket? The one with no cigar burns."

"Wait!" Mariah sits up quickly. "I didn't tell you that so you'd go running back to her! What happened to loving her and letting her be?" When Harry doesn't reply, Mariah grabs her arm, pulling her back to the bed. "Harry please." Mariah spreads her legs over the edge pulling Harry in between them and wrapping her arms around Harry's waist. She presses her head to Harry's stomach and looks up at her, eyes wide. "Please don't leave me."

"Do you really think there is anything left here?" Harry asks. "For either of us."

"I don't want to be alone."

"I don't think you will be for long. But this isn't love, Mariah. This isn't company or friendship or happiness or anything. It makes us both so terribly unhappy."

"Oh God." Mariah drops her head. "Am *I* the one you're loving and letting go?"

"Let's say that."

Mariah lets out a sigh, so long and heavy that her breasts leaven again. "Fine," she says at last. "I will take your dog to your brother's, but I will make him tip me."

"As you should." Harry kisses her quickly on the cheek, then returns to the wardrobe. "Now, have you seen *any* of my trousers?"

32

The only thing more humiliating than staying at the dance, Emily decides, would be to leave—nothing confirms or inflates a rumor like running from it. So she forces herself to stand, alone with her back to the wall for a reel, a quadrille, another reel, a sixdrille, and a three-couple set, forgoing her usual demure glances and instead casting withering looks at anyone who dares glance her way.

At long last, the final song before the intermission is finally called—a waltz. And, as all around her gentlemen offer their hands to ladies, kissing their knuckles and guiding them onto the floor with their skirts looped over their elegantly cocked hands, Emily can bear it no longer. She had hoped to make it to the interval and slip out discreetly, but her nose burns with the effort it is taking not to cry. She tucks her unmarked dance card into her bodice, pushes an errant pin back into her hair, and turns for the door.

But just as she does, she feels a soft touch on her arm as, behind her, someone says, "May I have this dance?"

She turns, expecting a leering stranger or a boy on a dare from his friends—*ask the murderess to dance!*

But there, at her shoulder, is Harry.

Harry, in one of the fine suits Emily had run her fingers along in the wardrobe in her room, the brocade as black as onyx, gold buttons shimmering in the candlelight. She must have bound her breasts, for the starched white shirt lies almost flat across her chest, and her neckcloth has been pressed into slicing folds. She's unwigged, and her cropped hair curls softly around her ears and at the back of her neck, despite the effort she's gone to slick it down with pomade.

Emily's mouth trembles. She's sure her pulse can be seen in her neck. She tries to take a breath and finds she cannot draw one deep enough. "What are you doing here?"

"Asking you to dance," Harry replies. "If it's not too bold."

All around them, couples positioning themselves on the dance floor look their way curiously. Several of the men who had gaped at her earlier crane their necks to see who is offering their hand to Miss Emily Sergeant. The women peer at Harry from behind their hands. Emily sees one of them whisper to her friend *Who is that?* Though she cannot tell if it is said in admiration or derision.

Emily had expected that if she ever saw Harry again, she'd be angry. She'd want to slap her and scream at her, her heart so full of hatred for the way Harry had deceived her that any love there would be forced out of her heart like tenants evicted from an overcrowded house. There was simply no room to contain both.

So Emily is shocked to find that more than anything, she wants to rest her head on Harry's shoulder. She wants to take Harry by the lapels of her coat and run her fingers through the short hair at the back of her neck. She wants to touch Harry's lips with the tips of her fingers.

Emily wants to hate Harry. She wants to make a scene, shout at her and tell her to leave. She wants to ask her to stay. She wants to dance with her, wants to be held by those strong arms like she was when Harry carried her through the rain. She wants no one else in this room to matter. She's somehow certain they won't, if she can just dance one waltz with Harry.

Emily wants so much.

"If you do not want—" Harry says just as Emily says, "Let us dance."

As they take their positions among the other couples, Harry places a hand on the small of Emily's back, and Emily places hers on Harry's shoulder. Harry moves to tuck Emily's other hand behind her own back, but winces sharply.

"Are you all right?" Emily asks, alarmed.

Harry holds her chin to her chest for a moment, and when she speaks, her voice is tight. "You'll have to forgive me. My shoulder isn't yet recovered fully. May I, instead?" Her hand brushes Emily's waist.

"Of course."

Harry does not keep to the edges of the dance floor, as Emily might have chosen to. She carries them forward into the middle of the crowd, her footsteps assured and her head high, turned just slightly from Emily's so their cheeks are parallel to each other.

"Did you tell anyone?" Emily says quietly.

Harry turns her face to Emily's, and Emily feels the brush of Harry's nose against her temple. "No. I swear."

Emily reaches up and puts a hand lightly upon Harry's lips. "Do not swear. I believe you."

"You were right," Harry says softly.

"What about?"

"I had designs on Rochester," Harry says. "That's why I sent those men after you at the Majorbanks's. And when Collin introduced us, it crossed my mind that I could use my influence to put

Rochester off you. It was cruel, and I'm sorry. When I realized I wanted to do no such thing, I did not tell you the truth for fear that . . . well, that what would happen at the race would transpire. You would discover my deceit, and never want to speak to me again."

"Yet here we are," Emily says. "Speaking."

"The remarkable nature of that is not lost upon me." Harry's head cants. "I'm not marrying Rochester. My initial plan to do so was made in haste and desperation. I thought I wanted someone with whom I could be wed and yet remain on my own."

"You deserve that," Emily says. "You should not have to marry someone who would ask you to compromise yourself."

"I know," Harry replies. "But I see now that they are not diametrically opposed."

"So why not marry Rochester?" Emily asks. "What changed?"

"I met you." Harry ducks her face, chin to her shoulder, then says, "I do not deserve your forgiveness. But I ask for it anyway. Emily Sergeant, please forgive me for the harm I caused you. I regret most profoundly anything I did to make you feel less than what you are: the most desirable woman in London. I hope you find someone deserving of your magnificence. And if that's Rochester, I'll throw rice at your wedding. I'll bring the flowers. I'll bake the cake. Whatever makes you happy, Miss Sergeant. That's all I want."

Emily's heart feels as though it's swelling in her chest. Like a letter lost in the post for years, her resentment has returned to her hardly legible.

Harry steps back, and Emily realizes the song has ended. She wants to shout at the quartet to please add another verse, for this cannot possibly be their last moments together.

Harry bends over Emily's hand, still cupped in hers, and kisses her knuckles. "You look beautiful tonight," she says. "As lovely in white as you ever were in yellow."

Emily looks at Harry, in her brocade coat, her expression grave, though she gives Emily one final wink before she steps back. Emily is afraid her heart may fly from her chest for the way it is stretching, arms out, toward Harry. "Enjoy your evening, Miss Sergeant."

"No," Emily whispers, and Harry pauses in the act of turning for the exit.

"Pardon?"

She has reached the limits of her strength. She cannot conjure even the memory of language.

"Miss Sergeant," Harry says, but before she can say another word, Emily turns and flees the ballroom.

33

Harry prepared herself for a variety of possible reactions from Emily upon their reunion, from stoic silence and refusal to take Harry's hand, to screaming obscenities, perhaps even violence—this was, after all, a woman who, upon their first meeting, had thrown her shoes.

She had not imagined Emily would take her hand and dance with her.

Even more surprising—that Emily should then turn and run.

At which Harry's resolve to let Emily Sergeant leave her life dissipates.

Harry follows Emily out of the ballroom and halfway down the colonnade that runs parallel to it, catching up to her just before she reaches Bennet Street. "Miss Sergeant, wait!"

She grabs for Emily's arm, but Emily rounds on her and snaps, "Don't touch me."

Harry steps back at once, raising her hands.

Emily swipes at her eye with her wrists—she's crying, why is she crying, has Harry made Emily cry? This whole endeavor is beginning to feel like a sleeveless errand.

But when Emily speaks, her voice is strong. It reminds Harry of the first time they met, under the wisteria at the Majorbanks's ball, when Emily had told her to sod off and Harry had gone cross-eyed.

"What did you do that for?"

"Do what?"

"Dance with me."

"I wanted to apologize."

"But why now?" Emily's face is shining, cheeks poppy red. "Why here?"

"I . . ." Harry swallows. The colonnade is empty, and the low rumble of sound at their backs from the ballroom feels vast and muted, like they're standing beside the ocean. "I didn't want you to be alone."

"Who says I can't be fine on my own?"

"I know you *can*," Harry says. "But you don't have to be." She wants to take Emily by the hand, but Emily is pacing the width of the path like a tiger in a menagerie, and Harry is too afraid to reach between the bars of the cage for fear of losing a finger.

"You know, I was fine before I met you," Emily says, her voice pitched. "I could have been fine my whole life. I could have married some man and been his wife and had his children and lived in his house and it would have been so damn fine, but then you had to show up, you mad, stubborn, difficult woman."

Harry swallows. "I didn't mean for my coming tonight to upset you."

"Tonight?" Emily's laugh is threaded with hysteria. "You think this is about *tonight*?"

"Is it . . . is it not?" Harry struggles to grasp the meaning of Emily's words, but she might as well be snatching for the back of a runaway carriage. "Miss Sergeant, forgive me, but I do not understand why you're angry with me."

Emily scoffs and swipes at her eyes again. "If only."

"If only what?"

"If only I was angry at you."

"Then what is it?"

Emily stops her pacing. Turns to face Harry. Her eyes shine in the candlelight. "Do you really not know?" she whispers.

And it is then, before Harry has a chance to answer, that Emily Sergeant takes Harry's face between her hands and kisses her.

34

As soon as their lips meet, all of Emily's muddled emotions—regret, relief, happiness, joy—dissolve into the singular feeling of Harry's mouth on hers. Harry puts a hand on Emily's back, like she had while they waltzed, the other rising to cup Emily's neck. Her fingers twine in Emily's hair, palm trembling as she flexes her fingers, as though she has to stop herself from clutching. And Emily finds herself enveloped in those strong arms she has so admired since the day she saw Harry riding at Regent's Park. Her arms and her scent and her fierce tenderness, and Emily could die here and want nothing else in life, now that she has been held and touched and kissed by Harriet Lockhart.

Emily feels herself sinking, her body bowing against Harry's like trees in the wind. She has never been kissed like this. She has not been kissed at all since . . . since Thomas. He invades her thoughts suddenly, his nimble hands and stubbled jaw. What good has ever come from thinking she loved someone? She had thought she loved Thomas and that had tipped her whole life off course.

She should pull away. She should tear herself from Harry's arms, wipe her mouth, and walk away without another glance. She needs a husband. She needs a future. She needs security and a reputation and distinctly *not* these arms and this mouth and this clarifying touch and the shuddering thrill of living the rest of her life in the shade of this kiss.

I cannot do this, she thinks. *I cannot again be distracted by another unsuitable lover.* She cannot sail this close to the dark shores that once nearly scuttled her. She has come too far—patched her sails and flown different colors and learned to twist into the wind rather than against it. It would be madness to change course now. She cannot let someone else come into her life and ruin her heading. She loved unsuitably before, and no good came from it.

But what she felt for Thomas in comparison to what she feels for Harry is like comparing a teaspoon to the ocean.

And what has she gotten from a lonely life at sea? Who says a marooner's rock can't be her home? She can throw anchor in whichever port she likes. She can drop her anchor in the middle of the goddamn ocean if it pleases her. And Harry surely is an ocean. She stretches as far as Emily can see.

And so, when Harry asks, "Would you come home with me?"

Emily says, "Yes."

35

Collin's house is empty when they arrive. Havoc sleeps soundly before the fire, exhausted from their earlier adventure to Harry's room and presumably his return home with Mariah. His snores are so loud he must not hear their footsteps, or Harry's certain he would have followed them as they climb the stairs to Harry's bedroom and shut the door.

Harry shucks off her jacket and tosses it across the bench of her dressing table. She reaches for Emily, but stops when Emily cries, "Wait!"

Harry freezes, one hand raised between them. Her fingers tremble.

But then Emily retrieves Harry's jacket from the bench and shakes it out. "You can't leave it all rumpled. It's far too fine."

Harry watches as Emily folds the jacket carefully and sets it upon the window seat, wondering when taking proper care of one's clothes became so arousing.

Emily turns to Harry. "There."

"Anything else you want to tidy up?"

Emily makes a show of looking around the room. "You could do for some dusting. I'll get a cloth."

"Oh hell." Harry grabs Emily around the waist as Emily pretends to start for the door, and Emily shrieks, letting herself be pulled into Harry's arms. She twists around so they are face to face, hips together, and Emily's gaze is so heavy Harry wants to wrap it around herself like a blanket.

"What now?" Emily whispers.

"Now?" Harry says. "I kiss you." Harry takes Emily's hand in hers and kisses it like they are being introduced at a ball, then takes the glove between her teeth and tugs it off. She touches her mouth to Emily's palm, lips skimming the heel of her hand, and holds their hands together between them until Emily presses it to Harry's cheek. *Oh that I were a glove*, Harry thinks. She touches her nose to the soft corner of Emily's jaw below her ear, weaving her fingers through Emily's hair. When she pulls, Emily tips her head back like she is catching rain on her face.

Harry kisses Emily's cheek. Her jaw. The angled bones of her shoulder. She pushes back the sleeve of Emily's dress and rests her cheek there, the skin like the pearled inside of a seashell, as she murmurs her name. She can taste Emily's perfume. She wants it to rub off on her. She wants to wake in the morning exhausted and bruised and carrying the scent of Emily.

Emily falls backward upon the bed, unfurling like a spool of thread with her arms thrown over her head. Harry climbs atop her, one knee on the mattress as she pushes Emily's skirts up to her waist. Beneath her chemise, Emily's legs are white and dimpled, her knees round caps and the skin behind them soft as sable gloves. Harry cups Emily's calf, sliding her stockings down one leg, then the other. The ribbons of her garters flutter to the floor. Harry strokes the soft inside of Emily's thigh with the backs of her fingers, watching as the fine hairs there rise. These places that not even the sun has touched before, now hers. Harry's own skin trembles at the thought. Her breasts feel heavy and piqued as she runs her hands along Emily's thighs, and then between her legs. Emily's breath trembles. Harry kisses the crease of Emily's leg, the space below her navel, the brittle peaks of her hip bones.

Emily shudders, reaching out suddenly and seizing Harry's shirt. "Take this off. Please, take it off now."

"Anything for you, Miss Sergeant."

"Oh God, you villain!" Emily pounds a fist against Harry's chest with a stifled moan. "Calling me *Miss Sergeant* when you have me in your bed."

"Does it *bother* you, *Miss Sergeant*?"

"Oh, damn you!"

"No, don't curse at me," Harry cries, catching Emily around her wrist and pressing her hands to Harry's heart. "I can't bear it, this will be over before it's begun."

Emily sits up and Harry finds she is kneeling over Emily's lap. Emily had felt so fragile in her arms when they danced, but suddenly, she feels strong, taking Harry's weight on her bare thighs. Harry cradles Emily's face in her hands, pushing her hair back before she kisses her. She feels Emily's hand between them, open across her skin.

"Undress me," Emily says, her mouth against Harry's.

"As you wish," Harry replies. "Miss Sergeant."

36

The impossibilities of this night are stacked so thick and deep Emily can hardly see through them.

The first, that she should kiss Harry. That Harry should kiss her in return, the second. That Harry should take her to bed, the third.

And that feeling of Harry straddling her—of the weight of Harry's hips against hers, she in nothing but her chemise and Harry in even less. Impossible to even imagine before this moment.

Emily throws her head back so her hair tumbles from its pins and cascades off the mattress. Between her own breaths, she can hear the soft plink as each one hits the floor.

Harry leans over her, and Emily marvels at the shape of Harry's shoulders, divots and swells of her bones forming a topography beneath her skin. Her breasts, her hips, her soft belly, the shape like an inverted heart.

Harry slides her lips down Emily's body, pausing when they touch Emily's breast, and Emily thinks wildly that Harry must be able to feel her heartbeat through her lips, so weighty inside her it feels like a pulse of liquid. Harry will drink it and swallow it.

Harry sinks to her knees between Emily's legs, then takes Emily's hips between her hands and slides her down the slick sheets. Emily's chemise rides up until it is bunched at her breasts. Emily stares up at the bed hangings, any attempts to catch her breath foiled when she feels Harry's tongue running up the inside of her thigh, then up the creases between her legs before gliding to the peak. She can feel the elicit throb, almost too much sensation to be borne. She wants to pull away. She wants to lean into it, push her hips up to meet Harry's mouth.

As if sensing her thoughts, Harry licks her, and Emily feels the ground swell down to the soles of her feet. Harry's breath is inside her, along with the soft press of her tongue. Emily shudders, tightening her muscles to stop her legs involuntarily clenching around Harry as she sucks and strokes Emily with her mouth.

The swells pause, and Emily raises her head as Harry sticks two fingers into her mouth to wet them.

"Do you like this?" she asks.

"I don't know," Emily replies.

Harry slides a finger inside her, and Emily grabs Harry's hair as her body caves with pleasure. "Oh God, yes, I do, yes." Emily clenches around Harry's fingers, and now it's Harry who curses.

Harry slides another finger in, deeper this time. "Is it too much?"

"It's not. God, it's not—"

Emily feels like she is about to rise off the bed. Harry skims her thumb against Emily as her fingers crook inside her, and Emily's whole body tenses. She wraps her legs around Harry's neck, heel digging hard into Harry's shoulder, and Harry laughs, so breathless it is air more than sound. "You're so eager," she murmurs, withdrawing her fingers so slowly that Emily feels herself clench around the sudden emptiness. Her body cries out for Harry.

"This is new to me."

"It's beautiful." Harry kisses the inside of Emily's knee, then presses her fingers into Emily again. This time they slide in easily, without any spittle.

"Harry," Emily gasps, and it feels like she's been hoarding that name in this tone, bookended by sighs, since they met. She has her hands in Harry's hair, grasping for purchase on the short strands. She pulls harder than she means, but Harry only laughs with pleasure.

"What I'd do to you," Harry says, "if I had two good shoulders at present."

Emily laughs too, the sound pebbled when Harry begins to thrust her fingers in and out, slowly at first, but with increasing speed when Emily gasps with pleasure. Then with her fingers still inside Emily, Harry pulls herself up onto the bed, resting her weight just enough on Emily that their breasts are together. She hooks her legs over Emily's, pushing them into the mattress, holding them still as she fucks her, and Emily writhes. She feels like she's sinking through the mattress and falling through the floor, and she grabs for something—anything—to hold on to. Harry's thumb presses into her as she leans down and kisses Emily's breast, once again, right over her liquid heart.

In the dim light, Harry looks slick and oiled. Her lips shine like she has just bitten into a ripe fruit. Bruises still shadow her ribs from her fall at the steeplechase, and Emily is reminded of a map, light and dark like land and sea. She wants to make a new world together, and this night—this here and now—will be the first steps on a new continent.

Emily gasps and moans and practically screams until the moment of summit, and suddenly she finds her throat empty. The feeling drives the breath from her lungs, the sensation from her skin. She felt greedy all the while Harry was touching her, desperate for more, and now she's overwhelmed by the capacity of her body to contain so much.

Harry pulls her fingers out of Emily, puts them to her mouth, and sucks them. She wants to turn herself inside out and let Harry feast on her. She'll gladly be tasted. Devoured.

Harry lies down and takes Emily in her arms, holds her open mouth to Emily's shoulder. Emily's whole body feels gelatinous and confectionary. Her thighs stick together as she shifts, the slickness coating her like a glaze.

"Would you like a biscuit?" Harry asks, which, as far as postcoital conversation, is not what Emily had expected. Harry untangles herself and climbs out of bed, groping along the floor for her shirt.

"What?"

"I think there's some steak and ale pie left from luncheon as well."

Emily pulls the bedclothes up over her mouth.

Harry's eyes narrow. "What?"

"Nothing."

"What are you laughing at?"

"I'm not."

"You are, you little hyena." Harry yanks the bedclothes fully off Emily, and she shrieks at the sudden cold. Harry pounces on top of her, pinning her to the bed, and Emily's laughter shifts into a heavy sigh as she feels Harry's bare legs against hers. "What," Harry says, nuzzling her face into Emily's neck, "are you laughing at?"

"It's just . . ." Emily resists the urge to bite down on Harry's earlobe. "None of this is anything like I imagined it would be."

"Is that a good thing?" Harry asks, raising her head.

"It's good," Emily replies, then kisses Harry, quick and light, on the mouth. "It's so much better."

In the kitchen, Emily sits on the table with her feet on the bench, wrapped in Harry's dressing gown, as Harry, naked, slices cheese and negotiates its ownership with Havoc, whose chin rests on the table beside her as he follows her movements with the focus of a sniper. Emily watches Harry as she works—the curve of her back, the muscles of her shoulders and the cords of her thighs. The way her ass dimples when she flexes.

Harry catches Emily staring at her and grins. "Stop looking at me like that."

"Like what?"

"Like you're having unchaste thoughts. I'll have no choice but to indulge them."

Emily laughs, tucking her hands under her thighs. "Nothing unchaste, I'm only wondering."

When Emily doesn't continue, Harry prompts, "What have you been wondering?"

"Ever since I met you. I think I have been wondering," Emily says, "what it might be like to love you."

Harry turns quickly to the hearth, before Emily can get a good look at her face, but when she speaks again, her voice has gone soft. "I suspect it's rotten work."

"Is it?"

"Mm." Harry hands Emily a plate, cutlery balanced along the edge. "I'm notoriously bad tempered when woken before noon. I put out my cigars on the furniture and buy expensive shirts before I pay my rent and never pick up my socks."

"That's fine."

"And," Harry says. "I'm prone to moods and selfishness. I'm

hideously childish, especially when slighted, and I have been known to brood—"

Emily interrupts her. "Someone ought to love you, and I'd like it to be me."

Harry turns from the hearth, and with the flames in the grate leaping behind her like dancers, and Emily thinks of the first time she saw Harry, silhouetted in gold wisteria.

"So perhaps," Emily says, "you'll let me try."

Harry leans forward and presses a kiss to Emily's forehead. "Darling," she says, "it would be the greatest honor of my life to be loved by you."

37

Five days!

Five luxurious, languid, improbable days of nothing but swanning around together, mostly naked and almost always in bed, until the sheets smell briny and the windows are steamed. The only communication they have with the world outside their doors is the card Emily sends to her cousin that their quarrel is mended and she has fallen into Harry's bed. Though perhaps not stated so bluntly. Emily had read it aloud for Harry's appraisal of its tact, but she had been wearing nothing, sitting at the desk in Harry's room with a leg pulled up beneath her, and Harry hadn't been able to focus.

Five days, and Harry cannot remember a longer stretch of uninterrupted happiness in her entire life. Emily sleeps late and makes tea and teaches Havoc to sit in exchange for bits of ham. She reads books, beats Harry at cards, folds Harry's shirts, wears Harry's shirts, and lets Harry take those shirts off her. They go to bed early. They rise late. They walk Havoc and go out for bread in the morning and little else.

Harry had not known how happy she could be to do nothing with someone. To speak gently. Share confidence. Life, it would seem, can be quiet and Harry can be content with that. As long as it is Emily here with her. All the things she had not let herself notice in Emily, let alone admire, for she knew how quickly she would tip over into obsession, suddenly overwhelm her. The angle of Emily's chin when she reads. The way she sips her tea, holds her hat, talks with exuberant gestures when she tells Harry about her strange dreams in the morning.

The first night they slept together, Harry had found herself lying awake, considering what would happen if she refused the prince's offer and stayed instead with Emily. By the end of their delirious stretch holed up together, she's decided. She does not want to be a dog on the prince's lead for her whole life. She cannot live beholden like that, her existence dependent on the whims of the monarchy.

Now that Harry has Emily, she has a reason to say no. She'll never even have to tell Emily what she gave up, lest Emily feel conflicted or guilty or angry or anything other than blissfully, completely, unquestioningly in love with Harry.

But something stays her hand each time she considers putting pen to paper to inform her father of her intentions. She had hoped to voice the plan to Collin first—not because she requires his approval, but because she wants to hear herself say it aloud, and watch his face as she does. Perhaps he may even have advice worth hearing, as the only other person she knows who is living in this same—albeit less restrictive—shadow. Though his even hand typically aggravates her, she finds herself suddenly craving it.

But in their five days of seclusion, she has not seen any evidence of his presence in the house. She would assume he returns late and departs early to avoid the carnal utopia fomenting in his upstairs guest bedroom, but he never seems to eat anything she leaves out in the kitchen, nor his coat on the rack or shoes by the door. In the wee hours of one morning, she half wakes in the dark, certain she's heard him come home, only to realize the sound is Havoc ramming his head against the bedroom door to be let in.

Harry tells herself she's grateful he's made himself scarce, no matter the reason, but she's starting to grow concerned. Then, just as quickly, feels silly for that. Collin can take care of himself—hasn't he spent years cold-shouldering her specifically to prove that? Besides, as long as he's gone, Emily will keep walking around wearing Harry's dressing gowns with nothing underneath, eating eggs on toast that Harry makes for her, and keeping hair unpinned so it falls in ringlets over Harry's knees when Emily nestles her head between them. Harry will not let errant preoccupations over her brother's whereabouts wake her from this dream.

Though Collin, as it happens, is not the first horseman of Harry's apocalypse. It instead arrives on the doorstep in the form of the Duke of Edgewood's boy assassin.

He is armed this time not with a pie, but a gift box tied with a blue ribbon like a fancy hat delivered from a milliner. When Harry opens the door he clutches the box against him like he might use it as a shield.

"Well." Harry leans against the doorframe, surveying him. "We meet again."

The boy holds out the box.

"Let me guess," Harry says without taking it. "The Duke of Edgewood sends his regards."

"I didn't know what would happen," the boy says, his voice quavering. "I'm so very sorry."

"You hit me with a pie; there are only so many possible outcomes."

"Not that." He shoves the box at her again. "Please take it." His gaze glances across her face, not meeting her eye but taking in her faded bruises and flat nose.

Harry's stomach drops. She takes the box.

"Who was that?" Emily calls when Harry carries the box into the living room and sets it on the sofa.

"Remember that boy who hit me with a pie?"

Emily comes to stand beside her, Havoc hot on her heels, keen to explore any deliveries first with his nose, then possibly his tongue. "Is this from the duke?" Emily asks, blocking Havoc with her knee. "The one you dueled?"

"The very same." Emily reaches for the lid but Harry snatches her hand. "Hold on there."

Emily shoots Harry a raised eyebrow. "What exactly do you think is inside?"

"I dunno. Something bad. A snake?"

Emily reaches out and shakes the box. It rattles in a distinctly unsnakelike way. "If you're afraid—" Emily starts, but Harry brushes her off.

"No, no, it's my death threat. I'll do it." Harry undoes the ribbon on the top. "Cry 'God for Harry, England, and St. George,'" she says, and pops the lid off.

When nothing inside moves, Harry, Emily, and Havoc all lean over the box to better see the contents. A thread of drool from Havoc's lip catches on the corner and stretches like a kite string.

"What is it?" Emily asks.

The object inside is perplexingly snake shaped, but far too limp and flat to be a serpent, unless it was first smashed by a dictionary. Emily shifts the paper, revealing the silver buckles on one end, and suddenly Harry realizes what it is.

She picks up the leather strap and lets it hang over her hands like a sash.

"That son of a bitch," Harry mutters.

"What is it?" Emily asks.

"The girth from my Derby saddle," Harry says, showing Emily the spot where it's been cut, cleanly until the very edge, where it was left to snap on its own. "The bastard cut it—or his man did, because he's far too much of a milksop to get his own hands dirty. That's why my saddle tipped. It's why I fell. Damn!" Harry throws the girth into the chair. Havoc quietly retrieves it and begins to gnaw upon it.

"You need to tell the authorities," Emily says.

"I need to tell Alexander," Harry says. "It was his horse—he'd be the one to press charges. And Collin. Good lord, where is Collin?"

"I thought you said he was working," Emily says. "What is it he does, exactly?"

"Unclear, but I suspect it doesn't keep him away from home for a full bloody week. God, what if something's happened to him? If Edgewood is trying to ruin me completely, he may come for my brother as well." And why hasn't she been more concerned? What sort of carnal drunkenness of five whole days in bed with Emily Sergeant had made her forget that she was in the wake of a disrupted horse race, with her brother possibly missing, and her in need of a husband? She wants to slap herself across the face.

"Do not fret yet. Not until we know more things with certainty." Emily takes Harry's hands in hers, their palms together and fingers interlaced. "Shall we go to Collin's office?"

"I have no idea where his office is!" Harry says, panic rising in her voice. "Why did I never ask him where his office is?"

"Because you are only recently reacquainted, and your relationship is complex." Emily rubs her hands down Harry's forearms. "If not Collin, then let's go to the duke and see if he might help us."

"Yes," Harry says. "Yes, of course. God, what would I do without you?"

"You'd have worked it out on your own," Emily says, then adds, "eventually."

Harry kisses Emily on the cheek, then reaches down to pry the girth from Havoc's maw.

Best not to eat the evidence.

38

When Harry sees Alexander Bolton striding toward them across the Regent's Park riding ground, his hair slick with sweat and a towel draped around his neck, she wonders how she had ever thought she wanted to marry him.

"Harry!" he calls in greeting, raising a hand to them. "And Miss Sergeant. Still the unlikeliest couple of the Season, I see."

"We know what happened at the Derby," Harry says.

Alexander's smile falters. "What?"

"The Duke of Edgewood interfered with the race," Emily explains as Harry tosses Alexander the girth. "He tampered with the strap on Harry's saddle. That's why she fell when Matthew jumped."

"Edgewood?" Alexander frowns. "I hardly know him. What grievance has he against me?"

"His quarrel is with me," Harry says. "We fought a duel and he lost an eye."

"Ah, well!" Alexander claps a hand to his chest and laughs. "What a relief. I knew it was no fault of Matthew's. Nor yours, obviously."

He flashes them his broad, boyish grin. Neither Harry nor Emily smiles in return. Emily stares at Alexander with her mouth slightly open, and before Harry can work out what to say, she barks, "He tried to kill Harry, and that's a relief to you?"

"To be fair," Alexander says, "it does sound as though she tried to kill him first."

"We dueled," Harry interrupts. "It was a mutual attempt! I did nothing wrong unless you would blame me for being the more competent with swords."

"You always find a way to boast, don't you?" Alexander hops up onto the fence and pulls off one of his boots, tipping it upside down until fine dust streams out. "Why does it matter? The race was lost. They won't call for an amateur race to be run again because you claim to have proof that a man with a grudge against you intervened."

"It's not a claim," Emily says. "He sent the proof."

Alexander holds up his hand. "Miss Sergeant, with all due respect, I'm not sure what this has to do with you."

"Harry could have died," Emily snaps, voice rising. "And you're acting as though this was all some sort of harmless misunderstanding."

Alexander laughs, then says to Harry, "She is altogether different than I first thought. I can see why you like her." Harry hates the way he's talking as though Emily isn't here, instead addressing Harry in that chummy, laddish way simply because she's got the shortest hair here. Alexander tugs his boot back on, hops down from the fence, and dusts his hands on his britches. "What would you have me do, Miss Sergeant?"

"Alert the authorities," Emily says. "Have the results contested."

"It's hardly worth the trouble."

"Weren't you collecting bets?" Harry asks. "I suspect it might be worth the trouble to those whose coin you took."

"Bit late for that, I should think. And it's not my debt anymore. Your brother took care of that for me."

Cold dread trickles through Harry like the first drops of rain dotting the pavement in a storm, a harbinger of bad weather on its way. "What has Collin got to do with this?"

"Didn't he write you?"

"He doesn't have to write me, I'm staying with him and he hasn't been home in days. Where is he? Come back here, you prick," she calls, for Alexander had begun to slink away, "and tell me where my brother is!"

Alexander stops, staring at Harry as though trying to work out if she's having him on. Then he says, "He's been taken to the Marshalsea."

"The debtors prison?"

"No, the spa—of course the prison."

"On what charges?"

"On what charges? Are you daft?" Alexander looks to Emily, as though she might join him in amazement over Harry's stupidity, but she folds her arms and glares at him. He turns back to Harry. "Don't you know what your brother does?"

Harry can feel her teeth vibrating with how hard she's clenching them. Has Alexander always been this infuriating and petty, or has she simply never been on the receiving end of it?

"Collin's a bookmaker," Alexander says when Harry doesn't respond. "He takes bets on everything from the passage of laws in Parliament to card games. He came to me at the Majorbanks's party and asked if he might be the intermediary for the bets I was taking at the Milton Derby, in exchange for a cut of the winnings."

All the blood leaves Harry's head with a *whoosh* that she feels in her eardrums, and she almost staggers. She can hardly make sense of the words in relation to her virtuous, captious brother. He had sneered at everything from her career to her rooms to her drinking glasses, while all this time he's been making his name as an illegal intermediary for the ton's underbelly, not just encouraging vice but profiting from it. What a patheticly short high horse from which he had looked down at her.

"Gambling isn't illegal," Emily says. "On what charges was he arrested?"

"My race didn't quite play out the way I hoped it would, thanks to your duke's vendetta," Alexander says. "And I couldn't pay my vowels. Collin's creditors took him to court, and since he's been operating without a license to avoid tax, he's been put away."

"But it's your fault," Harry says. "It's your debt, he's just the intermediary."

Alexander shrugs. "I can't be arrested, I'm a duke. And Collin's name is on all the forms."

"So pay your creditors and get my brother out of the Marshalsea," Harry says. "You're letting him take your flogging for you."

"I haven't any money."

"You're a duke," Emily says, parroting his cadence.

"Yes, and if you were better at fortune hunting, Miss Sergeant," Alexander replies, "you'd know those two things don't always go hand in hand."

Emily looks as though she'd like to leap across the paddock and tackle him to the ground. "How dare you."

But Harry has already worked it out. The words *fortune hunting* had sent the cogs of her mind spinning. Why else would the penniless duke have changed course so abruptly after his Derby loss and abruptly decide to accept her proposal of marriage unless he knew?

"When did Collin tell you?" she asks Alexander.

His grin doesn't falter. "Tell me what?"

Harry pauses. She has only just regained Emily's trust, and cannot bear the idea of risking it by exposing the full truth of her peculiar social position and how it relates to the duke. "You know."

But Rochester, like Mariah, can read Harry too easily. He looks positively giddy as he points to Emily. "Oh does *she* not know? Go on, Harry, do share. It's not your patrilineal line you should be ashamed of. Can you imagine proudly telling people you're the daughter of a whore, then you find out your father's—"

"Stop," Harry says.

Emily looks at her, confusion in her eyes and something else too—the tiniest hint of retreat, a protective withdrawal into herself—and Harry knows this carriage cannot be uncrashed. And Emily must hear it from her, not Rochester. "It was recently revealed to Collin and me," Harry says, "that our father is the Prince of Wales, about to be crowned king of England. He offered us both a house, title, and land so long as we behave, and I am married by his coronation. And when this profligate weasel"—she kicks the toe of her boot in Alexander's direction—"found out his sure-bet racehorse didn't win, he suddenly became very interested in my stale marriage proposal. Now why might that be?" She pivots back to Alexander, who doesn't even have the decency to look ashamed. "Your father finally cut you off, did he?"

"He'd been threatening for so many years, but I never thought he actually would," Alexander replies. "But apparently coming to London and buying a racehorse was the straw that broke his back."

"I should have told you," Harry says to Emily. She wants to take her hand, but in the presence of Alexander, the gesture feels far too intimate. Emily is staring at Harry with wide eyes, her full lips parted. "I didn't want you to know that's why I was pursuing Alexander. And then I didn't want it to ruin everything between us."

"But it has anyway, hasn't it?" Emily says quietly.

Harry can't bear to look at her, so she rounds on Alexander again. "Did you turn Collin in yourself?" she demands. "Or did you let nature take its course as you waited for me to come running to you?"

Alex lifts a shoulder. "I had to make one last trip to see my father. Make absolutely certain I wouldn't be forgiven before I tied myself to you. Besides, the longer I wait, the more desperate for matrimony you become."

Harry bites her tongue, then changes course, softening her voice in an attempt to appeal to whatever friendship had once existed between them. "Alex, please. After everything we've done for each other for so many years. I know you're . . ." She pauses, struggling to find the truth in the words *good man* and afraid the lie will be so obvious on her face it will undercut her appeal to his decency. ". . . Not a bad man. Please, do what is right. The debts unpaid are yours. Turn yourself in so Collin can be set free."

"Or, instead," Alexander says, "you marry me. It's the best either of us can hope for."

Harry wants to hit him. She almost does—but she can't risk two Lockharts in prison, and Harry wouldn't put it past Alexander to call the constabulary if she bloodied his nose.

And more than that, she wants to travel backward in time, to the moment she received the letter from Alexander—*back in London, thought I might see you*—and remember him as he always was: vain and brash and selfish. She'd throw that letter into the fire. She'd tear it to pieces and eat it.

"You need to get Collin out of prison," Harry says. "Beg your father. Sell your goddamn horse. This is your fault—you can't let Collin take the blame."

"I cannot help you, Harry," Alexander says. "Unless . . ." He makes a show of starting to bend the knee in proposal.

But he's barely touched grass when Emily shoves him by the shoulders, pushing him off balance so he falls backward into the dirt. "Go to hell, Rochester."

Alexander laughs, humorless, as he examines his skinned palms. "Harry, you always know how to pick the best bitches, don't you?"

"I'd rather be a bitch than a mongrel like you," Emily retorts. She turns for the paddock gate, and Harry follows, feeling dizzy with anger and shock and also wishing the moment were not so fraught, because if Emily had agreed, she certainly could have done with a quick snog behind the stables.

"I'll see you soon, Harry," Rochester calls to their retreating backs. "Next time you throw yourself into my bed."

"I'd rather go down on an unstuffed sofa," Harry shouts back at him. "At least it would be harder than your cock!"

39

"Why didn't you tell me?" Emily asks.

They are sitting on a bench in Regent's Park, far from the riding grounds, both of them staring forward at the burbling fountain at the end of the path. The sky overhead is brilliant and cloudless, but, in spite of the day's warmth, Emily wants to press herself into Harry's side, tuck her head into her shoulder and never again raise it. Around them, children play, chased by nannies. Women stroll with parasols and men tip hats to them. The world moves on, oblivious.

Harry runs her hands through her hair, leaving a trail of curls standing up straight. "I couldn't very well tell you at first, or you'd know I was after Rochester too. And when I came to find you at Almack's, I didn't want to seem as though I was making an excuse; what mattered was that I hadn't told you the truth. And these past few days, I didn't want it to matter. It doesn't matter!"

"Of course it matters," Emily says. "It's terribly selfish for the prince to put you in such a position. Of all people, he should understand how conformity can be a prison." She presses her index fingers to the bridge of her nose. A part of her wishes she was crying, as though such an ordinary reaction might make the whole situation less absurd, but her eyes are dry. "Perhaps he will be a great king—perhaps he already is, he's been regent for years. But everything I've ever heard of him mostly discusses his taste for excess and decadence."

"You read the gossip columns about Prinny?" Harry asks with a small smile.

"Sometimes, but it's well-known back home, as he's often in Brighton with his degenerate friends. Thomas met him once." Emily pushes a strand of loose hair from her eyes. "He spoke of it all the time. They all did—all those laborers on Tweed's turnpike. The day the prince regent visited their building site when his carriage broke an axle, and he shared a meal with them. Thomas gave me a ring he claims he stole from the prince that day, but I never believed that's where he got it. It was so small and tarnished."

"God, your Thomas really was a scoundrel."

"The other men were so amused that the prince thought it was a gesture of his own great humility to dine with the common people, when really he was having a meal with criminals."

"Criminals?" Harry repeats.

"Tweed staffs his building sites with criminals," Emily says. "He bribes prisons to release them to him, works them half to death, and refuses their wages. They cannot take him to court or they'll be discovered to be escaped convicts and rearrested."

"Was Thomas a criminal?" Harry asks.

Emily nods. "A pickpocket in his youth, who looked older than he was so he was imprisoned with grown men. The others on Tweed's sites were so much worse. Thieves and arsonists and molesters of women."

"Emily," Harry says, "you cannot marry this man."

"I know," Emily says.

"I can find some other way to scrape together enough money to bail Collin out of prison," Harry says. "I'll sell everything I own to keep you from him."

"Hal," Emily says, but Harry presses on.

"Run away with me." She seizes Emily's hand between both of hers and clutches them to her chest. "Let's go. Right now."

"Where?"

"Wherever you want. Away from Robert Tweed and your horrible little hamlet and my brother and Prinny and all the meddling twats of London society. We can live somewhere no one will ever find us. We will change our names—Rosalind and Celia, like in *As You Like It*. I always thought they had a bit of a thing. We'll take the name of Sappho and live off our wits."

"What are you asking me?" Emily says. "To be your wife? Your lover? Your companion?"

"To stay," Harry says quietly. "I'm asking you to stay."

"I would," Emily replies. "You know I would. The same way I know you cannot sacrifice so much for me. Your whole future would be secure if you took your father's offer. You'll be able to do anything you want."

"Well." Harry offers her a sad smile. "Not anything."

The idea of fleeing together thrills Emily, certainly, but under any scrutiny, it will collapse like a cream-filled choux.

"What about Collin?" she asks.

"Sod Collin," Harry says. "He got himself into this mess. He can get himself out."

But Emily had watched Harry check the rack beside the door each morning for Collin's jacket and make too much food at every meal like a third guest might join them. She cannot ask that Collin be the price Harry pays for their happiness. Much as Emily feels about her parents, she knows that often the only thing more difficult than standing by your family is abandoning them.

"You can't do that," Emily says quietly.

Harry releases a heavy breath. "No I cannot, dammit."

They sit in silence. A flock of birds in a nearby tree takes flight, and the shadows on the path ripple as the branch bounces with their weight. *If only,* Emily thinks, *life could be distilled so simply that happiness and duty were always perfectly aligned.*

Harry sits up so suddenly Emily jumps in surprise. "*You* marry Collin!"

"What?" Emily laughs, so absurd is the notion. "To what end?"

"To rid yourself of Robert Tweed. To marry suitably. Collin will be some sort of landed gentry if we can get him out of this mess without Prinny finding out."

"And you think Collin will be amenable to this?"

"Once he hears what I'm doing to free him from the Marshalsea, he'd be an absolute clodpole to refuse."

"So you mean to extort your brother into marrying me?" Emily leans back on the bench. "How romantic."

"Don't think of it like that. This way, you and I can be . . ."

"Related by marriage?" Emily offers.

"No! I mean, yes. But not . . . we could be . . ."

Emily looks over at Harry. Her face is alight with hope, but Emily cannot muster the same. "Lovers?"

"Does the name for it matter? It's all we'd ever be, whether or not we married other people. Collin's a bang-up cove. A bit judgmental and a prude and will make you go to bed before nine, and, it would seem, has a bit of a criminal history. But he won't be cruel to you. You can take him home to your parents and they'll adore his boring suits and dry anecdotes. And if you and I decide to go our separate ways, no matter—Collin and I can easily fall out again."

"And then I'll be stuck married to a man I . . ." Emily can't think of a word to adequately express it. Even *like* feels too strong. "Don't hate?"

"It's better than the alternative, isn't it? I know it's not . . . ideal. But what is? Even if there was no Tweed or prince or my brother or anything, this is as far as we could ever travel. We can be lovers, we can be partners, but I'll never be someone you wed in a church."

When Emily doesn't reply right away, Harry lights up again, this time with another idea. "Or I marry Rochester and you refuse Tweed because you'll come live with us in our estate as our . . ." She trips on the next word, clears her throat, then says, "our friend. My friend. And if you decide you want to leave—tomorrow or a year from now or decades in the future—I'll give you an allowance. I'll buy you a home, whatever you need to be free and independent."

Emily swallows. The whole thing makes her feel vaguely ill. "What about my parents? I have to marry or they'll never recover their reputation. They may even lose their claim to their own land due to a broken contract with Tweed. And you can't marry Rochester after what he's done to your brother. You cannot think his abuse would stop there. He'll always take advantage of you."

"So then we return to you marrying Collin," Harry says. "It's the only solution."

And Emily knows she's right. The possible futures a woman of her age and station can hope for are already so limited, yet here are ways to circumvent them all and live on her own terms. Emily should be thrilled. But instead, she feels the same emptiness she had upon seeing Alexander at the Derby. She can't even muster joy as a pretense.

An arranged marriage with Collin Lockhart would be nothing like one to Tweed, but it is still a pale version of the same shade. Before she came to London, she thought all she wanted was anyone but Robert Tweed. But now she knows what it's like to stand on her own two feet, to reach for what she wants and claim her desire. And now she wants more than *not* Robert Tweed. She wants a life with someone she loves. She wants to be unfettered and belong to herself. Never again does she want to define herself by a Robert Tweed or Collin Lockhart or Thomas Kelly. Now that she has lived in London as free as she has felt since she was seventeen, she cannot imagine going back. It has taken all her courage to turn her back to the sun, but now that she has, she finds everything else is illuminated.

But she does not know how to say any of this to Harry, whose eyes shine with hope. Harry, who has kissed the inside of Emily's wrist and untied the sash of her dressing gown and rubbed the arches of her feet and looks at her like she is a work of art.

"Emily," Harry says, and Emily snaps, sharper than she means to, "Give me time to think."

"We don't have time—"

"Give me at least a moment!"

Harry presses her hands to her forehead, then says, "I have to go see Collin."

"Of course." Emily's shoulders sink. "Of course, you must go to him."

"And I'm going to ask him to marry you in exchange for getting him out of prison." She looks sideways at Emily. "You don't like that. I can see it in your mouth."

"I need to think it over, that's all. You've caught me by surprise."

"What is there to consider?" Harry asks. "This saves you from marrying Tweed."

"By offering me a different coerced marriage, or the life of a kept woman."

"That's not—" Harry breaks off, pressing a thumb hard to her lips before she speaks again. "They're not the same as marrying Tweed."

"They're not," Emily agrees, though they aren't that different either. She's simply substituting one jailer for another. One man for another. It's the difference between a locked door and a bolted one. "But you must give me time to think it over."

Harry purses her lips. "I'll have to speak to the prince about lending me money before I make arrangements at the Marshalsea—and pray to God that he never connects the need to Collin."

"How long do you think that will take?" Emily asks.

"No more than a week, I should hope."

"Then I'll see you at the end of it all."

"What?"

"I need time."

"No, please." Harry grabs Emily's arm, as though holding her in place. "Come home with me at least."

"Harry."

"I know, I know." Harry's grip loosens, and she raises her hands in surrender. "Five days? Will that be enough?" Her throat pulses as she swallows hard, and Emily knows Harry wishes it were minutes instead.

"Five days," Emily says. "I'll come to you with my answer, no matter what it is, in five days."

Neither of them move. They sit side by side, staring down the path, before they turn to each other at the same moment. And Emily is overwhelmed by how full she feels when she looks at Harry. Like she might spill over and flood the city. This beautiful woman who could have anyone has chosen her.

"Whatever your answer is," Harry says, "I want you to know,

the time I have spent with you has been the greatest joy of my life."

"Mine as well."

"I wish it could last forever."

"I don't think joy has to," Emily says, and touches her fingers to the back of Harry's hand. "I don't think it can. That's why it matters."

"I love you," Harry says.

And Emily smiles. "And I you."

40

The cost of bailing Collin out of the Marshalsea is too great for Harry's limited means, but she manages to scrounge together enough to bribe the turnkey into letting her enter the debtor's prison to visit her brother. She has heard stories about the strangeness of the place—that it's a city more than a prison, with the look of an Oxbridge college from hell, and businesses and gangs and a social infrastructure all its own. But seeing it and knowing that her brother is here among all these shrunken, huddled figures, resigned to their fate more often than fighting it, makes her feel ill.

As she stands outside the prison's taproom, sweating in the heat, waiting for her brother to be brought to her, all she can think of is how much she wishes Emily were with her.

When Collin is brought out, he is not in chains, though Harry realizes as soon as she sees him that prison trappings would have been less alarming than seeing her brother look so himself, but undone. The dark shadow of a beard creeps across his jaw, and Harry can see a crust of dirt around his ears and the collar of his shirt. His clothes are stained, and one arm of his coat has been ripped nearly off. Harry goes to him, though neither of them reach to embrace, which means they end up walking across the dining room in awkward proximity.

They sit on opposite sides of the scarred pub table. It wobbles on uneven legs when Collin folds his hands upon the top. Harry can't think of a thing to say. All this way, all that money, and now she's here and she has no words. Around them, residents of the Marshalsea play cards, drink, chat, and laugh like it is any barroom rather than a place they are forced to stay, subjected to thumbscrews and starvation and rats eating through their flesh at night.

"Are you hurt?" she finally asks, and Collin shakes his head. "Or hungry? Can I buy you a drink?"

"I didn't want you to come here." Collin's hands flex into fists. Dark crescents of dirt ring his nails.

"Why? Because you're guilty?"

Collin dips his chin. "In so many words."

"I'm going to get you out of here."

"With what money? Rochester owes money to half the men in London after the Derby, which means *I* owe half the men in London. And the amount compounds every day. Debt is not a hole one easily digs oneself out of."

"They do if their father is the sodding prince regent."

A vein in Collin's forehead throbs. "Please don't involve him. I cannot imagine I would fall under his definition of respectable if I must ask for an advance on my inheritance to be bailed out of debtors prison. It would negate the inheritance from which I'd have to borrow against."

"Then he'll lend it to *me*," Harry says. "He needn't know it's for your bail." Collin raises his head, but before he can get too drunk on hope, she adds, "But you have to do something for me in return."

Collin nods. "That's fair."

"It's not small."

"Neither is getting me out of prison."

Harry takes a breath. "I need you to marry Emily Sergeant."

Collin looks momentarily confused—he likely thought she was going to ask him for his house or pocket watch or to stand on a box at Speakers' Corner and declare Harry had and always would be right about everything. Then comprehension dawns across his face, and his eyebrows lift. "Are you two speaking again?"

"Bit more than that."

"Good." Collin nods. "You've been mooning over her for weeks."

"I'm not marrying Alexander Bolton," Harry says.

"Thank God."

"And neither is Miss Sergeant. But she needs to marry someone, and I think that should be you."

"Harry, I'm not marrying your lover so you can keep sleeping with her."

"Then you can stay in prison and lose your inheritance." She leans forward, elbows on the table, which nearly collapses on its shaky legs. "It's not just for me—you'd be saving her from a dangerous marriage to a dangerous man. If it also means she has a husband who is tolerant of her particular proclivities and allows me to remain in her life, well that's good too."

"And who will *you* marry?" Collin asks. "In order to collect the inheritance you're borrowing against."

"I'll ask His Majesty to pair me off with someone. Maybe he can find a nice sodomite among the nobility and we can disguise each other."

"And you'd be happy with that?" Collin asks. "As would Miss Sergeant?"

What she would be happy with is a summer with Emily. Another year to court her in every season, with snow in her hair and her face splashed with autumnal colors. She wants to hold Emily's hand in a public square and kiss her after performances and wear her ring and introduce her to the prince. What she wants is a different world. But she says to Collin, "It's the best I can hope for."

"What does *she* want?"

"She wants out of her marriage contract with a villain." Harry presses her palms into her knees. Then, since they're airing grievances, decides to ask as well, "Why didn't you tell me about your business?"

"Because this"—he raises his hands to indicate the Marshalsea, but also seemingly his existence as a whole—"is not how I hoped my life might turn out. I wanted to be better than where I came from. I wanted to do better than . . ."

He trails off, but Harry picks up for him. "Better than Mother, you mean? Better than me? She wasn't ashamed of who she was or the life she lived. Neither am I. You're the only one who finds where you come from disgraceful."

"I know," Collin replies. "Maybe this is my punishment for that. I tried to make a legitimate business for myself, but it's just so bloody hard to outrun where you came from. It's hard to get a job without references and apprenticeships or a father to buy you a post. I could do the bookkeeping without a license or an exam, just had to be good at figures and pay out on time." He pinches the bridge of his nose between his thumb and forefinger. "It's just in our blood, isn't it? People like us aren't meant to succeed."

"No," Harry says firmly. "You can blame many things on our mother, but not your own bad decisions. Those are yours, Collin. You cannot live your whole life defined by the way we grew up, even if it's just comparing yourself against her. She's not a point of reference for your self-worth. And neither am I."

Collin hangs his head, and Harry prepares for a retort. But all he says in return is, "You're right. I'm sorry."

Two sentiments Harry has never heard Collin express, let alone sound so sincerely like he means them. His fists are pressed together on the table, so rather than take his hands, she stacks her own fists on top of his. He smiles, eyes still down.

"I'm going to talk to our father," Harry says. "I'll ask him for the money without revealing why."

"Please, don't," Collin says. "You have no idea the sums Alexander is holding over my head."

"And then you'll propose to Miss Sergeant," Harry continues like he hadn't spoken. "And she will say yes. Then she'll be rid of her undesirable fiancé back in Sussex and you'll be free and I'll be married off to someone to be determined."

Collin sighs heavily. "And that's the best we can hope for?"

"Yes," Harry says, for she can see no other way forward, no matter how many times she turns the situation over in her head. "It's all that's out there for people like us."

The corner of Collin's mouth turns up at his own words parroted back at him. "Bastards and Sapphists?" he asks, and Harry smiles too.

"I'd drink to that."

41

To Harry's surprise, the prince regent agrees to meet her personally at Longley Manor.

She had hoped to be passed off to some minor financial adviser and that she wouldn't have to disclose quite as much of the story of why she pressingly needs to borrow money from the crown, or look anyone in the eyes while doing it. But the prince sends a card—the same hand spelling out *Longley Manor* on the same stationery she had received in late March, for the meeting that unstoppered the drain of life as she knew it.

Harry arrives before the prince, accompanied by Havoc and Matthew—borrowed from his stables in Regent Park without asking Alexander—both of whom she considers letting inside the manor as a symbolic representation that the house is hers to do with as she likes. In the end, she decides to leave them in the yard. It may not end up being her house after all—and if it does, she'd rather not start with horse shit in the parlor.

She stands alone in the sitting room, realizing only once she sees it how much she had counted on the house being hers. She banked since March upon the knowledge that she would marry Alexander and she would have Longley. The title. The money. The unchanged version of herself that could keep carrying on alone. Wasn't that why she had quit the theater, given up her home, finally unshackled herself from Mariah Swift?

But now there is Emily, with her blue eyes and bright laugh and soft mouth curling around a curse, and there is everything Harry is when she's with her. Harry has slept well and laughed often, not just in the past few days but all along the delirious slide into the moment of their first kiss. Emily had swept into her life like autumn, and as leaves did, Harry had fallen.

A marriage of convenience. How had she ever thought it would satiate her? Especially now that she knows the alternative.

It overwhelms her suddenly, and Harry lies down on the floor, her knees up and her hands thrown over her face.

She is alerted to the prince's arrival by Havoc's delighted barking in the yard, and a moment later, His Majesty's royal shadow darkens the doorway. His trousers, she's gratified to see, are smeared with drool and dog hair.

Harry sits up, arms looped around her knees. "Hello, Father."

The prince inclines his head. "And here I hoped you wouldn't be alone."

"Did you think I called you here to present my intended? I would have insisted we do that at the palace, and you provide sandwiches."

The prince eases himself down onto one of the covered chairs. The material bunches under him. "You're hurt."

Harry looks down at herself, as though there might be blood on her shirt. Then she remembers the flat bridge of her nose and the scrape across her forehead that is still not entirely faded. "I was thrown from a horse."

"I hope you weren't kept from the stage."

"I've resigned, actually. Quit the company. I thought that would be the respectable thing to do."

"I appreciate the sacrifice."

"Oh sod off." The prince's eyebrows rise, and Harry laughs. "Don't pretend to be sorry you've ruined my life."

"Have I?" He scratches his chin. "I thought I was helping."

God, Harry thinks, if anyone was likely to assume money could be a bandage over a bullet hole, royalty would be at the top of the list.

The prince clasps his hands and leans forward with his elbows on his knees. The dog hair transfers itself from his trousers to his coat sleeves. "Now, what is it that I can do for you? If not give you my blessing to wed."

Harry rubs her hands through her hair. "I need a loan. Or perhaps we could call it an advance on my inheritance."

"What for?"

"A friend is in trouble."

"What sort of trouble?"

"I'd rather not say."

"What sort of friend, then?"

"I'd rather not discuss that either."

The prince's nostrils flare. "Well, what can we discuss? How goes your search for a husband—is that on the table?"

Harry pushes her hands through her hair again, though she knows it must be standing at all sorts of odd angles. "Therein lies the second matter I mean to raise with you. I was hoping you might choose one for me."

The prince tips his head. "Oh?"

"I don't know many suitable men, and I'd rather not guess at where our definitions of suitable will overlap, so make your selection and I'll consent."

The prince strokes a hand over his chin, surveying her in a way that makes her want to start a coup. "I was hoping," he says after a moment, "you might find someone for yourself. I don't wish you to be unhappy in a marriage."

"Rushing me into it for the sake of an inheritance you could bestow upon me without terms would suggest otherwise."

She had just been thinking how impressive it was that he could hold his smile so neutral and so still—had he been made to practice such vacancy in his youth?—when it slips, just a little, like the toe of a boot catching uneven pavement. He looks, for a moment, almost reflective—something she would have thought he pays someone to feel on his behalf. "You must understand that my terms are for your own benefit."

"I do *not* understand," Harry replies with her own blank smile. "Please enlighten me."

"There are limitations on the protections extended to women in regards to an inheritance. The best way to protect what is yours is for you to have a man and then a succession line on your side."

"If only we knew someone in a position of national power who could change said limitations rather than ensure his daughter is yet another victim of them."

Is he going to storm out? Surely she has pushed him too far this time. But all he says is, "You're giving a lot of cheek for someone who has come to ask for a loan."

"It's been a long day. Week. Year—when did we meet?" Harry pushes her hands through her hair. "That's the stretch of time that has worn me down."

The prince leans back upon his sofa. The afternoon light through the windows falls in bright streaks across his dark hair. "May I make an observation?" he asks.

"I don't suppose anyone has ever stopped you."

"I think you're in love."

Harry folds her arms, resisting the urge to deny too vehemently lest she reveal herself. "And what makes you think that?"

"Because I too once loved unsuitably," the prince replies. "And it all sounded very much like this." He leans forward, elbows on his knees in what it takes Harry a moment to realize is meant to be a pose of confidence. "I fell in love with someone my father deemed unsuitable."

"What was her name?"

"Maria." The corners of his mouth turn up, as though around a spoonful of sweet pudding. "Maria Fitzherbert."

"Why did your father not approve?"

"She was a commoner," he replies. "And twice widowed. And a Catholic."

"But you loved her?"

"I did." He fiddles with the ring on his finger, sliding it past his second knuckle, then back absently. "We tried to marry. We *did* marry. But my father had it declared invalid."

"That must have broken your heart."

"It was the thing to be done. I had a duty to my country and my family. I needed an advantageous marriage to make up for some unwise debts I had accrued."

"And now you are married to a woman you hate so much you have barred her from being coronated queen alongside you."

The prince's eyebrows slope. "Where did you read that?"

"It's in every paper!" Harry says. "The two of you have not been able to stand being in the same country, let alone the same room, for years. You fight each other in the press for guardianship of your daughter when the royal edicts don't move fast enough."

"Careful, Miss Lockhart," he says, and for the first time, he sounds as though he may mean it, but she truly doesn't care. Somehow, in offering her the world, he's given her so little to lose.

"You cannot say you want your children to be happy and force us into the same situation you were shoved into. At least tell me the truth—you want me to reflect well on you, you want me to be respectable, you want me to be controlled, but please God spare us both the embarrassment of pretending you are doing any of this because you want me to be *happy*." She says the word with such vehemence she accidentally spits, decides pausing to wipe her mouth will undermine her venom, and plows on. "It doesn't always have to be the same as it was, you know. Just because your father forced you to leave the woman you loved because she had the wrong family name or not enough land or too red hair or whatever he decided made her arbitrarily unsuitable—never mind that you loved her. Just because his father probably did the same to him and his father before him. To say nothing of all the sisters and mothers who have been forced into bed with men who mistreat them and belittle them and—this is getting somber."

Harry presses her hands to her cheeks and stares hard at the floor for a moment, giving her racing heart a chance to slow. She should not have spoken so boldly, for a whole host of reasons, not the least being that she still needs him to give her money—oh God, the money!—but she's already come this far. What's one more nail in the treasonous coffin? So she swallows and finishes. "You can change things. Nothing has to stay the same just because that's the way it's always been."

She can almost hear the sharpening of the executioner's axe in the silence that falls between them. When she finally finds the courage to glance up at the prince, she expects him to be wearing the sort of scowl most only see in prelude to being sent to the Tower for life. She almost takes a knee in preemptive apology—or so he can behead her more easily. He certainly looks shocked—though by her sentiments or the boldness in expressing them, she isn't certain.

She starts to apologize for both, but before she can, the prince asks, "Am I wrong?"

Harry raises her head. "About what?"

"You're in love, aren't you?"

Harry considers lying down on the floor. Perhaps pulling the neck of her shirt up over her face and screaming as well. Everything she said, and *this* is what he lingers on? "Your Grace, I am, and I can confidently say there is no world in which you'd declare this a proper match for me."

"But you are in love?"

It's the first time someone has asked Harry this question, and despite the impossibility of her answer mattering, or perhaps because of it, she is overwhelmed by her desire to fall to her knees and proclaim aloud her love for Emily Sergeant like a soliloquy in a Shakespearean play. Let her feelings into the sunlight, sparkling and radiant. "Ardently," she replies. "Passionately. Unbearably. So much that it makes me ill and stupid and happy and better. I am so much better when I'm with her. Loving her feels like looking at the stars."

The prince studies her for a moment, and Harry clears her throat, preparing to restate her request for her prince to find her a suitable husband, now that he knows why she's asking, but then the prince smiles and says, "Love makes you feel small and overwhelmed by the vast firmament of the sky?"

"Full of wonder," Harry replies. "I've never felt part of anything so big before. Now." Harry pushes herself to her feet, brushing her palms off on her breeches. "If you'll excuse me, I have a friend to get out of jail, and two arranged marriages to see to."

"Two?" the prince asks.

"Well, you must pick me a husband," Harry says. "If you know any dukes who identify as confirmed bachelors looking for a wife to make them look like less of a sod at royal functions, I'm happy to be that bulwark so long as you let me keep seeing my lady. I promise she and I will be discreet. Simply the best of friends, the way ladies are. And I've got to save her from marrying a lecherous cretin who wants her child-bearing hips and family land in Sussex so he can build an access road to your favorite seaside town of Brighton. Yet another complication in my life I can thank you for. I'll be sure Mr. Tweed knows you're to blame when his construction project fails to manifest. He can take his complaints all the way to the palace."

She starts for the door, determined to at least get a good storm out without looking back, but on the threshold, she hears the prince say, "Would that be Mr. Robert Tweed?"

And goddamn it, Harry has no choice but to turn back.

42

Emily and Violet walk the western trails of Hyde Park, lapping the perimeter of the green three times while Violet listens patiently to Emily's story, unedited, beginning to end. She had kept to herself for the first few days following parting ways with Harry, shut away in her bedroom in hopes that she might find her answer in quiet contemplation, but after four days, she is as muddled as before. When she finally emerged from her room, Violet was already waiting with their parasols.

"I told her I'll have my decision to her by the week's end," Emily finishes.

"So, tomorrow?" Violet asks.

Emily nods. "But I still have no notion what that decision will be."

"First," Violet says, "I must ask you something important." Violet leans in and asks, her mouth against Emily's ear, "Were there dildos, or was it mostly tongue?"

"Violet!" Emily slaps her cousin's arm. "Vulgar!"

"What?" Violet bites the finger of her glove. "I've always wondered!"

"How did you know it was even possible?" Emily asks. Then, much quieter, "And how do you know what a dildo is?"

"Because I haven't lived my whole life in a tiny Sussex village where the same aunties who rocked me in childhood now spread vicious rumors about my suitability as a bride!" A pause, then Violet adds, "Also, I bought a book in preparation for my wedding night and it was much more extensive than I expected."

Emily rolls her eyes. "Someone should have told *me*. I've only just learned the word *Sapphist,* and it would seem I am one."

Violet loops her arm through Emily's. "Do you love her?"

"I do," Emily says sadly. "I can't remember ever being this happy before."

"That's the somberest declaration of happiness I've ever heard."

"Because there is no future for us."

Violet squeezes her arm. "Marrying Mr. Lockhart could allow you to remain in her life."

"I do not want to be forced to marry anyone, even a good man like Collin Lockhart. I want to choose for myself."

"But that choice is legally unavailable."

"I know." A gust of wind strikes them, and Emily and Violet both clap their hands to their bonnets, holding them in place. "I wish I could go backward in time and do everything differently."

"Such as what?"

She tries to trace her time in London backward, pin down the moment that falling in love with Harry had become inescapable, but nothing seems far enough. "Never meet Thomas?" Emily offers at last. "Never go to that village fair? Never let him bed me?"

"Thomas?" Violet's brow puckers. "What has Tom Kelly got to do with any of this?"

"When given agency in my own life, I always choose unsuitable people," Emily says. "He was just the first. I have proved again and again that I cannot be trusted. Which is perhaps why I should let this all go."

"Unsuitability is as much a part of love as mutual respect and trust. It's the fabric of the thing. No one ever falls for someone suitable." Violet encourages a duck off the path in front of them with her foot. "If there was no inheritance to consider, would you stay with Harry?"

"It's not that simple."

"Why not? You love each other. You make each other happy."

"Because Harry needs money from the prince to see her brother freed from the Marshalsea. And because I am promised to Tweed! And what about my parents? I have already put them through so much shame; can you imagine what would happen to them if I ran away with a woman? They'd bear as much shame as before."

Violet stops walking and Emily turns back, unsure what has stopped her. "Emily." Violet folds her parasol and clamps it under one arm so that she is free to take both Emily's hands in her own. "What happened with Thomas was not your fault."

Emily laughs without meaning to, a harsh cackle that takes her by surprise, but she hadn't expected such an outlandish statement from her sensible cousin. "I killed him," she says, though she feels silly for explaining it.

"It was an accident," Violet says. "You defended yourself against his advances. You may have been the cause, but that does not mean you were at fault. I'm sorry if I never said that to you." Violet squeezes her hands. "I should have."

"But I let him court me," Emily says, for if Violet thinks her blameless, she surely doesn't understand. "I let him come to me. I invited him into my bed, I was going to marry him."

"None of that means you are to blame," Violet says. "You had the right to tell him no. Having bedded him before does not mean he is entitled to you in perpetuity. You said no. He ignored you. You acted in your own defense." Another breeze tears a strand of

Violet's hair free from her bonnet and whips it in front of her face, but she makes no move to push it away. Her eyes are fixed intensely on Emily. "People act as though shame is a disease. They're terrified of catching it. Not everyone in town blames you—most people never did. It's just a few meddling biddies making a show, and everyone else being too afraid to stand against them."

"It is not so easy," Emily says, her voice thick. She cannot believe any of this. She doesn't dare. If she does, her entire past will shatter and reform. Will she even know herself without Thomas Kelly's shadow hanging over her? "You cannot simply offer me atonement."

"Then you must find a way to give it to yourself," Violet says. "You have spent years walking around with this shackled to you. Even here, you cannot let yourself be free of it. You can be sad for it, you can be sorry, you can regret it, but you cannot let it define you. Nor can you let what others say bear so much weight." She puts a hand to Emily's cheek. "You fought back. That is proof of your strength. Of knowing your own worth."

A door opens inside Emily's heart, just a crack. A sliver of light shines into a long-shadowed corner.

"I wish it had ended differently," she says.

"Of course," Violet replies. "But that does not mean you have to carry it forever."

Emily presses a hand to her eyes, like she is shielding them from the sun, when really she is trying to push tears back. For so long, she has scratched repeatedly at the Terrible Thing she had done and wondered why the wound wouldn't heal. Her past had been a bodily sensation. She had felt it every day on her skin, under her nails, in the lines of her palms.

But Harry had held her and kissed her and taken those palms in hers. She had seen Emily in darkness and told her how lovely she looked in black.

She feels restless. She wants to run, like she once had through the trails of the Ashdown Forest, her hands trailing along the branches and searching their shadows for Thomas Kelly. Instead she starts to walk, strides as long and quick as her tight skirt will allow.

"What do I do?" she asks, voice hoarse, as Violet catches up to her and loops a hand through Emily's arm once more. "I don't want to marry Tweed, and I don't want to marry Collin. I cannot marry Harry but neither can I ask Harry to give up her inheritance or her brother's freedom. I cannot ask her to choose."

"Why not?"

"Because I'm afraid she'd pick me," Emily says. "And regret it."

"That would be her choice," Violet says. "You are not coercing her by asking, Emily, you must ask people for what you want. You must tell them what you need and let them give it to you and trust they do not mean you harm. In a perfect world, with no questions of money or sex or inheritances, what would you want?"

"I would want to be with Harry."

"So does it matter if it isn't marriage?"

"Of course it matters!" Emily says. "Marriage is everything. The whole world is centered around who you marry and marrying well and marrying for happiness and position and security and protection and life. It's the only thing that gives a woman any existence."

"Life is only centered around marriage in our very small and particular corner of the world," Violet says. "You think you are the first person in history who has had to bend the boundaries to make a space for themselves? I know your whole world—your whole life, particularly since Thomas—has been centered around marriage, but it doesn't have to be. You can change that. You can make a choice for everything to be different. What's stopping you?"

"The world—" Emily says, but Violet interrupts with a wave of her hand like she's clearing away a cloud of pipe smoke.

"—is made up of a bunch of rules that change all the time! Men wore dresses in the Bible and sold their daughters into slavery. Sod convention! Your life need not make sense to anyone but you, so long as you are happy."

They have reached the edges of the park, falling into silence as they turn onto their street. When they reach home, Emily stops them on the doorstep and kisses her cousin upon the cheek. "I do love you," she says.

Violet smiles. "And I you."

"Tell me everything will turn out all right."

"It might not," Violet says. "The world will not remake itself for you, but neither should you remake yourself for the world."

Emily presses her forehead to Violet's shoulder. "Then what am I to do?"

"Make your own world," Violet says, and touches Emily under the chin. "The two of you."

Violet pushes open her front door and Emily follows her inside, her head spinning. It takes her a moment to notice the ornate walking stick leaning beside the door, though Violet is already frowning at it.

"Were you expecting company?" Emily asks as she hands Violet her parasol and bonnet.

"Not that I know of. Martin?" she calls.

"In the parlor!" her husband's voice replies. "Is Miss Sergeant with you?"

Which is when Emily notices the silver top of the cane. A rabbit head, ears tucked back and eyes glazed.

Rabbits always scream when cornered.

"Yes, where is Miss Sergeant?" comes a second voice from the parlor. "I've come all this way to see her."

Emily feels the ground tip beneath her. She had once thought herself Persephone, but never has she felt it so acutely as now. Six months of spring, and now here is the lord of the underworld to drag her back into his dark domain. Her time is up and the flowers will never bloom again.

Robert Tweed has come for her.

43

Emily promised she would give Harry her answer in five days' time.

But five days come and go, and Harry has walked the varnish off Collin's floorboards with her pacing, Havoc always on her heels, mooing in supportive distress.

"There is a reasonable explanation, I'm sure," she tells Collin on the morning of the sixth day. "As she said she'd come no matter what she chose."

Collin, whom Harry liberated from the Marshalsea the same day she met their father at Longley, is stretched out on the sofa looking like he'd very much like to take a nap if only Harry would stop sniveling. "Perhaps something came up with her cousin and she's been delayed."

"Perhaps," Harry says. "Or perhaps she decided she'd had enough of me."

"That seems unlikely."

Harry throws herself into a chair across from Collin, fingers knit together behind her head. She feels the strain in her shoulder. "How are you feeling?"

Collin raises his head and looks around, as though she might be asking someone else. "Who, *me*? I thought I was only here to offer you reassurance."

"My apologies," Harry says, resisting the urge to roll her eyes at him. "I've had much on my mind lately."

Collin drags his hands down his face with a sigh. "I feel like a bit of a goosecap, I suppose."

"I was more inquiring after your health."

"Ah." Collin lets his head fall back against the arm of the sofa. "Of course."

"You had a fever when you came home—"

"Well in that regard, I'm well."

"But we can talk about your . . ." Harry balls her hands into fists around the knees of her trousers. "Sensitivities. If you want to."

Collin drops an arm over his face. "Pay me no mind."

"No, tell me." Harry scoots her chair closer to the couch. "Why do you feel silly?"

Collin sighs, then says, "Because I made a bad bet on a bad man. I trusted the wrong person and spoiled things for you and Emily. And I was an ass to you."

"All true."

Collin chuckles.

"Everyone trusts the wrong person at some point," Harry says. "Alexander fooled us both."

"I know," Collin says. "I'll just have to let it ruin my life for a bit longer before I allow myself to be forgiven."

"Try not to linger upon it. The best thing to do is allow yourself to move forward." Harry lets that sit between them for a moment before she asks, "Is it going to ruin your life further if you marry Emily for me?"

"No, no," Collin says. "I like Miss Sergeant quite a lot. She and I will be well matched. I never expected to marry for love, even before the prince got involved."

"And if she and I keep carrying on?"

"We've known couples with more unorthodox arrangements," Collin says. "I don't mind her affairs if she doesn't mind mine." He raises his head and says seriously, "But you know it will be easier for me. Not just because you're both ladies together, but because it's always easier for men and their dalliances."

"I know."

"I know you do. And I know she does. But just be absolutely certain this is what you both want."

"Do we have any other choice?" Harry slumps in her chair, feeling suddenly gelatinous. "Though it may not be my choice if Emily never comes. What if she's lying dead in a ditch somewhere?" she says just as Collin closes his eyes again. "What if she was struck by a cart or took a fall or got lost and is wandering around the city calling out my name?"

"You're so dramatic." Collin rolls over, face away from Harry. "Just go to her."

"What if this silence is my answer and she's chosen to leave me?"

"From what I know of Miss Sergeant, she wouldn't go back on her word. Go to see her at her cousin's."

"I can't."

"Why?"

"Is that not a bit . . ." Harry sticks a nail between her teeth. "You know. Pathetic?"

Collin sits up and glares at her. "You're concerned because you care for her. What's pathetic about that?"

Harry wants to pull out her own hair by the fistful. How can she feel so shy over seeing someone whose gigg she had recently licked in excess? Surely they were past the point of embarrassment and doubt. "Why have I lost my ability to be cool and aloof? I used to be so good at that when it came to women."

"Because you love her," Collin replies. "And the only way to attain love is by embarrassing yourself deeply and asking for it. No great love story ever began with two people being rational and calm around each other."

Harry watches as Collin pulls up a pillow around his ears. Since Harry is no longer pacing, Havoc rests his head on the cushion next to Collin's knees, then starts to heave himself atop him on the sofa.

"Damnation." Harry pushes herself to her feet, slapping the back of Collin's head lightly as she passes. "You are tiresome."

"Where are you going?" Collin calls, and Harry shouts in return, "To embarrass myself!"

HARRY RINGS THE bell of Violet's house, then resists the urge to knock as well, in case the bell wasn't heard.

Nothing is amiss, she tells herself, struggling for a new reassurance with each toll of the bell.

It does not mean she has left you.

Or forgotten you.

Or that her feelings do not run as deep as yours.

She reaches for the bell cord again just as the door opens. Martin, as sour-faced as he had been when they had previously crossed paths, glares at her across the threshold. She's certain he recognizes her, but can't quite remember from when or where, which is probably to her benefit.

"Mr. Palmer." Harry takes off her hat. "Good morning. I've come to see Miss Sergeant. Is she at home?"

"Miss Sergeant is not available to callers."

Harry's heart sinks. Emily's absence had been a sign after all—*How stupid to pursue her!* "Any callers?" she asks. "Or just me?"

"She's occupied with preparations for her departure."

"Departure?" A different sort of dread floods Harry's heart. "Where is she going?"

"She's returning to Sussex," Martin says, then adds—with savage pleasure, or is that just her imagination?—"with her fiancé."

Robert Tweed is here. He has come for Emily. Harry wants to thump Martin over the head so she can dash past him and into the house. It was not her pursuit that had been foolish—it was that she hadn't come sooner.

"Please," Harry says. Martin starts to shut the door, but Harry sticks her boot in the frame, stopping its progress. "Let me see her."

"Leave my home this instant, or my hand shall be forced."

Martin pulls on the door, but Harry is taller and stronger and manages to shoulder it open and push past him. "Intruder!" Martin hollers as she charges across the entryway.

"Is that your forced hand?" Harry asks. "Hollering for reinforcements?"

"Martin!" Harry and Martin both freeze as Violet appears on the stairs, glaring at them as she takes her skirt in her hand and hurries down. "What the devil is going on?"

Martin points to Harry. "An intruder! In our home!"

"Oh calm yourself." Violet takes Harry by the arm, a quick squeeze calming Harry enough that she allows herself to be led from the entryway. "I'll see her out the back," Violet calls over her shoulder to Martin, as she steers Harry through the house.

Violet stops when they reach the kitchen and turns to Harry, who wastes no time in demanding, "Where's Emily?"

"Out with Tweed purchasing their bishop's license," Violet

says. "I tried to send you word—so did Emily, but Tweed's been a tyrant about our communications, which inspired the same in Martin. He tried to order me to wear blue this morning. Can you imagine?" She flicks the sleeve of her pink dress. "These men."

"Emily can't marry Tweed," Harry says. "We have to do something."

Violet's lips purse. "I don't know what we can do to stop him."

"I'll take her away. She can marry my brother."

"Under what licensure? Have the banns been read? Will a hasty wedding by the end of the day fall under your father's idea of moral uprightness?"

"Why did Tweed come for her? Why now?"

Violet rolls her eyes. "Apparently my husband had *moral concerns* about Emily's behavior and felt it his duty to send a report to her betrothed that inspired him to come himself."

"Oh for God's sake."

Violet takes Harry's hands and squeezes them hard. "She loves you. Know that."

"I do," Harry replies. "I wish it was enough."

"Only in stories," Violet replies with a sad smile.

They're interrupted by the sound of the front door opening, followed by men's voices in the hall. Violet glances over her shoulder, then says to Harry, "Wait here," before she turns on her heel and leaves the kitchen.

Harry waits, afraid to move lest she reveal herself. Snippets of conversation, mostly Violet's voice, float into her from the hallway. "Gone, yes . . . Luncheon soon . . . I have to see to the baby, Emily could you make us some tea?"

Footsteps across the stones, and Harry realizes what's happening a moment before Emily appears in the kitchen doorway in a gray dress, her hair pinned back so tightly cheekbones cast shadows. She looks like herself cast in wax, skin pale and her eyes red rimmed.

When she sees Harry, she throws a hand over her mouth to muffle her gasp. Tears flood Harry's eyes, and she opens her arms to Emily, who falls into them, burying her face in Harry's coat.

"I should have gone with you when I could," Emily says. "I was so foolish."

"You still can."

"Not now that he knows. Now that he's here. I should have agreed to marry Collin as soon as you proposed it." Emily's voice breaks. Harry can't see her face, but she can feel Emily's tears soaking through her shirt. "How silly to think I had a choice. Silly to come to London at all and think I could change anything."

"Stop." Harry takes Emily's face in her hands and kisses her on the forehead. "You cannot let despair overtake you."

"It's not despair—it's realism. I'm being honest about my lot for the first time since . . . maybe my whole life." Emily rests her chin on Harry's chest, looking up at her. "Thank you, for everything."

"Emily—"

"I love you. I always will."

Emily pushes herself up on her toes and kisses Harry. Her lips taste of salt, and Harry cups the back of Emily's head with a gloved hand, the other on the small of Emily's back. She wants to lift Emily into her arms and carry her away.

"It sounds as though you're saying goodbye," Harry says.

"Aren't I?"

"Please, we can find a way—"

"Miss Sergeant," says a voice from the kitchen doorway, and too late, Harry and Emily step apart, "do not forget I do not take my tea with—"

The man in the kitchen doorway is stocky but broad shouldered, with a weak chin and crooked nose, like someone had tried to draw Napoleon from memory. Emily wipes her face quickly with the back of her hand, taking another step away from Harry, but it's too late. He saw them. He stalks into the kitchen with a heavy stride, just as Violet hurtles in behind him, a moment too late.

"So," says the man, striding toward Harry. "You are the knave who has been fucking my betrothed."

"Mr. Tweed," Violet says. "Do not be crass in my home."

"Do you know that this whore is promised to me?" Tweed jerks his chin in Emily's direction. "Do you know what happened to the last buck who bedded her? I would not take the risk if I were you. She needs a firm hand."

Harry wishes she had brought Havoc. If ever there were a moment to let slip the dogs of war. "She is not yours," she says. "Nor mine. She belongs to herself."

Tweed laughs, then says to Emily, "Miss Sergeant, come here." Harry watches in helpless horror as Emily, head bowed, crosses to his side. "Tell this swain you'll have no more of him," Tweed says, jamming a finger in Harry's direction. "Say it!"

"Harry," Emily says quietly. "Please, you should go."

"Emily," Harry says, and the name wilts on her tongue like a plucked petal.

"You said she belongs to herself," Tweed says. "And now she has made her choice. If you are a gentleman of any kind, you will cease your attempts to coerce her and leave."

"If you are a gentleman," Harry snaps in reply, "you will realize that when a lady runs to London to escape her intended, that is not the start of a happy marriage."

"This is not your concern."

"It is," Harry says. "Because I love her, and I want her to be happy, even if it's not me she's happy with. And by God, I won't let you ruin her life."

"How dare you." Tweed rips off his glove and flings it at Harry. It falls short and flutters to the ground between them. "I challenge you."

"Do you?" Harry raises her chin. "A duel?"

"No, don't," Emily says at the same time Violet shrieks, "Are you mad? You'll both be killed!"

"A duel indeed!" Tweed ignores Violet and grabs Emily by the arm, pressing her to his side. "Epping Forest. Pistols at dawn."

"Harry," Emily cries. "Don't! Please, just go!"

"At the Cuckoo's Oak!" Tweed cries before Harry can reply, dragging Emily after him as he stalks from the kitchen. "Make peace with your God, sirrah!"

44

Emily sits on her bed, watching Robert Tweed secure the locks upon her windows. "Since we know your history," he says, holding up the key and shaking it on its ring.

Their return to Sussex has been delayed another day, but only so her betrothed can kill her lover—it's so comically Shakespearean. Her bedroom door will be locked as well, with not even her cousin allowed inside, Tweed informs her, until he returns tomorrow from Epping Forest, upon which he will wash Harry's blood from his shirt, finish directing the porters with their trunks, and then take them both back to Middleham and straight to the chapel.

Tweed is a known marksman in the Downs, and Harry had only won against Edgewood because they dueled with featherlight foils. Though it's promising that Tweed's poor eyesight prevented him from identifying Harry as a woman from the opposite side of the kitchen. Or perhaps he had only seen what he expected.

If Harry kills Tweed, she'll be arrested, or have to flee the country. At the very least, her inheritance will surely be forfeit.

There is no way this ends but in tragedy. Shakespearean indeed.

When Tweed arrived, Emily confessed she had come to London looking for a different husband. He screamed at her and shook her by the shoulders before confining her to her room. He was convinced that she had taken a lover in the city. Harry's arrival had only confirmed that.

Tweed assured her that if she did not marry him, he would ruin her life. He would ruin her family's lives. They had a contract for her marriage, and he would take the Sergeants to court to see it upheld. He would not be jilted. He would not be a cuckold. Her absence had already caused enough of a stir in town, and there was no world in which Tweed would return to Middleham without Emily in the carriage beside him.

"Pardon me." Tweed and Emily both turn to find Violet standing in the doorway, her box of hairpins held against her stomach. "Emily," she says. "I thought I might plait your hair for you before bed."

"I do not want the two of you alone together," Tweed snaps, "as you have already conspired against me."

"You're welcome to stay and observe," Violet says sweetly. "But there's nothing nefarious one can get up to while plaiting, I assure you."

Tweed scowls. "Be quick about it."

Violet kneels on the bed behind Emily, taking her time unfastening Emily's hair from its coiffure before combing through it with her fingers. Her cousin has never before fixed Emily's hair before bed, and Emily waits for Violet to whisper some secret words in her ear, or provide some wisdom or advice or concealed weapon with which she can stab Tweed through the eye when he next leans in to kiss her. Some explanation for this pretend ritual. She'd take anything. Even a single word of love or encouragement, though she hardly feels she deserves it.

But Violet ties a ribbon at the end of her plait and tucks it over

Emily's shoulder in silence. She squeezes Emily's arms, and Emily turns to her mirror as Violet leaves the room. In the reflection, she watches Tweed approach her, and her muscles stiffen. She feels his hands upon her shoulders, resting lightly. He doesn't grip her, yet her skin feels suddenly thin as pastry.

"I believe," Tweed says, "it is customary for you to wish me luck before my duel."

"Good luck, sir," Emily says simply, praying that will sate him, and he will leave her be.

But then he adds, "Perhaps you might give me a token to wear with me when I duel. Something your buck will recognize as yours and know I carry your heart with me." He stalks over to her trunk, where her dresses are folded in preparation for travel. He shakes out each and tosses them across the bed beside her, until he emerges with the dandelion yellow dress she had worn to the races, so riotous and bright and singular.

Tweed holds it out to her, draped between his arms in a way that makes Emily think of carrying a body. "Cut a strip of fabric from this for me, Miss Sergeant."

Anger pricks Emily's eyes. How infuriating that rage should manifest as tears.

When she doesn't move, Tweed shakes the dress at her. "Quickly, please. Or I might think you are going against me."

Emily takes the dress from Tweed and lays it across her dressing table, then retrieves her scissors from her sewing box. They're so small, it will take ages to cut a panel large enough for Tweed to deem it adequate.

Emily makes the first snip, and thinks of Harry in the dress shop, unlacing her corset. Harry's hands on her waist. The way she could not stop herself from staring at the pale globes of Harry's breasts pushing up from beneath the material cinched under her arms. That queer thrill of desire she had not allowed herself to feel, let alone name, in years.

Another snip, and she feels Tweed's hand caress the back of her head. A shudder goes through her, and it occurs to her how similar the physical reaction of love and fear are, for she had shuddered at Harry's touch too, but for different reasons. "When you wake, I will likely be gone," he says, "to kill that villain with whom you have so unwisely taken up. Then you and I shall return to Middleham posthaste. And you will never again behave the way you have during your time in the city."

Another snip. The yellow fabric frays at the edges.

"Is there anything you wish to say to me?" Tweed asks.

So many things, but she voices none. Where is the spine she thought she had grown? Turned back to pudding. She hasn't changed. Nothing has changed. How foolish to think a few months and the transformative power of love or whatever poetical tripe could change her entirely. She would always shrink under Tweed's hand, and the weight of her own reputation.

"Harry will not answer your summons," Emily says. "You need not go to the forest tomorrow."

Tweed laughs. "How admirable that you still wish to save him. I shall go and see for myself, I think, whether he would rather be dead or a coward. That will suffice." He snatches the dress from the table, material sliding through Emily's hands like water, and tears parallel to the strip she has carefully cut. He yanks the stripe of material free, then wraps it around his wrist. Emily balls her hands into fists.

"There." Tweed holds his arm up to the lamplight in order to better admire the band. Emily wonders if he will wear it to sleep that night, wrapped around his hand and tucked under his cheek.

Oh that I were a glove.

"Be ready to depart when I return," Tweed says as he turns for the door, but pauses on the threshold. "How I pity you," he says, his eyes meeting hers in the mirror. "You really do pick the rankest of men."

If this were a theatrical drama, Emily thinks as she hears the door close and then bolt behind him, this would be the moment she would leap to her feet, unfurl the rope of bedsheets she had woven in secret, pick the lock on the window, and shimmy down to freedom. She would run to Harry and take her in her arms and kiss her deeply before running away to become exiles together. Or she would break the window and slit her wrists on the shards, drink the poison, stick a dagger through her own heart rather than live without love. She would let a snake coil itself around her neck and sink its fangs into the same spot Harry had last kissed her. It would be a tragedy, yes, but a poetic one.

She drops her head onto her arms on the desk, feeling too empty even to cry.

And hears a small *thunk*.

She sits up. The ribbon has fallen from her plait and fluttered to the floor, but something heavy dropped with it. Aside from the sound as it landed, she felt the weight too. A pin? It sounded far too heavy.

Emily drops onto her hands and knees, groping beneath her dressing table until her fingers brush cold metal and she stands, victorious, holding a key up to the light.

Emily almost laughs out loud. Hadn't Violet told Emily, months ago, that she'd made copies of every key in the house for her fear of locking the baby in by accident? She has twice misplaced the key to the front door and had to use one of the spares hidden in the garden. And now her clever cousin has gone and slid the spare key to her room into her hair.

Here is her escape, should she choose to take it. She can leave, now. She can go back to Harry.

But if she spurns Tweed, he will hunt her forever, the hound after a rabbit he had long ago vowed he would be. She has seen his dogged pursuit of her father's land and the great lengths he would go to for it. There is no reason to believe he'd behave any differently in his pursuit of her. Had he not made that clear when he had sat, dry eyed, at his wife's funeral? When he'd sat on Emily's father's couch and squeezed the blood from her hand? He'd be a murderer before a fool.

She could have left with Harry that morning when she had appeared like a ghost in the kitchen. She could have left with Harry when they first fell into bed together. She could have left the moment Tweed had come to call at her parents' house, the moment Thomas had been pronounced dead at her bedside. It would have been difficult, but she could have made her way as a woman in the world. And over and over, she has made excuses. She stayed because of the love she has for her parents, her desire for an ordinary life, to protect Harry's future.

She had never run because it would ruin her reputation.

But there is no one as concerned about Emily's reputation as Emily herself.

How many times must she be presented with a chance to save herself—whether that chance was a trip to London or a beautiful woman or a literal goddamn key to a locked door, a symbol so on point it makes her want to scream—before she realizes that the only thing standing in her way is herself and the fear burned into her flesh like a brand of what people would think of her? How much longer will she continue to sacrifice herself on the altar of her own reputation?

In her younger years, before optimism had started to feel less like a necklace of precious jewels and more like a millstone roped around her neck, Emily had walked the Ashdown Forest that bordered her parents' farmland and imagined herself Rapunzel. A beautiful girl alone and waiting for destiny to carry her one true love through the forest to her. Now, though, the childhood fantasy only strikes her as deeply ironic. Rapunzel's tower was a prison, not romantic solitude, and she can see now there is no folkloric spell keeping her confined. She is her own captor. One can be both princess and witch, prisoner of a tower built with her own two hands.

She presses the key into her palm until it leaves an imprint upon her skin. Let anyone say what they want about her. Call her a murderer or a whore, unmarriable or unladylike or unworthy. She is through defining herself by the measurement others take of her.

Tonight, she is tearing down her tower.

45

Emily realizes too late just how similar all the trees of Epping Forest look.

Though she hired a boy from a nearby estate to lead her to the Cuckoo's Oak, she sent him back before they had gone all the way, for fear he'd see Tweed and the doctor assembled and realize a duel was happening. He might call for help or try to stop Emily from going on and call attention to them and her whole plan—if you could call it that—would be ruined.

"You'll know the Cuckoo's Oak," the boy had assured her when they parted. "One hundred paces ahead, with a trunk like an ewer and a whole mess of branches in every direction starting nearly from the ground."

But she has walked what she thought were one hundred paces, and all the sodding trees look the sodding same, and none pitcher-like, with or without a mess of arms. When she had left the Palmers' house in the indigo hours before dawn, she had worried she'd be unable to sufficiently conceal herself. Darkness—or at least the wan light of early morning—would be her greatest ally. That, and the resin Mariah Swift had used to help Emily affix false whiskers to her face when she had appeared on her doorstep in the middle of the night.

Mariah had no questions when Emily had asked her for a disguise that could pass, from a distance, as a second in a duel. She had simply disappeared for a half hour down to the Palace costume shop—during which two different ladies' voices had called out to her from behind the bed screen—then returned to Emily with a hooded greatcoat and a soldier's uniform from an unspecified country but almost certain a century out of date, and a helmet that Mariah said, to her best guess, would be worn in a war of the future. She then sat Emily down at her dressing table to affix whiskers to her face and braid her hair tightly against her head before concealing it beneath a cap. Emily's only addition to the duds was Thomas's ring on its chain around her neck—partly for symbolic reasons, partly because she had read a story about a soldier in the Napoleonic wars whose wedding ring on a chain around his neck had stopped a bullet, and she would take any armor available.

After an hour of costumery, Emily had looked at herself in the mirror and seen . . . exactly herself. But Mariah had promised that, were one not expecting to see her, it would do. Particularly if the light was flat and the sky overcast, and the weather at least is on her side now, because though it is summer, the morning is cold and wet. Fog sits low over the forest floor, and the ground is spongy as a pincushion beneath her boots—Harry's boots, several sizes too big so that Emily's feet nearly slide out with every step.

Now all Emily must do is offer herself as Harry's second when she arrives at the dueling ground—Harry, she is certain, will not come, for her entire inheritance and Collin's too is now resting upon her morality, and accepting an invitation to an illegal duel is irrefutably not within the bounds of good behavior. She will then ask Tweed's second—likely the valet he had brought with him from Sussex—to negotiate a peace, and advise the second that Tweed is soliciting a duel with the daughter of the prince regent, and for his own sake should quit not only the duel, but London itself. To escape royal persecution, he really should quit the country and never return, or risk the full wrath of the law.

If it all goes well, it will not untangle the whole knot, but it will buy her time. She can get back to Harry, and perhaps they can get the license she'd need to marry Collin. Perhaps the prince might help.

Or, should Tweed's second refuse peace, Emily will duel in Harry's place. There is a pistol in her pocket, stolen from the Palmers' mantelpiece. It is heavy and antique, handed down from Martin's grandfather as he had told her several times to fill uncomfortable silences in the evening.

And should Tweed's aim be as good as he seems to think . . .

She remembers him sitting on the sofa beside her in her parents' house, forming his fingers into the shape of a pistol and pressing it to her chest.

A sharp wind curls through the trees and she claps a hand to her whiskers lest they blow away.

Mustn't think of death. Not yet.

Through the fog, at last she sees it. A wide-bellied oak, with a riot of thick limbs exploding from the trunk so close to the ground Emily could have stepped up onto the lowest one with hardly any effort. Then she sees the lone figure sitting on one of those branches, hunched shoulders cocooned in a dark coat and top hat pulled low. His back is to Emily, but she recognizes the scrap of yellow fabric tucked into his sleeve.

Tweed.

The realization sinks into her like fog through her shirt, and she stumbles on the path, nearly leaving one of her boots behind. Tweed raises his head, and Emily panics. Where is his second and the doctor? Where is the equipage that she had planned to keep between them so she would never need to address him directly for fear of giving herself away? Are they coming? Are they close by? Are they tying up their horses or pissing in the woods? Should she hide or approach? She cannot get too close when it is Tweed alone, for while she may pass as a slight and effeminate gentleman to strangers through the fog, this disguise will not pass muster at any proximity—like all Mariah's work at the Palace, it is best viewed from the gallery. And Tweed will know at once who she is.

Around them, the forest is silent. Tweed and Emily are alone.

The yellow scrap flashes around his wrist again as he reaches up to catch his hat before a gust of wind can blow it off.

And Emily makes a choice.

She reaches into her pocket and withdraws the pistol. It is heavier now than it felt lifting it off the mantelpiece, and she can feel the etching in the metal plates like scars. She knows it's loaded—Mariah even checked on her behalf while telling Emily the story of the three and a half men she herself had shot. Two bullets, one in each barrel.

Emily raises the pistol and levels it with the back of Tweed's head.

"Do not turn." Emily pulls back the hammer on the pistol, a sound that reminds her of snapping the necks of chickens in their farmyard. On the low branch, Tweed freezes. "Robert Tweed, of Middleham, Sussex," Emily says, pitching her voice as low as she can. "There is so much for which I should like to hold you to account." Her throat dries around the next words and swallows hard before her voice has a chance to break. "Shall we start with your crooked business dealings, in which you have used various means from bullying to arson to convince farmers of the Sussex Downs to sell you their land so you can build your road to Brighton, then employing criminals to work on those roads? Criminals who assaulted young women and you did nothing? And of course today, soliciting an illegal duel with the daughter of the prince regent."

Tweed begins to turn, but rage catches Emily's heart like a piece of kindling and sets her alight. "I told you not to turn!" She fires the first bullet into the air. The sound is so loud she almost drops the pistol in surprise. Tweed flinches too, clapping both hands to his face. "Raise your arms so I can see you are not reaching for your weapon!" Emily shouts, trying to sound like a confident man who has fired artillery many times before, perhaps in a war somewhere, and not like her hand is now tingling and her ears are ringing so loudly she's not sure if she's actually shouting or if that's only in her head. Tweed obeys. "Yes, his *daughter*, you miserable cretin. Try to get your pigeon brain around that. Your precious Emily Sergeant is a Sapphist as well as a murderess and hellion and she will never marry you because she is worth so much more than a fiend like you!"

She's gone too far, but *oh hell,* how good it feels to say! Besides, she cannot give up her position now—she must stay the course.

"So." Emily clears her throat and again drops her pitch. "I have been sent to give you this message for your own good. Leave the country. Cease your pursuit of Emily Sergeant. Do not again trouble Harriet Lockhart or her father, the king, will see that you are pursued and prosecuted for soliciting an illegal duel with his daughter who is under his protection for the rest of your small, miserable life. Make your choice now, then leave."

Silence. An owl swoops low and lands on a high branch of the oak. The dawn light is shifting, and the fog looks pearled as the inside of an oyster shell.

Tweed does not move. He leaves his hands in the air, that yellow sash fluttering against his black-gloved hand.

The thought flits across Emily's mind: What if she shoots him? What if she really is a murderess? She has been called it for years, blamed and accused and punished for something that had not been her fault. And never could have been, because even in this moment, her finger does not even twitch for the trigger. She cannot imagine it.

At last, Tweed lets out a heavy breath, then throws his head to the sky. Emily only has a moment to think that she hadn't realized his ancient joints were quite so nimble to allow for such a stretch when he cries, "Fine then. Shoot me."

And it is not Tweed's voice.

Nor is it Tweed's stance as he straightens to his full height rather than the crouch he has maintained since hearing Emily cock the gun. Nor is it Tweed's hands pulling off their gloves, dropping them to the forest floor, and tugging the yellow sash from their sleeve as they turn to Emily and proffer it to her. Emily thinks she must be imagining things, and the fog combined with her own resolute delirium has conjured this half-obscured apparition like a forest sprite from Oberon's court. She has breathed too deeply the fumes from her gummy facial hair. She is still asleep in her cousin's house and this phantom has come to her at night.

Because how else could Harry be striding across the dell to her, how else could she catch Emily when her knees begin to wobble beneath her and press her to her chest in a fierce embrace?

"Harry," is all Emily manages to breathe.

"Hello, darling." Harry grins down at her. "You've changed so much since last I saw you. Is that a beard?"

"Chops," Emily replies.

"Really?"

"They might have migrated. Mariah did them for me."

"That explains why you're wearing my boots."

"You must go!" Emily says. "Tweed will be here—"

But Harry interrupts her. "He's gone."

"Gone?" Emily repeats. "Where?"

"He's been arrested by order of the prince regent," Harry explains. "He challenged me to a duel, for God's sake! The courts are historically lenient in such matters unless a man actually dies, but as you mentioned, I am—how did you put it? The king's favorite Sapphist bastard? We may be able to paste on a few other charges as well—what a list you had! I'll have to write them down." Emily's cap has begun to slip down over her eyes, and Harry pushes it back, her thumb lingering upon Emily's temple. "Tweed will be persecuted to the fullest extent of the law. And as publicly as possible too, just to be certain that he's no longer a respectable candidate for you to marry."

Emily presses her face to Harry's chest, and breathes as deeply as she can, filling her lungs with Harry's familiar scent. "How did you know I would come?"

"I didn't," Harry says. "I went to Violet's to find you, and we discovered you'd gone. Once she explained that she'd given you a key and we realized you'd also taken a pistol, we suspected you might try to intervene in the duel. Collin's at the house, in case you were to turn up there, and Violet was checking coach lines to Sussex, in case you had gone home."

Emily takes the scrap of her dress still in Harry's hand and twists it around her own until their palms are pressed together. "Tweed wasn't sleeping with this, was he?" Emily asks, and Harry laughs.

"Tied around the handle of his pistol."

"More fitting for the Middleham Murderess," Emily says, and her breath stutters at a sudden realization. "Harry, what if I had shot you?"

"You wouldn't have," Harry says. "Not me, nor Tweed. I know you wouldn't."

"You think so much of me."

"Someone's got to." Harry opens her coat, wrapping it around them both so that Emily can feel the heat from her skin through her shirt. When Emily raises her face, Harry kisses her, deep and long and all-consuming, the way Emily had thought she would never be kissed again. To be kissed this way at all, even once, felt like more than most get in their lifetime.

"The beard is a lark," Harry says, mouth still close to Emily's. "It's like snogging a peach."

Emily laughs, nestling her forehead into Harry's neck. "I'm so tired."

"I can imagine." Harry presses her lips to the top of Emily's head. "Have you the strength for one last stop before bed? I'd like to show you something."

46

Emily follows Harry up the stairs of the mysterious manor house to which Harry has brought them without question, like she is being led through a dream. Perhaps as a result of the sleepless night, the tense, pent-up energy of waiting to face Tweed, or a combination of both, but it is only when Harry opens the front door without knocking that it occurs to Emily where she has been brought.

"This is the house," she says.

Harry nods. "Longley Manor."

"*Your* house?"

"No," Harry says, "but we won't be prosecuted for trespassing. Come see."

She tugs Emily's hand, gently leading her inside.

An involuntary gasp escapes Emily's lips as she stares up at the high ceilings, the windows—coated in grime, yes, but the sunlight still finds its way through. "It's beautiful! But. Oh dear." She stops, staring up at the murals on the ceiling with her nose wrinkled. "Those wicked-looking cherubs will have to go."

Harry nods. "It would be first on the list."

"And the gardens!" Emily drags Harry through the foyer and into what must be the dining room, for a long table shape is covered by a drape. The chandeliers above are furred with dust, and large windows look out across a veranda. Beyond that, the grounds, overgrown and unkempt but blooming with wild clover and rampion.

"Obviously I'd add a hedge maze," Harry says, resting her chin on Emily's shoulder as they look out. "In which my guests can have clandestine meetings with their lovers."

"And all this light!" Emily leads Harry to the opposite end of the room, which opens into a large ballroom, this too paneled with windows that look out across the grounds. The door to the garden is open, letting in an aroma of damp soil and wildflowers.

The wainscoting of the ballroom is cracked and the paint is faded, but the size alone is so grand it steals her breath. Emily's hand falls from Harry's as she twirls into the center of the room beneath the brass chandelier, caked in years of old wax. She wants to throw a ball in here. She wants to walk toe to toe and see how many steps it takes her to cross it. She turns to where Harry is leaning in the doorway, watching her with a smile on her face that reminds Emily of afternoon sunlight, the exact hour before sunset that makes the whole world glow. "How will you decorate it?" she asks.

"Paper hangings," Harry says, sweeping a hand through the air. "And portraiture. A whole mess of them there." She indicates the opposite wall, the first guests would see when they walked in.

"Portraits of who?" Emily asks.

Harry points to each imagined frame in turn. "Me. You. Havoc. Then a series of me and you and Havoc, dressed in Renaissance attire, acting out tableaus from Shakespeare. And we'll put a grand piano here. No—two pianos! And a bunch of tasteless vases. Perhaps a costume closet."

"What exactly is this room being used for?" Emily asks.

"Whatever we'd like." Harry grabs Emily by the hand and spins her. "We could even put a big bed in here. Or a very small sofa. And every night Havoc will sit upon the giant bed and I'll take up on the very small sofa." She leans against the wall where the small sofa will be and slides down, and Emily joins her. "And every night, I shall take you upon my lap." She puts her hands on Emily's waist, and Emily obligingly straddles Harry, kneeling over her with her face above Harry's. "And every night I will tell you that you, Miss Emily Sergeant, are the love of my goddamn life."

"Dear me," Emily says. "What will your husband think of that?" She had meant it to sound light, but it strikes her heart with the strength of a blacksmith's hammer, and suddenly she finds she's crying. She claps a hand over her mouth, trying to stifle the sobs, but the sound leaks out between her fingers.

"Don't." Harry takes Emily in her arms, kisses her cheek. "I'm sorry, I didn't mean to upset you."

"You didn't." She scrubs at her eyes with the heels of her hands. "I'm crying because I'm exhausted and I'm emotional and I love you and I miss you and . . ." She grips a fistful of Harry's coat. "I love you. I already said that, but once more. For good measure."

"You needn't miss me," Harry says. "I'm not going anywhere. Neither are you, now that Tweed is gone."

"But it will never be the same as it was."

"Maybe that's a good thing. Maybe there are better things ahead."

Emily scoffs. "Husbands?"

"The best thing," Harry says, and reaches out to press her hand against Emily's before lacing their fingers together, "is that there will never be a version of me that did not know you. From now on, every day that passes, I will be the Harry that has been known and loved by Emily Sergeant. Whether we part now or are together until the day we die. There will never be a year I don't mark your birthday or think of you when I see dandelions or remember the way you take your tea. And I like myself better, now that I've loved you."

Emily settles onto the floor beside Harry, tipping her head onto Harry's shoulder. "You have such a soft heart."

"Don't tell anyone."

They sit in silence for a while. Emily stares up at a beam overhead. It looks soft and rotted, and she notices a starling has nested in one of the growing cracks. "The house really is quite dilapidated," she says. "Prinny should give it to you without conditions, considering the work it will take to restore it."

"He really should, shouldn't he," Harry says. Then, raising her head from where it's tipped against Emily's, she calls across the room, "Did you hear that, Father? Miss Sergeant thinks you should give me the house without condition, on account of it being a pit."

"Does she?" calls a voice from the veranda. Emily looks up as, through the door open to the garden, the prince regent appears, a stick in one hand and Havoc on his heels, leaping with joy as he waits for it to be thrown.

"This dog," the prince says, holding the stick over his head, "is comparably sized to my horse."

Oh God, the prince regent. Here, in Harry's house. *His* house, she corrects herself.

And—*Christ on toast!*—he has just walked in on her and Harry cuddled up on the floor together in a way that is distinctly sapphic.

Harry, however, seems unconcerned. She climbs to her feet, then holds out a hand to Emily, who is so stunned she has forgotten how her body works. Harry has to practically lift her up before she remembers how to find her footing. "Miss Emily Sergeant," Harry says, "may I introduce you to my father, George, shortly to be coronated king of England?"

The prince inclines his head. "How do you do."

"And, my dear father, this is Miss Emily Sergeant, who needs no introduction as I've gone on at length to you about her many fine qualities." Emily wants to step on Harry's foot. How obvious could Harry be, particularly after the prince had seen them snuggled up like kittens on the floor together?

"It's very good to meet you, Miss Sergeant," the prince says. "I have, indeed, heard so much about you."

Emily tries to bow, but Harry holds her upright. "No need," she says.

"I don't think that's your decision, Miss Lockhart." The prince gets a running start back onto the veranda, then flings the stick as far as possible into the yard. Havoc bounds after it, leaping into the overgrown garden, where he is immediately swallowed by the foliage. The prince rubs his shoulder, then returns to them with a smile. "But she's right—no need for formalities here."

Emily doesn't know what to say. She can't look him in the eye. She feels the need to curtsy so badly she is beginning to go boneless in Harry's arms.

"And," the prince says. "I believe we have someone in common, much to both our detriment. A Mr. Robert Tweed."

Emily looks up. She can feel her heart in the back of her throat. "I do know him, Your Majesty. We were—are—engaged to be married."

"Oh, I think *were* is the correct tense," the prince says. "Considering the trouble he's now in, I cannot imagine he would be considered a suitable match for a fine lady such as yourself any longer."

"Your Majesty," Emily says, "if I may ask . . . How are you acquainted with Mr. Tweed?"

Out in the garden, Havoc lets out a delighted bark. The prince glances over his shoulder, then says, "Several years ago I was robbed when I stopped at one of his building sites. A ring of great sentiment was taken from me. It was never recovered." He hooks his hands in the pockets of his coat, head bowed. "He insisted it was not taken and I must have lost it somewhere else, and refused to let his men be searched. He was a very unpleasant man and unsympathetic to my loss. I have always remembered that."

"Could you not have forced him to submit?" Harry asks.

"I had him investigated," the prince replies. "Evidence was found that he was not paying his workers, but no one would stand against him as a defendant so the case was dropped. But now that he has solicited an illegal duel against Harry, we were able to arrest him. And he will be prosecuted to the fullest extent of the law, Miss Sergeant, I assure you."

He smiles at her, and before Emily can consider the ramifications of her statement, she says, "Your ring."

The prince raises an eyebrow. "What of it?"

"It was a silver band."

"Indeed," he replies. "How did you . . ."

But Emily is already pulling the chain from beneath her shirt, looping it from around her neck, and holding it out to him. "I knew a builder on his site," she says. "He gave it to me, as a token. He said he stole it from the prince, who stopped to luncheon with them, but I admit I did not believe him. It's so small for a man."

"Because it wasn't mine," the prince says. He takes the ring by the chain, holding it to the light for a moment before he touches it with the tip of his finger, as delicate as if it's a soap bubble. "It was given me by a woman I loved in my youth. A woman I was forced to part from. I used to wear it on a chain around my neck, just as you have."

"I'm sorry it was stolen from you," Emily says.

"I'm very glad to have it back." The prince rubs the ring between his thumb and forefinger, forehead puckering as he stares at it. "Thank—" he says, but his voice breaks around the word, and he stops and clears his throat into his fist. "Excuse me." He holds up the ring and brandishes it a few times, as though he'd like to say more. But instead, he simply finishes, "Thank you."

Emily nods.

"Will it do anything to further incriminate Tweed?" Harry asks.

"You needn't worry," the prince replies. "He may not serve long in prison, but his legal fees will be expensive, and many of his assets in Sussex will be seized. No longer a fitting candidate to marry a woman as fine as you, Miss Sergeant."

Emily feels her eyes welling again. Harry squeezes her shoulders.

"However," the prince says. "I do think a marriage between you and my son Collin Lockhart, would be an asset to you both."

Emily's heart sinks, but she manages to sound at least adjacent to happy when she says, "Indeed, Your Majesty, he is a good man. I would be very lucky."

"As would he. As would I, to add you to the ranks of my nobility." The prince turns, casting a warm smile upon Harry. "And, Harry, as requested, I have several men for you to meet. All upstanding gentlemen, friends of mine. But none so upstanding that you'd find them dull." He winks. "I think you'll find a good match among them."

Harry gives him a broad grin in return. "Oh, no thank you."

"Pardon?"

"I said no thank you," Harry replies. "I no longer need you to find a man for me to marry."

"Did you not request my introductions?" the prince asks.

"I did, but I've changed my mind. I shall not marry a man at all."

The prince folds his arms. "So you're refusing my offer?"

"No, I'm accepting it." Harry's grin goes wider. "I plan to marry suitably and move into this house and conduct myself according to your moral standards, however much it pains me."

"I know it's unorthodox, but if you work it out with your brother, what happens between you and Miss Sergeant is no one's business but yours. I'll not—"

"That's not good enough for me," Harry replies. "Because I love Emily. I want to spend the rest of my life devoted to her. I want to worship her. Build cities for her and erect monuments to our love on every corner. I want people to tell each other stories about the terrible things we did for our love."

Emily's arms break out in gooseflesh.

"Your stipulation," Harry continues, "was that in order to claim my title and estate, I must be married by your coronation to a partner you deemed suitable, was it not?"

"Correct," the prince replies.

"Harry," Emily whispers, her voice hoarse.

"And Miss Sergeant here," Harry says. "Just now, you said she was a fine woman."

"I did," the prince replies.

"Well then, Father," Harry says. "I would like to marry Emily Sergeant."

Emily cannot breathe. Her heart feels liquid inside her, spreading down her arms, into her belly, rising to her throat like she is a tub filling with water. If she opens her mouth, no breath will come out, just a heartbeat.

Harry's fingers tighten around hers. "With Your Grace's permission, of course," she says. "Remembering that you have deemed her fit and fine and a suitable bride."

"That would not be my concern with such a partnership," the prince says.

"How is this different from being too Catholic or common or too whatever else your father decided was wrong with your Maria?" Harry asks, and the prince's eyes flit to the ring still in his hand. "It doesn't have to be this way because this is how it always was. That's not a good enough reason."

"There would be complications," the prince says slowly, "with the legalities—"

But Harry—*the cheek of her!*—interrupts.

"I have already considered this. Your bestowment of Longley Manor and its title could include a legal provision that the ownership belongs to your daughter rather than her nonexistent husband. It's unusual, but not unheard of."

"And what if something should happen to you?" the prince asks.

"Then we add yet another provision—God, don't you just love a provision?—that should I become infirmed or incapacitated or simply in the event of my inevitable death, my legal partner, Miss Emily Sergeant, will be protected by the title and land as a wife would in the event of her husband's death. Surely your solicitors could come up with linguistic maneuvers that would protect Miss Sergeant and my relationship and holdings as if it were a marriage, even if the law doesn't recognize it."

The prince stares at Harry, face contorting. He seems to be on the verge of speech, but then Havoc reappears, trotting through the veranda doors, covered in tarry mud up to his belly and carrying his stick, which he drops proudly at the prince's feet.

Harry presses herself against Emily, and for all her bluster, Emily can feel Harry trembling. Emily too is trembling. Her lips shake with the effort it is taking not to grin like a fool. If it works, if it doesn't, it hardly matters—or rather, of course it matters, her whole future will reshape in these next few moments. But what matters more is to hear Harry say such things. To call her thus. To go to such lengths to give her the future she wants, to listen to what Emily asked for in a marriage and try to remake the world to give it to her. Emily has never felt loved like this.

The prince looks down at Havoc and runs a thumb along his bottom lip. "You have failed to consider one thing, Miss Lockhart."

Harry goes still as a sighted hare. "Have I? Damnation. What's that?"

The prince loops the chain with Maria's ring around his neck, then picks up Havoc's stick gingerly. He starts toward the door, Havoc bouncing after him. "If you asked her to marry you," he calls as he slips out onto the veranda, "will Miss Sergeant say yes?"

Emily's heart leaps like a falcon lofted off a glove. She turns to Harry to ask if she too has just heard and understood the same impossible thing Emily has.

But Harry has already fallen to her knees before her. "Do you want to take the false chops off first?" Harry asks. "Or shall I proceed regardless?"

Emily takes Harry's face in her hands. She wants to remember Harry in this moment forever. Her lips. Her bright eyes. The dark hair curling across her brow. The way her smile tests the limits of her face. The way she is looking at Emily, like she is impossible and brilliant and hers.

Harry takes both Emily's hands, pries them from her cheeks, and presses her lips to the inside of Emily's wrists.

"Emily—" she says.

"Yes," Emily replies before she can even ask.

"Yes?" Harry asks, and Emily takes Harry's face in her hands and raises her to her feet.

"Yes," she says, and Harry folds Emily into her arms and kisses her.

A NOTE FROM THE AUTHOR

Lady Like is a blend of history, fiction, and fantasy. While none of the characters are real people—except the prince regent, who is a mix of facts and fictional characterization—their lives and experiences are based on the reality of queer women in early nineteenth-century England.

While Georgian England was not particularly hospitable to queer people, queer women have always existed, and so have their friends, allies, and advocates. When crafting the characters for this book, I was inspired by well-known lesbians of the era like diarist and business owner Anne Lister, sculptor Anne Seymour Damer, actress Kitty Clive, and the bons vivants Eleanor Butler and Sarah Ponsonby, known in society as the Ladies of Llangollen. While none of these women were able to be married with legal protections, and while they likely encountered homophobia and prejudice, their sexuality was never a secret and is part of their legacy.

In crafting Harry and Emily and their lives, I drew on works by authors of the time who presented erotic desire between women, such as Aphra Behn, Maria Edgeworth, and Eliza Haywood. I also read accounts of people assigned female at birth who chose to live as men, such as Giovanni Bordoni and Charles Hamilton. It's hard to know whether these people—called "female husbands" in the

Regency era—chose to live as men to reflect their gender identity or to make living with their lovers legally possible.

Like much of queer Western history, gay women's stories have largely been erased. Romantic relationships between women were often classified as passionate friendships, and though homosexuality was criminalized, legal action was typically not pursued against queer women. Many were also masked by marriage to men, likely in part because of the need to hide, but also because of how difficult it was for women to live securely without a husband. There are very few records of sapphic spaces in the way there are records of molly houses and gay cruising grounds for men from this time.

As a lover of both historical fiction and stories with central queer characters, I often find myself frustrated that when LGBTQ love stories appear in historical narratives, homophobia—both internalized and societal—is the main source of conflict for the couple. When I started working on this book, I decided to write a novel where the insurmountable obstacles standing in the way of love were never based in homophobia. I wanted queer characters who have the same breadth and complexity of obstacles in their way as their heterosexual counterparts, and for them to get the same happy ever after of all Regency romance novels—marriage. So while it may not be the most historically accurate choice, I intentionally left homophobia out of my Regency love story, and, inspired in part by women like Anne Lister and the Ladies of Llangollen who married their female partners, ended it with a proposal.

I know that history was not always kind to the marginalized, but at my core, I believe people will always find a way to know themselves, and live happy and free with those they love. To quote John Green, "True love will triumph in the end—which may or may not be a lie, but if it is a lie, it's the most beautiful lie we have."

LADY LIKE

Mackenzi Lee

Dial Delights

*Love Stories
for the
Open-Hearted*

Even More Information on the Queer Regency

Well, you asked for it. Or you didn't, but here it is anyway—some of the true stories that inspired *Lady Like*.

First, let's get this out of the way: Because the Regency era (technically a period that only lasted from 1811 to 1820 in England, in spite of how expansively we use it to label our romance novels) was over two hundred years ago, definitive records of lesbianism from this time period are scant. In addition to the vast gulf between our modern understanding of sexuality and gender and the one that existed at the time, sometimes lesbians burned any record of their own relationships. Sometimes their families did in shame after their deaths. Homophobia pervades scholarship in every generation. Many modern historians are still tying themselves in knots to prove how women who lived together their whole lives before being buried side by side were just good friends. And, because of the nature of literacy and recordkeeping at the time, most of the records we have are of affluent white women.

However, Regency England was a diverse place, though not necessarily in the way *Bridgerton* would make you think it was (the ton was pretty white). And though many stories of queer women may have been lost or can't be definitively verified because very few of these women irrefutably wrote "I love you in a gay way" (some did—we'll get to Anne Lister), we have every reason to believe that there were queer women of all kinds in eighteenth- and nineteenth-century England, and many of them were able to live lives in the open with their partners.

In spite of the rosier ideas of sexuality presented in this book, homosexuality was illegal and punishable under law in Regency England. However, since ideas of sexuality were wrapped up in the sex act itself and the law couldn't conceputalize sex without a penis involved, women were able to fly under the radar more often, and legal action was less likely to be taken against lesbians.

So with all those disclaimers out of the way, here are some extended notes on the real historical people who inspired the fake historical people who populate *Lady Like*.

Anne Lister

If you know one Regency lesbian, congratulations, that's one more than most people. Also, it's probably Anne Lister, because there's a great TV show about her called *Gentleman Jack*, which you should watch. You should also read Emma Donoghue's fabulous novel about her, *Learned by Heart*, as well as Anne's own diaries, published as *I Know My Own Heart*.

Anne was born in 1791 to a minor landowning family in Yorkshire, England, and had the privilege of having both a home education and being sent to a girls' school at age 13, where she started keeping diaries.

Over the course of her life, Anne wrote millions of words of diary entries, most in complex codes of her own devising that combined Greek and Latin letters, mathematical symbols, and punctuation. The code was so complicated that it wasn't fully deciphered until the 1980s. Anne's diaries give readers a unique look into life at the time. She wrote about everything—her day-to-day as an estate manager; her inheritance and management of her beloved family home, Shibden Hall; her love of travel and mountain-climbing and wearing men's clothes; and her relationships with the people in her local town of Halifax.

And, most relevant to this book, she wrote about her life as a huge flaming lesbian. At school, she recorded her dalliances with the other female students in the rare definitive sort of language that no historian can argue wasn't super gay—statements like "I love and only love the fairer sex and thus beloved by them in turn, my heart revolts from any love but theirs." She wrote about how she wanted a wife, her crushes on the women of Yorkshire, tallied her orgasms with crosses in the margins, and documented her various seduction techniques, such as casually mentioning books with queer overtones to potential partners to see how they would react. And while she was considered a bit of a local weirdo by the people of Halifax, many were more concerned that she was a business owner and woman who wore trousers than that she was a lesbian. She was able to live largely out in the open without persecution in her community.

After a series of failed love affairs, Anne settled down with and married Ann Walker. There was no legal recognition of their union, but the ceremony was held in a church and it was real to them (that historical tidbit inspired me to end *Lady Like* on a proposal of marriage too). They lived together in Shibden Hall until Anne died of a fever while traveling.

The Romantic Friendship

But what of the romantic friendship, you might ask. Weren't societal conventions surrounding female friendships at the time more affectionate? Women spoke grandly of their love for each other, kissed on the lips, shared beds, and held hands with their friends! That was just how things were done! Does that mean that they weren't also super gay?

Well, some probably weren't. Some were. And when you look closely enough, you can tell the difference. I always feel weird assigning definitive sexualities to historical figures who were real people and didn't have the same vocabulary or internet access or therapy that we do, but we can look closely at their lives, compare them to other records of the time period, and draw conclusions based on evidence we have.

For example, let's talk about Georgiana Cavendish, Duchess of Devonshire, a noblewoman known for her charisma, political influence, beauty, unusual marital arrangement, and love affairs. In 1774, at the age of seventeen, Georgiana entered an unhappy yet profitable marriage with William Cavendish, the fifth Duke of Devonshire, one of the richest men in Britain. With her husband's bottomless pockets at her disposal, Georgiana could indulge her passion for fashion and soon her elaborate hairstyles became all the rage among women throughout England. She also indulged her passion for gambling, which she was less good at—she ran up huge debts over the course of her life.

Throughout her marriage, Georgiana openly took many male lovers, but also had plenty of those pesky romantic friendships with women that may or may not have been gay. On more than one occasion, she went beyond ordinary Regency girl crushes, which we can deduce from the strength of her language. Georgiana wrote to her "friend" Mary Graham, "You must know how tenderly I love you . . . I am falling asleep and must leave you now, but I want to say to you above all that I love you, my dear friend, and kiss you tenderly." Which feels like a bit more than just friends to me. We can also assume she blurred the lines of friendship and romance based on her straight friends' reactions to these advances. For example, the Countess of Jersey, upon receiving one of Georgiana's passionate letters, replied, "Some part of your letter frightened me." And their relationship deteriorated after that.

But not everyone was turned off by her overtures. Lady Elizabeth Foster, known as Bess, moved in with Georgiana and her husband, and became her husband's mistress while seemingly keeping up a romantic relationship with Georgiana as well. Georgiana wrote things like, "You hear the voice of my heart crying to you? Do you feel what it is for me to be separated from you? . . . Oh Bess, every sensation I feel but heightens my adoration of you." Upon Georgiana's death, Bess wrote that Georgiana "was the constant charm of my life. She doubled every joy, lessened every grief. Her society had an attraction I never met with in any other being. Her love for me was really passing the love of woman." How very Anne Lister of her.

Let me save you the google—yes, there's a film, *The Duchess*, about Georgiana starring Keira Knightley, and no, it's not as gay as you'd hope.

"She Visits Mrs. Damer"

Anne Seymour Damer was an eighteenth-century English sculptor patronizingly called a "female genius" by nepo baby Horace Walpole (son of prime minister Robert Walpole, and Anne's godfather, who was noted for being a little *you know* himself. He was a cool guy, but "female genius"? *Come on*). Born in 1748 to an upper-class family, Anne had a rough entrance into society when she married a man who hated budgets almost as much as he loved gambling. When he took his own life in part because of gambling debt, Anne was able to remain independent and single due to money given to her by her father-in-law.

Anne spent her life being an all-around interesting, adventurous, cool lady. She showed her art at the Royal Academy, became pen pals with Joséphine Bonaparte and visited Napoleon in exile, was captured by pirates, and asked to be buried with her sculpting tools and her dog. She inherited her godfather's—he of the patronizing Female Genius quote—mansion, called Strawberry Hill, where she set up herself and her girlfriends, including . . .

Elizabeth Farren, born to an apothecary in Ireland and plucked from the regional theater circuit to become a star of Drury Lane. She spent most of her career at the Haymarket Theatre, playing more than 100 characters from Shakespeare to contemporary theater. She married an earl and had three children, but that didn't stop her from having affairs with several men before taking up with Anne Seymour Damer. However, the pair faced scrutiny and public ridicule. In 1795, society gossip Hester Piozzi wrote that "whenever two ladies live too much together . . . 'tis a Joke in London now to say such a one visits Mrs. Damer" and that Mrs. Damer was "a lady much suspected for liking her own sex in a criminal way." Cruel caricatures, ballads, and pamphlets—the era's tabloids—eventually sent Elizabeth back to her husband, leaving Anne heartbroken and alone. But it also left Anne open to meeting the great love of her life, Mary Berry.

No, not the beloved *Great British Baking Show* judge. Great British nonfiction writer Mary Berry, with whom Anne spent the last thirty years of her life. Though the press sometimes came between them and they had to separate temporarily so the rumor mill would die down, they were able to live most of the rest of their lives together at Strawberry Hill. "You need hardly have told me," Anne wrote to Mary, "(tho' I like to hear it) that your soul when unconfined flys to me, for I have felt it hovering about me a hundred times here, in all my walks alone, whenever contemplating your favourite seat, always when going to bed at night (my constant opportunity of reading over your letters)."

And while Hester Piozzi's snide comments about visiting Mrs. Damer were meant to ignite rumors, she wasn't wrong. Strawberry Hill became a known haven and safe space for women artists, many of whom were sapphically inclined.

One of these women, though not gay, was Kitty Clive, another comedic actress from the Drury Lane circuit who was the first stage star in Georgian England to make music the basis of her stardom. Kitty had a beautiful soprano voice that made her a star of the London theater circuit at age seventeen. Composers like Handel wrote arias specifically for her and she even collaborated with many of them to rewrite music so it would fit her style and persona, leading and creating new forms of English musical theater. Kitty eventually entered into a lavender marriage with George Clive, and throughout her career, she championed female playwrights, called out anti-women bias in the theater, led campaigns against theater owners to make sure actors were paid fair wages, and reinvented herself several times, Taylor Swift–style, when her reputation was tarnished by gossip, ageism, and sexism.

Her good standing with the public helped improve the reputation of actresses in general. When she retired from the stage she took up residence in Little Strawberry Hill and joined Anne's sapphic set. There's no evidence Kitty was a lesbian, or even bisexual, but she definitely ran in the circles. Kitty was a major inspiration for Harry, and her work laid the groundwork for a woman like Harry to exist.

Eleanor Butler and Sarah Ponsonby, the Ladies of Llangollen

The Ladies of Llangollen are the stuff of historical sapphic romance novels—and not just because they are the queer Regency's most cottagecore love story.

Eleanor Butler was a high-born Irish woman with a family castle and too much education, while Sarah Ponsonby was an orphan taken in by distant relatives. The two met in 1768, and sparks flew right away. To avoid unwanted marriages and the wandering hands of Sarah's guardian, they ran away to Wales, where they made their life together as a couple outside Llangollen. They called their new home Plas Newydd, or "New Mansion," and lived there with their loyal maid Mary until all three died (and were all buried under the same grave marker, which you are welcome to read into whatever you would like).

In the same way the queer experience varies wildly depending on where you live today, so it did in Georgian England, and Llangollen was chill about their resident forest lesbians. While some newspapers wrote about how admirable it was that these virtuous women had chosen a life of virginity (lol), and some others made snide comments about what kind of affection these women shared exactly or which of them was the man in the relationship (some things never change), Sarah and Eleanor did their own thing and ignored the noise. They made their home a little rural commune where they hosted a rotating cast of famous visitors, including Wordsworth, Byron, Shelley, the Duke of Wellington, Lady Caroline Lamb, Queen Charlotte, and even our friend from several paragraphs ago, Anne Lister. They became known all over Britain, and people traveled long distances to meet the ladies, join their salons, and witness a lifestyle that they assumed was extraordinary but in the end, everyone agreed, was pretty boring. Which is exactly how the ladies liked it.

Also they named all their dogs Sappho.

FEMALE HUSBANDS DESERVE A MENTION!

Because of Different Times, the eighteenth and nineteenth centuries entertained the concept of Female Husbands, which likely overlaps with our modern understanding of trans and nonbinary identity. At the time, a female husband was defined as a woman living as a man who married a woman. It's impossible to know now how many of these people would today identify as transgender men if they had had that vocabulary or how many were women who chose to live as men to maintain relationships with other women. And the trouble with most of the surviving stories is that we only know about them because of court records, and usually they only went to court when women accused their "female husbands" of deception. For more reading on this, I would recommend the book *Female Husbands: A Trans History* by Jen Manion—the subject is fascinating, complicated, and not present in *Lady Like* but still an important element of the queer Regency!

FOR FURTHER READING

I cannot recommend highly enough everything written by Emma Donoghue, particularly her enormously helpful book, *Passions Between Women: British Lesbian Culture 1668–1801*, which, in spite of focusing on a period just before *Lady Like* is set, was formative in setting the tone of the book.

Gentleman Jack: The Real Anne Lister by Anne Choma is also a great read, as are Anne's diaries, collected and edited by Helena Whitbread, and available online in full.

For the definitive biography of the fascinating Kitty Clive, who provided a lot of inspiration for Harry, check out *Kitty Clive, or the Fair Songster* by Berta Joncus.

For great stories of great women from the Regency that are a little less academic than the aforementioned texts, I recommend *Mad and Bad: Real Heroines of the Regency* by Bea Koch.

Additionally, for these extended notes, I used https://www.english-heritage.org.uk/ and their excellent podcasts and resources on LGBTQ history, as well as the British Museum's online collection and www.regencyhistory.net.

Mackenzi Lee is the *New York Times* bestselling author of ten books, including *The Gentleman's Guide to Vice and Virtue*, a Stonewall Honor book, New England Book Award winner, and an NPR and *Vulture* best book of the year. Her short fiction and nonfiction have appeared in *The Boston Globe, Atlas Obscura, Teen Vogue,* and *Bust Magazine,* among others. She holds a BA in history and an MFA in creative writing from Simmons College. *Lady Like* is her adult debut.

mackenzilee.com
instagram.com/themackenzilee

DIAL DELIGHTS

Love Stories for the Open-Hearted

Discover more joyful romances that celebrate all kinds of happily-ever-afters:

dialdelights.com

◉ @THEDIALPRESS

▶ @THEDIALPRESS

Penguin Random House collects and processes your personal information. See our Notice at Collection and Privacy Policy at prh.com/notice.